FORBIDDEN . . .

"You're a pretty girl, Hallie. Your skin is so smooth and clear." He lifted a finger to stroke her cheek. "Your nose is perfect, not too big, not too small. . . ." His finger slid down her nose, light as a raindrop. "Your lips are soft. . . ."

Hallie swallowed hard as his callused finger outlined the curve of her lower lip. Why was it suddenly so hard to breathe, to think? Her heart was pounding as if she had been running for miles, her whole body tingled in the most delicious way. She felt the prick of conscience, warning her that it was wicked to let him touch her.

"Soft," he said again, and before she realized his intent, he was leaning toward her, one hand cupping the back of her head so his mouth slanted over hers, blocking everything from her sight but his face.

She was too stunned to pull away. Eyes wide open, she sat there and let him kiss her. . . .

Hawk's Woman

Madeline Baker

A TOPAZ BOOK

TOPAZ

Published by the Penguin Group
Penguin Putnam Inc., 375 Hudson Street,
New York, New York 10014, U.S.A.
Penguin Books Ltd, 27 Wrights Lane,
London W8 5TZ, England
Penguin Books Australia Ltd, Ringwood,
Victoria, Australia
Penguin Books Canada Ltd, 10 Alcorn Avenue,
Toronto, Ontario, Canada M4V 3B2
Penguin Books (N.Z.) Ltd, 182–190 Wairau Road,
Auckland 10, New Zealand

Penguin Books Ltd, Registered Offices:
Harmondsworth, Middlesex, England

First published by Topaz, an imprint of Dutton NAL,
a member of Penguin Putnam Inc.

First Printing, July, 1998
10 9 8 7 6 5 4 3 2 1

 REGISTERED TRADEMARK — MARCA REGISTRADA

Printed in the United States of America

In loving memory of my
Appaloosa mare,
Candy,
who fulfilled a lifelong dream
and gave me
eighteen years of pleasure
I miss you, girl

Chapter 1

Convent of Mary Magdala
Colorado 1867

He looked dead. Surely no one could lie so still and look so horribly pale and still be alive.

Hallie McIntyre felt her stomach clench as she stared at the man's shirtfront, at the dark splotch of dried blood that made an ugly brown streak on the light blue wool, at the fresh stain that gleamed wetly in the twilight. She sighed, regretting that she had found him too late to be of any help.

Rising slowly to her feet, she straightened her skirts. Men were a rarity in her life and she couldn't help wondering who this man was, and where he had come from, and how he had come to be lying there in the mud in the middle of Sister Dominica's vegetable garden.

She offered a quick prayer, then removed her heavy black shawl and draped it over the body, automatically making the sign of the cross as she did so. Whoever the stranger was, his soul was in the hands of Almighty God now.

She was turning away when she heard a low groan.

The sound sent a shiver down her spine. She glanced over her shoulder, certain she had imagined it. He couldn't possibly be alive. But dead men didn't move, didn't groan with pain, the sound filled with such raw agony it made her ache inside.

She heard him swear under his breath. And then she heard him whisper a name. A woman's name. *Anna.*

She was wondering if it was his wife's name when he flung out one arm, dragging her shawl away from his face, and she saw that he was indeed conscious, and staring up at her.

"Oh, my." Startled, she would have fled had his right hand not snaked out to imprison her ankle.

"Where am I?" The words were harsh, as though they had been torn from his throat.

Stark unreasoning fear flooded through Hallie as she stared down at the long-fingered hand clasped tightly around her ankle.

"Let me go." She tried to pull her foot away. "Let me go!" She tugged again, harder, and then, as panic overwhelmed her, she began to struggle in earnest.

He swore a vile oath when the toe of her heavy black shoe smashed into his side, but he didn't let go of her foot.

"Please," Hallie begged. "Please let me go."

He shook his head weakly, his grip tightening around her foot. "Where am I?"

"If I tell you, will you let me go?"

"Maybe."

"You're at the Convent of Mary Magdala about five miles south of Bitter River," Hallie replied, her words coming in a rush. She tried to draw her foot from his hand again, but to no avail. How could he be so badly hurt, and yet so strong? "I told you what you wanted to know, now let go of me."

He grunted softly. "Need . . . water."

Hallie pasted what she hoped was a reassuring smile on her face. "I'll get you some, I promise," she said, speaking each word slowly and distinctly, "but first you'll have to let me go."

"Don't tell anyone . . . I'm . . . here."

"I won't," she said quickly. Too quickly.

He focused his hooded gaze on the intricately carved

wooden crucifix that hung from a braided cord around her waist. "Swear it."

Hallie's gaze slid away from his. "I swear."

She was lying, and he knew it. As soon as he let her go, she'd take off as fast as her feet could carry her to tell whoever was in charge that there was a gunshot stranger lying flat-out in the dirt.

"I don't mean you any harm, girl." He took several slow deep breaths. "Just keep your mouth shut and let me . . . let me rest here awhile . . . and I'll be on my way."

She tilted her head to one side. "You're in trouble, aren't you?"

A long sigh escaped his lips. "More than you can imagine."

Hallie stared at the big sun-bronzed hand that imprisoned her ankle. In spite of the stranger's weakened state, he had a grip like iron. It frightened her, until she gazed into his eyes, dark brown eyes that were filled with anguish and quiet desperation.

He eased his hold on her ankle, though he didn't release her. "Please," he begged softly, "just keep quiet until I'm gone."

The faint note of pleading in his voice tugged at her heart. She had the feeling that he hadn't asked for, or been granted, many favors in his life, and that he didn't really expect one now.

"All right," she said, meaning it this time. "I won't say anything to anyone."

"Promise me?"

"I promise."

His hand fell away from her ankle and he went suddenly limp.

Hallie gazed down at him, certain he was really dead this time, and glad, way down deep inside, that she would never have to look into those eyes again. Such haunted eyes, filled with pain and bitterness; eyes filled with torment and the shadow of death. Perhaps he would find peace now. . . .

She blew out a sigh when she saw the shallow rise and fall of his chest. A trickle of fresh blood oozed from the wound low in his right side. He wasn't dead, after all. No doubt she would have to do a penance for wishing him so.

She chewed on her lower lip a moment, then lifted the edge of his shirt. Picking up a handful of rain-damp earth, she pressed it over the wound to curb the bleeding.

When that was done, she made her way to the well and lowered the big old wooden bucket. She should find Reverend Mother, Hallie thought as she drew the bucket from the well and made her way back to the stranger. Promise or no promise, the man needed more help than she was capable of giving.

She wondered again who he was, and how he had come to be at the convent. They were a good distance from town, and she hadn't seen a horse. Surely he hadn't walked all the way from Bitter River in his present condition. She had never seen anyone who was badly injured before, never seen so much blood. Never been alone with a man . . . especially a man like this one. To her knowledge, only two kinds of men carried guns: lawmen and outlaws. And this man didn't look like a lawman.

He was lying as she had left him, his eyes closed, one hand pressed over his wound, the other tightly clenched at his side. It wouldn't have surprised her to discover he had passed into the next world, considering how much blood he had lost.

But he wasn't dead. His face was damp with perspiration; his shirt was soaked with rain and sweat and blood.

"Mister?" She knelt beside him. "Mister?"

His eyelids fluttered open and he stared up at her as if he had never seen her before.

"I brought you some water." Slipping one hand under his head, Hallie lifted him up a little, then held the dipper to his lips.

He drank greedily and asked for more.

"I don't think you should drink it so fast," Hallie admonished, and even as she spoke the words, he turned his head to the side and retched so hard, it made her own stomach ache.

He didn't look dangerous now, only weak and sick. She wiped his mouth with a corner of her shawl, then offered him the dipper again.

He drank more slowly this time, emptying the dipper twice before his head fell back and his eyelids closed again.

Hallie blew out a sigh. What was she going to do with him? She couldn't leave him out here. It would be full dark soon. A rumble of thunder heralded another storm coming. What should she do with him?

She glanced at the small whitewashed chapel located beside the main house, then shook her head. If she put him in there, she would just have to move him again before Sunday worship service.

The shed? No, Sister Dominica kept her gardening tools in there.

The barn! That was the answer, Hallie decided. It was her job to feed the horses and milk the cows. None of the other sisters ever went into the barn, except for Sister Ayanna, but that good sister had slipped on the back step and broken her leg the week before and was confined to her bed. Sister Dominica was allergic to hay. Sister Marguerite was afraid of the cattle. Sister Ruth, Sister Paul, and Sister Monique were too old and feeble to do more than say their prayers. Sister Barbour rarely left the kitchen. The other sisters had been summoned to the Mother House in New Mexico to await new assignments.

Yes, she thought, he would be safe in the barn.

"Mister?" She shook his shoulder gently. "Mister, wake up."

He grunted softly, then stared up at her through eyes glazed with pain and weariness.

"I can't carry you. You have to get up."

He stared at her blankly for a moment, then nodded.

Hallie slung her shawl over her shoulder, then eased him into a sitting position. It took him a minute to catch his breath.

With her help, he managed to gain his feet. She hadn't realized how tall and broad he was. Standing, he loomed over her like a dark cloud. It wasn't easy, getting him to the barn. He leaned heavily upon her, his footsteps unsteady, his breath coming in labored gasps. She had to stop several times so he could rest. Each time they paused, she glanced anxiously over her shoulder, afraid someone from the house would see them.

She looked up at him as she guided him the last few feet. Sweat poured down his face, his skin was the color of the old parchment scrolls in the library. His arm was heavy where it rested across her shoulders. His fingers bit into her arm as he endeavored to keep his balance.

There was a sharp crack of lightning, followed by a low rumble of thunder, and then it began to rain.

Hallie was more than a little out of breath by the time they stumbled into the barn. As gently as she could, she lowered him onto a pile of straw in one of the empty stalls.

In spite of her best effort, he landed heavily on his right side, the air whooshing out of his lungs along with a string of the most vile curse words Hallie had ever heard.

By the time she had him settled, she was ready to utter a few curse words of her own.

Moments later, she heard the sound of the convent bell calling the sisters to the evening meal.

"Mister? I've got to go. I'll be back as soon as I can. Mister?"

Bending down, she placed her hand on his chest, reassured by the slight rise and fall of his chest. She didn't know whether he was asleep or unconscious, but there was nothing she could do for him now. If she didn't get back to the house right quick, Reverend Mother was sure to send someone looking for her, or, worse yet, come herself.

Rising, Hallie glanced down at the bloodstains on her apron and skirt. Changing clothes would make her late to dinner for sure, but there was no help for it. She couldn't go in looking like this.

Covering the man with her shawl, Hallie offered a quick, fervent prayer for his recovery, then ran across the fields to the convent, the presence of the stranger in the barn weighing heavily on her conscience.

Clay groaned softly as he opened his eyes and looked around. Where the hell was he, and how had he gotten there? He searched his memory. He remembered escaping from jail, being chased, getting shot, but that was all.

He frowned. There'd been a woman. A girl, actually, with dark brown hair, and light green eyes. Or had they been brown? She had worn a shapeless gray dress and a big white apron and some kind of covering over her hair. He shook his head, wondering if he had imagined her.

He shifted his position on the straw and pain jolted through him, the force of it making him sick to his stomach. He swallowed the bile that rose in his throat, cursing the man who had shot him as he did so.

Staring into the darkness that surrounded him, listening to the sounds of his own labored breathing, he wondered if he was going to die.

Minutes passed. Chills racked his body and he drew the heavy wool shawl more closely around him, grateful for the warmth it provided. He was plagued by a relentless thirst. The ache in his side throbbed continuously, monotonously.

Closing his eyes, he prayed for an end to the pain that assaulted his body, for relief from the relentless need for vengeance that gnawed at the very depths of his soul.

It was after nine before Hallie managed to sneak out of the convent.

She had spent the last hour in the chapel with her sisters. Each evening, after dinner, the nuns gathered to say the rosary and meditate before bedtime. It was the time of the Grand Silence, a silence that was not to be broken until after refectory in the morning.

Instead of saying her prayers, Hallie had spent the time thinking about the man in the barn. His presence weighed heavily on her conscience. Twice, she had contemplated going to see Reverend Mother to confess, but she had promised the stranger she wouldn't tell anyone he was there.

Now, clutching a small burlap bag filled with food and medicine in one hand and a small oil lamp in the other, she ran across the muddy ground toward the barn, taking care not to step on the edge of the blanket dangling over her arm. Was he still alive? She should have told Mother Matilda about the stranger as soon as she returned to the house, yet every time she had started to say something, she had remembered the haunted expression in the stranger's dark brown eyes when he had begged her not to tell anyone he was there. She wondered ruefully what her punishment would be when Reverend Mother found out about the man in the barn. Months, perhaps years, of scrubbing floors and emptying chamber pots rose in her mind, but she couldn't worry about that now.

She closed the door behind her, then placed her oil lamp on an overturned crate beside the stall door and turned up the wick.

For the third time that day, she looked at the man and wondered if he was dead.

Dropping the blanket on the floor, she rummaged in her bag, withdrawing a small jar of water, several clean clothes, a bottle of carbolic, a pair of scissors. Moving carefully, she began to lift his shirt so she could examine his side.

She gasped in alarm as his hand closed over her wrist.

"Who are you?"

"My . . . my name's Hallie," she stuttered, her heart pounding with trepidation. "I found you. In . . . in the garden. Don't you remember?"

He stared at her. "Hazel eyes," he murmured, and releasing her hand, he fell back on the straw.

Mouthing a silent prayer, Hallie peeled the shirt away from the wound. Doing so caused it to start bleeding again and she pressed a piece of toweling over the ragged gash to absorb the blood. The scent of the blood, the sight of it, made her stomach churn. She swallowed the bile rising in her throat.

When the bleeding stopped, she washed the wound and the surrounding area with strong soap and water, then daubed it with carbolic. After covering the ugly hole with a compress of soft cloth, she wrapped a wide strip of material around his middle to hold it in place. Next, she opened one of the packets the doctor had prescribed to ease the pain of Sister Ayanna's broken leg. She emptied the packet into a cup of warm water and held it to the man's lips. He drank the bitter concoction without complaint.

With his wound taken care of, she removed his boots and socks. For a moment, she contemplated his trousers. They were filthy, torn in several places, and stained with blood. For modesty's sake, hers if not his, she was reluctant to remove them; for the sake of cleanliness, she was just as reluctant to leave them on.

In the end, she took a deep breath, turned her head to the side, and yanked them off, then quickly covered him with the blanket. She caught a quick unintentional glimpse of a pair of long hairy legs and noted, with a blush that singed her cheeks, that he didn't wear anything underneath the trousers.

When she had made him as comfortable as possible, she stood up. She regarded him for a moment and then, with a weary sigh, she offered a quick, heartfelt prayer for his recovery and hurried back to the house, thinking that all this sneaking around was certainly wearing on a body, both physically and spiritually.

It was late by the time Hallie managed to sneak out to the barn again. She had not planned on going back to the barn before morning. No one would question her leaving the house then, as it was her duty to tend the animals, but something, a premonition, perhaps, had urged her to check on the stranger one more time.

Setting her lamp on the overturned crate, she studied the man lying in the stall. Since she had come to the convent almost five years ago, she had seen very few men who weren't priests. Curious, she studied the stranger for a moment. His hair was long, black as the wings of the ravens who sometimes raided Sister Dominica's gardens. A long white scar puckered the left side of his neck, running in a jagged line from just behind his ear to his collarbone.

He seemed to be resting comfortably, and she was about to leave when she noticed the fine sheen of perspiration on his face and neck and shoulders. His breathing was shallow and uneven.

Kneeling beside him, she placed her hand on his brow. His skin felt hot and damp beneath her palm. Fever. She had snuck into the infirmary after dinner and thumbed through one of Sister Mary Teresa's books on healing, hoping to find some wondrous remedy, but it hadn't told her anything she didn't already know: a fever was to be expected after serious trauma; the patient should be given plenty of liquids and periodically sponged with cool water.

"You're a lot of trouble, you know that?" Hallie muttered, and immediately felt a rush of guilt as the words from the Gospel of Saint Matthew rose up in her mind: *Inasmuch as ye have done it unto one of the least of these, my brethren, ye have done it unto me . . .*

Chiding herself for her uncharitable feelings, she walked out to the well, filled the big old oaken bucket, then returned to the barn.

One of the least of these, she thought, and sitting down on the straw, she dipped a rag into the cold water. After wringing it out, she dragged the damp cloth over his chest and belly, over his shoulders and down his arms.

She had never seen a man's bare chest before. Or bare arms, or shoulders or legs, either. She had never dreamed a man's body could be beautiful, and she couldn't help staring, couldn't help admiring the naked expanse of so much male flesh. She held out her arm, comparing it to his. They were both arms, with hands and fingers, yet vastly different. Her arm was smooth, softly rounded, the skin pale and unblemished. His arm was much larger, corded with muscle, the skin dark bronze and bearing several small scars.

Her gaze moved over him again, noting his skin was dark all over. He had a broad chest, lightly covered with dark curly hair. A flat belly ridged with muscle. Impossibly wide shoulders.

She tried not to stare, but she knew those images, sinful as they were, had been forever imprinted on her mind, waiting to haunt her the moment she closed her eyes. But she didn't have to close her eyes. He was there, before her, long and lean and bronze. And helpless. And yet, even at rest, he looked dangerous. He had big, capable-looking hands. Strong hands, she thought, remembering how his fingers had wrapped around her ankle, holding her fast.

She dipped the rag in the bucket again and gently wiped his face. It was a hard face made up of sharp planes and angles. His brows were slightly arched, his nose was a little crooked, making her wonder if it had been broken, and how. Thick black bristles sprouted from his jaw and upper lip, giving him the look of a Barbary pirate whose picture she had once seen in a book. She wondered how he had gotten the scar on his neck.

Lifting the edge of the blanket, she sponged his legs. Long legs covered with fine black hairs.

He was going to die. The thought grieved her for some reason she couldn't name. He was going to die because he was badly hurt, because she didn't know how to help him, because she had foolishly promised not to tell anyone he was here.

A cold wind kicked up outside, rattling the barn

doors. Thunder rolled across the skies like the sound of angry drums, and then the storm broke. Rain pummeled the roof. She could hear it striking the ground in the stall across the way. Reverend Mother kept talking about getting the hole in the roof fixed, but it never got done.

Hallie lost track of the time as she sat there, repeatedly drawing the cool cloth over the man's body in an effort to lower his fever, listening to the sound of the rain pounding the barn, dripping through the hole in the roof. The man babbled incoherently. Her cheeks burned at some of the words he used. He spoke in English and sometimes in a harsh guttural language she didn't understand.

Once he cried out the woman's name, sobbing "Anna, I'm sorry, Anna, so damn sorry" and then, to her utter amazement, he began to cry.

Hallie stared at him in astonishment. Never before had she seen a grown man weep, or heard such heart-rending sorrow. It brought a lump to her throat, made her wish she could comfort him somehow. He must have loved the woman very much, she thought, and wondered what it would be like to love a man and have him love her so desperately in return.

Just before dawn, he lapsed into a restful sleep.

With a weary sigh, Hallie stood up and left the barn, thinking it was a good thing Reverend Mother didn't make bed checks during the night. With any luck, she would be able to sneak into her room with no one being the wiser.

Pausing outside, Hallie drew in a deep breath. The storm had passed. The sky was blue and clear, the earth smelled fresh and clean. It was going to be a beautiful day.

With a sigh, she stretched the kinks out of her back

and shoulders, then lifted her skirts and picked her way across the muddy ground. She had just enough time to clean her shoes and change her clothes before morning prayers.

Chapter 2

A shimmering ray of bright golden sunlight woke him. For several moments, Clay hardly dared breathe, paralyzed by the constant throbbing ache that engulfed him. Where the hell was he? He had a vague memory of a girl bending over him, of bells chiming in the distance.

He glanced at his surroundings—at the peaked roof overhead, the unpainted wooden walls that enclosed him on three sides. The strong scent of animals and manure told him he was in a barn; a barn badly in need of repair. There was a large hole in the roof across the way, the door to the stall in which he lay hung askew. The faint stink of moldy straw told him it had been a while since the place had been properly mucked out.

Gritting his teeth, he tried to sit up, then fell back on the straw, a pithy curse escaping through his clenched teeth. Damn, his whole right side felt like it was on fire.

Panting hard, he closed his eyes, waiting for the first rush of pain to pass. He didn't know where the hell he was, but the urge to be on the move rode him hard. He had no doubt that Mason Clark and the posse from Bitter River were still looking for him, and he had no desire to be at Clark's mercy again. Mercy! That was a laugh. The man didn't know the meaning of the word.

He had been on his way to Wyoming when he decided to stop at a saloon in Bitter River to wash the trail dust from his throat. Bitter River was a small town, located about eighty miles from the Wyoming border, and Clay had felt reasonably sure that he could rest there for an hour or two. He had rarely been more wrong in his life. The three weeks he had spent locked up in the Bitter River jail had been pure hell, and if Mason Clark wasn't the most sadistic lawman Clay had ever met, he was certainly in the top two.

Clay blew out a deep breath. He didn't remember much of what had happened on that wild ride out of town. His horse had taken a bullet but hadn't gone down right away. Clay had pushed the animal hard, hoping to lose the posse in the woods that flanked the road. He had managed to cover another couple of miles before the game little mare he'd stolen from behind the jail played out.

Clay had slit the animal's throat to put it out of its misery, then doubled back the way he had come, hoping the posse would keep heading south toward the border, hoping they wouldn't find his horse, hoping the storm would unleash enough rain to wipe out his tracks. He had walked as far as he could, then crawled on his hands and knees. Exhausted, his vision blurred, he had continued on, drawn by a sound that could only have been angels singing.

He glanced around again. He didn't know where he was, but it sure as hell wasn't heaven.

When the pain receded to a manageable level, he struggled to stand up, only then realizing he was stark naked.

He was sweating profusely by the time he made it to his feet. Breathing heavily, one hand pressed hard against his right side, he leaned against the side of the stall and admitted that, even if he'd been fully dressed, he wasn't up to going anywhere.

The door to the barn opened with a groan of protest, admitting a rush of fresh air and a splash of sunlight.

Instinctively, he dropped into a crouch, the ache in his side forgotten as his hand reached for a gun that wasn't there. Damn!

He heard footsteps heading in his direction. Light footsteps, moving cautiously.

Not knowing what to expect, he looked up, his breath catching in his throat when he saw the young woman staring at him over the side of the stall.

Having grown accustomed to women who wore paint and powder and lots of it, the girl should have looked downright plain. Instead, he thought she looked like an angel, with her smooth clear skin and luminous hazel eyes fringed with long, dark lashes. A short white veil framed a fine-boned, heart-shaped face. Maybe he *was* in heaven.

She stared at him, her eyes as wide as saucers as she took in his state of undress.

Muttering an oath, he grabbed the blanket and wrapped it around his hips.

"You're not gonna faint on me, are you?" he drawled, watching as her face went from bright red to pasty white.

She shook her head. "I . . . you . . . that is, you're awake," she stammered.

"You sound surprised."

"I thought you would probably be dead," she replied candidly.

Clay grunted softly. "Not yet. Who are you? Where am I?"

"Who are you?"

"I asked you first."

"My name is Hallie McIntyre." She made a vague gesture with her hand. "You're in our barn. Now, who are you?"

"Doesn't matter who I am."

"What happened to you? How did you get hurt?"

"Don't take this wrong, girl, but my business is none of your business."

Color bloomed in her cheeks again, more from annoyance than embarrassment, he guessed.

"I brought you something to eat," she said, holding up a small covered pail, "but I'm not sure you deserve it."

"Keep it then."

She grimaced at him, then came around the stall and stood in the doorway. She wore a long gray wool dress covered with a white apron. A wooden crucifix hung from a narrow black cord around her waist. Heavy black shoes peeked from beneath the hem of her dress. He stared at the veil.

Damned if she wasn't a nun. And he was at a convent. He remembered now. The Convent of Mary Magdala outside of Bitter River. Funny place for a convent, he mused, out in the middle of nowhere. No doubt the angels he had heard singing were her Sisters.

He swore under his breath. It was a foul oath, and it brought a new rush of color to the girl's cheeks. "What the devil are a bunch of nuns doing out here, anyway?"

The girl crossed herself, her eyes wide and offended. "We're a teaching order," she said. "Or we were. We haven't had much success here, and we're slowly being disbanded and sent to other houses."

"Who are you supposed to be teaching?"

"The Indians."

Clay grunted softly. His people put no trust in the white man, or his God.

"Why won't you tell me your name?"

"It's Clay." It was a lie, but he couldn't take a chance on telling her the truth, even though it was doubtful that she would have heard of him. "What've you got in there?" he asked, jerking his chin toward the pail.

"It's not much," she said, handing him the dinner pail and a spoon. "Just some soup."

"Obliged." He reached for the pail, choking back a groan as the movement pulled on his injured side.

His hand brushed hers, and she drew back as if she'd been snake bit.

"Who's Anna?"

His head jerked up and he stared at her through narrowed eyes. "Where did you hear that name?"

"You called for her when you were unconscious. Is she your wife? If you'll tell me where she lives, I might be able to notify her of your whereabouts."

Clay shook his head. "No," he said, his voice ragged.

"But she must be worried . . ."

"I said no."

She regarded him curiously for a moment, then shrugged. "I'll be back later to collect the pail and check on your wound."

Clay nodded.

The girl licked her lips, then glanced over her shoulder. "I . . . uh, that is, what kind of trouble are you in?"

"What makes you think I'm in trouble?"

"You told me you were. Don't you remember?" He shook his head, and she shrugged. "Well, you did. Are you sure you don't want me to let your wife know where you are?"

"I'm not married," he said, his tone warning her not to pry any further. "Did you take my gun?"

She backed up until she was out of his reach, then nodded.

"Where is it?"

"I hid it."

"Has the sheriff been here?"

She shook her head.

"Does anyone else know I'm here?"

"No."

"Why didn't you tell the head nun?"

A faint smile curved Hallie's lips as she imagined Reverend Mother's reaction to being called the head nun.

"I was afraid Reverend Mother might ask me what I was doing out in the garden when I was supposed to be washing the windows in the rectory."

"What were you doing?" he asked, curious in spite of himself.

"Digging for worms."

"Worms?"

"For bait. I was going fishing this morning. And I didn't tell Reverend Mother you were here because I promised I wouldn't. Don't you remember anything?"

He grunted softly. Nun or not, he hadn't really expected her to keep her mouth shut.

The pail was warm in his hands. A fragrant aroma teased his nostrils. Removing the lid, he scooped up a spoonful of soup. It was thick with vegetables and beef, and he wolfed it down, unable to remember the last time he'd had a decent meal.

"Oh, I forgot!" She reached into her pocket and withdrew a thick slice of bread wrapped in a white napkin. "Here."

Clay stared at the hunk of warm fresh bread. It reminded him of all he'd once had, all he had lost. "Thanks."

"You're welcome."

He'd thought she was leaving, but she continued

standing there, her hands in the pockets of her skirt, quiet and still, while he ate. Never in all his life had he seen a woman who looked so serene, or known one who could remain quiet for so long.

He sighed with pleasure as he dropped the spoon in the empty pail. Head resting against the back of the stall, he closed his eyes. Nothing like a full belly to make a man forget his troubles for a while.

"I need to examine your wound."

"Help yourself, Sister."

He heard the soft rustle of her skirts as she knelt beside him, felt the brush of cloth over his skin as she made sure the blanket covered him from the waist down. He flinched as she began to remove the blood-stained bandage.

He watched her from beneath heavy-lidded eyes. She had brought a small bucket of warm water inside the stall with her. Her hands were small and fine-boned, incredibly gentle as she washed the dried blood from his side. She studied the wound for several seconds, her brow furrowed, then she reached into one of her voluminous pockets and withdrew a small jar and several strips of cloth. With infinite care, she spread a layer of thick yellow salve over the wound, covered it with a pad of soft cloth, then wrapped the other strip of cloth around his middle to hold it in place.

Clay jerked his chin at her pockets. "You wouldn't happen to have a bottle of whiskey in there, would you?"

She looked at him as if he had just asked her to produce a handful of rattlesnakes. "Of course not."

"Too bad," he drawled. "I could use a drink."

"Alcohol is the devil's own brew."

Clay nodded. "Can't argue with that, Sister, but I could sure use some. Purely medicinal, I assure you."

She looked skeptical. "I can bring you some laudanum, if you like."

He considered it a moment, then shook his head. Better to endure the pain and keep his wits sharp.

"Can I get you anything else?"

"I need my gun."

She shook her head. "No."

"Dammit . . ." He took a deep breath. "I need it," he repeated, his voice calm and rational, "in case I have to defend myself."

"You're perfectly safe from me," she replied tartly.

He couldn't help it, he laughed, the sound quickly turning into a groan as slivers of pain pricked his side.

"Are you all right?" Hallie asked doubtfully. At his nod, she gathered up the soup pail, dumped the soiled bandages in the water bucket, and walked out of the stall.

He could hear her voice as she went to the other end of the barn. He frowned a moment as he wondered who she was talking to, then grinned as he realized she was talking to one of the animals. Leaning back, he closed his eyes. He followed her mentally as she went out back to feed the chickens. A few minutes later, he heard her climb the ladder up to the loft. There was a soft rustle as she dropped hay into the troughs in the horses' stalls. Romeo and Juliet, she called them, though they were both geldings. Juliet was a pretty little chestnut with one white stocking and a blaze face; Romeo was a big blood bay with good conformation and a bad temper.

Romeo and Juliet . . . he fell asleep, smiling.

With a sigh, Hallie sank back on her heels and regarded the kitchen floor. She had been late to morning prayers again and her penance had been to scrub the floors in the infirmary, the kitchen, and the laundry room. No small task, that, but at last she was done. She wondered what the penance would be for not telling Reverend Mother there was a wounded outlaw hiding in the barn.

She dropped the cloth in the pail, then carried it outside and dumped the soapy water in the flower bed located to the left of the kitchen door. Sister Dominica claimed the soap kept the bugs away. Hallie had long ago decided it must be true, since Sister Dominica's primroses and daisies flourished.

It had been a long day. Before scrubbing the floors, she'd had to help Sister Paul do the laundry, and then she'd had to help change the sheets on Sister Ayanna's bed.

Pressing a hand to her aching back, she stared toward the barn, wondering how her patient was doing.

"Clay." She murmured his name aloud. It was a nice name for a man who, in all likelihood, probably wasn't very nice at all. She thought of his gun, hidden at the bottom of her clothes trunk under her winter cloak. It was a huge weapon, heavy, with plain walnut grips and a long barrel. She could hardly lift it.

He occupied most of her waking thoughts, that man, and troubled her sleep, as well. Her dreams were like none she had ever had before, haunted by dark brown eyes and vivid images of bronzed male flesh. She was sure she should confess those dreams to Father Antoine, but she just couldn't do it, couldn't tell that kindly old white-haired priest that she was having dreams that no cloistered woman should be having.

Last night, she had dreamed that Clay kissed her. And what was even worse, she had liked it. She, who had renounced men forever, who would soon take on the vows of poverty, chastity, and obedience.

Clay . . . why was she so drawn to a man she hardly knew?

Removing the sleeve guards and work apron she wore to protect her dress, she went into the larder and wrapped several slices of bread and meat and cheese in a cloth, then went out to the barn. It was time to feed the stock. And the man.

Clay heard the barn door open, and then the familiar sound of Hallie's footsteps treading softly. He settled the blanket over his hips, wishing, simultaneously, for his gun and his trousers.

She entered the stall, tentative as always, bringing the scent of sunshine and soap with her.

"How are you feeling this evening?" she asked.

"Better, thanks to you."

A fleeting smile crossed her lips as she handed him a clothwrapped bundle.

He nodded his gratitude as he took it from her hand.

She stood just outside the stall, her arms folded, her hands hidden in the habit's wide sleeves, while he ate. She didn't watch him, yet he could feel her stealing surreptitious glances in his direction, as if she expected him to leap to his feet and attack her. The thought brought a wry grin to his lips. He could barely stand up long enough to relieve himself. He was in no condition to attack her, even if he was of a mind to. Which he wasn't. Good Lord, a nun!

She stepped forward to take the napkin when he was done. His fingers brushed hers and she froze, her eyes wide and scared as she met his gaze.

"Dammit, girl, I wish you'd relax. I'm not gonna hurt you."

She nodded, then jerked her hand away and took a step backward.

"You are the most confounding woman I ever met,"

Clay muttered. "You save my life, and then act like I'm gonna bite your head off first chance I get."

She didn't say anything, just stared down at him, reminding him of a doe poised to take flight at the slightest provocation.

"Why haven't you called the law on me?" he asked.

"I promised not to tell anyone you were here, remember?" She looked at him in exasperation. "If you didn't expect me to keep my word, why did you make me give it to you in the first place?"

"Beats the hell out of me," he muttered. "If you'll bring me something to wear, I'll move on."

"You're not strong enough."

"I can make it."

"Maybe," she said doubtfully. "But I can't bring you anything to wear. There aren't any men's clothes here."

Clay swore under his breath. "What'd you do with the clothes I was wearing?"

"I . . ." She took a step backward, putting herself out of his reach. "They were ruined. I burned them."

"Burned them!" He blinked at her in disbelief. She had burned his clothes. He glanced down at the blanket that covered him and had a quick mental image of himself facing Bob Sayers wearing nothing but a gun belt and a sheepish grin.

"They were past mending, and stained with blood."

He glared up at her. "So, what do you suggest I do? Borrow one of those shapeless gray things of yours?"

Hallie pursed her lips to keep from smiling as she tried to picture him in one of her dresses. Even though she had not yet taken her first vows, she wore the habit of a postulant.

"Dammit," Clay growled, "it's not funny."

"I'm sorry," she said contritely. But she couldn't stay the laughter that bubbled up in her throat as she imagined him in one of her dresses, his hairy legs and bare feet peeking from beneath the hem.

"Did you burn my boots, too?" he asked irritably.

"No. I hid them up in the loft."

Well, that was something. He had paid good money for those boots. "Maybe you could ride into town and get me a pair of pants?"

She shook her head. "I can't. I'm not allowed to go into town alone." A faint grin tugged at Hallie's lips as she imagined accompanying Reverend Mother on one of her rare trips to town and trying to explain why she needed to stop at the mercantile to buy a pair of men's trousers.

"Well, that tears it! What do you suggest I do, then? I can't hide out in here forever."

"Well . . ." She chewed her thumbnail for a moment, her expression thoughtful. "Father Antoine will be here on Wednesday to hear our confessions and drop off his laundry. Maybe I can borrow a pair of his trousers."

Hallie stifled the urge to laugh as she pictured Clay wearing a pair of the good father's pants. Father Antoine was shorter than she was, and almost wider than he was tall.

"I seem to be an endless source of amusement for you," Clay muttered irritably.

Hallie shrugged. It was true, she thought, though amusing wasn't the word she would have picked. Still, her life had been infinitely more interesting since his arrival, certainly more exciting. Even dangerous.

"I've got to go." Hallie plucked the napkin from his lap and slipped it into one of her voluminous pockets. "Sister Barbour will be expecting me to help her with dinner."

"Any chance of you bringing me my gun in the morning?"

"No. Good night."

"Yeah, good night," Clay replied morosely, and wondered if he would ever have a good night again.

Chapter 3

Hallie stood with her arms folded, doing her best to keep her face impassive as the sheriff from Bitter River paced the floor. Mason Clark was a big man, with dark hair and cruel eyes. A jagged scar ran down his left cheek. He wore a brown shirt, a black leather vest, tan britches, a yellow slicker, and a black Stetson he hadn't bothered to remove. His black boots were covered with mud.

Hallie stared at his spurs, feeling a surge of pity for his horse as she imagined the large rowels raking the animal's flanks. His badge of office gleamed brightly on his shirtfront.

The lawman had been in the parlor when she returned from the barn. Reverend Mother had explained that Sheriff Mason Clark was looking for a prisoner who had escaped from jail.

"The man we're looking for is a half-breed," the sheriff had informed Hallie when she entered the room. "Goes by the name of John Walking Hawk. Ever heard of him?"

Hallie shook her head. John Walking Hawk. Was that Clay's real name? "What did he do?"

"It's not our concern, Hallie," Reverend Mother said, reproof evident in her voice. "Whatever that man has done is none of our concern."

"Yes, Mother. I'm sorry."

Hallie tried not to appear too interested as the sheriff took Reverend Mother aside and spoke to her for a few minutes.

Mother Matilda nodded, then turned to face the sisters. "The sheriff wishes to speak with each of you," she said quietly. "Please, Sisters, be seated."

Obediently, the sisters sat down. Hallie sat on the sofa next to Sister Dominica, her hands buried in the pockets of her skirt to still their trembling.

The sheriff started with Sister Monique, who was the oldest nun in the convent. He had to shout to make himself heard and after trying three times to make her understand, he shook his head and moved on.

He had no better luck with Sister Ruth. "A pan?" she asked dubiously. "You're looking for a pan hiding in the convent?"

Sister Paul's voice was barely audible as she assured the lawman that the only man she had seen in the last week was Father Antoine.

Sister Barbour looked the sheriff right in the eye, as if daring him to doubt her veracity when she told him there wasn't a man within five miles.

Sister Marguerite was next. Her cheeks turned scarlet as the sheriff asked if she had seen the man they were looking for. She replied, in a whisper-soft voice, that the only man she had seen in the last twenty-two years had been the priests who looked after the welfare of her soul, and the doctor who treated her rheumatism.

Sister Dominica swelled up like a banty rooster, her whole demeanor expressing outrage that Sheriff Clark would think she even knew a man, let alone one who had been convicted of a crime.

And then it was Hallie's turn. Her heart began to pound with dread as the sheriff's gaze settled on her. She had never been any good at lying.

"What's your name?" the sheriff asked. He stood in

front of her, one big hand resting on the butt of his pistol.

"Hallie Josephine McIntyre."

"I understand you're the only one here who spends much time outside. Have you seen a man prowling around?"

"No," Hallie said. That much was true. She hadn't seen Clay prowling around.

"You're sure? Big man, dark-skinned, with long black hair? Got a real nasty-lookin' scar on his neck, runs from here to about here." The sheriff ran a blunt-tipped finger from beneath his left ear to his collarbone.

Hallie shook her head vigorously. "I haven't seen anyone prowling around."

The sheriff grunted softly. "We're not sure he headed in this direction. The storm washed out his tracks."

Hallie didn't say anything, just continued to look at him, her heart racing, her palms damp with sweat. What would she do if they searched her room? She groaned inwardly. What if they found the gun in her trunk? She thought of Clay, lying naked and defenseless in the barn. Maybe she should have returned his weapon, but what if she had, and he killed someone? She would be responsible. And what if he were killed. . . .

The sheriff grunted softly, obviously annoyed that she couldn't help him. "I doubt you all have anything to worry about. The sonofa . . . ." He glanced at Sister Barbour's shocked expression and a dull red flush climbed up his neck. "That is, he's probably over the border by now. I doubt even that dumb 'breed would be stupid enough to head back in this direction, but you never know."

He turned back toward Reverend Mother. "Thank you for your time, ma'am. If you don't mind, we'll take a look around, just to be sure."

"As you wish, Sheriff." Mother Matilda smiled graciously. "We have nothing to hide."

While the sheriff and his men searched the convent room by room, Hallie went into the kitchen on the pretext of getting a drink of water, then slipped out the back door and made her way toward the barn. She fought the urge to run, afraid that might look suspicious if anyone from the house saw her.

Stepping into the barn, she closed the door, then hurried toward the last stall.

"You've got to get out of here," she said. "The sheriff . . ."

Clay was on his feet before she finished speaking. "I don't suppose you brought my gun?"

"No. There wasn't time to get it."

"Is there any other way out of here?"

"A door in the back. Hurry."

Grabbing the blanket, Clay wrapped it around his middle, damned if he'd let Mason Clark catch him buck naked. Exiting the stall, he headed for the back door, staggering a little.

With a sigh of exasperation, fearful he would be discovered, Hallie wrapped her arm around his waist.

"Lean on me," she said, and practically dragged him out of the barn.

"Now where?" Clay asked.

Hallie thought a moment. The sheriff and his men would probably search the shed and the chapel. "Do you think you could climb a tree?"

"I don't know, but I'm willing to try." Hell, he'd try anything she suggested, because he for damn sure wasn't going back to jail.

She led him down a small hill, across a narrow ravine, and up the other side. A huge old tree grew a few yards from the ravine, its heavy branches close and thick with leaves.

"Hurry!"

Teeth clenched, Clay reached for the lowest branch and swung himself up, swearing under his breath as the strain tore at the wound in his side. The blanket fell away from his hips to land in a dark blue puddle on the ground, but he kept going, the rough bark scraping against his bare flesh as he climbed higher, higher, until, looking back, he couldn't see anything but branches and leaves. If he couldn't see the ground, hopefully, anyone standing on the ground wouldn't be able to see him, either.

He heard the sound of footsteps and guessed Hallie was making her way back to the barn. Shivering from the cold, his side throbbing, he clung to one of the branches, and waited.

Hallie sat at the table, glad, for the first time since she had come to the convent, that there was no talking in the refectory. It was the time of the Grand Silence. Though she had not taken her vows, Hallie had observed the Rule ever since coming to the convent. Until Clay.

Hallie ate the food placed in front of her, hardly aware of what she was eating. All she could think of was Clay, stuck up in that tree. Sister Dominica had told her the sheriff and his men had made a thorough search of the convent, poking into closets, looking under the beds, checking behind the big cast-iron stove in the kitchen. They had searched the attic and the basement. They had even searched Mother Matilda's room.

Hallie had made it back to the house just as the sheriff and his men were about to search her room. She had stood beside her bed, hardly daring to breathe, as one of the deputies peered under her cot. She had felt light-headed when he glanced at the small trunk at the foot of her bed, but it wasn't big enough to hold a grown man and he hadn't bothered searching it.

When the sheriff was satisfied Clay wasn't hiding inside the convent, he had told his men to check around outside.

They were going to search the barn. She had a sudden mental image of Clay's boots lying on a pile of straw in the loft, the blanket he'd dropped folded over the stall door. She had made it back to the barn mere moments before two of the sheriff's men. She barely managed to shove Clay's boots and the blanket under the straw in Romeo's stall before the two deputies arrived.

She had been brushing Juliet when the two men entered the barn. She had tried to look unconcerned as they checked the stalls, looked in the tack room, climbed up into the loft, then went out the back door.

She had listened to the low murmur of their voices as they looked around, studying the ground out back. Clay had told her to turn the cows out before she went back to the house, explaining that the milling cattle would obliterate their footprints leading to the ravine.

The younger of the two lawmen had tipped his hat in her direction when he returned to the barn. "Sorry to have bothered you, Sister."

Hallie had smiled at him, her throat so tight she couldn't speak.

Now, she fretted over the need to finish her dinner, to join her sisters at evening prayers. It would be at least another hour before she could sneak away. She wondered if Clay was still up in the tree, or if he had managed to make his way back to the barn. She wondered why he had been arrested, wondered if she had made a terrible mistake in hiding him from the sheriff. What if Clay was a bank robber? Or worse? She didn't know anything about him. What if, when he was stronger, he murdered them all while they slept? She shook the thought from her mind.

It was almost eight-thirty by the time she managed to sneak out the kitchen door.

Lifting her skirts, she ran across the damp ground as fast as she could manage while carrying a lantern and a sack of food.

She opened the door and slid into the barn. "Mister, are you here?" She took a few steps inside, peering into the empty stalls that lined both sides of the barn. "Clay?"

He wasn't there. Depositing the lamp and the sack inside the last stall, she went out the back door, then hurried toward the tree where she had left him hours ago.

"Clay?" She peered up into the tree branches. "Clay, are you up there?"

"Yeah."

"Can you get down?"

"I got up here, didn't I?"

She held her breath, listening to the rustle of leaves as he descended the tree. Too late, she realized she had neglected to bring the blanket with her.

"Clay, wait!" But the warning came too late. Moments later, he was standing in front of her, stark naked in the moonlight. But it wasn't his nudity that drew her eye. It was the bandage swathed around his middle, or, to be more exact, the bright red stain that was spreading over the darker one. He was bleeding again.

Pulling off her shawl, she wrapped it around him. "You must be freezing."

He didn't deny it. He was hurting bad and cold clear through. Only the thought of going back to jail, of being at the mercy of Mason Clark again, had kept him up in that tree.

"Come on, we've got to get you back inside."

"Sheriff gone?"

"Yes. Hurry. You're bleeding again."

"I've got to admit, I've been better," Clay allowed, and knew he would consider himself damn lucky if he made it back to the barn without passing out. He was colder than a Colorado winter, and hungry enough to eat a horse, tail and all. The wound in his side ached with hell's own fury, and he couldn't stop shaking.

Inside the barn, Hallie settled him in the last stall, then covered him with the blanket and her shawl. He couldn't decide how he felt about having her fuss over him. On the one hand, it irritated the hell out of him to know he was dependent on her for food and shelter; he hadn't been dependent on anyone else since he was fourteen. On the other hand, he kind of liked the way she hovered over him, clucking like a mother hen with one chick. It had been a long time since a woman coddled him, a long time since anyone cared if he lived or died. . . .

She was sitting beside him now, spooning hot soup into him, her beautiful hazel eyes dark with worry. He noticed her lashes were long and thick, the way she worried her lower lip between her teeth while she fed him.

When he had warmed up some, she removed the bandage and examined his wound. The bleeding had stopped. He watched in tight-lipped silence as she carefully washed away the dried blood, patted his skin dry, then replaced the sodden bandage with a clean one. She had beautiful hands, gentle hands.

"I'll bring you another blanket," she said. "I think it's going to rain again."

Clay nodded. He could smell the storm in the air.

"You should rest now."

When she stood to leave, he reached out and clutched the hem of her skirt. "Stay awhile."

She shook her head. "I can't."

His hand fell away from her skirt. "Go on then," he

growled, annoyed with himself for wanting her to stay, and even more annoyed for asking her. "Get the hell out of here."

Hallie stared down at him. She had the strangest notion that his gruff demeanor was intended to mask a deep loneliness he didn't want her to see.

She glanced at the door. Then, with a sigh, she sat down beside him on the straw.

He regarded her through narrowed eyes. "Thought you were goin'?"

"I can stay a few minutes. Reverend Mother expects me to be late for prayers anyway. Why is the sheriff after you?"

"I told you not to pry into my business, Hallie."

"I'm not prying . . ." she began in a huff, and then she shrugged one shoulder. "Well, maybe I am, just a little, but I . . . I saved your life. I lied to the sheriff for you. I think I've got a right to know what kind of man you are."

"You've got every right, Hallie, and I can't thank you enough for what you've done, but it's better if you don't know." *Better for you. Better for me.*

"It must be something terrible, if you won't even tell me what it is."

"Terrible?" He considered that a moment, then sighed. "Yeah, I guess you could call it that. Do you want me to leave?"

She should have said yes. Reverend Mother and the good sisters had warned her time and again that worldly men were not to be trusted, that they only wanted one thing from a young woman. But surely Clay wouldn't hurt her. Besides, meeting him, caring for him, was the most exciting thing that had ever happened to her.

"Well?"

"No," she said, her voice barely audible. "I don't want you to leave."

"How long have you been a nun?"

"I'm not a nun yet. I'm a postulant."

"What's that mean, exactly?"

"It means I've decided to devote my life to God, but I haven't taken any vows yet.

"He grunted softly. "Why do you want to be a nun anyway?"

"What else should I be? Besides, everyone expects it. I've lived here since I was thirteen. The sisters are all so kind, and they seem so happy, so at peace." Hallie shrugged, wondering if she would ever find that same serenity. "I want to be like them."

"Where are your folks?"

"I don't remember much about my father," she said bitterly, and wondered if the pain of his desertion would ever go away, if she would ever be able to forgive him for the anguish he had caused her mother. "He abandoned us when I was four."

"What happened to your mother?"

"She passed away a short time later." The doctor had said she died of pneumonia, but Hallie knew her mother had died from a broken heart. "I lived with my grandmother until she died."

Grandma Hastings had tried to explain her father's behavior to Hallie. She had made lots of excuses for Frank McIntyre, saying he had been too young to accept responsibility, that he was just a born wanderer. But Hallie had known the truth. He just hadn't loved her.

"I was thirteen when my grandmother died," she went on, "and I didn't have anyplace to go, so I was sent here. The sisters have been very kind to me."

"How old are you now?"

"Seventeen."

He swore under his breath. She was still a kid. "Don't

you want to see a little of the world before you give it all up?"

She shook her head, but he saw the sudden interest in her eyes.

"I thought it was a sin to lie."

"I'm not lying," she said, and then her shoulders slumped, as if in defeat. "Maybe I am."

"Lots of pretty country out there," Clay said. "Rivers and mountains and big cities." He tugged on the hem of her drab gray skirt. "Pretty clothes in rainbow colors."

Hallie sighed. She didn't mind being shut up behind convent walls, but she did have a secret yearning to wear pretty colors, to own a red dress with a plunging neckline and a bustle draped in silk roses. To have a grand adventure, the kind she had only read about in books. But it would never happen. When she took her final vows, she would trade in her drab gray dress and short white veil for a somber black habit and veil, and the only color in her life would be the blue sky and the flowers in Sister Dominica's garden.

She thought of her life as it was now, a life controlled by the tower bell. The bell woke her at five every morning, called her to prayers and meditation morning and evening, sent her to meals, and tolled her to bed at night. Once she had taken her vows, she would be subject to the Grand Silence, required to keep silent from evening prayers until after breakfast the following morning.

"You're too young to turn your back on the world," Clay said. "Too young to turn your back on life when you haven't even lived it yet."

Hallie drew her gaze from his and stared at her hands, folded in her lap. She had been the youngest one at the convent even before the other sisters had been called back to the Mother House. It had never bothered her until now. She had been grateful for their love. They had coddled her and fussed over her. Instead of having one mother to care for her, she'd had twenty.

"You're too young, and too pretty, to hide yourself away from the world."

She looked up, startled. "You think I'm pretty?"

Clay frowned at her. "Don't you think so?"

"I wouldn't know."

"What does your looking glass tell you?"

"There aren't any mirrors in the convent." She hadn't seen her face in a mirror since she had come to this place, only a wavy, distorted image of herself reflected in a windowpane from time to time, but that was all. Vanity was a sin.

Clay grunted softly. "You're a pretty girl, Hallie." He lifted a finger to stroke her cheek. "Your skin is smooth and clear. Your nose is perfect, not too big, not too small . . ." His finger slid down her nose, light as a raindrop. "Your lips are soft . . ."

Hallie swallowed hard as his callused finger outlined the curve of her lower lip. Why was it suddenly so hard to breathe, to think? Her heart was pounding as if she had been running for miles, her whole body tingled in a most delicious way. She felt the prick of her conscience, warning her that it was wicked to let him touch her.

"Soft," he said again, and before she realized his intent, he was leaning toward her, one big brown hand cupping the back of her head as his mouth slanted over hers, blocking everything from her sight but his face.

She was too stunned to pull away. Eyes wide open, she sat there and let him kiss her. Heat flooded her cheeks. Her insides fluttered like the wings of a hummingbird. There was a peculiar roaring in her ears; an incredibly sweet warmth blossomed in the very center of her being and spread outward, like ripples in a pool. It was a most pleasant sensation, quivery and exciting and a little frightening.

Tentatively, she kissed him back, amazed by the sudden heat that suffused her from head to toe as she pressed her lips to his, by the inexplicable need to wrap her arms around him and draw him closer, to press her body against his.

Clay muttered an oath as he broke the kiss. He had kissed a few women in his time—whores and virgins alike, but not one of them had ever affected him like this, or caught fire so quickly. It wouldn't have surprised him if they had both gone up in flames.

Hallie stared at him in wonderment as she touched her fingertips to her lips. She had been kissed by a man for the first time in her life, and she felt as if the whole world had suddenly shifted.

"I think you'd better go," Clay said, his voice gruff.

Hallie's conscience screamed that he was right. It was a terrible sin to let him kiss her, and a worse sin to have enjoyed it. And what if she were caught out here in the barn, in his arms? Reverend Mother or one of the other sisters could come looking for her at any moment. Father Antoine would be shocked by her next confession. But none of that seemed to matter.

"Would you kiss me again?"

"What?"

"Kiss me," Hallie whispered, and leaning forward, she pressed her mouth to his, hoping he could kiss away the unfamiliar ache throbbing deep within her.

She was a quick study, Clay mused. Awareness sizzled between them like chain lightning. Knowing it was wrong, yet helpless as a moth to resist the inviting glow of a flame, he drew her into his arms, groaning softly as her elbow brushed against his wounded side. But the pain was soon forgotten in the quick rush of desire that engulfed him from head to heel as he felt the lush curves hidden beneath the shapeless gray dress. Her breasts were warm and soft against his chest. Little moans of pleasure rose in her throat as he deepened the kiss. Her hungry little sounds excited him still further. Her eyelids fluttered down, and his arm tightened around her waist, drawing her closer, closer, until she was nestled snugly in his lap, her weight a sweet, sweet torture.

She was drowning, smothering in sensations she had never dreamed of. Hallie clutched at his shoulders, needing to anchor herself to something solid as the world she knew spun out of control, out of focus. She pressed herself wantonly against him, needing to be closer, wishing she could crawl inside him, but not knowing why. Her hands slid restlessly up and down his arms, kneading muscles that were rock hard, yet quivered beneath her fingertips. His tongue traced the curve of her lower lip, and a delicious heat unfurled deep in her belly, the flames licking upward, outward, until her whole body seemed to be on fire.

Drugged by her kisses, Clay drew her down in the straw beside him, one hand sliding up and down her thigh, delving beneath her skirts. She wore thick black cotton stockings and his hand climbed up, up, seeking the soft smooth skin of her inner thigh, while his other hand searched for her breast.

And then, in the deep valley between her breasts, his questing fingers brushed against her rosary beads. Muttering an oath, Clay jerked his hand away as if he'd been burned.

She looked up at him, her lips swollen, her eyes hazy with desire.

Clay straightened her skirts. "You'd better go," he said gruffly, "before someone comes looking for you."

Confused and hurt by his abrupt dismissal, Hallie stood up and brushed the straw from her skirts.

Clay turned on his side so she couldn't see the aching evidence of his desire.

"Go on," he said, deliberately making his voice harsh. "Get!"

She stared at him a moment, the hurt in her eyes like a knife in his gut, and then she turned and ran out of the barn.

Left alone in the darkness, Clay stared after her, stunned by what had happened between them. Another few minutes, and he would have had her flat on her back with her drawers down and her skirts bunched around her hips.

Damn! He had enough sins to answer for without ravishing a nun.

Chapter 4

Hallie knelt at the altar in the quiet, candlelit chapel that was located on the first floor of the convent, her head bowed, her hands clasped around her rosary. She had been there for over an hour, trying to pray for forgiveness, but the words seemed locked in her throat. She had let Clay kiss her. But that wasn't the worst of it. Oh, no. One kiss might be explained away, forgiven even. She had never been kissed by a man before. She had been naturally curious to experience what she had been missing, what she would be renouncing forever when she took her vows, and kissing Clay had been her first, possibly her only chance to discover what kissing was like before she became a Bride of Christ. No, one kiss didn't seem such a grievous sin.

It was the second kiss that was causing her so much spiritual anguish. Surely it had been the Devil and all his angels at work. What else could have prompted her to do such a dreadful thing? Yes, it had to be the work of Satan, tempting her with sins of the flesh. She thought of Clay constantly. Her dreams were filled with images of bronzed male flesh, of long, long legs and muscular arms, dreams no cloistered woman should be having.

She knew she should speak to Reverend Mother, knew she should seek out Father Antoine and confess her sins and beg for absolution. But, and this was the worst of it, the part she couldn't comprehend, kissing

Clay hadn't felt like a sin. It had felt wonderful and right. And surely she couldn't be held responsible for her dreams.

"Hallie?"

Turning her head, Hallie saw Reverend Mother kneeling beside her.

"You've seemed rather preoccupied these past few days," Reverend Mother said kindly. "Is something troubling you, child?"

Hallie nodded. She had never been able to lie to Mother Matilda.

"Do you wish to tell me what it is?"

"Not now, Reverend Mother."

"Is it a spiritual matter that troubles you so?"

"Not exactly."

"I see." Reverend Mother placed her hand on Hallie's shoulder and gave her an affectionate squeeze. "Come and see me when you're ready, child. My door is always open."

"Thank you, Mother."

"And try not to be late for dinner."

"Yes, Mother."

Reverend Mother made a firm sign of the cross on Hallie's brow, then rose gracefully to her feet and left the chapel.

With a sigh, Hallie buried her face in her hands. What was she going to do?

"You're awfully quiet tonight," Clay remarked.

"Am I?"

"Is something bothering you?"

"You're the second one to ask me that today," Hallie said irritably. She looked at him, her gaze running over his broad chest and shoulders with feminine appreciation. *Sins of the flesh,* she thought, and quickly glanced away. She had to find him something to wear, and soon.

"Want to tell me about it?"

"No!"

Clay frowned as twin flags of color appeared in her cheeks. "No need to bite my head off," he muttered, and then, in a sudden flash of insight, he knew what was causing her so much distress. "You're not stewing over that kiss, are you?"

Embarrassed that he had read her thoughts so easily, Hallie turned away, her hands pressed to her flaming cheeks.

"Hallie, it was just a kiss. It didn't mean anything."

"Oh!" She had thought of nothing since, and now he was telling her it hadn't meant a thing to him. He probably kissed every girl he met. Mortified, she sprang to her feet.

"Wait!" He grabbed a handful of her skirt, anchoring her in place when she would have run out of the stall. "I didn't mean it like that."

"Let me go!" She lashed out at him with her foot, the toe of her hard-soled shoe landing with a solid thud against his injured side.

With a yelp, he turned her loose, his hand pressing against the wound as shards of white-hot agony exploded through his side.

"Oh, Clay, I'm sorry." Instantly contrite, she knelt beside him. "Here, let me take a look."

He took a deep breath and blew it out between clenched teeth. "I'm all right."

She nodded, then glanced away, feeling more miserable than she ever had in her life. No doubt she would go to hell for her wicked thoughts. The Devil was probably laughing at her.

"Hallie?"

"What?" She refused to meet his eyes.

"There's nothing wrong with kissing. It's perfectly natural, perfectly normal. People do it all the time."

"It's not perfectly normal!" she exclaimed. "Not for me."

"Why? Because you're gonna be a nun?"

"Exactly. I'm not supposed to think about such wicked acts."

"There's nothing wicked about kissing. I'll bet even the head nun thinks about it once in a while."

Hallie stared at Clay in horror. "She does not!"

"Ask her."

"I can't ask her that."

Clay shrugged. "She may be a nun, but she's still a woman."

"You're horrible."

"Yeah, that's what they all say."

Hallie looked at him curiously, her embarrassment forgotten. "That's what who says?"

"You, for one."

"Who else?"

"Practically everybody who knows me."

"I don't believe that."

"It's true."

"What's true? That everyone says it? Or that you're horrible?"

"Both," Clay said, grinning.

Hallie stared at him, thinking how handsome he was. Even the thick black bristles that shadowed his jaw couldn't detract from the masculine beauty of his face. She longed to reach out and touch him, to let her fingertips slide down his arm, to trace the shape of his lower lip, to run her hands over the width of his shoulders.

"Stop it," Clay said.

"Stop what?"

"Looking at me like that."

For the second time that night, she felt a rush of heat climb up her neck and infuse her cheeks. "Like what?"

"Like I'm dessert."

"I'm not!" she exclaimed, mortified that he had caught her staring.

"I'd like to nibble on you, too, Hallie. You look good enough to eat."

"You mustn't say such things to me," she said primly.

"Mustn't I?" His gaze slid over her. "I'd like to start at your lips and work my way down to your toes."

"Stop it!" She clapped her hands over her ears, not wanting to hear more, but she couldn't shut out the images his words conjured in her mind. She liked his kisses, liked them far too much, thought of them, and him, far too often.

"Hallie? Hallie, I'm sorry."

She folded her hands in her lap, then slid a glance in his direction. "Do you really think I'm pretty?"

"Pretty as a spring flower."

Warmth spread through her at the compliment. Even if it wasn't true, it was nice to hear. Mother Matilda had once told her she was "a pretty little thing," but it was different, more meaningful, coming from Clay. "I'd better go."

"Yeah." Clay settled the blanket over his hips, then lifted his knee so she couldn't see the telltale evidence of his lustful thoughts. "I think you'd better. Thanks for dinner."

With a nod, Hallie stood up. "Good night, Clay."

"Night, Hallie."

He watched her leave the barn, then swore under his breath. Damn! That girl had him feeling as randy as a billy goat. He had to get some clothes and get the hell out of here before he did something stupid.

For Hallie, the next few days were nerve-racking. She was on edge every minute, afraid Reverend Mother would find out about Clay, afraid Clay might try to kiss her again, afraid she would let him. He was healing rapidly now. Soon, he would be well enough to leave.

With that in mind, she had taken a wool blanket from the storage room and spent every spare minute sewing Clay a pair of pants, no easy task, since she had never been more than a barely adequate seamstress.

In all honesty, she had to admit she was sewing the pants mostly for her own peace of mind. It was most disconcerting to see him walking around the barn wearing no more than a blanket wrapped around his lean hips. She had never imagined that seeing a man's bare arms and chest could be so distracting, or that her fingers would itch to stroke that same chest, to slide over those wide shoulders, to test the strength of those arms, feel them wrap around her and hold her close . . .

She found herself thinking about him while she knelt at the altar, while Sister Dominica read the scriptures aloud in the evening, while she helped Sister Barbour prepare dinner. He filled her thoughts while she made the beds . . . especially when she made the beds, wondering what it would be like to lie beside him in the night. She saw his face when she closed her eyes to say her prayers.

Sister Dominica shook her head, declaring it was just spring fever and would pass soon enough.

Reverend Mother decided Hallie was suffering from the miseries and prescribed a tonic.

But nothing helped. Hallie agonized constantly over the wicked thoughts that plagued her days and haunted her dreams. Some mornings she woke up, certain she had sinned during the night, so real were her dreams. She longed to talk to Reverend Mother, but she lacked the courage to do so, and there was no one else. The other sisters had been nuns for years and years. They were such dear, sweet, righteous women. Surely they had never been tormented by the wicked yearnings that troubled her.

Hallie glanced at the clock in the kitchen. It was time for evening prayers. Tonight, after chapel, she would go straight to her room.

She wouldn't sneak out to see Clay.

She wouldn't think of him.

She wouldn't dream of him.

She had finished the trousers the night before and had started making him a shirt out of a discarded habit she had found in the scrap basket. If she worked hard, she could have the shirt done by tonight, and then he could go, and she would never have to see him, or think of him, again.

Clay waited until all the lights were out in the convent, and then he slipped out the back door of the barn, the blanket wrapped around his waist, the edge flapping around his ankles.

Standing outside, he closed his eyes and took a deep breath. The night was cool and clear, fragrant with the scent of damp earth and wet grass. He could smell the smoke rising from the convent chimney.

He started walking toward the shallow ravine behind the barn. He cursed softly as he stepped on a rock. He needed some clothes. He needed his boots, and his gun. He needed to get the hell out of here.

He walked along the edge of the ravine, thinking how good it felt to be outside, how lucky he was to be alive. He lifted a hand to his neck, grimacing as he imagined a noose there. Damned lucky.

He tried not to think about Hallie but couldn't help wondering why she hadn't come to see him before she went to bed. She usually came out around eleven to collect his supper dishes. He told himself he didn't miss her. She was just a kid—a kid who was going to be a nun, for crying out loud. And he was a man on the run with a reward on his head and a noose waiting for him if he got caught.

He grimaced as he thought of the days and nights he had spent locked up in Bitter River's jail. Mason Clark might be a good lawman, but he was also the most vicious, cruel man Clay had ever had the misfortune to run across. His one regret was that he hadn't had a chance to kill the man.

Pausing, he stared into the distance, remembering the first night he had spent in jail. Clark had been goading him, taunting him about being a half-breed, describing the last hanging he had carried out in lurid detail, laughing about how Hector Hernandez had died, kicking and puking. *That's how you'll go,* Clark had declared. *Wait and see.* Clark had been turning away when Clay reached through the bars and grabbed the lawman by the collar. Jerking him back against the bars, he wrapped his arm around Clark's neck, squeezing, squeezing. He might have killed the man right then if one of his deputies hadn't come in. Coughing and choking, Clark had staggered away from the cell. When he turned to face Clay, there had been murder in his eyes. For a moment, Clay had thought he was gonna cheat the rope after all, that Clark would shoot him where he stood. Instead, the lawman had cuffed his hands to the bars; then slowly and deliberately, he had laid into Clay, his meaty fists driving home with relentless intensity, until Clay sagged against the bars, held upright by the shackles around his wrists.

He swore under his breath as he turned back toward the barn. He had to get out of here. Tomorrow, he would tell Hallie to bring him his gun and if she refused, he'd threaten to bust into the convent and search the place room by room until he found it. Once he was armed, he would take one of the horses and ride out tomorrow night after dinner. He'd get some clothes somehow, steal them if he had to. He grunted softly. He was getting good at stealing. And lying. Even killing was getting easier . . . He swore under his breath. Killing would never be easy But sometimes it was necessary.

The barn loomed ahead of him. Juliet whinnied softly as he neared the animal's stall. He paused to scratch the horse between the ears, grateful for the gelding's company. He had examined the horses earlier in the day and though Juliet had a sweet temper, Romeo was better suited to a man of his size.

"It's time to move on, old man," he murmured, and giving the gelding a final pat on the neck, he made his way through the dark to the stall he'd been sleeping in.

It was time to leave this place. Time to finish what he had started.

Time to get his daughter back before she forgot who her father was.

Chapter 5

He woke to the familiar sound of Hallie humming softly as she milked the cows. He should have got up early and done it for her, he thought. Maybe tomorrow . . . and then he remembered that he wouldn't be there tomorrow.

With a sigh, he closed his eyes and went back to sleep. It was the sound of the barn door opening that woke him the second time. Grabbing the blanket that had slipped away during the night, he sat up and settled it over his hips.

Hallie appeared in the doorway a few moments later. "I brought you something to wear." She placed a neatly folded pile of clothing on the floor inside the stall. His boots, cleaned and polished to a high shine, were on top of the pile.

"Where'd you get this stuff?" he asked.

"I made them for you." She lifted one shoulder and let it fall. "I hope they fit. I'm not much of a seamstress, and I didn't have anything to use for a pattern."

"I'm obliged. Thank you." He dragged a hand over his jaw. "I don't suppose you've got a razor anywhere?"

She shook her head. "No, I'm sorry. I'll be back in a few minutes with your breakfast. I couldn't carry everything at once."

"Is something wrong?" he asked.

"No, why?"

He shrugged. "I don't know. You usually stick around awhile."

"Oh, well, I . . . I've got a lot to do today."

Clay nodded. "Thanks for the clothes. Hallie?"

"What?"

"I'll need my gun back."

"I'll bring it before I go to bed," she said, then hurried out of the barn as if the Devil himself were snapping at her heels.

Clay frowned, wondering if he had said or done something to upset her, and then wondered why he cared. He was leaving tonight and he would never see her again.

Hallie bent to her task with fervor, determined not to think of Clay. He was a wanted man, one who lived by the gun, and she had no business daydreaming about him, or about any other man. Once he was gone, her life would go back to normal. She wouldn't think of dark brown eyes fringed with thick lashes, or muscles covered with copper-colored skin, or long black hair brushing a pair of wide masculine shoulders. She wouldn't hear his voice in her head telling her she was pretty as a wildflower, or yearn to feel his kisses again. She would stop wondering what it would be like to be his wife, to give birth to his children, strong sons and beautiful raven-haired daughters. . . .

She shook her head, annoyed that she was thinking of him again.

She finished changing the sheets on her hard, narrow cot, then went upstairs to change the sheets on Sister Ayanna's bed.

The elderly nun smiled at her as she entered her cell. "Good morning, my child," she said cheerfully.

"Good morning, Sister Ayanna. How are you today?"

"Better, thank you."

"I've come to change the sheets on your bed."

"Bless you, child."

Hallie helped the frail nun out of bed and settled her into the hard chair that was the room's only other piece of furniture. A large wooden crucifix hung from the wall behind the bed.

Hallie smiled at Sister Ayanna as she spread a blanket over her lap. Like all the other nuns, Sister Ayanna was always happy and cheerful. With a sigh, Hallie wondered if she would ever attain that kind of inner peace and serenity.

She glanced around the room as she removed the soiled linen from the bed. She had never given much thought to the future, had always assumed she would take her vows and join the Sisterhood. Now, she looked at the barren walls, the sparse furnishings, and wondered what it would be like to spend the rest of her life in this place, or one like it, to never wear pretty clothes or see a city or marry and have children. . . .

Shaking such thoughts away, Hallie finished changing the sheets and helped Sister Ayanna back into bed.

"Can I get you anything?" Hallie asked as she plumped the pillow.

"No, I'm fine, child. I have my Prayer Book and my rosary."

"All right. I'll see you later."

"Yes, God willing."

With a nod, Hallie went to change the other beds. To keep from thinking about Clay, she sang her favorite hymn while she worked. Reverend Mother always said a song to the Lord was counted as a prayer of righteousness.

When she finished changing all the beds, she carried the sheets down the narrow winding stairway to the laundry room.

Sister Marguerite was up to her elbows in soap suds. She smiled at Hallie. "Just leave them there, child," she said cheerfully.

Hallie dumped the dirty linen on the floor near the washtub. "I have some free time," she said. "Would you like some help?"

"Why, thank you, Hallie, that would be nice."

Rolling up her sleeves, Hallie picked up one of the sheets and dropped it in the vat of hot soapy water.

"The house seems quiet, with so many of our sisters gone. It must be exciting for them. Imagine establishing a new house, seeking out new souls." Sister's Marguerite's pale blue eyes glowed with zeal at the thought. "Perhaps we'll go to join them soon."

Hallie nodded. Next year she would become a novice, charged to obey all the Holy Rules of the community. "Did you ever . . ." She hesitated, suddenly afraid to voice her doubts aloud

"Ever what, dear?"

"Ever wish you hadn't become a nun?"

"Oh, my no! I knew it was to be my vocation from the time I was a young girl. My mother was against it. I had six brothers. The eldest is a priest, but I was her only daughter and she wanted me to stay at home. But Father said it was my calling, and she would have to accept it. I doubt she ever did."

"I wish I had brothers or sisters," Hallie remarked.

Sister Marguerite nodded. "It's sad, being alone in the world." She leaned over and patted Hallie's hand. "But you're not alone anymore," she declared with a smile. "I wonder what Sister Barbour is cooking up for supper."

Hallie was proud of herself as she made her way out to the barn late that afternoon. She hadn't thought of Clay all morning. Well, she amended, hardly ever.

He was currying Romeo when she entered the barn. "You don't have to do that," she said. "It's my job."

"I needed something to do."

"Oh." She observed him for a moment. The trousers she had made for him were a trifle short, but otherwise the fit wasn't too bad. She hadn't felt up to tackling buttonholes or a collar, so the pants had a drawstring, and the loose-fitting shirt slipped over his head. The wide vee neck of his shirt exposed a generous expanse of dark skin. She stared at the puckered white scar on his neck, wondering what had caused it.

Clay grinned at her. "Thank you for the clothes, Hallie."

Color suffused her cheeks at his praise. "You're welcome. I'm sorry I'm not a better seamstress."

"They're fine." He didn't care about the fit; he was just glad to be wearing something besides a blanket.

She shrugged and looked away, only to have her gaze drawn back to him again. "Does your side still hurt?"

"A little."

"Then you shouldn't be doing that."

She moved forward to take the currycomb from his hand, froze as her fingers brushed his. Startled by the awareness that sizzled between them, she stared up at him, her eyes wide and uncertain.

He stared back at her, the intensity in his gaze bringing a flush to his cheeks.

"I've got to go," she said, the words tripping over themselves in a rush.

She whirled away from him, only to come to an abrupt halt when she came face to face with Reverend Mother.

"What is going on here, Hallie?" Mother Matilda asked sternly. "Who is this man?"

"He . . . I . . . that is, I . . ."

"Afternoon, ma'am." Clay interjected smoothly. "I came by looking for work. I was just trying to convince this young woman to hire me. I'm good with animals."

The nun raised one brow. "I see. Hallie?"

"Yes, Mother, that's right. He . . . he said he could shoe the horses and . . ." She pointed toward the roof. "And fix that hole. You know it needs fixing badly. And . . . and he could look after the cattle."

"That's right, ma'am," Clay jumped in. "I'm right handy to have around."

The nun regarded him for several moments. She was a tall, spare woman, with a narrow face, sharp gray eyes, and straight brown brows. He had the uncomfortable feeling that she could see right through him, clear down to his soul. It was hard to determine her age, but he thought she must be at least fifty. She carried an air of authority that would have put an army sergeant to shame.

"Handy?" she repeated. "Indeed? What's your name, young man?"

"Clay Evans, ma'am."

"How much would you expect to be paid for your labors?"

"I don't need any pay, ma'am, just a place to bed down for a few days, and something to eat."

"Are you of our faith, Mr. Evans?"

"My father was."

"And have you strayed from our beliefs?"

"Yes, ma'am, I'm afraid I have."

"Perhaps we can bring you back to the fold," Reverend Mother remarked, the faint trace of a smile on her lips.

Clay grinned. "I doubt it, but I give you leave to try."

"Very well. We shall try it for one week and see how it works out."

"Thank you, ma'am."

"There's a room in the basement that you may use. It's small, but definitely more comfortable than the barn. Hallie, make up the bed."

"If it's all the same to you, ma'am, I'd just as soon sleep out here."

Reverend Mother glanced at Hallie. "Yes, perhaps that would be better. Hallie, Sister Barbour needs you in the kitchen."

"Yes, Reverend Mother."

Clay watched Hallie leave the barn. He could feel the Reverend Mother watching him.

"Hallie is a young, impressionable girl who will be taking her first vows very soon," the nun remarked. "She has no knowledge of men." She pinned Clay with a hard look. "I should like to keep it that way."

"Yes, ma'am."

"Very well. I shall expect you to look after the chickens and the livestock. I should like you to repair the hole in the roof of the barn as soon as possible." She pointed toward the southwest corner of the building. "You'll find shingles and a hammer over there, along with a box of nails."

Clay nodded. He already knew where everything was. He'd had a lot of time on his hands the last few days and nothing to do but explore.

"We'll expect you in the refectory for meals."

"I think we'd all be more comfortable if I ate out here."

"Undoubtedly, but it will be less work for Sister Barbour if you take your meals with us. We rise at five in the morning here in the convent, Mr. Evans. Breakfast is at six. Please don't be late. We take our midday meal at half-past noon, and dinner is at five. There is no talking during meals."

Clay nodded. He had the distinct impression that the

only reason she wanted him to join the nuns at meals was so she could keep an eye on him. "Yes, ma'am."

"I would appreciate it if you would bathe and shave before coming to breakfast."

"I'm afraid I don't have a razor."

"I shall ask Sister Barbour to find you one." She regarded him for a long moment, her eyes narrowed. "Don't make me regret my decision, Mr. Evans."

"No, ma'am."

With a nod, she lifted her hand and, with a spatulate thumb, firmly traced the sign of the cross on his forehead. Then, with a last speculative look in his direction, she left the barn.

"Damn," Clay muttered, "what the devil have I got myself into?"

He started his job as convent handyman the following morning after breakfast.

Mother Matilda herself had roused him from bed at five, informing him that there was a tub of hot water waiting for him in the kitchen. He was to bathe and shave while the sisters were at prayers.

Too sleepy to argue, he had crawled out of his blankets and made his way up to the house. Sitting in a small wooden tub, his knees practically knocking against his chin, shaving himself with a razor that was none too sharp (where had a nun found a razor in the first place?), he had called himself ten kinds of a fool for not riding out during the night. He'd had every intention of doing so. Instead, he had made all kinds of excuses why he should stay put for another couple of days: his side was still tender, he owed the convent for the food he had eaten, staying would give him time to regain his strength. He refused to admit he was staying because of Hallie.

Hallie. She had stared at him across the breakfast table as if she had never seen him before. Discomfited by her intense scrutiny, he had gobbled his breakfast like a hog and excused himself from the table.

He had fed the stock, collected the eggs from the hen-house behind the barn, milked the cows. Eight brown cows with placid brown eyes. Hallie had told him they sold the extra milk to the people in town as a way to earn money for the convent. One of the local farmers came by each morning to collect it.

He found a ladder behind the barn and began working on the hole in the roof that afternoon. It didn't take more than ten minutes for him to realize he wasn't up to the job. Every swing of the hammer pulled on the half-healed wound in his side, but he'd said he would do it, and he kept doggedly on, resting frequently.

He skipped lunch. The thought of climbing down the ladder and back up again was just too daunting.

He was on the last row of shingles when he heard a cough behind him. Glancing over his shoulder, he saw one of the nuns peering at him. Behind thick spectacles, her dark blue eyes regarded him with blatant distrust.

"Reverend Mother said you might like a drink, since you've been working so hard," the diminutive nun remarked.

Clay stared at her, wondering how she had managed to climb up the ladder in her voluminous black skirts and hold on to a glass of what looked to be lemonade at the same time.

"Thank you, Sister," he said. He reached for the glass, noting she made certain their hands didn't touch.

"You're welcome," she replied curtly. She studied him through narrowed, suspicious eyes. "I don't know what we need *you* for," she said in a most uncharitable way. "I could have fixed the roof."

Clay offered her his most charming smile. He knew

the power of that smile. It had served him well with the ladies in the past. "Be a shame to put those pretty hands to such rough work."

Her cheeks flushed bright red, but she didn't look away, or bat her eyelashes, or do any of the other coy things women usually did when a man flattered them.

"Don't break the glass," was all she said.

With a wry grin, he watched her climb down from the ladder and return to the convent, her dark skirts hardly moving. He wondered if she was walking, or floating over the ground.

From his vantage point, he looked out over the convent grounds. The main house was large and square and needed a good whitewashing. A tall wooden cross rose from the peak of the roof. The chapel stood to the left of the house, small and neat. Primroses grew in neat beds on both sides of the front door. Behind the house, there was a small rough-hewn wooden building. Hallie had told him it was a storage shed. Sister Dominica kept her gardening tools there. A high wall surrounded the property. The stout wooden gate he had crawled through was open, inviting. Had it been closed and locked the night he had escaped from jail, he would likely be dead now.

He finished the lemonade, put the glass where it wouldn't get broken, and went back to work.

At dusk, he climbed down the ladder. His back ached. His shoulders ached. His side burned with renewed intensity, but he had finished reshingling the damn roof.

Feeling like he was two hundred years old, Clay hobbled into the barn. Using a corner of the blanket, he wiped the sweat from his brow, wishing he had access to a shot of whiskey and wondering what the chances were of taking two baths in the same day.

He whirled around as the barn door swung open, felt a surge of gladness when he saw Hallie standing there.

"Reverend Mother thought you might like to, ah, wash up before dinner. Sister Barbour has some water warming on the stove."

Clay grinned. "Like an answer to a prayer," he muttered. "How are you, Hallie?"

"Fine, thank you." She tried not to stare at him, but she couldn't keep her gaze from running over him. She had thought him handsome before, but now, clean-shaven, with his long black hair freshly washed, he was simply beautiful. She drew her gaze from his face, but it didn't help. She couldn't stop thinking about the strong, square jaw that had been hidden beneath his whiskers, couldn't stop remembering what his skin felt like; couldn't keep her lips from remembering the touch of his mouth on hers. "The water should be ready after you've milked the cows."

Clay nodded, acutely aware of the fact that she was having a hard time keeping her eyes off of him. The thought pleased him, though it annoyed him that he couldn't stop staring at her, either, any more than he could keep from remembering how she had felt in his arms, all warm skin and soft curves.

"I'll help you with the milking, if you like."

He was going to refuse, but he was too tired, too sore in every muscle, to turn down an offer of help. "Thanks. I'd appreciate it."

"You didn't have to finish the roof all in one day, you know," Hallie remarked as she pulled up a stool and sat down beside one of the cows.

"It smells like rain," Clay replied, taking his place beside the next cow.

"Oh." Hallie sniffed the air, but all she could smell was hay and manure. "Reverend Mother offered to let you sleep in the basement. Why did you refuse? Surely it would be more comfortable than sleeping out here."

Clay's hands stilled. How could he tell her the truth? And what was the truth? That he wanted to sleep in the barn so he wouldn't be so close to her? Or that he wanted to sleep in the barn so that she could sneak out to see him if she was of a mind to?

"Clay?"

"I just thought it would be easier on everyone if I slept out here."

"Oh." She thought of all the nights she had crept out to the barn to bring Clay something to eat, to make sure he was all right. Was he hoping she would keep coming out to see him in the middle of the night? She tried to concentrate on the task at hand, but the silence between them, broken only by the sound of the milk squirting into the pails and the occasional swish of a tail, made her uncomfortable.

"Sister Dominica doesn't think you should be staying here. I heard her talking to Reverend Mother this afternoon."

"Sister Dominica," Clay mused. "Is she the little feisty one who brought me the lemonade?"

"Yes. She's our gardener."

Clay grunted softly. He had the feeling that, in spite of her diminutive size, Sister Dominica would be a formidable enemy, should she choose to be one. "You don't think she'll slip hemlock into my soup, do you?"

Hallie laughed. It was a warm, pleasant sound, one that seemed to seep under Clay's skin and wrap around his heart, warm and soft as silk. He glanced over his shoulder and his gaze met hers. How pretty she was, with her hazel eyes sparkling and her cheeks flushed.

The laughter died in Hallie's throat as her gaze met Clay's. There was a fire in his eyes, a pulsing heat that sizzled between them, bright as a rainbow, hot as the sun in midsummer. It warmed her clear down to her toes.

"Hallie . . ." Hardly aware of what he was doing, Clay stood up and moved toward her.

She stared up at him as though hypnotized as his hands folded over her shoulders, lifting her to her feet, drawing her into his arms.

Her head fell back, granting him easy access to her lips. She heard him swear under his breath, and then he was bending toward her, his mouth slanting over hers. Her heart fluttered wildly as she waited for him to kiss her. His lips were warm and firm and eager. His tongue slid over her lower lip, igniting a hungry flame deep inside her that made her press herself against him. Her breasts flattened against his chest, his arms tightened around her, drawing her closer to the hard length of his body.

She moaned softly as his tongue slid into her mouth. It occurred to her that she should be shocked by such intimacy, that she should push him away, slap him, make him stop. But the feelings tumbling through her were too new, too intense. Too pleasurable. Stop? She hoped he would never stop. . . .

The sound of the convent bell calling the sisters to the evening meal jerked her back to the present.

She twisted out of Clay's arms, mortified at what had happened between them, what she had allowed to happen between them.

"Hallie . . ."

"No!" She shook her head as she pressed her hand to her lips and then, with a strangled cry, she lifted her skirts and ran out of the barn.

Clay swore under his breath as he stared after her. What the devil was he going to do about Hallie?

What in heaven's name was she going to do about Clay? The thought kept Hallie awake far into the night. She had made a fool of herself at supper. She had tried so hard to pretend he wasn't sitting across from her at the table that she had knocked over her water glass, then spilled soup in her lap. Sister Dominica had looked at her, tacitly chiding her to be more careful; Reverend Mother had broken the silence to ask if she was feeling well. She had been close to tears by the time the meal ended and had hurried away from the table as soon as possible.

How could she even think about becoming a nun when she felt like this? The burden of sin lay heavy upon her shoulders. She had lied to the sheriff. She had lied by omission by not telling Reverend Mother about Clay. She had let Clay kiss her three times . . . and she yearned to kiss him again.

She tossed and turned on her hard narrow cot, unable to get comfortable, unable to relax, unable to do anything but think of Clay . . . Clay, whose real name was John Walking Hawk. The sheriff had said he was a half-breed. Funny, she had never noticed Clay looked like an Indian, but, of course, he did. His hair was long and black and straight, his skin was coppery-red. She had never known an Indian before, although she had seen a Cheyenne woman once. The woman's husband had beat her up and she had come to the convent seeking shelter. Hallie had seen her from a distance a few times, a pretty, dark-skinned woman who never smiled, who had jumped every time there was a loud noise. She had given birth to a baby boy a few weeks after she arrived. The baby had been born dead, and the Indian woman had died the next day. Hallie had overheard Sister Dominica tell Sister Ruth that it was a blessing for both the mother and child, especially the child.

A half-breed, Sister Dominica had said, her voice

filled with pity. *No one loved a half-breed, so it was better that God had called him home.*

Hallie's last thought before sleep claimed her was to wonder if anyone had ever loved Clay.

Chapter 6

The sound of the big bell calling the nuns to breakfast woke him in the morning. Feeling as though he were about a hundred years old, Clay walked up the narrow rock-lined path that led to the kitchen's back door. Every muscle in his body ached. He'd been a fool to push himself so hard. The hole in the roof of the barn had been there for a long time; another couple of days wouldn't have mattered. The floorboards in the barn were already ruined. Another soaking wouldn't have made them any worse. He winced at the thought of pulling them up and replacing them. Maybe he'd wait a few days.

He glanced up at the sky as he wiped his boots off outside the back door. It was going to rain again before nightfall.

The nuns were already seated when he arrived at the refectory. He murmured an apology to the Reverend Mother, then took his place at the table, his gaze seeking Hallie. She glanced away, then bowed her head as one of the nuns—he thought it was Sister Ruth—began to pray.

Clay bowed his head. It had been years since anyone had blessed the food he'd eaten, years since he, himself, had said a prayer, or given much thought to the welfare of his soul . . . a soul that was surely beyond redemption now.

Breakfast was a quiet meal. It seemed odd, to be surrounded by so many silent women. He kept his gaze on his plate, but he could feel Sister Dominica glaring at him.

He rose as soon as the meal was over, but Mother Matilda's voice stayed him before he could leave the room.

"Mr. Evans?"

"Yes, ma'am?"

"Hallie tells me you have finished repairing the roof."

Clay nodded.

"That's quite commendable. I had expected it to take you several days. What will you do next?"

"Replace the flooring in the barn. Most of it's rotted."

"I see. I shall have to order the material from town."

Clay nodded again.

"When you have time, I should like to have the walls in the kitchen painted. There are several gallons of whitewash in the basement."

"I'll take care of it."

Mother Matilda smiled at him. "Hallie, one of the town ladies donated a generous amount of cotton cloth to the convent. I should like you to make new curtains for the front parlor."

"Yes, Reverend Mother."

"If there's any material left over, perhaps you could make new curtains for the kitchen, as well. The old ones are looking quite tattered."

"Yes, Reverend Mother."

"It's raining," Sister Barbour said. "Praise the Lord."

A murmur of Amens rose from the other nuns. It was the wettest spring Hallie could remember, but they sorely needed the rain.

"I'll get started in the kitchen right away."

Reverend Mother stood up. "Come, Sisters, we have the Lord's work to do."

Clay's gaze met Hallie's as he turned away from the table, and a surge of awareness passed between them. Hands clenched, he left the room.

Sister Barbour was delighted that Clay was going to paint the kitchen. She was a tiny woman, with flashing brown eyes, a small nose that turned up on the end, and hands that were always fluttering. She reminded Clay of a sparrow.

"It's been years since it was done last," the good sister told him as she cleared off the countertops and covered the stove and her worktable. "Your coming here was surely a Godsend."

Clay grunted softly. A Godsend, indeed. If they only knew.

Sister Barbour took down the old curtains and folded them in a neat pile. Clay was certain they would not be tossed out, but would be put to some other use, rags for cleaning, he mused, or perhaps a shirt for the next outlaw who passed by.

"Well, I'll leave you to work in peace," Sister Barbour said, clutching the bundle of old curtains to her chest.

"I'll try not to make a mess," Clay said.

She smiled at him, then hurried from the kitchen. The nuns were all polite to him, he realized with a grin, polite but nervous. Of course, they probably didn't get too many male visitors other than their priest. Yeah, they all walked on eggs when he was around, except for Sister Dominica. She wasn't the least bit intimidated by him. And she didn't trust him at all.

With a sigh, he dipped the brush into the bucket of whitewash he'd brought up from the basement and began to paint. It was a task that didn't require much concentration and he found his mind wandering, remembering things he didn't want to remember. He had spent years with Summer Rain, yet no single day stood out in his mind as clearly as the last one they had spent together.

"We will be fine while you are gone," Summer Rain said. She smiled up at him, her dark eyes filled with love.

"I'll bring you back a new dress," he told her. "And a doll for Anna."

"I do not need a new dress." Summer said. "You should buy something for yourself. A new shirt, perhaps."

"A blue dress." Clay caressed her cheek, let his fingers comb through the heavy fall of her hair.

"A red shirt," she had replied playfully. "You will be careful?" She had always hated it when he went to town. She knew how the whites felt about half-breeds.

"I'll be careful." He kissed her and held her close. Had he known somehow that he would never hold her like that again?

He kissed her one last time, then swung his daughter up in his arms and hugged her tight.

"Be good while I'm gone, sugar," he said.

Anna nodded, solemn as only a five-year-old child can be solemn. "Will you bring me a peppermint?"

"Sure."

He kissed them both one more time, then swung into the saddle and rode out of the valley. How many times had he wished that he had told Summer how much he loved her before he left, that he had kissed her and held her close just one more time? That he had just stayed home that day. . . .

"Clay? Clay?"

He turned with a jerk, wondering how long Hallie had been standing there, calling his name. "What?"

"Reverend Mother asked me to see if there was anything you needed."

He shook his head.

"Are you sure?"

"I'm sure."

She cocked her head to one side, regarding him thoughtfully. "Something's wrong, isn't it?"

"Nothing you can fix."

"Sister Barbour asked if you could maybe stop for a while so she can prepare our midday meal."

"Sure."

"Clay . . ."

"I'm fine, Hallie."

He cleaned up his mess, aware that Hallie was standing there, watching him.

"I don't want anything to eat," he said, heading for the door. "I'll be back in an hour to finish up."

"Clay, wait . . ."

But he couldn't wait. He needed to get out of there.

He opened the back door and walked out into the rain, wishing it could wash away his rage, his hurt, the awful need for vengeance that was eating away at him.

Taking refuge in the barn, he forked the horses some hay, then stood outside Juliet's stall, absently stroking the horse's neck, while his thoughts went back in time.

He had been born in an Indian village in the fall of 1847. His father had been a French trapper, his mother a Lakota medicine woman. Clay had grown up in both worlds. His mother had taught him the ways of the People, and also taught him about the white man's God that his father believed in. Yellow Buffalo Woman had seen nothing wrong in worshiping both *Wakan Tanka* and the Great Spirit that the whites called Jesus. His father had taught him to speak French and English; his mother had taught him to speak Lakota.

Clay had spent his early years with the Indians. As he

had grown older, his father, Jean Pierre, had started taking him along when he went to check his traps. Clay had visited the white man's cities, and if the *wasichu* were less accepting of him because of his mixed blood than were the Lakota, it didn't matter. He was happiest among his mother's people.

He grew up and became a warrior. He learned to hunt, to fight, to live off the land. He learned to read and write the white man's language. And he fell in love. . . .

Her name was Summer Rain and she was the most beautiful creature he had ever seen, tall and slender as a willow, with ink-black hair, a shy smile, and dark, dark eyes that saw only him.

They were married a year later, and the year after that, their daughter was born. They named her Anna because Summer Rain thought it was pretty.

The following spring, Clay's father had decided it was time to leave the Indians. The fragile peace between the Lakota and the whites had been broken and Jean Pierre predicted that things would only get worse. Jean Pierre had asked Clay and his family to join them. Summer Rain had not wanted to leave her parents and her sisters, but Clay had insisted. Summer was pregnant again, and he wanted to take her away from the land of the Lakota, away from the war with the Bluecoats that was sure to come, to a place where she would be safe. . . .

Safe. His hands clenched into tight fists. His wife and unborn child were dead, and he blamed himself. Even knowing it was not really his fault, even knowing that, had he been there, he would likely have died, too, did nothing to ease his guilt. His wife and his unborn child were dead and he should have been there to protect them or die beside them.

He bowed his head, resting his forehead against the gelding's neck. He had gone to town to buy supplies. In his absence, six men had come to their cabin. They had stolen everything of any value, raped his wife, and put a torch to the house.

He had known, as soon as he rode into the valley, that something was wrong. A heavy stillness lay over the land.

When he saw the smoke, he had urged his horse into a gallop. Anna had come running toward him, sobbing incoherently.

Dismounting, he had tried to pick her up, but she had grabbed him by the hand, tugging hard, crying for him to follow her.

He had found Summer Rain lying in the dirt alongside the house, her clothes torn, one eye swollen shut. Her thighs had been streaked with blood. He had wrapped Summer in his jacket, then gathered her into his arms, choking back his tears as she told him what had happened. Six men had come to the house, asking for food. When they discovered she was alone, they had raped her, then set the house on fire. Nothing remained of their home but a pile of smoldering ash.

He had held Summer in his arms, assuring her that everything would be all right, knowing she had clung to life for Anna's sake. But he was there now, and she was slipping away. With her dying breath, she had begged him to take Anna back to the People where they would be safe.

He had buried Summer in the new dress he had bought for her. Anna had stood beside him, tears streaming down her cheeks, as he filled in the grave. He had taken a last look at the place that had been his home, then, with Anna mounted before him, he had ridden down the valley to his parents' spread, intending to leave Anna with his mother while he rode into town to tell the sheriff what had happened. But the marauders had been there, too.

He had buried his parents in a single grave behind

the house; then, drained of tears, drained of every emotion but the need for vengeance, he had ridden into town and told the sheriff what had happened, demanding that he form a posse and go after the men who had killed his family.

But the lawman had just shrugged his shoulders. *Ain't no law against killin' Injuns.*

What about my father? Clay had demanded. *He was a white man.*

Squaw man, you mean, the sheriff had retorted, his voice heavy with disdain. *Now, go on, get out of here.*

Outraged by the sheriff's refusal to help, driven by a dark need for revenge, he had taken Anna to the People and left her with her grandparents.

Returning home, he had picked up the outlaws' trail. It had taken him a little over two years to hunt the men down. But he had found them, all but one. They had not died easy, and now he was a wanted man himself, with a price on his head, and a little girl he hadn't seen in over two years. . . .

"Clay?"

"Go away, Hallie."

"Won't you tell me what's wrong?"

"What makes you think there's anything wrong?" He glanced at her over his shoulder, then blew out a deep breath. "It's that obvious, huh?"

She nodded. "If you don't want to talk to me, maybe you could talk to Reverend Mother, or Father Antoine."

"I don't think so."

"It might help."

"Nothing can help."

"Oh, Clay, that's not true." She closed the distance between them and laid her hand on his arm. "When was the last time you went to confession?"

If she hadn't looked so earnest, he would have laughed out loud.

"I don't know what's bothering you, but I know you'll feel better if you talk to Father Antoine. He's such a wise man. I know he can help you."

Clay grunted softly. After years of hearing the confessions of cloistered nuns, hearing Clay's confession would probably give the old man a severe case of apoplexy.

"Well . . ." Hallie nibbled on her lower lip. "If you don't want to discuss it with Father Antoine or Reverend Mother, maybe you could talk to me."

"Hallie, listen, I know you're just trying to help, but I don't want to talk to anyone."

Her hand fell away from his arm and she took a step backward. "I'm sorry."

"Hallie . . ."

"No, it's all right." She blinked rapidly, refusing to cry. She wouldn't let him see how much his rejection hurt. She wouldn't. "I have to go help Sister Barbour in the kitchen."

He started to call her back, then swallowed the words. It would be better for them both if she left now, before he weakened, before he dragged her into his arms and tried to forget the past in her sweet embrace.

Chapter 7

Clay rose early after a restless night, quietly cussing Hallie McIntyre. Thinking of her, wanting her, had kept him awake most of the night. Pulling on his boots, he stepped outside.

For a moment, he stood there, breathing in the cool fresh scent of early morning, letting the peace and beauty of a new day break over him as he watched the rising sun trail her fingers across the broad sky canvas, leaving bold slashes of crimson and ocher and bright pink in her wake.

A flicker of movement caught his eye and he turned to see Hallie walking toward the side gate, skirts swishing, her short white veil fluttering in the breeze. She swung a bucket in one hand, a long slender pole rested on her shoulder.

Frowning, he followed her out of the gate and down a narrow, barely discernable path that led through a stand of timber. After about a quarter of a mile, she turned to the left and disappeared from sight.

Curious now, he followed her from a distance lest he alert her to his presence. A few minutes later, he reached the end of the trees and found himself at the top of a small knoll. Looking down, he saw Hallie. She was standing at the edge of a slow-moving stream, fishing.

On silent feet, he walked down the hill, then ghosted

up behind her. "Does Reverend Mother know you're here?"

Hallie gasped, the pole dropping from her hands as she whirled around.

"Clay! Darn you, you made me drop my pole."

"Here, I'll get it."

He stepped around her and pulled the slender wooden pole from the water. "Look here," he said with a grin, "you've got a fish."

She grinned back at him as he removed the hook from the fish's mouth, then dropped the trout into the bucket.

"You come here often?" Clay asked.

Hallie nodded. "Reverend Mother likes trout for breakfast on Friday."

"I'm surprised she lets you come out here all alone."

"Why? No one ever comes here."

He cocked one brow. "I'm here."

"So?"

Clay shook his head, wondering what Mother Matilda was thinking to let Hallie leave the safety of the convent. True, they were a good distance from town, but that didn't mean anything. The main road wasn't far away. No telling who might take a notion to stop here and rest a few minutes in the shade, or water their horse. There were plenty of men who wouldn't think twice about taking advantage of a woman they found alone and defenseless. Men like Ryker and Sayers.

Clay took a deep breath. Hallie was Mother Matilda's worry, not his. He would be leaving in a few days and he'd never see her again. He couldn't afford to care. "Got another worm?"

"Sure." She pulled a jar out of her pocket and handed it to Clay. Inside were a half-dozen long red worms, all knotted together.

He baited the hook with a fat one, tossed the line in the water, then handed the pole to Hallie.

A few minutes later, she pulled in another trout.

Somewhat gingerly, Hallie removed the hook, then dropped the fish into the bucket with the other one.

Clay watched, amused, as she baited the hook, her face scrunched up with obvious distaste as she tried to attach the wriggling worm to the hook.

"You want me to do that?" he asked.

"No, I can do it." She looked up at him and smiled. "I always feel so sorry for the worm. Do you suppose it hurts?"

Clay shook his head. "I don't know. I never gave it any thought."

"I guess you think I'm silly for worrying about it."

"No." His gaze moved over her. "I think you're beautiful."

Hallie stared at him, the worm's fate forgotten. Lost in the admiration in his dark brown eyes, she made no protest when Clay took the pole from her hands and tossed it aside. Never taking his eyes from hers, he removed the short veil that covered her hair and laid it aside.

"Beautiful." He ran his fingers through the heavy silk of her hair, then drew her, ever so slowly, ever so surely, into his arms.

Desire sizzled between them, hot, devastating, burning away every other thought. Hallie leaned into him as though drawn by a string, helpless to resist the yearning of her own flesh. Her pulse pounded like distant thunder in her ears.

"We shouldn't do this," Clay muttered and then, unable to help himself, or to withstand the sweet lure of her lips a moment longer, he bent his head and kissed her.

Hallie swayed against him, her eyelids fluttering down as Clay's mouth closed over hers. She had been waiting for this, hoping for this, ever since the last time he had kissed her. It was wrong, she knew it was wrong. Wrong to want his mouth on hers, wrong to glory in the feel of his arms tight around her. He groaned low in his throat as her tongue slid over his lower lip.

"Hallie!" He gasped her name, his fingers kneading her back and shoulders. She tasted so good, felt so good in his arms, he knew he would never get enough of holding her, kissing her.

His hands slid down to cup her buttocks and he pulled her up against him, molding her body to his.

And now it was Hallie's turn to gasp as she felt the rigid evidence of his desire pressing against her belly. She clasped her hands behind his neck, afraid her legs would no longer hold her.

"Clay. Oh, Clay, you make me feel so . . . so . . ."

He swore under his breath, then pushed her away. He was breathing hard, looking at her as if he hated her.

"Dammit, Hallie, what are you trying to do to me?"

"What?" She shook her head, her heart pounding, her body tingling all over. "I don't understand."

Heaven help him, she'd never looked more appealing than she did now, with her hair mussed from his hands and her lips swollen from his kisses.

He swore again, then ran a hand through his hair as he sucked in a deep, calming breath. "I know you don't. Grab your pole and I'll walk you back."

"But I'm not done."

"Yes, you are."

With a harrumph of annoyance, she grabbed her veil and her fishing pole and flounced up the hill.

Clay watched the tantalizing twitch of her hips. "Heaven help me," he muttered and then, shaking his head at his foolishness, he grabbed the bucket and followed her up the narrow trail that led back to the convent.

* * *

Clay fidgeted in his seat. The night before, after dinner, Mother Matilda had taken him aside and insisted, gently but firmly, that he attend Sunday Mass "for the good of his immortal soul."

"And for my own peace of mind," she had added softly.

"I'd rather not, if it's all the same to you," Clay had replied.

Mother Matilda had smiled at him, a sweet saintly smile. "Do you remember when I asked you if you had strayed from the true faith, Mr. Evans?"

Clay had nodded, acutely conscious of Hallie's regard.

And then Reverend Mother had played her ace in the hole. "Then perhaps you remember that you also gave me your permission to try and bring you back into the fold?"

In the end, it was easier to surrender than fight.

With a sigh, Clay sank lower in the pew and wished he'd just kept his big mouth shut. He had taken a seat in the front pew and far to the side, sitting in the shadows in hopes no one would notice him. It was the first time he had been inside a church in years. Not since . . . He shook the memory from his mind, then rose to his feet as the nuns began to sing.

His gaze moved over the small congregation. In addition to the nuns, there were maybe a dozen people he guessed were from Bitter River and the surrounding ranches, mostly older women dressed in severe, unrelieved black, their heads covered by lacy mantillas.

Though he hated to admit it, he was suddenly glad to be there. The sweet voices of the nuns wrapped around him as they sang praises to the Holy Mother and her Blessed Son. The scent of prayer candles, the serene faces of the plaster saints near the altar, all whispered peace to his troubled soul.

He slid a glance at Hallie, standing across the aisle from him, her arms folded, her gaze fixed in rapt attention on the stained-glass window behind the altar. How beautiful she looked, and how young. The white veil she wore seemed to emphasize her purity. Goodness shone from her face. Goodness and innocence.

The song ended and he sat down. He paid little attention to the words of the priest. Even if he had understood Latin, he doubted he would have given much heed to what the man had to say. What did Father Antoine know of life? Shut away from the world, bound by vows of poverty, chastity, and obedience, what did the priest know of love, of loss? Easy to preach of love for mankind when you had no knowledge of hatred, when you had no idea what it meant to love a woman, or to watch that woman suffer through hours of pain to bring your child into the world. Easy to talk of hope and charity when you knew nothing of hate and despair. Easy to preach forgiveness when you'd never had anyone to forgive.

Clay stared, unseeing, at the priest, the tiny moment of peace he had experienced earlier shattered by memories of Summer Rain and the men who had killed her.

As soon as the last Amen was said, he bolted out the side door of the chapel.

He should have known Mother Matilda would seek him out.

"Mr. Evans?"

He looked up from the harness he was mending, but said nothing.

"You left rather abruptly."

Clay nodded curtly.

"I had hoped to introduce you to Father Antoine."

Clay shrugged, but said nothing.

"Was attending Mass truly so unpleasant for you?"

"Yes, ma'am, it was."

Mother Matilda folded her arms, the full sleeves of her habit falling forward to cover her hands. "I do not mean to pry, Mr. Evans, but perhaps it is the weight of a guilty conscience that caused your discomfort."

"Yes, ma'am," Clay replied tersely. "I'm sure it is."

"I asked Father Antoine to spend the night here, in case you felt the need to go to confession."

"I don't."

He looked up to find her regarding him through eyes filled with sympathy and compassion. He doubted she would look at him like that if she knew what sins weighed so heavily on his conscience.

"Father Antoine won't be leaving until tomorrow morning, should you change your mind."

Clay nodded, then turned his attention back to the halter he had been repairing. He could feel Mother Matilda's gaze resting on his bowed head and then, with a whisper of black serge, she turned and left the barn.

Clay swore under his breath. He didn't want her concern or her sympathy, didn't want her praying for his soul. But she would. She would pray for him and maybe light a candle or two. And though he wouldn't admit it, it gave him a sense of comfort to know there would be someone praying for him when he left here.

He grunted softly. There was someone else praying for him, he mused. Hallie. But all the praying in the world couldn't wash the blood from his hands, or keep him from fulfilling the vow he had made while he held Summer Rain, dying, in his arms.

The next morning found Clay working in the garden, pulling weeds, preparing the ground for the next planting. It felt good to till the earth, to feel the heat of the sun on his back. He thought about the days and nights he had spent locked in a narrow cell, seemingly endless days of listening to Mason Clark's gruff voice reminiscing about all the hangings he had seen. The Bitter River sheriff had gone into great, grim detail, relating the death of the last man he had hung, elaborating on how the condemned man's legs had barely held him up as he climbed the stairs to the gallows, how the man had stood there, puking his guts out, while the noose was looped around his neck, how he had begun to cry like a baby when the preacher asked if he had any last words.

Pitiful, Clark had said scornfully. *Just pitiful. Man had a reputation as a hardcase, but he wet his britches when they dropped the hood over his head. That's how you'll go, too, whining and begging.*

Worse than listening to the sheriff had been the long nights of staring at the dingy gray ceiling, his mind playing back the vivid images the sheriff's words had painted across his mind, images that had haunted his dreams. He had relived the bleak years since Summer Rain's death, the months he had spent tracking her killers. He had thought constantly about his daughter, wondering how she was doing, if she was happy, if she had forgotten him. Anna . . .

Removing his shirt, he tossed it aside, then stood with his face turned up to the sky. It was a beautiful day, warm and clear. A handful of spring flowers had poked their heads through the earth, making a bright splash of color near the kitchen door.

Anna had loved flowers. He felt a sudden yearning to see her, to hold her. But he couldn't go back for her, not until the last man was dead. It would be too painful to see her for a short time and then have to tell her goodbye again. He couldn't put her through that. Couldn't put himself through that.

He closed his eyes, a prayer to *Wakan Tanka* hovering on his lips. But he had lost the right to pray with the first man he had killed.

A tsking sound caught his attention and he glanced over his shoulder to see Sister Dominica glaring at him. "Have you no shame?"

"What?"

She jabbed an accusing finger in his direction. "Your shirt, Mr. Evans. Please, put it on."

"Oh," he replied, stifling a grin. "Sorry." Grabbing his shirt, he slipped it over his head.

"How did you get that scar on your neck?" she asked.

"Somebody took a knife to me." The memory of finding Jack Ryker flashed through Clay's mind.

"A near miss, from the look of it."

Clay nodded. Another inch to the right and he would have been a dead man.

The nun regarded him through narrowed eyes filled with suspicion. "The sheriff was looking for a man with a scar like that."

Clay left his stomach clench. "Was he?" He shrugged nonchalantly. "It's a rough country. Lots of men have scars, including the sheriff."

Sister Dominica nodded, acknowledging the truth of his words. "How soon will you be finished here?"

"You can start planting this afternoon."

"I've been taking care of this garden for ten years. I don't know why Reverend Mother insisted on having you prepare the ground."

"I know you work hard, Sister. Maybe she was just trying to lighten your load a little."

"Lighten my load?" She narrowed her eyes at him. "Are you saying I'm too old to be working?"

"No, ma'am," Clay said hastily. "But I need to do something to earn my keep, and I'm sure you've got lots of other chores to keep you busy." He flashed a smile. "Chores more fittin' for a lady like yourself."

"Humph! Don't waste your sweet talk on me, young man."

"No, ma'am, I wouldn't think of it," Clay replied. "You don't like me much, do you?"

She squared her thin shoulders. "No, I don't."

Clay grinned. "Well, that's honest enough. And it's too bad, 'cause I like you a lot."

"Oh, I never!" she exclaimed, and picking up her skirts, she walked back to the convent as fast as her legs could carry her.

"That was mean of you."

Clay turned to find Hallie grinning at him. "Where'd you come from?"

"I was eavesdropping," she admitted.

"Heard everything, huh?"

Hallie nodded.

Clay rubbed the scar on his neck. "You don't think she'll say anything to the sheriff, do you?"

"I don't know. How did you get that scar?"

"Knife fight, like I said."

She didn't know how to phrase the question burning on the tip of her tongue.

"Don't ask, Hallie, you won't like the answer. You'd better go. I've got work to do."

"Clay . . ."

"Go on, scoot."

She left in a huff.

Clay watched her walk away, remembering the night he had found Jack Ryker. Ryker had been snuggled in bed with a two-bit whore when Clay broke in on them. The girl had screamed and fled the room. Ryker had grabbed a knife from the table beside the bed and lunged at Clay. They had struggled over the blade. It had been a near thing. He still remembered the touch of cold steel at his throat, followed by a gush of warm blood. The thought that he was going to die, that Ryker would go on living after what he had done to Summer Rain, had infused Clay with a surge of strength and he had jerked the knife from Ryker's grasp and buried it to the hilt in the man's black heart.

Panting, bleeding, he had stood over Ryker's body until he heard the sound of excited voices and running footsteps. Hand pressed over the jagged wound in his neck, he had dived out the window and disappeared into the darkness. He'd been darn lucky he hadn't bled to death.

Clay blew out a deep breath. Five down and one to go, he thought. It was time to move on, before Bob Sayers's trail got any colder, before Sister Dominica acted on her suspicions, before Hallie burrowed her way any deeper into his heart.

Chapter 8

Hallie lay in her narrow cot, staring at the ceiling. As always, she was thinking of Clay. It was hard to remember a time when he hadn't been there, when he hadn't filled her every waking thought, invaded her every dream.

She was in love with him, she thought bleakly. Nuns weren't supposed to fall in love. She didn't know how it had happened or when it had happened, only that it had. She thought of him constantly, only felt truly happy when she was with him. Seeing him, being with him, filled her with joy and excitement; touching him made her feel warm all over, as if she had swallowed a ray of sunshine.

And now he was leaving. He had told her so this morning. It was time for him to move on, he'd said. His side was healed; he had made all the repairs to the convent that Mother Matilda had requested, and he was leaving first thing in the morning. And she would never see him again.

Before she could talk herself out of it, she slid out of bed, drew on her wrapper, and tiptoed out of the house.

As if drawn by a magnet, she made her way toward the barn and tiptoed inside. She had thought to find him asleep, but he was sitting in the stall where he bedded down, his back to the wall, one leg drawn up, his left arm resting on his bent knee.

Clay frowned when he looked up and saw Hallie standing in the doorway. "Something wrong?"

"No."

The light from the oil lamp hanging from a nail on the wall behind him cast his face in shadow. She fidgeted with the sash on her robe. She shouldn't have come here. What could she say to explain her presence?

"Hallie?"

"I . . . I just wanted to tell you good-bye. I'm . . . I'm going to miss you and I wanted . . . wanted to thank you for . . ." She blinked rapidly, sniffing back her tears. "For all you've done around here."

"Hallie." He rose to his feet, clenching his hands at his sides to keep from reaching for her. "You don't owe me any thanks."

"Yes. Yes, I do. . . ."

"You saved my life, Hallie. I should be thanking you."

She stared up at him, mute, her heart aching with the words she longed to say. *Don't leave . . . take me with you . . . I love you . . .*

"I'll never forget you, Hallie."

"I'll never forget you, either."

He smiled at her. And then, needing to touch her, he drew the tip of his finger along the curve of her cheek. "Will you say a prayer for me now and then?"

She nodded, afraid she would burst into tears if she tried to talk.

"Hallie . . ."

"I'm . . . I'm going to miss you!"

Clay swore softly as tears spilled from her eyes and cascaded down her cheeks. "Don't cry, Hallie." He reached for her and she burrowed into his arms, and into his heart. "Please don't cry."

"I can't help it," she wailed, and buried her face against his shoulder.

He was leaving just in time, Clay thought bleakly.

Another day or two, and he'd never be able to let her go. "Hallie, please. I'm not worth one of your tears."

"You are!"

"I wish I was."

"Why do you have to go?"

"There's something I've got to do."

"Can't you tell me what it is?"

He shook his head. He didn't want her to know what kind of man he was, wanted her to go on thinking there was goodness in him.

She looked up at him, her hazel eyes luminous, her lips slightly parted. And he knew he had to kiss her once more.

Slowly, he bent his head toward hers, giving her plenty of time to refuse, but she had no intention of refusing him. She tilted her head back a little, her eyelids fluttering down as his mouth closed over hers.

His arms tightened around her, drawing her body flush against his. It was a hot, hungry kiss, filled with promises he couldn't keep, dreams that could never come true.

She teased his lips with her tongue and he groaned low in his throat, every fiber of his body aching with need. Her sweetness washed over him, wiping out the memory of every woman he had known in the last two years.

Helpless to resist her, he drew her down on the blanket, his mouth fused to hers, his hands stroking her back, fumbling under her night rail, sliding up over the smooth curve of her thigh.

"What is the meaning of this!" Mother Matilda's shocked voice cut through the air like a scythe through corn.

With a gasp of horror, Hallie scrambled to her feet. "Reverend Mother!"

Clay swore under his breath as he sat up, swore again

when he found himself staring down the barrel of his own Colt. He glanced up at the peg where his empty holster was hanging, then shook his head ruefully. Talk about bad timing. Hallie had returned his gun the night before.

He looked back at the nun, wondering if she would actually shoot him.

Mother Matilda took a step back. "Hallie, come out of there," she said sternly.

Hallie glanced at Clay, then exited the stall.

Mother Matilda motioned for Clay to get up. "Please, Mr. Evans, don't misjudge me. I haven't always been a nun. I know how to use this."

"Yes, ma'am," Clay said soberly. "I believe you do." Moving slowly, he stood up. "Now what?"

"We're going to the house. Hallie, take the lantern and walk ahead of us."

"Reverend Mother . . ."

"Do as I say, Hallie Josephine."

"Yes, Mother."

In an agony of embarrassment, Hallie took the lantern and walked toward the barn door.

"After you, Mr. Evans." Mother Matilda eased back the hammer on the Colt. "And please, keep your hands up where I can see them."

Clay muttered a crude oath as he followed Hallie across the yard toward the house. At one point, he considered making a run for it, but something told him Mother Matilda would not be adverse to taking a shot at him. And he had a strong feeling she wouldn't miss. He could see, from the way she handled his Colt, that she hadn't been bluffing when she said she knew her way around firearms. And he didn't relish the thought of taking another bullet.

Sister Dominica was standing in the kitchen doorway

when they arrived, an I-told-you-so expression on her face, a fireplace poker tightly clutched in her hands.

"Now what?" Clay asked, glancing over his shoulder.

"The cellar," Mother Matilda said. She smiled at him, but there was no warmth in her eyes, no humor in the expression. "You know the way."

"Listen, can't we just forget about this?"

"I'm afraid not, Mr. Evans. I warned you to keep your hands off Hallie. I was willing to give you a chance."

"Just let me go, and I'll leave now. Tonight."

"The cellar, Mr. Evans. Hallie, give the lamp to Sister Dominica and go to bed."

Hallie stared at Clay, then, with a sob, she thrust the light into Sister Dominica's hands and ran down the corridor toward her room.

Clay stared after her, then, with a sigh of resignation, he walked down the hallway toward the stairs that led to the cellar. He couldn't let them lock him up. Sure as death and hell, Mother Matilda would send one of the nuns to town for Mason Clark first thing in the morning, if not tonight.

When he reached the bottom of the stairs, he started to open the door, then whirled around and made a grab for the gun.

With a started cry, Mother Matilda jerked her arm out of reach and twisted to the side. Out of the corner of his eye, Clay saw Sister Dominica rush to her superior's defense. He tried to duck under the poker, but the little nun caught him flush on the side of the head. Bright lights exploded behind his eyes, and then everything went black.

"Clay? Clay, are you all right?"

With a groan, he sat up, his hands cradling his head as he quietly cursed Sister Dominica. If the wiry little nun had been any stronger, she probably would have split his skull open. As it was, she had given him a lump on his head the size of a goose egg, and a hell of a headache.

"Clay?"

"I'm here."

"Are you all right?" Hallie's voice.

"Oh, yeah," he muttered, his voice edged with sarcasm. "Never been better."

"I'm sorry, Clay."

"It's not your fault."

"Clay . . ."

He knew, from the sound of her voice, that he didn't want to hear whatever she was going to tell him.

"I thought you ought to know, Reverend Mother is going to send Sister Dominica into town to get the sheriff in the morning."

A vile oath escaped Clay's lips as the full significance of her words washed over him. Feeling suddenly defeated, he stared into the pitch blackness that surrounded him. He'd been cheating death for almost two years, had hoped to find the last man responsible for Summer Rain's death before the law—and the hangman—caught up with him. Despair perched on his shoulder as he realized he would never see his daughter again.

"Clay?"

"Yeah."

"How bad are you hurt? Can you ride?"

He scooted closer to the door, the hopelessness of a moment ago dispelled by the promise of her words. "I can ride. Can you get me out of here?"

"I'll try. I'll be back as soon as I can."

"Hallie? Hallie?"

There was no answer. Fighting the nausea in his

belly, he curled up on the hard wooden floor. Maybe he'd get the chance to cheat the rope one more time.

Head throbbing, shivering from the cold, he stared into the darkness, remembering the day he had taken Anna back to the People to stay with Summer Rain's parents.

He had held her and hugged her close, his eyes burning and his throat tight with unshed tears as he tried to explain that he had to leave her. She had clung to him, trying bravely not to cry.

Ate, tokiya la he? she had asked, her dark eyes filled with confusion. Father, where are you going?

How did you tell a little girl who had just lost her mother that her father was leaving, too? He had tried to explain that he had some business to take care of and that he would return for her as soon as he could.

A part of him had wanted desperately to stay with her, but he couldn't stay, couldn't think of anything but avenging Summer Rain's death, of finding their trail before it disappeared altogether.

Finally, unable to bear the pain any longer, he had kissed Anna on the cheek, handed Anna to her grandmother, and walked away.

She had cried after him. *Ate! Ate!*

He had stopped, taken a deep breath, and glanced over his shoulder. Anna was reaching for him, tears streaming down her cheeks. Even now he could hear the anguish in her voice.

Ate. Ye sni yo. Ye sni yo! Father, don't go. Don't go!

Tears welling in his eyes, he had gone back and held her one more time. *Ceye sni you, cikala,* he had whispered. Don't cry, little one.

Summer Rain's mother, Cloud Woman, had taken Anna then, her eyes filled with compassion and grief. Cloud Woman had understood his need for vengeance. She didn't approve, but she understood. Summer Rain's father, Iron Shield, had offered to go with him, but Clay had refused. Cloud Woman and Anna needed someone to look after them.

One last hug, a last kiss, and he had ridden out of the camp, his heart cold and empty.

He had hunted the men who killed his wife with a single-mindedness that burned out every other thought. The seasons had come and gone, almost unnoticed. It took time, too damn much time, but he had found the men he sought—in a Kansas cow town, in a Texas border town, in a Wichita whorehouse, in a barber chair in Silverton. He had found them and killed them and ridden on. He wore out one horse and bought another. Wanted posters with his likeness on them began to show up after he killed the man in Wichita. And now there was only one man left. One man he hadn't been able to find in almost two years. . . .

He woke to the sound of someone rattling the lock. "Hallie?" He sat up, groaning softly. "Is that you?"

"Uh-huh."

"What are you doing?"

"I couldn't get the key. I'm trying to pick the lock."

He heard a scrape as she poked something into the lock again, heard Hallie mutter, "Stupid hairpin's never going to work."

In spite of the pain pounding through his head, he found himself smiling as she muttered to herself. And then, miraculously, the door swung open.

He blinked against the faint light offered by the candlestick in Hallie's hand. She was wearing one of her long gray dresses. Her hair fell loose around her shoulders. He'd never been so glad to see anyone in his life.

Hallie gasped out loud as she lifted the candle and saw the ugly lump on the side of his head. Dried blood was matted into his hair and smeared across his cheek.

"Oh, Clay, your poor head!"

"Sister Dominica's got a heck of a swing," he said ruefully. Lifting a hand to his head, he winced as he explored the lump, which felt even bigger than before.

"Does it hurt very much?"

"Don't worry about it. I'm all right."

"Can you walk?"

"She hit me in the head," he muttered. "She didn't break my leg."

"Hurry."

He stood up, one hand braced against the wall while a wave of dizziness washed over him. "Hallie, my gun. Do you know where it is?"

"Reverend Mother has it locked in her room. We don't have time to worry about that now. Hurry!"

Feeling like a soul being released from the bowels of hell, he followed her up the narrow staircase. When they reached the top, she blew out the candle, then led the way to the kitchen and out the back door toward the barn.

Inside, he threw a bridle over Romeo's head. The gelding flattened its ears, apparently annoyed at being roused in the middle of the night. He gave the bay a smack across the nose when it tried to nip his arm.

"Quit it," he muttered as he led the horse out of the stall. "I don't have time for your games right now."

He smoothed a blanket over the bay's back, cinched a saddle in place, lashed the blankets he had been using behind the cantle; then, with a sigh, he drew Hallie into his arms. She snuggled against him, warm and trusting as a puppy.

"That's twice you've saved my life, Hallie. I wish there was some way I could repay you."

"Take me with you."

He held her at arm's length and stared down at her. "What?"

"You said you wanted to repay me. Take me with you."

Clay shook his head in disbelief. "Are you crazy, girl?"

"No. I want to go with you. I want to see the country you told me about, the big cities. I want to wear pretty clothes. Please, Clay."

He blew out a deep breath. "Hallie, I can't take you with me. You must know that. I'm a wanted man. I can't take you sight-seeing. Besides"—he tugged on the sleeve of her dress—"you're gonna be a nun, remember?"

She gazed up at him, her hazel eyes silently pleading with him. "I don't want to be a nun, not anymore. Please, Clay."

"I'll come back for you if I can."

"No! I want to go with you now, tonight."

He shook his head, not knowing whether to laugh, curse, or cry. "Hallie, I wish I could take you with me."

"Honest?"

"Honest. But it's not possible. Not now." He tunneled his fingers through her hair, loving the silky texture. For one brief crazy minute, he let himself imagine what it would be like to take her with him, to give up his quest for vengeance, to find a little town where no one had ever heard of him and start over. It was a nice dream, but that's all it was, a dream, with no more substance than the narrow ray of moonlight shining through a crack in the side of the barn. He didn't have a damn thing to offer her, not a home, not a future. He was a wanted man with a price on his head.

"I'm sorry, Hallie. Dammit, I wish . . ." Hell, he wished a lot of things.

He swore under his breath as he crushed her to him. It was going to be light in a few hours. He had to go before Mother Matilda or Sister Dominica found him missing.

"Hallie . . ." There was nothing more to say. The tears shining in her eyes tore at the depths of his soul, but there was no help for it.

He kissed her once more, hard and quick, and then, taking up the reins, he led the gelding outside. He hesitated a moment, tempted beyond reason to grab Hallie and run like hell, and then he swung into the saddle and rode toward the gate.

He didn't look back.

Hallie stared after him, her heart breaking at the thought of never seeing him again. And then, before she could change her mind, she ran back into the barn and saddled Juliet. He had wanted to take her with him, he had said so. It was just his sense of honor that made him leave her behind, his fear that she might be hurt.

But she wasn't afraid. She was in love.

Climbing into the saddle, she rode out after him.

Chapter 9

Clay refused to think about Hallie as he rode through the darkness. She was a distraction he couldn't afford to indulge. He needed a gun, supplies, a change of clothes.

When he reached the road that led to Bitter River, he reined the big blood bay to a halt. Bitter River was the nearest town, but the memory of being imprisoned there was all too fresh in his mind. Still, it was the closest town; everything he needed could be stolen from the general store.

Running a hand through his hair, he swore under his breath. Damn! He had never been a thief and the thought of becoming one now rankled deep inside. True, he had ridden with the Lakota on horse raids, but stealing an enemy's horse was considered a coup. It wasn't like breaking into a man's home. The Lakota and the Crow had been stealing horses from each other for centuries.

Clay shook his head. As much as he disliked the thought of what he was about to do, he didn't really have any other choice. He needed food, a change of clothes, a gun and ammunition, some cash money.

If he'd had any sense at all, he would have taken what he needed from the convent. The sisters had plenty of food, as well as a small supply of cash from the milk they sold, but he couldn't bring himself to steal anything else from the nuns. It wasn't the Lakota way to steal from friends, or from those who had done you a favor, and, grudging or not, the good sisters had given him food and shelter. It was bad enough that he had stolen their best horse. He couldn't take anything else.

Leaning forward, he rested his forearms on the pommel of the saddle. Well, there was no help for it. The next town was three days' ride away, and while he might be able to go without food that long, he wasn't willing to take a chance on being caught out in the open without a weapon.

Muttering an oath, he urged the bay toward Bitter River.

It was after two in the morning when he reached the outskirts of town. It wasn't much of a town, just a wide dirt road that ran between a dozen or so clapboard and adobe buildings. The sheriff's office was at the far end of the street on the south side. The mercantile stood nearest to Clay. No lights shown inside; the shades were drawn.

Clucking to the horse, Clay rode around to the rear of the building. Dismounting, he dropped the reins to the ground, then stood at the back door, listening. All was quiet inside and out.

Heart pounding, he checked the window beside the door, grinned when he found it unlocked. Moving cautiously, he raised the window enough to allow him to climb over the sill.

Inside, he stood still a moment, letting his eyes adjust to the darkness, and then he moved through the store, quickly taking what he needed: a pair of whipcord britches, a gray wool shirt, a dark blue neckerchief, a black Stetson with a rolled brim. He found a gunnysack and filled it with foodstuffs, then threw in a box of matches, a tin plate, a cup, and a fork, as well as a good sharp knife, a small frying pan, a coffeepot.

He opened the cash register, disappointed to find there were only a few bills and some change inside.

In the back of the store, he found a glass-fronted display case that held a number of handguns. The cabinet was locked.

Clay rubbed his hand over his jaw, suddenly wishing Hallie was there to pick the lock for him.

Wrapping the neckerchief around his hand, he broke the glass, quickly selecting a new model Colt revolver resting in a hand-tooled leather holster. He buckled on the gun belt, then grabbed several boxes of shells and tossed them in the gunnysack.

He was reaching for a long black duster when he heard a noise overhead, followed by a man's voice telling someone to "stay put while I go have a look-see."

Clay swore as he grabbed the coat and sack and headed for the back door.

He heard the sound of footsteps as the owner of the mercantile came running down the stairs, the telltale snick of a gun being cocked.

"You! Hey, you there! What are you doing in here? Stop! Stop, or I'll shoot!"

Clay dove through the window, rolled to his feet, and vaulted into the saddle. Slamming his heels into the bay's sides, he headed out of town, a spate of gunshots chasing him like a swarm of angry hornets.

The sound of gunfire roused Hallie from the brink of sleep. Jerking upright in the saddle, she peered into the darkness. And then, through the heavy mist, she saw a rider thundering toward her. She heard the sound of hoofbeats, saw a bright flash, heard the sharp report of a rifle, and then Clay was out of sight. She heard angry shouts coming from the town, but there was no time to stay and listen. She had to follow Clay before she lost him in the dark. She'd come too far to lose him now.

For the second time that night, she gave the horse its head, confident the little chestnut would follow the big bay if given the chance.

It had been frightening, pursuing Clay through the dark of night when she first rode out after him. Doubts had plagued her, and she wondered if she had made a terrible mistake, if she should turn back, but racing through the dark had been exhilarating and her fright had soon turned to excitement. The sound of Juliet's galloping hooves had echoed the beat of her own heart. She was going with Clay.

Dark clouds had draped the moon, a heavy mist clung to her skin. Shivering, she had realized how foolish she had been to leave without a cloak, but there had been no time to run back to the convent for a scarf or warm clothing, no time to think. She had decided to follow Clay between one heartbeat and the next. She had saddled Juliet before she could change her mind, climbed onto the horse's back, and ridden away from the convent, determined to throw caution to the wind and follow the urgings of her heart.

She had reined Juliet to a halt near a stand of tall trees when Clay rode into Bitter River. She had expected him to go to the hotel; instead, he had ridden around to the back of the general store. Puzzled, she had decided to wait where she was.

And now she was following him again, racing through the dark toward an unknown destination. Toward the adventure she had always secretly craved. Laughter bubbled up inside her as she imagined how surprised Clay would be when he saw her.

Clay reined the bay to a halt in the shelter of a stand of timber. Patting Romeo on the neck, he cocked his head to the side, listening for any sound of pursuit. At first, he heard nothing but the sighing of the wind and then, growing ever louder, came the sound of hoofbeats.

He swore under his breath. It sounded like just one horse, and he swore again, cussing the owner of the mercantile for coming after him.

He drew his Colt, checked to make sure it was loaded, and waited.

The thud of hoofbeats slowed from a gallop to a trot to a walk. Peering into the darkness, Clay could just make out the figure of a lone horseman heading slowly toward him.

He held his breath, hoping the man would bypass him in the dark, but, as if pulled by a string, the rider headed straight toward him.

Holstering his Colt, Clay launched himself at the oncoming rider and they pitched over the side of the horse and crashed to the ground.

Soft curves heaved beneath him as a feminine shriek rang out in the stillness. Clay reared back, startled to find himself looking down into Hallie's astonished green eyes.

"Hallie!" What the hell are you doing here?"

"Following you, of course."

He stared down at her. "Following me? Are you out of your mind?"

"No. You said you wished I could come with you."

"I know, but . . ." He stood up, raking a hand through his hair.

"Clay?" Hallie sat up, smoothing her skirts, brushing a clump of dirt out of her hair. She had expected him to be happy to see her. "You're not angry, are you?"

Angry! Angry didn't begin to describe it. Damn, what was he going to do now?

"You can't go with me, Hallie."

"Why not?"

He blew out an exasperated breath. Why not? Hell, there were a dozen reasons, a hundred reasons, why she couldn't go with him.

Cursing softly, he began to pace. What *was* he going to do with her? He couldn't leave her out here in the middle of nowhere, alone, in the middle of the night. He couldn't take her back to Bitter River and risk being seen. And he for damn sure couldn't take her with him.

"Clay?"

He whirled around to find her standing in front of him. He couldn't see her expression in the dark, but he could sense her nearness, smell the warm womanly scent of her hair and skin. He was sorely tempted to drag her into his arms and kiss her, but common sense warned him this wasn't the time or the place.

"Mount up," he said curtly.

"Where are we going?"

"Beats the hell out of me, but we can't stay here." Shaking his head, he went to get his horse. Romeo and Juliet were standing side by side. Juliet whinnied softly as he approached.

"Why was that man shooting at you?" Hallie asked, coming up behind him.

"Later, Hallie."

Slipping his hands around her waist, he lifted her into the saddle.

The moon broke through the clouds, washing the earth with silver. Hallie watched as Clay swung effortlessly onto Romeo's back. And then she was following him through the moonlit night.

They rode until dawn, then Clay drew rein in a small copse of trees. Dismounting, he lifted her from Juliet's back, then stood gazing down at her, a bemused expression on his face.

"You're mad at me, aren't you?"

Clay let out a long, exasperated sigh. "No, I'm not mad." He shook his head. "I'm just trying to figure out what I'm going to do with you. Did you tell anyone where you were going?"

Hallie shook her head. "There wasn't time."

"Mother Matilda will be worried sick when she can't find you."

"I know, but there wasn't time to leave her a note." Hallie bit down on her lip. "She's always been so good to me. I should have taken the time."

"You should have stayed home, where you belong."

"I belong with you."

Afraid he would either spank her or kiss her if he didn't get away from her, Clay turned his back on Hallie and began unbuckling Romeo's cinch strap. He slapped the gelding on the nose when it reached around to nip at him.

"Stop that," he muttered crossly. Bad-tempered horses and stubborn women. He shook his head.

"There's some supplies in that sack behind my saddle," he called over his shoulder. "Why don't you rustle up some breakfast?"

"I don't know how to cook."

"Well, it's time you learned."

"Can you cook?"

"When I have to."

"Well, then, why don't you cook," she suggested sweetly, "and I'll finish unsaddling the horses?"

Clay glanced over his shoulder, certain she was joshing, but she looked dead serious. With a rueful shake of his head, he dropped Juliet's saddle on the ground, grabbed the gunnysack, and set about making breakfast.

Hallie could hear him muttering under his breath as

she unsaddled Romeo, draped the blankets over the saddles to dry out, then tethered the horses to a nearby tree. She checked Juliet's hooves and then Romeo's to make certain they hadn't picked up any stones, patted Juliet on the neck.

When she was finished with the horses, she walked to where Clay was hunkered down on his heels. He had a small fire going. Bacon was frying in a pan. The scent of coffee filled the air.

"Smells good," Hallie said. She sat down beside him, her skirts spread around her.

Clay grunted softly. Fishing a knife out of the sack, he pried open a tin of peaches.

Hallie's stomach growled as he turned the bacon.

"It's almost done," Clay said. Using the hem of his duster as a pot holder, he picked up the coffeepot, filled the tin cup, and handed it to her.

"Thank you." Hallie stared at the steaming liquid. She'd never tasted coffee before. She took a hesitant sip and grimaced. It was strong and bitter. "I don't suppose you've got any milk and sugar in that sack?" she asked, remembering that was how Mother Matilda drank hers.

"There's some sugar," Clay said. He dropped the sack in her lap. "Go easy on it."

She added a heaping teaspoon of sugar, but even that didn't seem to sweeten the taste much. "Here," she said, offering him the cup. "You drink it."

He took the cup and set it aside, then piled half the bacon and half the sliced peaches on the plate and handed it to her, along with a fork.

"Aren't you eating?" Hallie asked.

"I've only got the one plate. Go on, eat it while it's hot."

Feeling somewhat guilty, Hallie ate her breakfast. Clay ate the peaches in the can by spearing them with his knife; he used his fingers to eat his share of the bacon from the pan.

It wasn't the best breakfast she'd ever had, but it was filling. She couldn't help wishing for a glass of milk to wash it down.

"Think you could wash the dishes?" Clay asked.

"With what? There's no soap."

"We're roughing it. Just take them down to the river and rinse them out."

"But what about the frying pan?"

"Scrub it with sand, then rinse it off."

"Sand?"

"Just do it, Hallie."

"Sand," she muttered as she stood up and dumped the plate, cup, and fork into the skillet. "Whoever heard of washing dishes with sand?"

"Works on people, too," Clay remarked with a grin.

"Humph."

He watched her walk away, then put out the fire. He checked the ground, found a good flat spot beneath a tree, and spread his blankets. Lying down, arms folded beneath his head, he gazed up at the branches and wondered what he was going to do about Hallie.

He was still wondering when he fell asleep.

He woke to find Hallie lying beside him. Propped on one elbow, her chin resting in her hand, she smiled when she saw he was awake.

Feeling self-conscious, Clay scowled at her.

"Good morning," she said cheerfully.

He grunted, wondering what she had to be so happy about.

"It's a beautiful day," she said.

"Is it?"

"Are you always this grouchy in the morning?"

"I'm not grouchy," he retorted.

Hallie raised one brow, but said nothing.

"So," Clay muttered, "what are we going to do about you?"

"What do you mean? What about me?"

"You can't go with me, Hallie."

Hallie stared at him. "Why not? I'm here."

Clay sat up and ran a hand through his hair. And even as he tried to think of how best to send her away, he was yearning to reach out for her, to draw her down beside him and drown his troubles in her nearness, to sip the sweetness from her lips, to feel her arms around him. But he couldn't.

He swore under his breath, knowing it was time to tell her the truth.

"Hallie, you asked me once what kind of trouble I was in."

"And you said it was none of my business."

"Yeah, well . . ." He shrugged. "I'm wanted for murder."

"Murder." *Thou shalt not kill.* She heard the words written in Exodus thunder in her mind, and then the words of another scripture came to her: *A time to kill, and a time to heal . . .* She sat up, hugging herself. "Oh, Clay."

"My name isn't Clay. It's John."

"I know. John Walking Hawk. The sheriff told me."

"What else did he tell you?"

"Nothing, really. Reverend Mother said we didn't need to know." She nibbled on her lower lip a moment. "Who did you kill?"

"I killed the men who murdered my wife."

"Anna?"

"No. Anna's my daughter."

"Daughter!"

Clay nodded.

Hallie stared at him, wondering if she knew him at all. "You said men. How many were there?"

"Six." His voice turned hard and cold. "Five of them are dead." He had killed the first one with his bare hands, shot three of them, killed the last one with a knife.

"You've killed five men?" *Thou shalt not kill. . . .*

Clay let out a deep breath, and then he nodded. "And I won't rest until the last one is burning in hell. Now do you understand why you can't come with me?"

She didn't know what to say. He had killed five men. *Vengeance is mine, saith the Lord.* He had a daughter. "Where is she, your daughter?"

"With her grandparents."

"How old is she?"

"She'll be seven in October."

"How long since you've seen her?"

"Almost two years."

There was no mistaking the pain in his voice, the anguish that twisted his features.

"I'm sorry, Clay . . . or should I call you John?"

"Call me whatever you want," he muttered absently.

"Why haven't you seen your daughter for so long?" Hallie asked, her voice thick with accusation.

"Hallie . . ."

"How could you leave her for so long? Don't you love her?"

"Of course I love her."

"Then you should be with her." Hallie clenched her fists as tears stung her eyes. "A little girl needs her father!"

"Hallie . . ."

"My father left me and never came back. My mother said he loved me, that he would come back to us. But he never did." Tears slipped down her cheeks and she brushed them away, angry that after almost twelve years, her father's rejection still had the power to hurt her. "I don't even know if he's still alive."

"Hallie, I'm sorry."

"I hate him!"

"Sure you do."

"Why, Clay? Why did he leave us? Why didn't he come back, like he said he would?"

"I don't know, honey, but I'm sure he had a good reason."

She sniffed. "Like you?"

"What's that supposed to mean?"

"You should be with your daughter, that's what I mean."

"Dammit, Hallie, don't you think I know that? Don't you think I want to be with her?"

"Then why aren't you?"

"Because my wife is dead and that bastard, Bob Sayers, is still alive. And I won't rest until he's dead, too. I can't."

"What if you never find him?"

"I'll find him."

"What if you don't? How many years will you waste looking for him? What if he kills you instead?"

Clay glared at her. She hadn't said anything he hadn't thought a thousand times, yet every word cut through him like a knife, until he was bleeding inside. "That's enough, Hallie."

"I'm sorry."

"Hallie, what am I going to do with you?"

"You don't have to do anything with me. I can take care of myself."

"Sure you can, but you can't stay with me."

"I don't need you," she retorted, stung by his rejection. "I don't need anybody."

With a sigh, Clay rolled out of his blanket and stood up, needing to put some distance between them before he took her in his arms and showed her what need was all about.

Chapter 10

What to do with Hallie? It was a thought that troubled Clay as they broke camp later that morning, and then it came to him, so easy, he didn't know why he hadn't thought of it before. As far as he knew, Bob Sayers was holed up in a town called Green Willow Creek, which was in Wyoming, about thirty miles on the other side of the Colorado border. All he had to do was keep Hallie with him until he reached Green Willow Creek, then he could put her on the first stage headed for Bitter River and send her back where she belonged.

He felt an enormous sense of relief to have reached a decision. Once Hallie was safely on the stage, he would send a wire to the convent telling Mother Matilda that her stray lamb was on her way home.

As soon as Hallie was safely out of the way, he'd finish his business with Sayers and then he'd light out for the North Platte and hope his daughter would forgive him for leaving her in the first place. As always, when he thought of Anna, he felt a sharp twinge of fear. So much could have happened in two years. The buffalo were scarce, there was the ever-constant threat of war with the whites, or with the Crow. Life was hard for the Lakota, especially for the very old and the very young.

What if . . . he shook the thought away. He wouldn't think of that. Couldn't think of that. If he did, it would drive him crazy. He would find her as he had left her, a sweet child with hair the color of a raven's wing and her mother's laughing brown eyes. And a smile to melt any father's heart.

They rode all that day, stopping only briefly to rest the horses and have a quick bite to eat.

Hallie had never seen such pretty country. Spring grass carpeted the prairie as far as the eye could see; the sky was a bright clear blue, the air warm, fragrant with the scent of sage. Wildflowers made splashes of color on the landscape, bright pinks and yellows, pristine white, soft lilacs.

She felt free for the first time in her life. No walls fenced her in; there were no rules to obey, no bells calling her to meals or prayers.

And she was with Clay. She slid a glance in his direction. He had changed his clothes, donning a pair of black whipcord britches and a gray wool shirt. He wore a dark blue kerchief loosely knotted at his throat, a black hat shaded his eyes. His long black duster was tied behind the saddle. *Thou shalt not steal.*

She regarded him curiously. He looked more dangerous now than he had at the convent, perhaps because of the gun he carried. The holster strapped to his right thigh looked very much at home there. *Thou shalt not kill.*

He had hardly said a word to her all day, apparently lost in a world of his own. What was he thinking? She wondered if he ever thought about the men he had gunned down. Five men. She wished she could forget that, but it kept gnawing at the back of her mind. There had been no regret in his voice when he had told her about the men he had killed. She wondered if he was thinking of the daughter he hadn't seen in almost two years. That was almost a third of his child's life. How could he leave her? How could vengeance be more important that love? But, of course, he had loved his wife.

He must have loved her deeply, to leave his child, to turn his back on everything except the need to avenge his wife's death. And such a horrible death. Hallie shuddered. She had little knowledge of the intimacies that went on between a man and a woman, could not conceive of rape. Kissing Clay was the full extent of her sexual knowledge. She tried to imagine what it would be like to be held and kissed against her will by a man she didn't know, to be forced to . . . what?

Lost in thought, it took her a moment to realize Juliet had stopped moving. "What's wrong?"

"We're gonna make camp here for the night."

"Oh." She glanced around. They were in a shallow draw, protected from the wind, and from the immediate view of anyone who should happen by.

She dismounted, then stood beside Juliet, stroking the gelding's neck.

"So, do you wanna try your hand at cooking tonight?" Clay asked.

Hallie shook her head. "I'd rather look after the horses."

"Suit yourself."

A short time later, she had the horses unsaddled and hobbled for the night. She fed them some grain she found in one of the packs, then went to sit beside Clay.

Dinner consisted of dried pork, hardtack, and more of the bitter black liquid that passed for coffee. She wondered if she would ever acquire a taste for it. Even sugar didn't seem to sweeten it much. Milk or cream might have made it more palatable, but, of course, they didn't have any.

It was full dark by the time they finished eating.

"You'd best get some sleep," Clay suggested. "We'll be leaving at first light."

She didn't argue. They had spent close to ten hours in the saddle and she was bone weary. Every muscle in her body ached, her thighs were chafed, her face was sunburned. But she didn't complain. Clay didn't want her there in the first place. Complaining would only make things worse.

She took the blanket he offered her and curled up on the hard ground, wondering why she had ever thought her narrow bed at the convent was uncomfortable. Compared to this, her cot seemed like a featherbed.

Wrapping one hand around her rosary, she began to say her evening prayers.

She came awake with a start. For a moment, she couldn't remember where she was, and then she heard a noise, a sharp cry, followed by a voice whispering, "no, no".

Sitting up, she glanced over at Clay. He was thrashing in his blanket, in the throes of a nightmare.

She scooted toward him, ducked under his flailing arm, and shook him on the shoulder. "Clay? Clay, wake up!"

She jerked backward as he grabbed his gun and thrust it in her direction. "Clay, don't shoot!"

"Hallie?" He swore under his breath. In the moonlight, her eyes were wide and scared.

"You were having a nightmare."

He slid the Colt back in the holster, ran his hands through his hair. "Yeah." He took a deep breath. "Sorry I woke you. Go back to sleep."

She grabbed her blanket and curled up in it once again.

With a sigh, Clay stood up and poked at the fire, then hunkered down beside it, his forearms resting on his knees. Damn, it had been months since he'd had that nightmare.

He stared into the glowing coals, wishing he had a

bottle of whiskey. *The devil's own brew,* Hallie had called it. And it was that. He had never really been much of a drinker, but there had been a few times, shortly after Summer died, when the only way he had been able to find relief from the pain of her death, from the nightmares that haunted him, had been to dive into a bottle and swim to the bottom.

He heard the soft sound of footsteps behind him, and then Hallie was sitting beside him.

"I can't sleep," she said, a note of apology in her voice. "Do you mind if I sit here with you?"

"No."

"It's so dark out here," Hallie mused.

Clay grunted softly. It was dark, all right. Black as the bowels of hell. As dark as the blood that stained his soul, as the hatred that burned like a cold flame in his heart.

"Do you want to talk about it?" Hallie asked.

"About what?"

"Your nightmare. I used to have nightmares when I first got to the convent. Reverend Mother told me if I talked to her about them, they would go away and I wouldn't have them anymore. And she was right."

"What kind of nightmares did you have?"

Hallie shrugged. "Mostly about my father, that I would find him someday, and that when I did, he wouldn't want me. Sometimes I dreamed that I found him and I'd be so happy, I'd run to him, and then, when he turned around, he'd be a ghost or some kind of monster." She blew out a sigh. "They seem silly now."

Clay studied Hallie's profile. Was Anna having nightmares, too, dreaming that her father would never come back? Did she think he didn't want her? That he was a monster?

He raked a hand through his hair, praying that

someday his daughter would understand why he'd had to leave her. That she would understand and forgive.

"Clay?"

"What?"

He turned to face her, his expression bleak. Hallie shook her head. "Never mind."

"The dream is always the same," Clay said. "I'm coming home from town and I hear Summer screaming my name, crying for help. But no matter how fast I ride, no matter how hard I try, it's like I'm mired in quicksand, and I can't reach her. I see those men holding her down, taking her again and again, and I can't do anything to stop it." He drew in a deep shuddering breath. "And when I finally get to her, it's too late . . . too late."

"I'm sorry, Clay, so sorry." She placed a tentative hand on his shoulder, thinking to comfort him.

And suddenly he was lying across her lap, his face pressed against her breasts, his arms locked around her waist. Harsh sobs racked his body.

"Oh, Clay." Feeling as though her own heart were breaking, she held him tight, one hand stroking his back, while his tears soaked the bodice of her dress.

She held him for a long time, knowing, somehow, that this was the first time he had let himself cry for his wife.

As if he were a child, she rocked him back and forth, murmuring soft words of comfort, assuring him that everything would be all right.

Gradually, his body stopped shaking and she knew, by his slow even breaths, that he had fallen asleep.

Moving carefully so as not to waken him, she scooted down until they were lying side by side. She drew both blankets over them and then, with his head pillowed on her shoulder, she stared up at the vast inky depths of the sky.

"God bless you, Clay," she whispered. "I hope you find the peace you're searching for."

He was embarrassed to face her in the morning. He woke first, surprised to find her in his arms. Gently, he eased away from her and stood up. Damn, he'd made a fool of himself last night.

Pulling on his boots, he removed the hobbles from the horses and led them out of the draw toward the water hole located a few yards away. He let the horses drink while he splashed cold water over his face and neck, then tethered the animals to a scrawny cotton-wood, leaving them to graze while he went in search of fuel for the fire. And all the while he thought about Hallie, and how he had cried like a baby in her ams, and how good it had felt to have her hold him while he shed the bitter tears he had kept locked inside for the last two years.

He had an armload of buffalo chips when he returned to their campsite. Hallie was sitting on one of the blankets, trying to comb the tangles from her hair with her fingers.

"Where've you been?" she asked.

"Gettin' some fuel for the fire," he said, dumping the buffalo chips on the ground.

"Oh." She stood up, shaking the dust from her skirts. She glanced around, then looked back at Clay, her cheeks pink.

"Up there," he said. "Bring the horses back with you."

She nodded, too embarrassed to speak. Last night, she had snuck off while he was asleep to relieve herself.

Climbing up the side of the draw, she hurried toward the first bush she saw and squatted behind it, thinking this was one part of having an adventure she could do without.

Romeo and Juliet whinnied at her as she approached

and she spent a few minutes scratching their ears while she admired the sunrise. The sky seemed to go on forever out here, making her feel small and insignificant.

In the distance, she saw a doe picking its way through the long grass, a spotted fawn at her side. Overhead, an eagle rode the air currents. She heard birds twittering in the cottonwoods near the water hole. Trees were scarce out here. Mostly there was just grass, miles and miles of grass that dipped and swayed to the music of the morning breeze.

Feeling as though she were in God's own church, she knelt on the ground and began to say her prayers, her thoughts wandering toward Mother Matilda and the other nuns. They were probably worried sick about her. She should have taken time to leave a note for Reverend Mother, but there was no help for it now. What was done was done.

Her fingers moved over the beads of her rosary as she prayed and then, remembering how she had held Clay the night before, the words died on her lips. He had turned to her for solace and her heart had swelled with love and tenderness. Holding him, comforting him, had been the most satisfying thing she had ever done.

Bowing her head, she resumed her prayers, adding one for Clay, and one for his daughter.

Clay looked up at the sky and frowned. Breakfast, such as it was, was ready. Where the devil was Hallie?

Strapping his gun belt in place, he climbed out of the draw and glanced around. He saw the horses, still grazing near the water hole. And then he saw Hallie. She was kneeling in the tall grass, her head bowed, her skirts spread around her like the petals of a flower.

Early-morning sunlight fell over her like a benediction, haloing her hair, casting golden shadows on her face and skirts. She looked like an angel fallen to earth.

He stood there for a long moment, jut staring at her, noting the way her nose turned up just a little on the end. Her cheeks were rosy from too much sun the day before.

"Hallie." Her name whispered past his lips, fervent as a prayer.

And, as if in answer to that prayer, she rose gracefully to her feet and moved toward him, her full skirts swishing around her ankles.

"Good morning, Clay."

"Mornin'."

She looked up at him, her hazel eyes shining. Radiant. That was the only word for her. She was beautiful, so beautiful it made his heart ache.

He cleared his throat. "Breakfast is ready."

"I'm starving," she said, then grinned as her stomach growled.

He couldn't help it. He grinned back at her. "Come on," he said, taking her hand. "Let's eat."

An hour later, they were riding north. Clay had insisted Hallie wear his hat to shade her face from the sun, and as the morning wore on, she was glad for its protection.

"Where are we going?" she asked after a while.

"Green Willow Creek," Clay replied.

Hallie frowned. "Green Willow Creek? That name sounds familiar. What's there?"

"Last I heard, Sayers was holed up there."

"Oh."

Clay slid a glance in Hallie's direction. It was evident from her expression that she knew why they were going to Green Willow Creek, and just as easy to see she didn't approve.

"How long will it take us to get there?"

Clay shrugged. "Two days, maybe three. You can't talk me out of this, Hallie, so don't even try."

"But, Clay, killing is wrong."

"Wrong for me, or for the men who killed my wife?

"For all of you."

"Hallie, let it go."

"I can't," she said miserably. "I don't want you burning in hell for all eternity."

"Don't you think my soul's already damned? I've killed five men. I doubt one more will make any difference."

"It isn't funny."

"No, it isn't."

"Then why can't you just . . ."

"Hallie, let it go."

There was no room for argument in his tone this time, and she lapsed into silence, one hand wrapped around her rosary. He had the feeling she was praying for him, asking mercy for his immortal soul. It annoyed him even as, perversely, it made him feel better.

She didn't speak to him the rest of the day. It was just as well, Clay mused. He needed to keep some distance between them, to remember that she was going to be a nun. Another couple of days riding across the barren prairie and she'd get over her foolish yearning for adventure quick enough. By the time they reached Green Willow Creek, he figured she would be more than ready to return to the convent.

At dusk, Clay drew rein in a small grove of cottonwoods. A narrow stream ran nearby. There was graze for the horses, wood for a fire.

As had become their habit, Clay prepared dinner while Hallie looked after the horses. A little more practice, and he'd make some woman a fine wife, he mused as he sliced a couple of potatoes and tossed them in the frying pan.

He held the pan over the fire, his gaze straying toward Hallie. She had the horses unsaddled and hobbled and now she stood between the two geldings, scratching their ears. Romeo, usually bad-tempered and snappish, stood with his head resting on her shoulder, a study in equine contentment.

Clay grunted softly, remembering all too clearly what it had felt like to rest his own head on Hallie's shoulder, to feel her arms around him, comforting him. Damn, now he was jealous of a horse! He must be getting soft in the head.

Cursing himself for being a fool, he added a handful of chopped onions to the potatoes.

"Smells good."

He glanced up to see Hallie standing beside him.

"Anything I can do to help?" she asked.

"Here." He thrust the coffeepot at her. "Go get some water."

"Yes, sir," she replied curtly, and flounced off toward the stream.

He watched her go, noting the sway of her hips, the petulant set of her shoulders, the way the setting sun glinted in her hair. She had removed his hat and her hair fell to her waist in thick brown waves. They would cut her hair off when she took her vows, he thought, and knew he'd regret the loss.

Damn! He had to stop thinking of Hallie, had to stop wanting her with every breath he took.

She tried to engage him in conversation during dinner, but he remained sullen and silent, his mind waging a tacit battle with the lustful urgings of his flesh.

As soon as the meal was over, he walked out into the darkness. How could he want her so badly, need her so much? He hardly knew her. And yet her innocence called to him, her innate goodness and compassion as hard to resist as her sweet curves and shy smile.

Hunkering down on his heels, he stared into the distance. Maybe he'd just been away from decent people for too long. Maybe he'd just been alone too long. Maybe he would feel the same way about any good, caring woman. And maybe cows would sing and birds would give milk.

He sat there for a long time, giving her time to get ready for bed, to get to sleep. He didn't want to see the concern in her eyes, didn't want to hear her sweet voice bid him good night.

If they pushed hard, they could be in Green Willow Creek tomorrow night. He would put Hallie on the first stagecoach headed south and send her back where she belonged before he did something they would both regret.

Chapter 11

Hallie sat beside the dwindling fire, waiting for Clay to return. It was scary, sitting there in the dark, alone. She was sure there was nothing to fear. After all, they hadn't seen anything more frightening than a couple of white-tailed deer all day; still, the land looked different at night, ominous somehow. She heard the howl of a wolf somewhere in the distance. The sound, alien and melancholy, sent a shiver down her spine.

"It's just noise." She said the words aloud, hoping the sound of her voice would give her some much-needed courage. "A little noise never hurt anyone."

And then she heard the wolf's howl again, closer this time. Soon, it was joined by another, and then another.

She stared into the darkness, felt her heart leap into her throat when she saw three pairs of yellow eyes staring at her.

Behind her, Romeo snorted and pawed the ground.

She heard a growl, and then another, the sound of snapping jaws.

Jumping to her feet, she clutched the blanket tighter. "Clay!"

"Shh, I'm here." As if by magic, he materialized out of the darkness.

"Clay, there are wolves out there."

"I know." He squatted on his heels across the fire from her. "They won't hurt you."

"They growled at me."

"What'd you do with the bones and scraps from dinner?"

"I threw them away." She pointed over her shoulder. "Over there."

He laughed softly as he added an armful of wood to the fire. "They're not after you," he assured her. "They're after the bones. I should have told you to burn them."

"Are you sure?"

"I'm sure. Go to bed, Hallie."

"But . . ."

"Hallie, I spent a lot of time living out here, and I've never known a wolf to attack a man." He smiled at her. "Or a woman. Now go on, get some sleep."

"What about Little Red Riding Hood?"

"It's just a fairy tale, Hallie, like Cinderella."

She glanced over her shoulder. She could see the wolves out there, hear them growling ferociously at one another as they fought over the bones and meat scraps.

"Can I sleep here, next to you?"

He hesitated a moment. "Sure."

She carried her bed roll to where he was sitting, spread it out, and crawled under the covers.

Clay slid a glance at Hallie, stretched out beside him, so close he could have brushed his fingers over her shoulder with no trouble at all.

He shoved his hands in his pockets to keep from doing just that, but he couldn't keep himself from staring at her, from noticing how long her eyelashes were, the way they lay like dark fans against her cheeks. Her hair fell around her shoulders in rich chestnut waves, sorely tempting his touch, as did the delicate curve of her cheek, the rise and fall of her breasts.

Damn! He turned his back to her, the wolves forgotten as he fought to control the sudden, overpowering need to slip under the blanket beside her and draw her into his arms, to kiss those sweet lips, to caress every curve, to explore every hill, every valley.

He tossed a stick of wood on the fire. She was trusting him to protect her. Little did she know she was in a lot more danger from the man sitting beside her than from the wolves prowling the darkness beyond the glow of the fire.

He woke in a foul mood. Hallie took one look at his face and wisely left him alone.

They rode all that day, galloping for long periods of time. Clay had told her if they rode hard, they would reach Green Willow Creek just after sundown. He was in a terrible hurry, she thought bleakly. Just couldn't wait to kill that last man. How could he do it? she wondered. How could he kill another human being? How did he sleep nights, with all those deaths on his conscience?

The thought no sooner crossed her mind than she recalled the nightmare he'd had, and how she had held him and comforted him. He had hardly spoken to her since that night, had been careful to avoid touching her. Was he angry because she had seen him at what he probably considered a weak moment?

She slid a glance in his direction as he reined Romeo to a walk, all that was female within her warming to the mere sight of him. He rode easy in the saddle, the reins loosely held in one hand. His profile was beautiful to see, sharp and clean, a study in masculine perfection. His hair, long and inky black, glinted with blue high-lights in the relentless glare of the sun. Her gaze moved from his shoulders down the line of his back, over a long muscular leg. She stared at the Colt strapped to his right thigh. How could she love a man who had killed five people? How could she keep him from killing again?

Leaning forward, she patted Juliet on the neck. "I do love him, you know," she whispered. "I just wish I knew how to help him."

A short time later, they stopped in the shade of a rocky bluff to rest the horses.

Hallie slid from the saddle, her back and shoulders aching, her legs feeling like rubber.

"Here." Clay handed her his canteen.

Hallie took a long drink. The water was lukewarm, but it was wet and she drank deeply. "How much farther?"

"Another couple hours."

She capped the canteen and handed it to Clay. "How do you know Sayers is still there?"

"I don't."

Hallie closed her eyes and sent a quick petition to heaven, praying that Sayers was gone, that no one would know where he was. Maybe then Clay would give up.

"What if he's not there? What then?"

"I'll find him," he replied in a voice that left no room for doubt. "I don't care where he goes, I'll find him."

Chapter 12

Green Willow Creek was a growing community. You could see, from some of the older buildings, that it had once been no more than a wide spot in the road, but it was flourishing now. Old one-story buildings, made of weathered wood, were quickly being replaced by new ones, some of which, like the Palace Hotel, were two stories high. Most of the establishments seemed to be saloons: The Dead Dog, The Three Queens, The Black Jack.

A trio of men sat on a bench outside a gambling hall called The Crazy Lady. They stared at Hallie as she rode by. It made her feel dirty somehow, the way they looked at her.

Riding on, she saw a barber shop, a mercantile, a feed store, and the sheriff's office.

On the opposite side of the street, she saw a millinery shop, a small newspaper office, a telegraph office, and another hotel called the Southwick. This one didn't appear to be as new or as grand as the Palace. There didn't seem to be a church, or a school. She saw a stage depot at the far end of town.

Clay drew rein in front of the Southwick Hotel and Dining Hall. He glanced at the jail, located across the street, felt a shiver of unease skitter down his back. Maybe they should have stayed at the Palace, he mused, but the place was too rich by half for his blood.

Dismounting, he tossed Romeo's reins over the hitch rack, then lifted Hallie from Juliet's back. After securing Juliet's reins to the rack, he slung the saddlebags over his shoulder and started up the stairs to the hotel.

Hallie followed close on his heels. She had never been inside a hotel before, and she glanced around the lobby, fascinated, while Clay talked to the man behind the desk.

The inside of the hotel had been freshly painted. A flowered carpet muffled her footsteps. Green and gold wallpaper covered the walls. Curved settees, tables, and chairs with dainty legs were scattered around the lobby. Several men in city-style suits were gathered in one corner. A cloud of cigar smoke hung over their heads.

She moved up to stand behind Clay, listening as he asked for two rooms adjoining, and then asked for a tub to be sent up to her room.

"Several of our rooms have tubs," the clerk said, pride evident in his voice. "You'll find one in Room Seven."

"Fine."

The clerk turned the register so Clay could sign it. "How many nights will you be staying with us, Mr. . . ." He glanced at Clay's signature. "Mr. Clayton."

"I'm not sure," Clay replied. He dropped the pen on the counter, then took Hallie by the arm. "I signed for you, sis."

"What? Oh, thank you."

"Rooms seven and nine," the clerk said. "I'll send the boys up with hot water for your bath immediately." He handed Clay the keys, smiled at Hallie. "I hope you enjoy your stay."

"Thanks. Have someone look after our horses, will ya?" Clay asked. "They're out front. A chestnut and a big blood bay."

"Yessir, I'll have a boy take care of it."

"Obliged. Tell your boy to look sharp. The bay's got a bad temper."

"Yessir."

Taking up his saddlebags, Clay headed for the stairs. They'd get cleaned up, grab something to eat, and then he'd see about getting Hallie a ticket on the next train or stage out of town.

He opened the door to room number seven and stepped inside. It was a large room, clean and fresh smelling. White lace curtains hung from the window, a matching spread covered the bed. There was a highboy and mirror, a rocking chair. A three-sided screen hid an enamel bathtub.

Crossing the floor, he opened the adjoining door and went into the other room. It was similar to Hallie's, save that the curtains and the comforter were green.

Clay dropped his saddlebags on the floor beside the bed, tossed his hat on the chair next to the window.

Hallie stood in the doorway, chewing on her lower lip. Clay turned away and looked out the window to the street below, aware of her gaze on his back, the silent condemnation in her eyes.

"How will you find Sayers?" she asked.

"Ask around. If he's here, someone will know." It wasn't a very big town. It shouldn't take long to find out if the man he was searching for was here.

"What if he's not here anymore?"

Clay shrugged. "I'll find him."

There was a knock at Hallie's door.

"That's probably the water for your bath," Clay remarked.

Clay continued to stare out the window. He heard Hallie open the door, the murmur of voices as three boys entered the room, the splash of water as they filled the tub. A few minutes later, a maid entered with clean towels.

"Clay?"

"Hmm?"

"I'd like to wash my clothes but I don't have anything to wear while they dry."

"I'll get you something over at the mercantile." He glanced over his shoulder, judging her size. "Take your time in the tub."

She nodded, a faint flush pinking her cheeks as she closed the door between their rooms.

Clay stared at the door, imagining Hallie getting undressed, reclining in a tub of steamy water, her body covered with soapsuds. Muttering under his breath, he grabbed his hat and left the hotel.

The mercantile was located in a large building crammed with shelves and counters. There appeared to be no rhyme or reason for the way things were stacked: tins of peaches and bottles of horse liniment shared a shelf along with packages of hairpins and boxes of imported cigars. He found a rack of ready-made dresses in a corner. There was only one that looked to be about Hallie's size, a dark green print with long sleeves and a modest neckline.

He plucked it off the hanger and started toward the front of the store, then paused when he saw a stack of nightgowns. He picked one off the pile and started for the counter again, then went searching through the store until he found a hairbrush.

He wasn't sure what else she might need, but it didn't matter. He couldn't afford to buy her anything else. Could no longer afford to buy her a ticket out of town, either. But that could be remedied at the poker table later.

He paid for his supplies, drummed his fingers on the

counter while the clerk wrapped his purchases in brown paper and tied the package with string.

Tucking the bundle under his arm, Clay left the store. He stood on the boardwalk a minute, then headed for the hotel. He'd get Hallie settled, take a quick bath, then go make inquiries as to Sayers's whereabouts.

Back at the hotel, he paused outside Hallie's door. "Hallie? You still in the tub?"

"No, I . . . I just stepped out." Even without seeing her face, he knew she was blushing again.

"I bought you something to wear. I'll leave it here, outside the door. Leave the water in the tub, will you?"

"All right."

Going down to the front desk, Clay asked the clerk to send another bucket of hot water up to Hallie's room, then went back upstairs. The package he had left outside Hallie's door was gone.

Unlocking the door to his room, he went inside. Too restless to sit still, he paced the floor, wondering if Sayers was still in town.

He paused at the window. Forehead pressed against the cool glass, he closed his eyes, his hands clenching as he thought of Summer Rain, of Anna.

"Just one more," he muttered. "Just one more and it'll be over."

He swore under his breath as he heard Hallie's voice, soft and sweet, in the back of his mind. *But Clay, killing is wrong. . . .*

Dammit, he knew that. He didn't need her to be his conscience. But he'd gone to the law, and the law had laughed in his face, so now he'd do it his way.

A rap at the door drew his attention. "Come in."

He moved away from the window, felt the breath catch in his throat as Hallie stepped into the room. The green dress fit right well, showing off the softly rounded curves that had been hidden beneath her shapeless gray habit. Her hair, freshly washed, fell in loose waves over her shoulders.

"Thank you for the dress, Clay."

"You look real pretty," he replied.

"Thank you." She blushed under his frankly admiring gaze. "One of the boys brought up some more hot water and some clean towels."

Clay nodded. He couldn't stop staring at her, couldn't keep from remembering the times he had kissed her, the way she had felt in his arms, warm and soft and all too willing.

"Thanks." He walked past her, closing the door behind him, knowing he had to put some distance between them before he gave in to the urge to drag her down on the bed, before she could see the path his thoughts were wandering.

Stripping off his clothes, he dumped the hot water into the copper tub.

"Should have asked for a bucket of cold water," he muttered. "Would have done me a lot more good."

It had been his intent to go looking for Bob Sayers once he got cleaned up, but he took Hallie to dinner in the hotel instead. He didn't miss the fact that every man they passed stared at her. The sooner he got her on a train bound for home, the better.

Her eyes fairly glowed as she looked around the lavish dining room. A crystal chandelier hung from the ceiling. A plush carpet covered the floor. There was flocked paper on the walls. The tables were covered with dark blue cloths.

Clay had to admit, it was the prettiest room he'd ever seen. To Hallie, accustomed to taking her meals in the stark dining room in the convent, it must look like something out of a fairy tale.

A woman wearing a blue gingham dress and a white apron came to take their order. She recommended the roast chicken dinner, and Hallie said that sounded fine. Clay asked for a steak, rare.

"I've never seen anything like this," Hallie whispered. "Isn't it elegant?"

Clay nodded. It was elegant all right. He'd be lucky to have any cash left after he paid the bill.

Hallie fidgeted with the edge of the tablecloth, uncertain how to behave in such a place. "Did I thank you for the dress?" She smoothed one hand over her skirt. It was the prettiest thing she had ever owned in her whole life. She treasured it all the more because Clay had bought it for her.

"I'm glad you like it."

"Oh, I do, I do." She glanced around the room, watching the people come and go. Such well-dressed people. Men in expensive suits and cravats, ladies in bright silks and satins. It seemed odd to see women wearing colorful gowns instead of severe black habits, to see them wearing bonnets adorned with flowers and feathers instead of veils. She ran her hand over her skirt again. The material was so much finer than she was used to, the green print so much more pleasing to the eye than the drab gray she had worn for the last four years.

The waitress arrived with their dinner and Hallie concentrated on her meal. She had never had trouble talking to Clay before, but now he seemed so distant, almost a stranger.

A handsome stranger. She saw the way the women looked at him, their gazes lingering on his face, measuring the width of his shoulders with their eyes. The men stared at him, too, their expressions wary, speculative, almost as if they were afraid of him.

Clay sat back in his chair. "You finished?"

Hallie nodded. She looked at the next table, and licked her lips. "Do you think we could have dessert?"

"Sure, if you want."

He summoned the waitress and ordered a piece of chocolate cake for Hallie, a cup of black coffee for himself.

He had to smile as he watched Hallie eat. She took small bites, savored each mouthful as though it might be her last.

"You can have more, you know," Clay said.

"Oh, it's so good. Here, taste it." She offered him a forkful.

Clay leaned across the table, his gaze on hers as she fed him. It was good. Rich and moist. He could have been eating dirt. All he could think of was how much he'd like to be licking the chocolate from Hallie's lips instead.

"Good, isn't it?" she asked.

Clay nodded. Pushing back in his chair, he stood up and tossed a dollar on the table. "Let's go."

"But I'm not finished."

"Wrap it up in your napkin and bring it with you."

Puzzled by his peculiar attitude, Hallie quickly wrapped her cake in her napkin and followed Clay out of the dining room and up the stairs to her room.

"Lock your door," Clay said. "And don't open it for anyone."

"Where are you going?"

"Out."

"Can't I come with you?"

"No. Go to bed, Hallie."

"But I don't want to stay here alone."

"You'll be all right. Just keep your door locked."

"Clay . . ."

"Dammit, Hallie, don't argue with me."

She stared up at him, her eyes filled with hurt, her lower lip quivering.

Feeling like the worst sort of heel, he turned and walked away.

Chapter 13

The saloon was dimly lit and smelled of stale cigar smoke, old sweat, and cheap perfume. A thick haze of blue-gray smoke hung in the air, a thick layer of sawdust covered the floor. There was the usual painting of a nude behind the long mahogany bar; this one had flame-colored hair, and a bullet hole in her right breast.

Clay stood just inside the swinging doors, getting the feel of the place. There had been a time when he'd been a stranger to places like this, but tracking Summer Rain's killers had changed all that. He had followed his prey from town to town, saloon to saloon. Along the way, he had learned much he didn't want to know.

Shaking away thoughts of the past, he made his way to the back corner of the room where a poker game was in progress.

"Mind if I sit in?"

The four men at the table shrugged, and Clay sat down. You could pick up a lot of town gossip at a card game, and right now he needed information as much as he needed a stake.

Playing poker and blackjack was something else he had learned in the last two years. To his surprise, he discovered he was a pretty good card player. Years of training to be a Lakota warrior had stood him in good stead at the card table. He knew how to keep his expression blank, how to wait out his opponent.

As always, he played conservatively, winning more than he lost. He said little, bought a round of drinks when he won a big hand. For himself, he nursed a beer. Only a fool clouded his mind with whiskey.

An hour passed, and then another. One of the men left the table. A few minutes later, a lanky redheaded man took his place. "Hey, Joe, Gil, Lem. Thought I'd find you all here."

"Shoot, Henry, it's Saturday night," the man called Joe replied with a good-natured grin. "Where else would we be? How was your trip?"

The newcomer grinned. "Fine, fine. The missus liked Kansas City. She's wantin' to move there now. Anything exciting happen while we were gone?"

"Dill Hampton busted out of jail day before yesterday," Joe remarked. Taking up the cards, he shuffled and dealt a new hand.

"Is that right?"

"Yep," Joe said. "He got hold of old Charlie's gun and lit out. Sheriff McIntyre was fit to be tied. I hear he fired Charlie on the spot, then rounded up a posse and lit out after Hampton."

McIntyre? Clay frowned. No, it couldn't be.

"Well, McIntyre's back," Henry said. "I saw him ride in just a few minutes ago, an' he was alone. Looked mad as hell, too."

"The sheriff," Clay said, "he been here long?"

Joe regarded Clay curiously. "Long enough. Why?"

Clay shrugged. "Name sounds familiar, that's all. Is his first name Carl?"

"No, it's Frank."

"Probably not the same man then. How long has he been sheriff?"

Joe made a vague gesture with his hand. "I dunno. Six, seven years, I reckon."

"Closer to eight, I'd say," Henry remarked.

Clay nodded, then picked up the hand he'd been dealt. Four queens and the ace of spades.

He spent another hour at the poker table, then took up his winnings and went to the bar. He ordered a beer, listening to the conversation around him. Once, he thought he heard the name Sayers, but he wasn't sure.

Finishing his beer, he put the glass on the bar and left the saloon.

Lost in thought, he made his way back to the hotel. Tomorrow night, he'd start asking questions.

In his room, he locked the door, tossed his hat on the chair, removed his gun belt. He went to the door that connected his room to Hallie's and knocked softly, not wanting to wake her if she was asleep.

The door opened almost immediately and Hallie stood there, a look of accusation on her face.

"I was beginning to think you were never coming back," she said.

"I wouldn't leave you here alone, Hallie."

"You were gone a long time."

"Yeah. What was your father's first name?"

Hallie frowned. "Franklin. Why?"

"I think he might be the sheriff."

Hallie stared at him, dazed. "My father's here?"

"It could be another man with the same name."

"But it could be him," she said, and remembered why the name Green Willow Creek sounded so familiar. She had overheard her grandmother mention it once, a long time ago. Had Grandma Hastings known where her father was all the time? "It's him. I know it is."

"Maybe, maybe not," Clay said. "Do you think you'd recognize him if you saw him?"

Hallie nodded. "I think so." Her mother had kept a picture of her father on the table beside her bed. Hallie had spent countless hours staring at that photograph, as if, by looking at it long enough, she might find the answer to why her father had left her.

"You okay?" Clay asked. "You look kind of pale."

"I'm fine." Clay was right. It might not be her father. There were probably a lot of men named Franklin McIntyre. But what if this man was her father? Excitement mingled with dread, making her feel suddenly nauseous.

"Yeah, well, you don't look fine. It's late. I think you should go to bed."

"What?" She looked at him blankly.

"Come on," he said, and taking her by the hand, he led her into her room and tucked her into bed. "Don't get your hopes up, Hallie."

She knew he was right, but she couldn't help it. Maybe God had sent Clay to the convent so that he would bring her here, to this place, so she could be reunited with her father. Hope quickly turned to doubt. What if this man was her father? What could she say to him? In all these years, he had never tried to get in touch with her. He probably wouldn't even want to see her. And yet, deep down, she knew it had to be him. It just had to be.

They ate breakfast in the hotel dining room the following morning.

Clay studied Hallie's face across the table, wondering if she had gotten any sleep the night before. Probably not, he decided, noting the dark shadows under her eyes.

"Hallie?"

"Hmm?"

"Eat your breakfast."

Hallie glanced down at the plate before her. She'd been so distracted with thoughts of her father, she hadn't noticed when the waitress brought their order. She ate the ham and eggs, hardly aware of what she was eating. She tried to remember everything her mother and grandmother had ever told her about her father.

Tall and handsome, her mother had said, with dark brown wavy hair and mischievous green eyes.

A wild and wicked man, her grandmother had said, but a man who'd had a way with the ladies. Grandma Hastings had always claimed the reason her father took off so suddenlike was because he was wanted by the law. Remembering that now, Hallie felt her hopes sink like a stone tossed into a river. If her father had been a wanted man, it was unlikely that he was now the sheriff of Green Willow Creek, Wyoming.

She pushed her plate away, her appetite gone.

"Something wrong?" Clay asked.

"No, I was just thinking about what Grandmother Hastings said about my father. She told me once she thought he was an outlaw."

"What made her think that?"

"I don't know, but if it's true, this man can't be my father."

"Why not?"

"Why do you think?"

"Shoot, Hallie, there's more than one sheriff out there who's been on both sides of the law."

"Really?"

"Really."

"Oh, Clay, what if it is him?" She twisted the napkin in her lap. "He probably doesn't want anything to do with me."

"He might have had a good reason for leavin'," Clay said, thinking of his own daughter. "Don't judge him until you hear him out."

Judge not, that ye be not judged. For with what judgment ye judge, ye shall be judged: and with the measure ye mete, it shall be measured to you again. How often had Reverend Mother used that subject as text for one of her spiritual discussions?

"Ready to go?" Clay asked. At Hallie's nod, he dropped a dollar on the table. "Come on," he said, taking her by the hand, "let's go for a walk."

It was a pretty day, bright and clear. Arm in arm, they strolled down the boardwalk. Hallie forgot about her father as she glanced around. She had never been in a town this big, never seen so many people. She saw women clad in cotton and gingham, their heads covered with floppy-brimmed bonnets, men in overalls and Texas hats, a slender Chinaman wearing strange-looking clothes and sandals and a pointy hat.

As they passed a saloon, she stared at a voluptuous woman lounging in the doorway. The woman had bright orange hair and wore a robe that gaped open, exposing a good deal of her bosom. A cigar dangled from a corner of her mouth. Her cheeks were rouged, her eyes outlined with kohl.

"Hallie, don't stare."

"She's smoking!" Hallie exclaimed.

"Yeah, well, that's not the worst thing she does," Clay said, tugging on Hallie's arm. "Come on."

"She's in her underwear."

Clay glanced over his shoulder. "That she is."

Hallie paused at every shop they passed, gazing at the merchandise displayed in the windows. Dresses and hats, boots, bolts of gaily colored cloth, rag dolls.

They passed a barber shop, a Chinese laundry, the newspaper office, several saloons, another hotel.

"Do you need anything?" Clay asked.

"What?"

He shrugged. "Female stuff."

Hallie shook her head. She had a dress, a night rail, a hairbrush, her rosary. What else did she need?

The stage depot was at the end of town. It had been

Clay's intention to put Hallie on the first stage headed south, but all that had changed now. He knew she wouldn't leave until she found out whether or not McIntyre was her father, and he couldn't blame her for that. She had a right to know.

They crossed the street, and started back up the other side. Clay watched Hallie's face as they passed one shop after another, smiling at the way her eyes lit up when they came to a candy store.

"Come on," he said, and went into the shop. "What do you want?"

Hallie looked at him as if he had just offered her the moon.

It took her ten minutes to make up her mind, and then all she asked for was a peppermint stick.

"That's all you want?" Clay asked incredulously.

"It reminds me of Christmas," Hallie said.

Clay grunted softly, then asked the lady behind the counter to fill a bag with a variety of sweets. He paid for the candy, then handed the sack to Hallie.

"For me?"

"I don't know anybody else in town," he muttered wryly.

Hallie clutched the brown paper bag as if it was filled with diamonds.

He felt her arm grow tense as they neared the sheriff's office.

"Wait out here," Clay said.

"But . . ."

"Just wait, Hallie."

He stepped inside the sheriff's office, feeling the hair raise along the back of his neck.

A man sat behind the desk. A man with close-cropped dark brown hair going gray at the temples, and green eyes. "Can I help you?"

"I'm lookin' for Bob Sayers."

The man stood up. He was almost as tall as Clay, broad through the shoulders. Solid as oak. He wore a green plaid shirt and black whipcord britches. There was a shiny six-pointed star pinned to his leather vest.

"Frank McIntyre," the sheriff said, extending a large, callused hand. "I'm the law in these parts."

"Clayton. Joe Clayton." Clay took the hand the sheriff offered. The man had a grip that could bend iron.

"Why are you looking for Sayers?"

"It's a personal matter. Is he in town?"

The sheriff shook his head. "He left a month or so ago. Headed for Virginia City, I think."

Clay ran a hand over his jaw. "Is he coming back?"

"I couldn't say. Where are you staying, Mr. Clayton?"

"The Southwick."

"What do you do for a living?"

"I'm a cattleman."

The sheriff nodded, then looked past Clay as Hallie peered in the doorway. "Can I help you, miss?"

"Come on in, Hallie," Clay said.

McIntyre's eyes widened as he glanced from Hallie to Clay. "Hallie? Did you say Hallie?"

Clay watched McIntyre's face as Hallie stepped into the room.

McIntyre leaned forward, his hands braced on the desktop. "Your mother . . ." he said, his voice tight. "Was her name Helen? Helen McIntyre?"

Hallie nodded.

"It is you." McIntyre sat down heavily, a colorful epithet escaping his lips. "You look just like her." He stared at Hallie like a man in a daze. "What are you doing here? How did you find me?"

"I came with . . . Joe. He's looking for someone."

"Hallie, I . . ." McIntyre ran a hand through his hair, obviously at a loss for words.

"Maybe I should leave you two alone?" Clay suggested.

Hallie started to protest, but Clay placed a finger over her lips, stilling the words. "I'll be right outside."

Hallie watched him walk out the door and then slowly turned to face her father. There were a few strands of gray in his hair, deep lines etched around his mouth, but, other than that, he looked much the same as he did in the photograph that had sat on the table beside her mother's bed.

"Hallie, I can't believe you're here."

"Why did you leave us?" She blurted the words in a rush. "Why did you run away? We needed you."

"Hallie, I'm sorry."

"You left and never came back."

"That's not true." He stood up and rounded the desk. "I did come back, but they told me your mother had died and no one knew where you'd gone."

"I went to live with Grandma."

"I couldn't find her," McIntyre said. "I had an address your mother gave me, and I sent your grandmother a letter, telling her I was coming to get you. But when I finally got there, she had left town, and no one knew where she'd gone. I looked everywhere I could think of."

"I don't believe you." Hallie glared at him. "You could have found me if you wanted to."

"Hallie, I tried. I even hired a detective to try and find you, but if was like you had just disappeared from the face of the earth. Don't you see? Your grandmother never liked me. She was afraid I'd come and take you away from her. That's why she moved away and didn't leave word where I could find you."

"That's not true," Hallie insisted, but she had a sudden memory of leaving Grandma's house in the middle of the night, the same night she had heard her grandmother mention Green Willow Creek to Mrs. Byard.

"Grandma liked you," Hallie said, unable to believe her grandmother had purposefully kept her from her father. "She said you couldn't help being a wanderer, that some men were just born to roam."

McIntyre shook his head. "She knew the truth about me, Hallie. I guess she just didn't want you to know that your father was an outlaw."

"An outlaw? It's true, then?"

McIntyre blew out a deep sigh. "Hallie, I . . . I was something of a hellion when I was younger. I got mixed up with a bad bunch and we pulled a couple of bank robberies. I never should have married your mother, but I loved her. I thought I could put my old life behind me and it would go away. I got a job. It wasn't much, but it put food on the table. One night I stopped at the saloon on my way home and someone recognized me. I didn't have time to tell your mother. I lit out of town and holed up in one of our old hideouts. By the time I made it back to town, your mother was dead, and you were gone."

"I don't believe you."

"Well, I guess I can't blame you, but everything I've told you is God's own truth. Tell me, Hallie, this man you're with, how long have you known him?"

"It's none of your business."

"I'm your father."

"Are you?"

"Dammit, Hallie . . ." McIntyre took a deep breath. "I'm sorry."

She shook her head, her hands tightly clenched. "Mama told me you would come back to us. Every night, she said, he'll come back tomorrow, Hallie, you'll see." Tears welled in her eyes and she brushed them away with an angry hand. "She said you'd come back, but you never did. She loved you so much, she didn't want to live without you. She died crying your name."

McIntyre took a step toward Hallie, but she backed away. "Hallie, I'm sorry. More sorry than I can say. I know it's asking a lot, but do you think you can forgive me?"

For if ye forgive men their trespasses, your heavenly Father will also forgive you.

"I don't know." She sniffed back her tears, not wanting him to see her cry, to know how badly he had hurt her by leaving.

McIntyre held out a placating hand. "Will you try?"

She blinked back the tears she couldn't keep from falling, nodded quickly, and ran out of the office.

Blinded by her tears, she ran headlong into Clay.

"Whoa, there," he said, reaching out to steady her. "Are you all right?"

"Fine," she said, and twisting out of his grasp, she ran down the boardwalk toward the hotel.

Clay glanced at the sheriff's office. Standing outside the open door, he'd heard every word. He paused, wanting to kill the bastard who'd deserted her, then turned and followed Hallie down the street.

When he reached the hotel, she was lying facedown on her bed, crying as though her heart would break. For a moment, he stood in the doorway and then, with a sigh, he crossed the room and gathered her into his arms.

He held her for a long while. He didn't say anything, just rubbed her back and stroked her hair, until her tears subsided.

"You know, Hallie, he might be telling the truth."

She sniffed, then shook her head. "He could have found me if he'd wanted to."

"What if he had? What kind of life could he have given you? You were a child, and he was on the run."

She didn't want to hear that. He knew it in the tensing of her shoulders.

"Think about it, Hallie. Sometimes we don't have a choice."

Clay looked out the window, his thoughts turning to Anna. Did she hate him for leaving her? How would he ever make her understand?

"Hallie?"

"I don't want to talk about it."

He nodded, then stood. "I'm going out for a while. I'll be back in an hour or so and we'll go to dinner. I'll have the clerk send up some hot water later."

"All right."

Leaving the hotel, Clay made his way to the saloon. Needing some time alone, he bought a bottle and took it to a back table. Sitting there, he thought about Hallie and how hurt and bitter she was, and then he thought about Anna. He tried to imagine what she was like now. She was almost seven years old; no doubt she had changed a lot in the last two years. Had she forgotten him? The thought ate at his soul like acid. What if he went back for her and she didn't know him, or worse, didn't want to know him? He thought about Summer Rain, remembering how she had died in his arms, her body bruised and bloody from what those animals had done to her, and he knew there was nothing else he could have done. He would never have been able to live with himself if he had let those men live.

"Mind if I join you?"

Clay looked up to find Frank McIntyre standing next to the table. "Suit yourself."

McIntyre sat down in the chair across from Clay. "I brought my own bottle." He poured himself a drink, tossed it back, and poured another. "Women," he muttered.

"Yeah."

"She hates me, doesn't she?"

"She thinks she does."

McIntyre stared at the contents of his glass. "I really did try to find her, you know. Old lady Hastings knew who I was, what I was. She hated me. Even if I'd known where to find Hallie, I doubt if the old lady would have let me take her." He shook his head ruefully. "I wouldn't have known what to do with a kid. Hell, I wasn't much more than a kid myself."

"How'd you get to be a lawman?"

McIntyre sat back in his chair. "It hit me hard when I couldn't find Hallie. I started drinking more than I should have, and then one day I woke up in a gutter with no recollection of how I'd got there, and I thought, what if Hallie could see me now? I was ashamed of what I was and I decided it was time to get my life straightened out. I quit boozin' and got a job haulin' freight, kept my nose clean. When I got a stake, I hired someone to find Hallie, but he came up empty." He shook his head. "I knew I'd never find her. I was drifting, looking for someplace to settle down, when I came here. The old sheriff got himself killed during a bank robbery. Nobody else wanted the job, so . . ." He shrugged. "I said I'd give it a try. That was just over eight years ago."

"You like it, being a lawman?"

McIntyre shrugged. "It's a living." He took a sip of his drink. "So, are you fixin' to marry my daughter?"

Clay nearly choked on his drink. "No, sir. I was fixin' to put her on the first stage headed home."

"Where might that be?"

"She lives in the convent outside Bitter River."

"Convent! Good Lord, you mean she's a nun?"

"Not yet."

McIntyre frowned. "Wait a minute. If she was in a convent, how the hell did she get hooked up with you?"

"It's a long story."

"I've got time."

"It's also a private story."

"You got something to hide, boy?"

Clay shook his head. "Just not much of a storyteller. I was doing some work at the convent. Hallie thinks she's in love with me. When I left, she followed me."

Clay made a dismissive gesture with his hand. "That's all there is to it." He sloshed the whiskey in his glass, took a drink, and stood up. "But now she's found you, and since you're her father, I guess that makes her your responsibility."

"Now, wait just a damn minute . . ."

Clay drained his glass and put it on the table. "Nice talking to ya, Sheriff."

Grabbing his hat, Clay left the lawman sputtering at the table.

Chapter 14

Clay headed back toward the hotel. Pausing out front, he glanced up at the window that was Hallie's, shook his head, and passed on by. He wasn't ready to face her, not yet. If it wasn't for the fact that Sayers might come back to town, he might have left Green Willow Creek right then and there and let McIntyre worry about Hallie. She was the lawman's daughter, he could darn well look after her.

Hallie. How had she planted herself so deeply under his skin in such a short time? When Summer Rain died, he had been sure he would never fall in love again. He refused to admit he might be falling in love with Hallie. She was a nice girl, and she was going to be a nun. She didn't need to get tangled up with a man on the dodge, nor did he think she would be too thrilled at the prospect of living with the Lakota. And that was where he was headed, just as soon as he finished his business with Bob Sayers.

Muttering an oath, he turned back toward town. He ducked into the first saloon he came to, scanned the room, and grabbed hold of the first soiled dove he saw.

"Come on," he said.

"What's your hurry, cowboy?" the girl asked in a throaty purr.

"Don't ask questions," Clay retorted. "I'll pay you double to keep your mouth shut."

"Okay, honey, whatever you want."

Clay paused at the top of the stairs. "Which way?"

She pointed down the hall. "That way. Second door on your left." She grinned up at him as he dragged her down the dimly lit corridor. "You are in a hurry, aren't ya? You gonna take time to open the door, or just kick it in?"

Clay took a deep breath. "Sorry." He let go of her arm, opened the door, and followed her inside. It was a small, ugly room. The walls were a dingy gray. A picture of a lady in a fancy ball gown and long white gloves, obviously ripped from some ladies' magazine, was tacked to one wall. A brass bed covered with a dingy yellow spread took up most of the room. The air smelled of strong perfume, stale sweat, and old lust.

"Make yourself to home," the dove said. She took off her slippers, put one foot on the bed, and began to peel off her stocking.

Clay kicked the door shut, his ardor and his anger cooling as he watched her. She was a lot younger than he had first thought, probably not more than a year or two older than Hallie.

Clay swore under his breath.

The girl glanced over her shoulder, then began to remove her other stocking in a slow, practiced move that was meant to entice him.

"That's enough," Clay said.

She smiled at him. "Sure, cowboy. You want to do it yourself?"

"No."

Her smiled wavered. "What do you want, then?"

"I've changed my mind."

She walked toward him, hips swaying, her eyes grown hard at the thought of losing a customer. She batted her eyelashes at him, then slid her arms up around his neck. "Let me change it back again."

Clay shook his head. "Not tonight." He reached into his pocket and withdrew a couple of greenbacks, which he stuffed into the cleavage between her ample breasts. "Maybe some other time."

"Whatever you say, cowboy." She kissed her fingertips, then pressed them over his mouth. "If you change your mind, come see me again."

"I'll do that," he replied with a wry grin. Leaving the room, he closed the door quietly behind him.

Outside, he took a deep breath, settled his hat on his head, and strolled down the boardwalk. He had promised to take Hallie to dinner, and that was just what he was going to do.

Hallie stood at the window, staring down at the street. Never, in all her life, had she felt so confused. After all these years, she had found her father. Why couldn't she just put the past behind her and start fresh? She wanted to, she really did, but she kept thinking about her mother waiting year after year for the man she loved to come back to her, and all the while he had been out robbing banks.

She rested her head against the window and closed her eyes. "Oh, Mama, what should I do?"

A rap at the door interrupted her musings. Crossing the room, she unlocked the door.

"You asked for hot water, miss?"

"What? Oh, yes, come in."

She stood aside while the boys filled the tub, then closed and locked the door. A nice hot bath was just what she needed to relax her.

Back in his room, Clay tossed his hat on the dresser and ran a hand through his hair. Tomorrow, he'd go see about buying a change of clothes.

He went to the door that connected his room to Hallie's and knocked softly. "Hallie, you in there?"

He frowned when she didn't answer, then called her name again, wondering if she'd gone out alone to see her father.

Still no answer. Curious, he turned the knob. He had expected the door to be locked, but it opened on well-oiled hinges. At first, he thought the room was empty, but then he saw her clothes, neatly folded, on the foot of the bed.

"Hallie?"

He crossed the room, his heart pounding loudly in his ears as he peered around the screen.

She was asleep in the tub. The water, cloudy with soap, covered her up to her chin. Tendrils of hair curled at her nape. He had a sudden urge to undress and slip into the tub behind her, to slide his arms around her waist and cradle her body against his, to . . .

Damn! She looked beguiling enough to tempt a Saint, let alone a sinner like himself. Turning away, he went back to his room, then rapped his knuckles on the door.

"Hallie?" he called loudly. "Are you in there?"

He heard a splash, and an image of Hallie bolting upright in the tub, soapy water sluicing down her shoulders and over her breasts, flashed through his mind.

"I'm taking a bath," she called, a note of panic in her voice. "Don't come in!"

"Let me know when you're done, will you?" Clay asked. "I'd like to wash up."

"Yes, yes, I will. Go away."

Hallie stared at the screen, imagining Clay standing on the other side. A sudden heat that had nothing to do with the temperature of the water suffused her. Grabbing the towel, she stepped out of the bathtub and quickly dried off. And all the while she thought about

Clay, waiting in the next room. Clay, washing with the same water she had used.

She dressed quickly, her gaze darting toward the connecting door time and again. Taking a deep breath, she crossed the floor and knocked on the portal.

It opened so quickly, she wondered if he had been standing there, just waiting for her.

She flushed as his gaze moved over her. "I'll wait in here while you wash up, if that's all right?"

With a nod, Clay stepped back so she could enter his room. "I won't be long."

Hallie nodded, wondering what Reverend Mother would think if she knew Hallie was in a man's room.

Clay closed the door behind him, and Hallie blew out a sigh of relief. She glanced around the room. His hat was on the chair, his boots were beside the bed.

She glanced over her shoulder, imagining Clay in her room. Undressing. In an effort to keep her mind from wandering down paths it had no right to follow, she focused her thoughts on her father. Maybe Clay was right. Maybe she was being unfair. What kind of life would she have had if her father had taken her away from her grandmother? They couldn't have settled down in one place, not when her father was on the run. She wouldn't have had any friends, wouldn't have been able to go to school. She had liked living with her grandmother. Of course, she had grieved for her mother and missed her father, but Grandma Hastings had loved her dearly.

Grandma . . . Had her grandmother packed them up in the middle of the night because her father was coming for her, like he had said? Had Grandma Hastings purposefully kept Hallie away from her own father, thinking it was in Hallie's best interests? Had she hated her father all these years for nothing?

Hallie picked up Clay's hat, running her fingertips

over the wide brim as she went to the mirror and gazed at her reflection. Reverend Mother said vanity was a sin, and Hallie knew she had spent far too much time looking in mirrors since they arrived at the hotel, but it had been years since she had seen herself in anything other than a window or a pool of water. Clay had told her she was pretty. Was she?

Head tilted to one side, she tried to see what he saw, but all she saw was a skinny girl with long brown hair and big hazel eyes. With an exasperated sigh, she plopped his hat on her head, then stuck her tongue out at her reflection.

"Come on, it's not that bad."

She whirled around at the sound of Clay's voice. "How long have you been standing there?"

"Long enough." He pushed away from the door jamb and walked toward her.

Hallie stared at him, her cheeks flaming. "You should have knocked."

"I did. Twice."

Her heart began to beat faster as he closed the distance between them.

"What do you see when you look in the mirror, Hallie?"

"What do you mean?"

He ran his knuckles back and forth along the curve of her cheek. "Do you see soft skin and beautiful hazel eyes?"

"Beau . . . beautiful?" she stammered.

His fingers slid down her neck, along her shoulder, and up into her hair. "Beautiful."

His gaze drifted over her face to rest on her mouth. Hallie drew in a quick breath, her lips parting, her tongue sliding out to moisten lips gone suddenly dry. He was going to kiss her. She knew it. And even then he was bending down, his mouth slanting over hers. His arm slid around her waist to draw her up against him, until they were pressed close together. His hat tumbled to the floor as his hand delved into her hair.

He deepened the kiss and she wrapped her arms around his neck, holding on for dear life as the world seemed to shift beneath her feet, leaving her feeling shaky and unsteady and breathless. She was floating, falling, plummeting through layers of sensation. His right arm was locked around her waist, holding her tight. His free hand skimmed over her back, restless as the night wind.

He drew back a moment, his dark eyes searching hers, and then he kissed her again, kissed her as if she was his only hope of salvation.

She leaned into him, wanting to be closer. His breathing was ragged, she could feel his heart pounding beneath her hand. He backed her against the wall, his body pressed against hers. One hand cupped her breast and desire shot through her.

"Clay . . . please . . . I want . . ."

"What, Hallie," he asked, his voice gruff. "What do you want?"

"I don't know."

"I know." He whispered the words against her neck.

"We shouldn't . . ."

"Yes." He kissed her throat, her eyelids. "Yes, we should." He groaned softly. "I need you, Hallie."

Need. Was that what she was feeling? She writhed against him and heat exploded through her, engulfing her, burning away all thought of right and wrong. Her hands delved under his shirt, sliding over smooth hot skin, and she was suddenly desperate to feel his skin against her own.

"Clay, I've never felt like this before . . . I . . ."

A sudden knock at the door penetrated the haze of desire. She opened her eyes, mortified at the thought of someone coming in, finding her in Clay's room, in Clay's arms.

A crude oath escaped Clay's lips as he released her. Dragging a hand through his hair, he crossed the floor. "Who is it?"

"McIntyre. I'm looking for Hallie. She doesn't seem to be her room."

"I think she's asleep." Clay glanced over his shoulder. Hallie was frantically straightening her skirts, smoothing her hair. Her cheeks were flushed, her lips swollen from his kisses. He swore again. Her father would only have to take one look at her to know what had been going on.

Clay motioned for Hallie to go into her own room. "She said something about taking a nap earlier."

With a nod, Hallie hurried into her own room and closed the door behind her.

Clay took a deep breath. Damn, how'd he get caught up in all this? He waited another few moments, then opened the door. "Come on in."

"Thanks." McIntyre stepped into the room and glanced around.

Clay leaned back against the chest of drawers, his arms folded negligently. McIntyre might have been an outlaw once, but he was all lawman now. It was evident in the way his gaze swept the room, missing nothing.

"I was hoping, that is, do you think she'd go out to supper with me?"

Clay shrugged. "I don't know. You'd have to ask her." He went to the connecting door and rapped his knuckles on the wood. "Hallie, you awake?" He knocked again, harder this time. "Hallie?"

The door opened and Hallie stood there, her hair mussed. She yawned behind her hand. "What's wrong?"

Clay stifled a grin. "Nothing. Your old man wants to take you to supper."

"I can ask her myself," McIntyre muttered. He cleared his throat. "What do you say, Hallie? I thought it would give us a chance to get reacquainted."

Hallie glanced at her father, then back at Clay. "Will you come with us?"

Clay shook his head. "No, you two go on."

"Please?"

He was about to decline, but then he saw the look of quiet pleading in her eyes and knew he couldn't refuse. The knowledge irritated him. With a sigh of exasperation, he glanced over at McIntyre. "You mind if I tag along?"

McIntyre shrugged. "No, I guess not."

"How about if we meet you in the dining room in, oh, ten minutes?"

McIntyre's gaze darted from Clay to Hallie and back again, and then he nodded. "Ten minutes."

Hallie's breath whooshed out in a sigh of relief when Clay closed the door behind her father.

"Close call," Clay said, grinning.

"It's not funny," Hallie snapped.

"No," Clay said, suddenly somber. "It's not. There was nothing funny about what he felt for Hallie, or about what had almost happened between them. He cleared his throat. "Listen, maybe I should skip dinner. Your old man wants to spend some time alone with you. You know, like he said, so you could get to know each other."

"If he'd wanted to get to know me, he could have stuck around when I was growing up."

"Hallie, give the guy a chance."

She glared up at him. "It's easy for you to sympathize with him, isn't it?"

"What's that supposed to mean?" he asked, his voice suddenly ominous.

"Nothing."

"Go on, say it. You think I'm just as bad as he is, don't you?"

"I didn't say that."

"But you're thinking it." Clay ran a hand through his hair. "Dammit, Hallie, what should I have done? Just let those bastards go? They killed my parents. They raped my wife and left her to die and nobody gave a damn."

"Clay, I'm so sorry."

He grabbed his hat off the floor and jammed it on his head. "I'll meet you downstairs."

Clay and her father were sitting at a table in the far corner when Hallie entered the dining room twenty minutes later. One look at their faces, and she had a strong urge to go back to her room. Her father looked morose; Clay's expression was sullen.

She was about to turn away when her father saw her. A broad smile lit his face as he stood up and waved to her.

Hallie took a deep calming breath and walked toward her father.

"Good evening, Hallie." He held out a chair for her. "I'm glad you came."

"Thank you."

McIntyre handed her a menu. "They serve a really good steak here."

Hallie made a soft sound of acknowledgment as she took the menu and hid behind it.

A few minutes later, a waitress came to take their order. Clay and her father both ordered steak, rare, and all the trimmings. Hallie wanted a steak, too, but she ordered chicken and dumplings instead. She knew she was being childish, knew Grandma Hastings would have said she was cutting off her nose to spite her face, but she wouldn't have ordered steak even it meant going hungry.

McIntyre sat back in his chair. "So, Joe here tells me he was going to send you back to the convent. Is that what you want?"

Hallie threw a startled glance at Clay. "Is that true?"

Clay glowered at McIntyre, then nodded.

Hallie blinked back the hot tears that stung her eyes. She wouldn't cry. She wouldn't!

"I hope you'll stay," McIntyre said. "I've got a small house behind the jail. I was hoping you'd come and stay with me."

"You want me to live with you?"

McIntyre nodded. "I know I've given you plenty of reason to hate me, Hallie, but you're here now and I'd like us to be a family. I know you're a big girl now. Maybe you don't need a father anymore." He took a deep breath. "You're all I've got, Hallie. I don't want to lose you again."

"You really want me to stay with you?"

McIntyre nodded.

Her first inclination was to say no. He had left her when she needed him most. But that no longer seemed as important as it once had. He had explained his reasons for leaving, and he seemed genuinely sorry that he had done so. Who was she to judge him? And, unlike Clay, he wanted her.

"Will you think about it, Hallie?" McIntyre asked.

"No."

"No?"

"I don't have to think about it," she said. "You're the only family I have, too." She blinked back her tears. "Every girl needs a father."

"Hallie." He covered her hand with his and gave it a squeeze.

It was probably a good thing the waitress arrived with their dinner, Hallie mused, or she probably would have dissolved into a sea of tears . . . tears of hurt and anger because Clay had been planning to put her on a train and send her away; tears of happiness because she had found her father at last.

Clay fumed as he cut into his steak. *Every girl needs a father.* The words slammed into him. He kept his gaze fixed on his plate, not wanting to see the happiness on Hallie's face as she was reunited with her long-lost father.

"The house isn't much," McIntyre said. "The place needs a woman's touch, you know what I mean? I've got an account over to the mercantile. If you need anything for yourself, or for the house, just put it on my account. I'll tell old Joe Spiceland it's okay."

"I don't need anything."

"I've got some money saved, Hallie. It would please me if you would spend some of it on yourself."

"But . . ."

"It's your birthday next week, why don't you . . ."

"You remember my birthday?" Hallie exclaimed.

"Of course I remember. It was one of the happiest days of my life."

She was going to cry. She couldn't help it.

"You okay?" McIntyre asked.

Hallie nodded.

"You sure?" he asked dubiously. "You look ready to bawl."

"Oh, Papa," she exclaimed softly, and burst into tears.

It was too much for Clay. He muttered something about looking after his horse and fled the dining room, his dinner untouched.

Outside, he took a deep breath, then started walking. He reached the end of town and kept going. Hallie had made peace with her old man, and he was happy for her and for McIntyre, too.

His foot struck a rock and he cursed under his breath.

There would be no happy ending for him until Bob Sayers was dead.

Every girl needs a father. . . . Hallie's voice, echoing in his mind.

"Don't give up on me, Anna," he whispered. "I'm coming."

Chapter 15

He had expected to find that Hallie had moved out of the hotel when he returned. Instead, she was in his room, asleep in his bed, her rich chestnut-colored hair spread like melted chocolate over the pillow.

Clay frowned as he tossed his hat on the chair and closed the door behind him. What the devil was she doing in here?

Sitting on the edge of the bed, he stared down at her. Her lashes were long and thick, making dark crescents against her cheeks; her lips were soft and pink and slightly parted.

Resisting the urge to kiss her, he placed his hand on her shoulder and shook her gently. "Hallie. Hallie, wake up."

"Hmm?" Her eyelids fluttered open and she gazed up at him. And then she smiled. "Hi, Clay." Her voice was sleep-roughened and warm with welcome.

"What are you doing in here?"

"Waiting for you." She blinked at him. "Are you mad at me?"

Clay frowned. "Why would I be mad at you?"

"I don't know. You left the dining room so abruptly, I thought maybe I'd said something to make you angry."

"No. Did you and your old man get everything settled?"

"Yes. I'm going to move in with him tomorrow morning. You'll come visit me, won't you?"

His gaze slid away from hers. "Sure I will."

"You're just saying that, aren't you?"

"Hallie . . ."

"I love you, Clay."

He smoothed a lock of hair from her cheek. "Go back to sleep. I'll bed down in your room tonight."

"Clay . . ."

"Go to sleep, Hallie. We'll talk about it tomorrow."

"You promise."

"I promise."

"Won't you kiss me good night?"

He clenched his hands, wondering if she knew what a temptation she was, lying there in his bed, all warm and sleepy-eyed. But of course she didn't. She was too young, too innocent, to be aware of the heated thoughts racing wildly through his mind.

Bending, he brushed his lips across hers. "Good night."

"Good night."

He went into her room and closed the door behind him. For a moment he stood there, picturing Hallie all curled up in his bed, waiting. Waiting for him. He could have slid under the covers and made love to her all night long. He knew it as sure as he knew the sun would rise in the east.

Unbuckling his gun belt, he hung it from the bedpost at the head of the bed, then ran his hands through his hair, wondering when life had gotten so complicated.

He was sitting on the edge of the mattress, taking off his boots, when he heard a muffled cry from Hallie's room.

Grabbing his gun from the holster, he padded across the floor and pressed his ear to the door. He heard a man's voice, the words low and indistinguishable, the unmistakable sound of a slap, Hallie's startled cry.

Clay eased back the hammer of his Colt and shoved the door open.

He took in the scene in one sweeping glance.

Hallie was sitting up in bed, her back against the headboard, the covers clutched to her breasts, her face fish-belly white save for the vivid red handprint on her left cheek.

There were two men in the room. They both whirled around, guns drawn. A jolt of recognition went through Clay as he stared at the man on the right.

Bob Sayers didn't waste time talking. His first shot splintered the door jamb near Clay's head. Clay dropped to the floor and rolled to the left. Coming up on his knees, he fired twice. His first shot hit the second man square in the chest, his second shot struck Sayers in the shoulder.

Hallie screamed as the door to her room burst open.

Sayers fired another round, then dove through the bedroom window.

Clay sprang to his feet and ran to the window, but Sayers was already out of sight.

"What the hell's going on here?"

Clay whirled around, gun at the ready, and came face to face with the manager of the hotel, who stood in the doorway, a shotgun cradled in his arms.

"Take it easy, Mr. Clayton," the manager said. He glanced around the room, the color draining from his face when he saw the body sprawled on the floor. "What's going on here?"

Clay muttered an oath as he lowered his weapon. "Two men broke into Miss McIntyre's room. I heard a noise and came in to see what was wrong." Clay gestured at the body on the floor. "I got one of them. The second one went out the window."

The manager looked at Hallie. "Is that right?"

Hallie glanced at Clay, then nodded. "Y . . . yes."

The manager grunted softly. "You two stay here. I'm gonna send my boy after the sheriff."

Clay nodded. Shaking out the extra blanket folded across the foot of the bed, he spread it over the body, then sat down beside Hallie. "What happened?"

"I heard a noise at the window, and . . ." She was shaking now. "And those two . . . two men came in." She looked up at him, her gaze wide. "They were looking for you."

Clay placed his Colt on the bedside table, then pulled Hallie into his arms and held her tight. "Go on."

"They wanted to know where you were. I . . . I said I didn't know . . ." She burrowed deeper into his arms. "The big one slapped me . . . and then . . . then you came in." Her hands clutched his shirt. "Is he dead?"

"Yeah."

"Who were they?"

"I don't know who this one is. The one who got away is Bob Sayers."

Hallie stared up at Clay. "Bob Sayers! But . . . he's the one you're looking for, isn't he?"

"Yeah."

"He might have killed you."

"Don't think about it."

"My father . . ."

"Don't say anything about this to your father, Hallie."

"But, Clay . . ."

"I mean it, Hallie. Just stick to my story. They came to rob you. I heard a noise, and I came in. One of the men took a shot at me, and I killed him. The other one got away. You got that?"

Before she could argue further, her father came running into the room, his shirttail flapping, his hair disheveled. He carried a rifle in one hand. "Hallie! Good Lord, girl, are you all right?"

"I'm fine. Joe . . ."

Frank McIntyre let out a huge sigh. "Clayton, how can I ever thank you?"

Clay shrugged. "No need."

"I don't suppose you recognized either of the two men?"

Clay shook his head. "No."

McIntyre nodded. "Hallie, did you ever see either one of them before?"

"No." That, at least, was the truth.

McIntyre walked over to the body and lifted a corner of the spread. "Clyde Sayers," he muttered, and dropped the blanket back over the dead man's face.

"Sayers?" Clay asked.

McIntyre lifted one brow. "You were looking for Bob, weren't you?"

"Yeah."

"This here's his brother, Clyde."

"No shit? I didn't know he had a brother."

McIntyre nodded and then, in a swift, well-practiced move, he raised his rifle and leveled it at Clay. "Put those hands up, nice and easy."

"What the devil's going on?" Clay asked. He glanced at his Colt, weighing his chances of grabbing it and firing before McIntyre cranked off a shot.

McIntyre jacked a round into the breech. "Don't even think about it."

Slowly, Clay raised his hands over his head.

McIntyre shrugged. "I don't know who you are or just what's going on here, but until I find out, I want you where I can find you."

"I'm not going anywhere."

McIntyre smiled. "That's for damn sure." He jerked his head toward the door. "Let's go."

"Papa, what are you doing?"

"Stay out of this, Hallie."

"But . . ."

"Lock the door behind us, Hallie. I'll be back as soon as I can."

"But . . ." Her gaze darted from her father to Clay and back again.

"Don't argue with me," McIntyre said, his voice sharp. "I've been a lawman long enough to know when there's something not right, and this stinks to high heaven. Let's go, Clayton."

Every nerve taut, Clay walked out of the room. Doors were open up and down both sides of the corridor. Curious faces peered at him as he walked down the narrow hallway toward the staircase.

"Go on back to bed, all of you," McIntyre said. "There's nothing to see."

The hotel manager stood beside the desk, a troubled expression on his face. "Everything all right, Sheriff?"

"Nothing to worry about, Garth. I'll send Milton over to pick up the body. Keep an eye on my daughter, will ya?"

The manager nodded. "Sure, Frank."

"Let's go, Clayton."

Clay crossed the lobby and stepped out onto the boardwalk. The street was dark and quiet. He glanced left and right, wondering if Sayers had lit out of town, or if he was lurking somewhere in the shadows, waiting to take another shot at him.

The jail loomed ahead. He thought of making a break for it. A bullet in the back would be quicker, more merciful, than a rope. It wouldn't take long for McIntyre to find out who he was.

McIntyre prodded him in the back with the barrel of his rifle. "Don't even think about it, son."

Clay felt some of the tension ease out of him. There was no escape. The realization brought an odd kind of peace, of acceptance. Of resignation.

The Green Willow Creek jail was pretty much like

the one in Bitter River. The main room held a large, badly scarred desk, a big black potbellied stove, a gun rack. A handful of posters were tacked to a bulletin board on one wall.

The cells, one large and two smaller ones, were located upstairs. They were all empty.

"Take your pick," McIntyre said.

Clay opened the door to the largest one and after a moment's hesitation, stepped inside. The rasp of metal against metal as McIntyre locked the door echoed in Clay's head like the crack of doom.

Hands shoved into his pockets, he turned to face Hallie's father. "Now what?"

"I'm goin' downstairs and check the wanteds." McIntyre shook his head, his expression rueful. "I have a feeling you could save me a lot of time and trouble if you'd just tell me who you really are."

Clay snorted. "I'm the man who just saved your daughter's life, that's who I am."

"I think maybe *she* saved *your* life." Suspicion darkened the lawman's eyes. "What the hell was my daughter doing in your bed anyway?"

"I don't know." Clay took a step forward and wrapped his hands around the bars. "She was there when I got back to the hotel."

McIntyre grunted softly. "She seemed to think you'll be moving on soon."

Clay's hands tightened around the bars. Damn. He felt like he was sinking into quicksand and there was no way out.

"Why don't you make it easy on both of us and just tell me what's going on?" McIntyre sighed in exasperation. "Okay, Clayton, suit yourself. You need anything?"

"No."

"I'll see you in the morning, then."

Clay watched McIntyre until he was out of sight, then

he sank down on the cot, elbows resting on his knees, his head cradled in his hands. Damn! Damn, damn, damn. He hated being locked up more than he hated anything else in his life. Shit! He could already feel that rope tightening around his neck.

Frank McIntyre stared at the flyer in his hands. It was a rough ink drawing, poorly printed, but there was no mistaking that face. He grunted softly as he tossed the poster on top of his desk. If that didn't peel the hide off the hog, he didn't know what did.

Sitting back in his chair, he propped his feet on a corner of the desk. Joe Clayton was none other than John Walking Hawk, wanted for killing five men.

McIntyre frowned, wondering how his daughter, who was supposed to have been living in a convent, had gotten hooked up with a ruthless killer like Walking Hawk.

Rising, he settled his hat on his head. The man with the answers was upstairs and he, by damn, meant to get them.

Clay sat up when he heard footsteps on the stairs. Moments later, Frank McIntyre was standing in front of the cell.

"You want to tell me your side of the story?" McIntyre asked. "Or do you want me to tell you what I know."

Clay shrugged. "Go ahead on."

"John Walking Hawk. Wanted for killing five men in the last two years. Two in cold blood. Am I right?"

"If you say so."

"I've always been a pretty good judge of character. You don't strike me as a cold-blooded killer, so why don't you tell me your side of the story?"

"Six men killed my parents. They raped my wife. She died from what they did to her. Bob Sayers was one of them."

"Bob? I don't believe it."

"It's true."

"He's lived here off and on for, oh, a year, year and a half. Never caused any trouble."

"That right? Then what was he doing breaking into my room?"

"I don't know, but I for damn sure intend to find out."

"Well, I know. He was hoping to get me before I found him."

"If what you say is true, why isn't the law after him for what he's supposed to have done to your family?"

"I went to the law when it happened," Clay said bitterly. "They didn't give a damn."

"The law's not always fair, I'll be the first to admit that, but I can't believe they'd turn the other way if what you say is true."

"My wife and my mother were Lakota," Clay replied, his voice curt. "Does that explain it any better?"

McIntyre dragged his hand over his jaw, his expression thoughtful.

"What would you have done in my place?" Clay asked.

"I don't know. Probably the same thing you did."

Clay stood up. Crossing the floor, he wrapped his hands around the bars. "Then let me out of here."

"I haven't always been a law-abiding citizen," McIntyre said. "I admit that. But my word's always been good." He tapped his forefinger on the badge pinned to his vest. "I took an oath when I pinned this on, and I've done my best to live up to it."

"I took an oath, too," Clay replied flatly. "I swore I'd avenge my wife's death."

"What about Hallie? Where does she fit into all this?"

Clay took a deep breath. "She doesn't."

McIntyre nodded. It was all too easy to see that Clay

cared deeply for Hallie. And just as easy to see that he wasn't happy about it.

"Let me out of here," Clay said. His hands tightened around the bars, his knuckles going white with the strain.

"I'll think about it," McIntyre said. "I can't promise more than that."

"Dammit, he's getting away!"

"I'm sorry. Get some sleep. I reckon Hallie will be here, come morning."

Clay didn't answer. Turning away from the lawman, he went to the window and stared into the darkness. Bob Sayers was out there somewhere. He cursed under his breath. He hadn't been this close to finding the man in two years, and now he was gone. What if it took another two years to find him?

What if McIntyre wouldn't turn him loose? Clay ran a finger around the inside of his collar. He could feel the noose settling around his neck, choking the life from his body, and he knew if he died, he'd always have two regrets: the years he had lost with Anna, and the fact that he had never made love to Hallie.

Chapter 16

Hallie woke bleary-eyed after a restless night. Every time she had closed her eyes, she had imagined Clay being led to the gallows. And when she had finally fallen asleep, she had the same nightmare over and over again. In her dream, she saw her father walking Clay to the gallows. She ran after him, calling his name, but no matter how fast she ran, she couldn't get there in time to save him, couldn't stop the hangman from putting the noose around Clay's neck, or from dropping a black hood over his head. Helpless and horrified, she stood at the foot of the gallows, watching Clay's body fall through the trapdoor and jerk to a stop.

It was only a dream. She told herself that time and time again as she washed her hands and face, brushed her hair, put on the green dress Clay had bought her. Clay . . .

Even though she was in a hurry, she took the time to kneel beside her bed and say her morning prayers, silently adding a petition for Clay's welfare.

It was early when she left the hotel. Most of the shops were still closed, though one early riser was already in front of his establishment, sweeping. He nodded at Hallie as she hurried by.

Outside the jail, she took a deep breath, then opened the door and stepped inside. Her father was sitting behind his desk, a newspaper in one hand, a cup of coffee in the other.

Crossing the floor, Hallie planted her hands on the scarred surface of the desktop. "I can't believe you arrested him."

McIntyre lifted one brow. "Good morning to you, too."

Hallie made an impatient gesture with her hand. "Don't good morning me. How could you lock him up?"

McIntyre tossed the newspaper on the desk, drained the last of the coffee from his cup before he said, "Hallie, he's killed five men. He admitted it to me last night. What did you want me to do? Just let him go?"

"Yes!"

"I can't do that."

She shook her head in exasperation. "I don't understand you. You're no better than he is."

McIntyre rose slowly to his feet. "What's that supposed to mean?"

"You were an outlaw yourself."

"That was a long time ago, Hallie, and I never killed anybody. I've turned my life around since then. It wasn't easy, but I did it. This town's been good to me. And I've been good for this town."

"Did Clay tell you why he killed those men?"

"He told me. Did he tell you?"

"Yes."

McIntyre grunted softly. "Did he tell you he killed two of them in cold blood?"

Thou shalt not kill. Hallie blinked at her father, not wanting to believe him. And then she squared her shoulders. She wouldn't believe it until she heard it from Clay's own lips.

"Listen, Hallie, I haven't notified Bitter River that he's here yet, but I did send a wire to the convent to let them know you're safe."

Hallie nodded. She should have done that herself. "What are you going to do with him?"

"I'm not sure yet. Have you had breakfast?"

"No."

"Come on, let's go get something to eat. I need to get some grub for my prisoner here, too."

"All right."

Mcintyre took the keys to the cell block and put them in his pocket, then followed Hallie outside and locked the office door behind him.

From the window in his cell, Clay watched Hallie and her father cross the street. One good thing had come from this ill-fated trip, he mused as he watched the two of them walk through the door to the hotel dining room. Hallie had found her father.

Turning away from the window, he began to pace the floor. Four long strides carried him from one end of the cell to the other.

He wondered how Anna was doing, what Hallie and her father were talking about, if McIntyre had notified Mason Clark of his whereabouts, if they would hang him here, or send him back to Bitter River.

Damn! He'd seen a man hanged once. It was a bad way to go, kicking and twitching at the end of a rope, slowly strangling to death if the drop didn't break your neck.

He went to the cell door, wrapped his hands around the bars and gave it a good shake, wishing he had the strength of Samson so he could bend the steel, wishing he had enough faith to work a miracle.

Muttering an oath, he began to pace again, his anger and frustration growing with every passing minute.

He had to get out of here!

Hallie ate her breakfast in silence. Several times her father tried to engage her in conversation, but she refused to cooperate. How could he talk about such mundane things as the weather and the possibility of a train coming to Green Willow Creek when Clay was in jail?

Finally, he pushed his plate aside and sat back in his chair. She could feel him staring at her. With a huff, she looked up and met his gaze.

"Okay, spit it out before you choke on it."

"There's nothing to say."

"Hallie, you're acting like a spoiled child."

"I am not!"

He grinned indulgently.

"Clay's a good man. You can't let them hang him!"

"You think you're in love with him, don't you?"

"I am in love with him."

"How do you know?"

"What do you mean?"

"You've never known another man. How can you be so sure he's the right one? How can you believe anything he says? Hell, his name's not even Joe. It's John. John Walking Hawk."

"I know that. But he said I could call him Clay. And I do love him."

McIntyre sat back in his chair, pleased that he had her talking to him at last. "Does he feel the same about you?"

"I think so. He hasn't said anything, but . . ." Color flamed in her cheeks as she remembered the kisses they had shared, the wanting that had burned bright and hot between them.

McIntyre grunted softly. "There's a difference between love and lust, Hallie. Be sure you know what that difference is before you jump into anything."

"What do you mean?"

"A man's needs are different from a woman's. A woman wants marriage and a home and a family, usually in that order. A man doesn't always want the marrying part, or care about the rest. Sometimes he just wants a little . . ."

McIntyre cleared his throat. Somehow, this wasn't a conversation he had ever envisioned having with his daughter. The thought that she'd spent the last four years in a convent didn't make it any easier. "Sometimes a man just wants a little . . . uh, physical relief, and any woman will do."

Hallie stared at her father, not sure what he meant.

"Didn't your grandmother ever talk to you about . . . uh, about marriage and, uh, what it means?"

"No."

McIntyre sighed. "I don't guess they talked about it much in the convent, either."

Hallie shook her head.

"Well, all I'm saying is a man most generally won't buy something if he can get it for free. You understand what I'm saying?"

"No."

"It's like this, Hallie. Sometimes a man will whisper sweet words to a woman just so's she'll let him . . . uh, take liberties . . . that is . . . there are some things that should only be done between a husband and his wife, but sometimes a man doesn't want to get married, so . . ." McIntyre picked up his coffee and took a drink, thinking he would rather face the whole McClellan gang single-handed than finish this conversation.

"Oh," Hallie said, eyes widening in comprehension. "You mean like fornication and consorting with harlots."

McIntyre choked on his coffee.

Alarmed, Hallie jumped to her feet and pounded him on the back. "Are you all right?"

"Fine," he gasped. "Where'd you hear words like that?"

"Bible study. Rahab was a harlot."

"I think we'd better finish this discussion later," McIntyre said. Picking up his napkin, he wiped his mouth, then signaled for the waitress. "Is that order to take out ready?"

"Yes, sir. I'll bring it right away."

"Thanks." Rising, he tossed a dollar on the table, certain that fatherhood was going to be a lot tougher than he had ever imagined.

At the sound of footsteps on the stairs, Clay stopped pacing. Even before he saw her round the corner, he knew it was Hallie.

She smiled when she saw him. "I brought you something to eat."

"Thanks, but I'm not hungry."

"Don't be silly. You've got to eat."

"Do I?"

"Clay!" She put the tray on the floor and slid it under the bars.

He had a vivid recollection of all the times at the convent when Hallie had snuck food to him in the barn as he picked up the tray. He lifted the cover, revealing a plate of ham and eggs and fried potatoes and a small pot of coffee. In spite of his words to the contrary, his stomach rumbled loudly.

"Go on, eat it while it's hot." She sat down on the floor, her skirts spread around her.

Clay sat down on the edge of the cot, acutely conscious of Hallie's gaze, of the thick iron bars between them. Feeling like a wild animal in a cage, he tried to ignore her presence while he ate. The food filled his belly, but he might as well have been eating ashes for all the pleasure it gave him. Every time he swallowed, he could feel the noose tightening around his neck.

When he finished eating, he put the tray on the floor, then sat with his back against the wall, his hands folded on one bent knee. His gaze moved over Hallie and he thought how pretty she looked. She was wearing the dress he had bought her. The color brought out the green in her eyes. Her hair fell over her shoulders in a mass of soft chestnut waves.

Her cheeks grew warm under his regard. "What are you staring at?"

"Just thinking how pretty you are."

"Thank you."

"Have you moved out of the hotel?"

"Not yet. I'm going to do that when I leave here."

"Your father's a good man, Hallie," Clay said gruffly. "Don't let what happened in the past ruin the present."

Hallie nodded. It was good advice. She only wished Clay would take it himself.

Clay blew out a sigh. "Has your father said what he plans to do with me?"

"No."

"Has he notified the law in Bitter River?"

"Not yet."

"What's he waiting for?"

"I don't know. I tried to get him to let you go, but he wouldn't."

Clay grunted. It had been a slim hope at best. In his travels, he had run across a lot of men who had ridden the outlaw trail at one time or another and then pinned on a badge. They tended to be a hard, unforgiving lot. Like drunks who had given up drinking, or preachers who had lost their faith, they bitterly renounced what they had once embraced.

"Hallie, you up there?"

"Yes, Papa."

"Come on down here."

Hallie stood up and moved closer to the bars. "I'll take that tray."

Rising, Clay picked up the tray and slid it under the bars. "Thanks, Hallie."

She gazed into his eyes and then, slowly, she reached through the bars and took his hand in hers. Slowly, she lifted his hand and rubbed her cheek against his palm.

"Hallie . . ."

"I love you, Clay," she said quietly. "I know everything will work out. I just know it." She reached into the pocket of her skirt with her free hand and withdrew her crucifix. "Here. Take this."

Clay frowned as he accepted the cross. "But . . ."

"I want you to have it."

With a nod, he slipped the cross into his pocket.

Hallie leaned closer to the bars. "Kiss me."

He hesitated only a moment, then he reached through the bars, his arms wrapping around her waist, his mouth descending on hers.

Clay closed his eyes. The touch of her, the warm sweetness of her kiss, drove everything else from his mind. His arms tightened around her waist, drawing her closer. Her hands moved restlessly over his back, her lips parted as he deepened the kiss.

She made a soft sound of pleasure and he answered it with one of his own. She was summer and sunlight, cool water on a hot day, hope in the midst of despair, and he clung to her in silent desperation, wishing he had met her sooner, under more favorable circumstances, wishing for a future that could never be.

Frank McIntyre rounded the corner of the landing, only to come to an abrupt halt when he saw Hallie locked in Clay's embrace. For a moment, he stood there, remembering the past, remembering what it had been like to be young and in love, when he couldn't keep his hands off Hallie's mother, when nothing mattered more than being with her. When what was right and what was wrong blurred in the face of the fierce desire that had burned between them.

After a moment, he cleared his throat, stifling the urge to laugh as they jumped apart. Hallie glanced at him and looked away, her cheeks flushed, her eyes bright. Clay glared at him.

"Sorry," McIntyre said, "didn't mean to intrude."

Hallie bent down to pick up the tray, certain she had never been more embarrassed in her life.

"Hallie, I've got a town meeting later this evening, so I thought we'd go over to the hotel and get your belongings," McIntyre said, "then stop by the mercantile so you can pick up anything else you might need."

"All right," Hallie agreed, still not meeting his eyes.

McIntyre regarded Clay a moment. "Can I bring you anything?"

Clay shook his head. "No." He didn't want to be in debt to McIntyre, didn't want to accept any favors he couldn't repay.

"You sure?" McIntyre asked. "It's no trouble."

"I'm sure."

"Well, suit yourself. Hallie, you about ready to go?"

She nodded. " 'Bye, Clay."

"So long."

She sent him a last, lingering look, then turned and followed her father down the stairs.

Chapter 17

Clay watched Hallie walk out of sight, then began to pace the floor again, his nerves strung tighter than a Lakota war drum. The cell seemed to close in on him, growing ever smaller with each step he took, each minute that passed.

He had to get out of here, and soon.

But how?

He went to the window and stared outside. There was a lot of activity on the street below: he could see several men clustered near the smithy, hear the faint sound of their laughter; women in cotton day dresses and bonnets moved up and down the boardwalk, going from shop to shop, pausing in the shade to speak to this friend or that. Children played on a side street across the way: a small boy throwing a stick for a spotted hound, another rolling a hoop, two girls who seemed to be arguing over a rag doll. Ordinary people doing ordinary things.

Damn! He had to get out of here, had to pick up Sayers's trail before it grew cold.

Frustrated beyond words, he flung himself down on the cot, one arm over his eyes. Surprisingly, he slept.

It was dark when he woke up. For a moment, he lay still, wondering what had awakened him, and then he heard voices downstairs: a man's voice, gruff with anger; Hallie's voice, shrill with alarm.

He rose quickly as he heard footsteps on the stairs,

and then he saw Hallie round the corner, followed by Bob Sayers.

"Clay! My father . . . I think he's dead. . . ."

"Shut up!" Sayers gave Hallie a shove from behind, and she stumbled forward, hitting her shoulder against the cell.

Clay reached out a hand to steady her. "Leave her alone, Sayers."

"You gonna make me?" Sayers asked, smirking.

Clay glared at the man. There was no point in making threats; he was helpless.

"You killed my brother," Sayers said. "You shouldn't have done that."

Hallie started to move, but Clay tightened his hold on her arm, silently warning her to keep still.

Sayers lifted his gun. "This is gonna be like shooting fish in a barrel," he mused. "Tell the girl to move aside."

"Do what he says, Hallie."

"No!"

"Do it."

Hallie glanced over her shoulder. "Can't I kiss him one last time?"

Sayers looked momentarily startled. "Kiss him! Don't tell me you're sweet on that dirty half-breed?"

"What if I am?" Hallie retorted. She glared at Sayers, fear for her own life dissolving in the certain knowledge that Sayers meant to gun Clay down in cold blood right before her eyes.

Sayers snorted disdainfully. "Go ahead, kiss him if it'll make you happy, and then I'll show you what it's like to kiss a real man."

Hallie turned to face Clay. She had come to the jail late at night in hopes of helping him escape. With that in mind, she had gone to the mercantile that afternoon and purchased a small derringer with some of the money her father had given her to spend on new clothes.

"Kiss me," she whispered urgently.

Clay bent down and Hallie wrapped her arms around his neck, kissing him hard, and then she trailed her lips over his cheek, ran her tongue inside his ear.

"There's a gun in my left pocket," she whispered, and then she kissed him again.

Slowly, Clay ran one hand down Hallie's back, then slid it around her waist and into her pocket.

"That's enough," Sayers growled impatiently. "Get away from him."

Hallie let go of Clay. Turning slowly to face Sayers, she began to wail, "Don't kill him, oh, please don't kill him."

"Shut up!"

"Please, I love him!" She lifted the hem of her skirt and dabbed at her eyes. "Please don't kill him, I can't live without him!"

Sobbing hysterically, she grabbed hold of Sayers's arm and pressed it to her breast, crying and pleading like a woman gone mad.

Sayers tried to shake her off. He turned to the side, as if to push her behind him, and in that split second, while his attention was diverted, Clay raised the derringer and fired.

The shot struck Sayers high in the back. With a grunt, he lurched forward, regained his balance, turned, and fired.

The sound of the second gunshot blended into the first so that they echoed off the walls in one long rolling report.

Clay reeled backward as Sayers's bullet caught him in the left shoulder, grunted with satisfaction as a crimson stain blossomed across the front of Sayers's shirt.

Hallie screamed as Sayers lifted his gun, then let his arm fall. He pushed her out of the way, then turned and staggered toward the stairs.

When she was certain he was gone, she ran toward Clay. "You're hurt!"

"I'm all right, Hallie. Get me out of here! He's getting away."

"Are you sure you're all right?" She stared at the blood soaking into his shirtsleeve. "Oh, Clay, my father . . ." Turning on her heel, she ran down the stairs.

"Hallie! Dammit, Hallie, get me out of here!"

But he was wasting his breath. She was already gone.

Hallie knelt beside her father. His face was ashen. Sayers had struck her father over the head with the butt of his gun. Blood oozed from the side of her father's head and dripped onto the floor.

"Papa? Papa! Oh, God, please don't let him die. Please. Hail Mary, full of grace . . ." She murmured the words as she took off her shawl and draped it over her father. He couldn't be dead. Not now, not when she'd just found him. She placed her hand over his chest, reassured when she felt the fluttery beat of his heart.

Rising to her feet, she left the office, closing the door behind her. She had to find the doctor.

It was darker than pitch outside. Even the saloons were closed. Lifting her skirts, she hurried down the street toward the doctor's house, which was located at the end of town, identified by a whitewashed sign that read A. SMITSON, M.D.

Opening the gate, she ran up the tree-lined path and pounded on the front door.

"I'm coming, I'm coming. Don't break the door down. Yes? What can I do for you?"

"Are you the doctor?"

"Yes."

"My father . . . he's the sheriff, he's bad hurt."

"Good Lord!" The doctor, a tall, thin man with wiry gray hair and blue eyes, grabbed his bag from the chair beside the door. "Let's go."

Back at the jail, Hallie stood behind the doctor, her rosary clasped to her breasts, while Smitson examined her father.

"Is he going to be all right?" she asked anxiously.

"Yes, yes, I'm sure he will be. Head wounds always bleed a great deal." He wound a length of gauze around her father's head. "I'll have to get him back to my office. That wound needs stitching, and I'll want some help carrying him when I get done here."

"I'll get someone," Hallie said. Going to her father's desk, she grabbed the keys from the drawer and ran up the stairs.

"Hallie, dammit, what's . . ."

"There's no time for questions now, Clay. I need your help." She thrust the key in the lock.

As soon as the door swung open, Clay bolted down the stairs and raced out the front door. He glanced up and down the street, but other than a few drops of blood, there was no sign of Bob Sayers. Muttering an oath, he turned back to the sheriff's office. Hallie was on the boardwalk, pacing back and forth. There were bloodstains on her dress.

"Hallie, how's your old man?"

"The doctor's with him now. I . . ." Hallie's voice trailed off. "Oh, Clay, your arm. . . ."

"I'm all right. He just nicked me. Come on, let's go check on your father."

The doctor stood up as Clay and Hallie entered the room. "What happened to you?" he asked, gesturing at Clay's arm.

"I'm okay." Clay looked down at Hallie's father. Mc-

Intyre was unconscious. The bandage swathed around his head was slowly turning red. "How's the sheriff?"

"I need to get him over to my office. That wound in his head has to be stitched."

"I'll help you carry him."

"Looks like you might need a few stitches yourself," the doctor remarked. "You take his feet. Ready? Careful now. Hallie, will you bring my bag?"

A half hour later, McIntyre was resting comfortably in the back room in the doctor's office and Clay's injury had been washed and bandaged. As he'd said, it wasn't bad. Sayers's bullet had gouged a long shallow furrow in the hard muscle of his arm.

Hallie stood beside her father's bedside, his hand clasped in hers. "How are you feeling, Papa?"

McIntyre grimaced as he lifted a hand to his head. "I've felt some better, I can tell you that." He glanced at Clay. "Where's Sayers? And what the hell are you doing out of jail?"

"He got away," Clay replied flatly.

McIntyre grunted softly. "You two want to tell me what happened?"

Clay glanced at Hallie. "Go ahead."

As quickly as possible, Hallie told her father what had happened, how she had bought a little over-and-under derringer for self-protection after the scare in the hotel room, how she had arrived at the jail only moments after Sayers had knocked her father unconscious. She related how Sayers had taken her upstairs, how she had passed the derringer to Clay, and the shooting that had resulted.

McIntyre cussed softly. He glared at Clay. "You're still under arrest, you know."

Clay shrugged. "I'm not gonna go back and lock myself up, if that's what you're thinking."

"I think I should have insisted the town let me hire

another deputy," McIntyre mused. "I'm afraid this isn't over."

"Damn right. It won't be over until Bob Sayers is dead."

McIntyre shook his head. "Sayers has got another brother, you know."

"No, I didn't."

"Yeah. His name's Will. He's the youngest of the three. Even if Bob lives, Will might not be too happy about you shooting up his kinfolk. I've always considered the Sayers boys to be a decent sort, but if what you say about Bob is true, you had best watch your back."

"Don't worry."

McIntyre looked up at Hallie. "How long am I gonna be laid up here?"

"The doctor said you should stay off your feet for three or four days."

"Three or four days! I can't lollygag around here that long."

"You'll do what the doctor tells you," Hallie retorted.

"Women," McIntyre muttered. He studied Clay a moment. "I guess you'll be leaving town now?"

"Yeah."

"Leaving?" Hallie exclaimed. "Why? Where are you going?"

McIntyre sighed wearily. "And you know I'll be coming after you."

"I'd rather you didn't."

Hallie stamped her foot, angry that both men were ignoring her.

"It's my job," McIntyre said. "If those men are guilty of killing your wife, I'll help you prove it."

"It's a little late for that now."

"It's never too late. Hallie believes in you, and so do I, but you have to answer for the men you've killed. I'm sure that, once all the circumstances are known, a judge will be lenient. You might have to serve a year, maybe two."

Clay thought of Anna, of the years he'd already lost. "I can't spare another year or two," he said, his voice bitter.

"You'll be caught sooner or later. Running now will only make it worse. Did you really kill two of the men responsible in cold blood?"

"No. I gave them all a chance."

"Clay, please listen to my father."

"Hallie, I can't stay." He shook his head. "I can't. I've left her for too long already."

"Her?" McIntyre's gaze flew to Clay's face. "Don't tell me you're married!"

"No. I have a little girl. It's time I got back to her. I've been away too long as it is."

"Clay . . ."

"I'm sorry, Hallie, I've got to go."

He shook McIntyre's hand, gave Hallie a quick kiss, and left the room.

Hallie bent down and kissed her father on the cheek. "I'm going to go tell Clay good-bye."

"Hallie, wait . . ."

"I can't. He needs me."

"He's no good for you."

"I don't care. I love him."

There was no one on the street at this hour of the night. Hallie stood in the shadows, watching as Clay crossed the street and headed for the hotel. She followed him a few moments later; then, her heart hammering with anticipation and trepidation, she made her way up the stairs.

His door was locked. Taking a deep breath, she knocked softly, wondering if he would answer.

"Who's there?"

"Me."

"Hallie?"

She had expected him to be surprised to see her, but now, seeing the look on his face, she had the feeling he had been expecting her.

"Come on in." He took a step back so she could cross the threshold, then closed and locked the door behind her.

Hallie glanced at the bed, then turned to face Clay. "I came to say good-bye."

"I sort of thought you would."

"Clay, please don't go."

"Hallie . . ."

"Please. I love you. I know you don't love me, but . . ."

"Shh." He placed his finger over her lips. "I do love you, Hallie. I wish to God I didn't."

"Oh, Clay . . ."

Somehow, she was in his arms, her tears falling like warm rain on his cheeks. Her body pressed against his and he heard a roaring, like thunder, in his ears. Just one kiss, he thought, surely he deserved one kiss of farewell. Her lips were sweet, so sweet, and he drank greedily, quenching a deep, deep thirst. Her goodness seeped into him, filling all the sad, empty places in his heart, lighting the dark lonely corners of his soul.

He clung to her, a drowning man seeking rescue, a sinner begging for salvation. He had been alone for so long, alone and lonely. For the last two years, he had thought of nothing but vengeance. Wasted years, he thought with bitter regret. Years he might have spent with his daughter. What had he accomplished since he left her? He had killed five men, but it hadn't eased the grief in his heart, or brought Summer Rain back to him. He'd missed two years of his daughter's life, Summer was still dead, and he was a wanted man with a price on his head.

"Hallie . . ."

He didn't deserve her, had nothing to offer her. He tried to tell her so, but she covered his mouth with hers, and the heat of her kiss drove all rational thought from his mind.

Her hands delved under his shirt, sliding up and down his back, drawing him closer.

"I love the way you feel." She unbuttoned his shirt and pressed her lips to his chest. "You're so strong." She pushed his shirt off his shoulders, trailed her fingertips down his arms, marveling at the rock-hard muscles that bunched and quivered beneath her hands. "So strong."

"Hallie, we shouldn't . . ."

"I know." She smiled up at him. It was wrong of her to touch him this way, but he was leaving and she might never see him again. Right or wrong, she wanted this memory to warm her on cold winter nights.

She took a step away from him and with hands that trembled began to unfasten the buttons on her dress.

Clay stood motionless, his mouth dry, as the dress pooled around her feet. "Wait," he said as she began to remove her petticoats, "let me."

His own hands trembled as he unfastened the ties to her petticoats. She placed a hand on his shoulder to step out of them and he tossed them aside, then very slowly, he removed the rest of her undergarments until she stood naked before him, her cheeks flushed, her eyes wide.

"Hallie, you're beautiful."

"Am I?" He had told her so before, but she never tired of hearing it.

He nodded. "The most beautiful thing I've ever seen."

"My turn." Her voice was barely audible as she unfastened his belt buckle.

"You don't have to do this."

"I want to."

He pulled off his boots, then stood there, his heart pounding like a runaway train, as she removed his belt, his trousers. He didn't wear anything underneath.

Hallie gasped, her gaze flying to his when she saw the obvious evidence of his desire. "It's so big!" she exclaimed, then clapped her hand over her mouth, mortified by what she had said.

Clay couldn't help it. He grinned at her, charmed by her innocence.

Embarrassed beyond words, Hallie turned her back to him. He was laughing at her!

"Hallie." He moved up behind her and wrapped his arms around her waist. "Sweetheart."

"Don't laugh at me, Clay."

"I'm not laughing at you," he said quietly.

She stared at his hands, locked around her waist. Big, capable hands. "I saw you naked once before," she confessed. "When you were unconscious. You . . . it wasn't so big then."

Clay blew out a breath. Once started, there would be no going back. Lowering his head, he brushed a kiss across her bare shoulder. "Maybe this isn't such a good idea."

"No, I want to." She turned to face him, delighted by the touch of his body brushing against hers. "But I don't know what to do."

"I'll show you," he said, and swinging her into his arms, he carried her to bed.

Stretching out beside her, he began to kiss her, his hand moving slowly along her thigh, over the curve of her breast. Gently, as though he had all the time in the world, he aroused her, his hands and lips paying homage to her beauty.

"Clay, oh, Clay . . ." She looked up at him, her eyes luminous, her voice breathless.

"Should I stop?"

"No. It's just that . . . I don't know. I feel all fluttery inside, as if I'm going to fly apart. I've never felt this way before."

"It's perfectly natural, sweetheart." He grinned at her, then kissed her again. "One of the differences between men and women is that, when I'm feeling the way you are, it shows."

A shy smile played over her face. She could feel his arousal pressing against her belly. "Clay, I want . . ."

"What do you want, Hallie? Tell me."

"I don't know."

"I know," he murmured. He caressed her cheek with the back of his hand, his heart aching for the pain he was sure to cause her, not just the physical pain of claiming her innocence, but the heartbreak that would follow when he left her. And yet, even knowing it was wrong, knowing he should leave now, while her virtue was still intact, he couldn't go, couldn't deny himself the pleasure he knew he would find in her arms, just as he couldn't resist the love shining so brightly in her eyes.

"It's going to hurt," he warned. "I'll be as gentle as I can, but it's going to hurt."

She nodded, and he knew her trust and her love were the most precious gifts he'd ever been given.

He claimed her lips in a long searing kiss as he rose over her, swallowed her gasp of pain as he breached her maidenhead.

He remained still for a moment, giving her body time to accept his, letting her get used to the feel of him inside her.

Hallie clutched at his shoulders. He had warned her it would hurt, and it had, but the discomfort was passing quickly and she was becoming aware of Clay again, of the weight of his body, the silky texture of his hair brushing against her skin. He was raining kisses over her face, her neck, her shoulders. She could feel little tremors running through him and wondered if he, too, was in pain.

She shifted beneath him, heard him groan against her neck, and then he was moving inside her, his voice low and husky as he whispered, "Sweet, so sweet."

Hallie closed her eyes, her hands moving restlessly over Clay's shoulders and back as his body melded with hers. Sensations she had ever dreamed of swirled through her, making her think of fiery comets streaking across the heavens, skyrockets on the Fourth of July.

He moved deeper within her, harder and faster. She writhed beneath him, desperately reaching, reaching for . . . for what? She clutched at him, fingers digging into his shoulders, embarrassed by the moan that rose in her throat.

"Clay!" she gasped his name, her body poised on the brink of a great chasm, only she didn't fall. Instead, she felt as though she were flying, soaring through rainbows. She lifted her hips, wanting more, wanting it to last forever.

She wrapped her arms around his waist, holding on for dear life, as the world exploded, then rained down upon her like stardust.

He cried her name as his life spilled into her, the sound one of regret and exultation, and then he buried his face in the hollow of her shoulder, his body convulsing.

Gradually, the world stopped spinning and awareness returned. She felt Clay's hand lightly stroking her hair. His body was slick with perspiration. She was embarrassed to realize hers was, too.

"Did I hurt you?"

"No." If there had been any pain, she couldn't remember it now. She ran her fingers through his sweat-dampened hair. "It was wonderful. No"—she held him in place when he would have rolled away—"don't go."

"I must be heavy."

"Please."

He lifted up a little, resting his weight on his elbows. "Hallie . . ."

"Don't you dare say you're sorry."

"I'm not. I just hope you don't regret it."

"I won't. Not ever. I love you, Clay."

"I know."

"Can I ask you something?"

He nodded. How could he refuse her anything after what she'd just given him?

"Have you made love to very many women?"

"No." With a sigh, he rolled over onto his side, carrying her with him. "I've only made love to three women, Hallie, and the second one doesn't count. There was no love involved, and it was a long time ago. I don't even remember her name."

It had taken place shortly after he left Anna with her grandparents. Grief-stricken, alone, more lonely than he had ever been in his life, he had sought comfort in the arms of a widow woman who had been equally lost and lonely. It hadn't really helped either of them.

Clay kissed the tip of Hallie's nose. "Anything else you want to know?"

She shook her head. Suddenly weary, she closed her eyes and snuggled against him. It felt so good to be in his arms, so right.

"Promise me," she murmured, "promise me that you won't leave without saying good-bye."

"I promise."

She smiled up at him, her eyes glowing with the look of a woman who had been well and truly pleasured. "I love you," she said. And then her eyelids fluttered down and she was asleep.

Clay glanced out the window. It was almost dawn. He should be going, but after two years, surely another few minutes wouldn't hurt. He'd just hold Hallie for a half hour or so while she slept, and then he would be on his way. . . .

Chapter 18

"**A**re you planning to marry my daughter?"

Clay opened his eyes to find Frank McIntyre glaring down at him over the unwavering barrel of a Colt .45. Clay slid a glance at Hallie who was sleeping soundly beside him, her head pillowed on his shoulder, one arm curled intimately over his chest. Damn, why hadn't he left town when he had the chance!

"Well?" McIntyre prompted. "What have you got to say for yourself?"

Clay made a vague gesture with his hand. "You look a lot better this morning than you did last night."

"Yeah? Well, my head feels like it's been run over by a train." McIntyre's finger caressed the Colt's trigger. "Can you give me one good reason why I shouldn't plug you here and now and save the county the cost of a new hangin' rope?"

Clay shook his head. McIntyre had every right to be angry.

"You've got two choices," McIntyre said. He glanced at Hallie, who was still asleep, and lowered his voice. "You can marry my daughter, now, this morning, or you can marry her this afternoon, but you are damn well going to marry my daughter."

Of all the things Clay had expected to hear, this would have been last on the list. "So," he drawled, "you're gonna make her a wife, then a widow?"

McIntyre shrugged. "I intend to see that you make an honest woman out of her. If she turns up pregnant after you're dead, I don't want people calling my grandchild a bastard, or sayin' nasty things about my daughter behind her back."

"What about Hallie?" Clay demanded, then lowered his voice as she stirred beside him. "Doesn't she have a say in the matter?"

Hallie pressed a kiss to Clay's cheek. "What matter?" she asked sleepily. "What are you talking about?"

She yawned, thinking she would like to go back to sleep for a few more minutes, and then she saw her father standing at the foot of the bed, gun in hand, his face as dark as a thundercloud.

Suddenly wide awake, she grabbed the sheet and yanked it up to her chin as a rush of heat flooded her cheeks. "Papa! What are you doing here?"

McIntyre stared pointedly at Clay, then looked back at his daughter. "I might ask the same question of *you,* miss."

Speechless, Hallie stared up at her father, certain she wouldn't have been more horrified if she had awakened to find Reverend Mother Matilda standing at the foot of the bed, looming over her like an avenging angel.

"Get dressed, Hallie," McIntyre said, his voice curt. "Then go downstairs and wait for me."

"But . . ." She slid a glance at Clay.

"Just do it," her father said.

Wrapping the sheet around her, Hallie slid out of bed. Her gaze slid between Clay and her father as she collected her rumpled clothing, then hurried into her room and shut the door. Heart pounding, she blew out a deep breath, wondering how she would ever be able to face Clay, or her father, again.

Clay sat up, his back braced against the headboard,

his gaze focused on the gun in McIntyre's hand. The barrel looked enormous from this angle, long and black and deadly.

"Don't even think about it," McIntyre warned. "Shooting you right now would give me a great deal of pleasure."

Clay crossed his arms over his chest and tried to look unconcerned. "Yeah, I'll bet it would at that."

Several minutes of awkward silence passed between them. McIntyre glanced at the connecting door, then pulled his watch from his pocket and checked the time.

When twenty minutes had passed, he rapped sharply on the door. "Hallie, get in here."

A few minutes later, Hallie opened the door and stepped into the room. "Papa, I can explain . . ."

"I doubt it," McIntyre retorted, his voice sharp. "We'll talk downstairs, young lady."

Hallie sent a helpless look in Clay's direction, wondering how he could look so calm in the face of her father's rage. She tried to think of something to say that would lighten the tension, realized it was hopeless, and left the room, quietly closing the door behind her.

McIntyre plucked Clay's gun belt from the bedpost and slung it over his shoulder, then backed up until he was standing beside the door. "All right. Get up and get dressed."

Muttering an oath, Clay slid out of bed and pulled on his shirt and pants. Sitting on the edge of the mattress, he stamped his feet into his boots, then stood up and shoved his shirttail into his trousers.

"Now then, this is how it's gonna be," McIntyre said, biting off each word as if it tasted bad. "We're going downstairs and have breakfast, then we're gonna mosey over to the preacher and you're gonna marry my daughter."

"And then what?"

"And then I'm gonna lock you up again."

"Won't be much of a honeymoon," Clay mused.

"You've already had it!" McIntyre snapped. He took a deep breath, searching for a calm that couldn't be found. "I want your word you won't make a break for it."

"You must be kidding."

"Suit yourself." McIntyre pulled a set of handcuffs from his back pocket. "Put 'em on."

Clay stared at the cuffs, the memory of being shackled and beaten while imprisoned in the Bitter River jail flashing through his mind. "All right, I give you my word."

With a nod, McIntyre shoved the handcuffs back into his pocket. "Let's go."

They took a back table in the hotel dining room. Hallie refused to meet her father's eyes, refused to speak to either man. Everything the good sisters had taught her during the last four years rose up to haunt her. She had willfully committed a mortal sin. There was no excuse for what she had done, none at all. She had known making love to Clay was wrong, and she had done it anyway. Even when he would have stopped, she had begged him not to.

She slid a furtive glance in his direction. He was sipping a cup of black coffee. He hadn't touched his breakfast. Apparently he didn't have any more of an appetite than she did this morning. Well, she couldn't blame him for that. She had never been so embarrassed in her whole life.

Her father finished his breakfast, pushed away from the table, and stood up. "You two ready?"

Hallie looked up, meeting her father's eyes for the first time since she had left Clay's room. "Where are we going?"

"You're getting married."

Hallie blinked at him in astonishment. "Married!" she exclaimed in disbelief.

"That's right, young lady. Married."

"Now?" The question emerged as a squeak.

"Right now." McIntyre plucked his hat off the back of his chair and jammed it on his head, then picked up Clay's gun belt. "Let's go get it over with."

Hallie folded her napkin in a neat square, placed it on the table, and stood up. Married! She would have argued with her father, would have pointed out that she was a big girl now and that he'd long ago given up the right to tell her what to do, except that she wanted to marry Clay more than anything. But did he want to marry her?

She looked up at Clay, trying to gauge his reaction to her father's ultimatum from his expression, but his dark eyes were fathomless, his expression implacable.

"I don't want to get married in this dress. It's all wrinkled."

"All right," McIntyre agreed. "We'll stop by the house and you can change."

Feeling numb, Hallie walked out of the dining room. She was going to marry Clay. Now. Today. She glanced over her shoulder. Clay was walking behind her; her father brought up the rear, one hand resting lightly on the butt of his gun.

When they reached her father's house, Hallie went into her bedroom and closed the door, wishing, for the first time, that she had never left the convent.

Clay stood in the middle of the whitewashed parlor, his hands shoved into his pants pockets. Even without being told, he would have known Frank McIntyre lived alone. There were no feminine touches to be seen— no flowers, no knickknacks, no rugs on the floor, no pictures save for one small tintype of a little girl with long dark hair and huge eyes.

Clay crossed the floor to get a better look. It was Hallie, there was no doubt about that. She was wearing a pinafore, a big bow in her hair. She was smiling at the camera.

"She was three," McIntyre said.

Clay grunted softly.

"They're mighty cute at that age," McIntyre remarked. Careful not to take his gaze from Clay, he hung Clay's gun belt on the hall-tree beside the front door.

Clay nodded. "Yeah." He turned to face the lawman. "Listen, if it's all the same to you, I'd just as soon you hang me here as send me back to Bitter River."

"Why? You in a hurry to swing?"

"Lets just say there's no love lost between me and the Bitter River sheriff."

McIntyre grunted. "I've heard stories about Mason Clark."

"Yeah? Well, they're all true and worse, and I've got the scars to prove it."

Clay swung around as Hallie's bedroom door opened, felt his breath catch in his throat as he saw her standing there. Her dress was pale pink, with a high neck, long sleeves, and a full skirt. Her hair was pulled away from her face, tied at her nape with a matching pink ribbon.

"Do I look all right?" she asked shyly. She had felt guilty about going shopping while Clay was in jail, but she had needed something to wear; now, seeing the look in his eyes, she was glad she had.

Clay nodded. "You're beautiful, Hallie." So beautiful, it made his heart ache.

"You look fine," McIntyre said, his voice thick with emotion. "Real pretty. Just like your mamma."

"Thank you," Hallie said. "Both of you." But she was looking at Clay, basking in the warm admiration she saw in his eyes.

McIntyre cleared his throat. "Let's go."

The Reverend Ronald Caskey looked momentarily taken aback when the sheriff asked him if he could perform a wedding immediately. Summoning a smile, the minister invited them into the front parlor and urged them to make themselves at home while he called his wife and daughter to come and witness the ceremony.

No one sat down. McIntyre stood near the front door, one hand resting on the butt of his gun. Clay stood in the middle of the room, his hands shoved into his pockets. Hallie stood beside him, looking uncertain.

It was a spare room. The walls were white. There was a lumpy brown sofa, a straight-backed chair, a small square table that held a vase of dried flowers, and a Bible. A rag rug covered the floor in front of the hearth. A picture of a sad-faced Christ hung over the fireplace, a motto, picked out in needlepoint, hung above the sofa. It read, *As for me and my house, we will serve the Lord.*

A few minutes later, Reverend Caskey returned, followed by his wife and daughter.

The reverend's wife was short and plump, with a riot of red-gold curls and bright blue eyes. "This is wonderful," she said enthusiastically. "Such a happy occasion . . ." Her voice trailed off when she saw the sober expression on the sheriff's face.

Clay glanced at Hallie as she placed her hand on his arm.

"I love you." She mouthed the words, her beautiful hazel eyes shining.

All the anger Clay felt toward her father, his outrage

at being married at gunpoint, melted away as he gazed into Hallie's eyes.

He took her hand in this and gave it a squeeze, then looked up as the minister began to speak.

He was hardly aware of the words the preacher uttered. He heard Hallie's voice, soft yet firm with conviction as she promised to be his wife, to love him in sickness and in health.

His own voice sounded foreign to his ears as he vowed to love and cherish her, "so long as you both shall live." That wouldn't be hard, Clay mused bitterly, he didn't have much time left.

He felt her hand tighten around his and when he risked a glance at her, he felt his heart constrict when he saw the tears shining in her eyes.

And then the minister was pronouncing them man and wife. Mrs. Caskey and her daughter hugged Hallie and wished her well, the minister handed her the marriage certificate, Frank McIntyre slipped the preacher a couple of dollars for his time, and it was all over.

McIntyre bade the reverend and his family good day and ushered Clay and Hallie outside.

"Go on home, Hallie," McIntyre said. "I'll see you later."

"Home!" she exclaimed. "I'm not going home. I'm going with . . . my husband."

"He's going to jail."

"Well, if you're going to lock him up, then you can just lock me up, too."

"Now, see here, young lady . . ."

"No, you see here. Clay is my husband now, thanks to you, and my place is with him, wherever that might be."

"Now, listen to me, young lady. . . ."

Clay stifled the urge to grin. Almost, he could feel sorry for McIntyre.

Smiling sweetly, Hallie slipped her arm around Clay's waist. "Shall we go?"

Frank McIntyre muttered something decidedly crude under his breath, then jerked his head toward the jail, indicating they should walk in front of him.

Stores were just opening up for the day. McIntyre nodded to the shopkeepers they passed, a stiff smile pasted on his face.

When they reached his office, he ushered Hallie and Clay inside, then closed the door.

"Upstairs, Clayton."

"Papa, please . . ."

"I'm sorry, Hallie." McIntyre looked at Clay, swore under his breath as he got a good look at the half-breed's face. Taking a step backward, he drew his gun. "Don't make me use this."

"Hallie," Clay said gently. "Go outside."

"No." She took his hand in hers and held on tight. "I'm staying here, with you."

"Please, darlin', just for a minute. I need to talk to your father. Alone."

For a moment, he thought she would argue with him; then, in a snit, she flounced outside and slammed the door behind her.

"So, what is it you want to say?" McIntyre asked.

"Turn me loose," Clay said quietly.

"Are you out of your mind? I can't do that."

"Those men I killed deserved to die."

"That's not for me to say."

"But you know it's true."

McIntyre shrugged.

"Look at it this way. If you notify Clark, he's gonna come after me, and you know Hallie's gonna insist on going back to Bitter River with me. Do you want her traveling that far with Clark or his men? With me in shackles? I didn't think so. And if you hang me here, she'll never forgive you. So, just let me go. I'll leave town, and you'll never see me again."

McIntyre snorted. "Either way, you're gonna break her heart."

"I know that! Don't you think I know that?" Clay ran a hand through his hair. "Look at it this way, if I leave her here, with you, it's me she'll hate."

"Think you're clever, don't you? Think I'd rather turn you loose than have my daughter hate me all over again."

"I know you've got no reason to believe me, but I'm trying to do what's best for Hallie."

"I'll have to think about it. Anything else you want to say to me?"

"Nope."

McIntyre jerked his head toward the stairs. "Let's go, then."

Clay glanced at the gun in the sheriff's hand, wondering what the chances were of overpowering the man and making a break for it. Slim and none, he mused. There was little chance of taking the lawman by surprise, just as he had little hope of overpowering him. McIntyre was a big man in his prime. He wouldn't go down easy.

"Don't try it," McIntyre warned. "I'd hate to make Hallie a widow the same day she became a bride."

"Yeah," Clay muttered laconically. "Me, too."

Resigned, he climbed the stairs and entered the cell at the end of the row. He flinched as McIntyre turned the key in the lock.

"I'll get Hallie," McIntyre said.

Clay nodded. "McIntyre?"

"Yeah?"

"Whatever happens, don't let Hallie be at the hanging."

"I won't. You can count on it."

"Thanks." Hands curled around the bars, he bowed his head and closed his eyes. He had to get out of here.

He listened to McIntyre's footsteps on the stairs, heard the muffled sound of voices, the quick tattoo of Hallie's heels as she ran up the steps. And then she was there, her smile like a ray of sunshine breaking through the clouds on a cold winter day.

McIntyre appeared a few minutes later. "Back away from the door."

Clay stepped back and McIntyre unlocked the door. Hallie flew into the cell, and into Clay's arms. "Thank you, Papa."

McIntyre shrugged. "I'll be back in a couple of hours to see if there's anything you need." With a rueful shake of his head, McIntyre locked the door, then left the cell block.

"Hallie, what the devil are you doing here?"

"Where else should I be?" she asked, her eyes bright.

"Anywhere but here."

"Call me old-fashioned," she said tartly, "but I believe a wife should be with her husband."

"Hallie . . ."

She looked up at him, a seductive smile playing over her lips as she wrapped her arms around his waist. "What?"

Clay swallowed hard, wondering when his angel had turned into such a wanton. Not that he was complaining, but . . . he glanced around, at the bare wooden walls, the rough plank floor, the steel bars that hemmed him in, the narrow cot with its thin mattress, the slop jar in the corner. Hardly a fitting place to bed his bride.

"I know, I wouldn't have picked this place for a honeymoon, either, but . . ." She slid her hand down his chest, lower, lower. She wanted him to make love to her again, wanted it more than her next breath. But what if he didn't want her? Their wedding had been less than romantic; it certainly hadn't been Clay's idea. What if he was sorry? The thought hit her like a blast of cold air. Abruptly, she let him go. "I'm sorry."

"Hallie." He drew her back into his arms. "I want you, too. It's just that . . ." He swore under his breath. "Hallie, you deserve so much more than this. Than me."

"Don't say that."

"It's true." He ran his knuckles over her cheek, his arms tightening around her waist. "God help me, but I love you."

She looked up at him, her gaze searching his. "Clay, oh, Clay . . ."

"I know, sweetheart. I know. I want you, too, but this isn't the place. What if your old man comes back?"

"He won't. He said he wouldn't be back for a couple of hours. He knows we want to be alone."

Clay grinned wryly. He wanted her more than anything in life. Here, or on silk sheets, it didn't matter. He wanted her. And she wanted him. He didn't know why; and at the moment, with her looking up at him, eyes shining with love, the reason didn't matter. What mattered was that she was here, now, and it might be the last chance he ever had to be alone with her, to hold her close.

"You're sure?" he asked.

"Very."

"I love you, Hallie," he murmured, and then he kissed her.

She was like fire and sun-kissed honey in his arms, hot and sweet, and he knew he would never get enough of her, not now, not ever.

Her eyelids fluttered down as she pressed herself against him, and everything else faded into the distance. It didn't matter that they were in an ugly little cell. Nothing mattered but his mouth on hers, his arms crushing her close to his hard, lean body, his words whispering that he loved her, and she knew she would live and die for this man, with this man, and no other.

He carried her to the cot and stretched out beside her, and all the while he showered her with kisses, sweet, gentle kisses that made her feel loved, cherished. Hot, passionate kisses that made her toes curl with pleasure.

Their clothes disappeared as if by magic. His hands played over her, clever hands that knew every inch of her, hands that knew what she wanted better than she knew herself.

She felt the desire ignite deep within her, building from a small flame to an inferno, heard the soft needy moans that rose in her throat. She clutched at him, caught up in a maelstrom of wanting . . . wanting . . . gasped with soul-deep pleasure as she reached the pinnacle and plunged over the edge.

He followed her a moment later, and then, together, they drifted lowly back to earth.

Hallie snuggled into his arms. Never had she felt so wonderful, so complete. She couldn't stop smiling, couldn't stop touching him, kissing him. And to think, if she hadn't met Clay, she would never have known such bliss, such ecstasy.

Reality returned slowly. Sounds from the street below drifted up through the iron-barred window . . . a boy crying, the rumble of a wagon passing by, the loud ring of the blacksmith's hammer, the whinny of a horse.

The cot creaked as Clay rolled onto his side. She

shivered as cool air whispered over her sweat-sheened flesh.

She opened her eyes, and wished she hadn't. Clay was watching her, his dark eyes filled with anguish, and she knew he was feeling guilty for making love to her on a jailhouse cot. But she wasn't sorry, would never be sorry.

Clay blew out a deep breath. "Hallie, we need to talk."

"No." She covered his mouth with her hand. "Not now."

He didn't argue. Instead, he reached down and pulled the blanket up over them. There was no point in lamenting what had been done. Better to enjoy her nearness while he could.

Wrapping her in his arms, he kissed her, hoping she knew how much her love meant to him.

"It'll be all right, Clay, you'll see."

"Sure."

She smiled at him. He didn't believe her, but she knew it was true. Somehow, some way, everything would work out.

Holding his gaze, she slid her hand between them, her fingertips trailing down his chest, over his belly, lower, lower. He sucked in a deep breath as her hand closed over him.

"Hallie!"

"Hmm?"

"What are you doing?"

She batted her eyelashes at him. "Doing? Who? Me?"

"Yes. You."

"I'm not doing anything." She grinned as she felt him swell within the circle of her hand.

Clay swallowed hard, surprised that he could want her again so soon, that he could want her so desperately.

"Should I stop?"

"No." Did his voice sound as strained to her as it did to him? He blew out a ragged breath. "Don't stop. Don't ever stop."

Chapter 19

Frank McIntyre stood at the cell door, watching Clay and his daughter. They were asleep in each other's arms, the blanket drawn over them. It didn't take a genius to figure out what they'd been doing for the last few hours. Their clothes were scattered on the floor and there was the unmistakable odor of spent passion in the air. It seemed impossible that his daughter, reared by nuns for the last four years, could be in love with an outlaw like John Walking Hawk, a half-breed Sioux who was wanted for killing five men.

McIntyre chewed the inside of his lip. He'd only known Clay a short time, but the man seemed a decent sort. He couldn't blame Clay for what he'd done, not if his story was true. Any man worthy of the name would have done the same thing.

McIntyre blew out a sigh. It wasn't up to him to sit in judgment. He was neither judge nor jury. It was his job to enforce the law, that was all. And John Walking Hawk was a wanted man with a price on his head.

McIntyre frowned, wondering why there were never any easy answers. He had three choices: he could hang Clay; he could send him back to Bitter River and let Mason Clark take care of it; or he could turn his back on his duty and let the man go.

Frowning, he rubbed his thumb and forefinger over

the six-pointed star pinned to his shirtfront. What mattered most, his honor, or his daughter's happiness?

It took him a moment to realize Walking Hawk was awake and staring back at him.

"Put your pants on," Mcintyre said, his voice pitched low so as not to wake Hallie. "We need to talk."

Clad only in his boots and britches, Clay followed McIntyre downstairs. He took the chair the lawman indicated, grimaced as McIntyre handcuffed his left wrist to the arm.

"That isn't necessary," Clay muttered.

"Maybe, maybe not." McIntyre dropped heavily into his chair behind the battered desk and propped his feet on the corner. "I want you to tell me everything that happened from the time you found your wife." A rueful smile flickered over the lawman's lips. "Your first wife."

"Why? You don't believe a word I say."

"Just do it."

Clay glanced out the window, surprised to see that the sun was going down, and then he began to speak, his voice low. He told how he'd seen the smoke from a distance, how he had found Summer Rain lying out in the yard, her clothes ripped to pieces, her thighs covered with blood.

"Anna was huddled beside her mother. I guess she'd seen it all. After I buried Summer, I took my daughter and rode out to my folk's place. They lived about three miles south of us . . ."

Hallie stood at the foot of the stairs, listening quietly as Clay told her father what had transpired the day his wife had died. She felt a lump rise in her throat as she heard the underlying grief in his voice when he described finding his parents murdered. She heard his sorrow when he spoke of leaving his daughter with her Lakota grandparents.

She blinked back tears when her father said, "I know just how you felt. When I left Hallie and her mother, I figured it would only be for a few days, weeks at the most. How could I have known I'd never see my wife again? And Hallie . . . I missed all her growing up years." Her father cleared his throat. "But we were talking about you. Go on . . ."

She pressed a hand over her heart when Clay told of the long days and lonely nights he had spent hunting the men who had killed his family. He could have gunned them down in cold blood, and after what she had heard, she would not have blamed him, but he hadn't. He had faced them all in a fair fight. She wondered now if, subconsciously, he had been seeking his own death, if he had been looking for an end to the sorrow and bitter regret that had been his constant companions for the past two years. And underlying every word, she heard the rage that still burned bright even though he had killed the men responsible.

There was a heavy silence when Clay finished his story, and then he said, "Okay, so now you know, but it doesn't change anything, does it?"

"Are you in love with my daughter?"

Feeling as if all the air had suddenly been sucked out of the room, Hallie held her breath.

"Yes."

Her father let out a sigh that seemed to come from the very depths of his soul. "I think you're telling me the truth, about everything."

"That'll be a real comfort when they slip that noose around my neck."

"You know damn well I can't hang you."

Hope and surprise rose up in Hallie and spilled from her lips in a wordless cry of joy. She clapped her hand over her mouth, hoping her father hadn't heard, but, of course, he had.

"Hallie? What are you doing, eavesdropping?"

Cheeks burning, she stepped around the corner into the main room of the jail.

McIntyre shook his head. "You always were a nosy little thing."

"I was not."

McIntyre grunted. "I remember when you were two and your mama sent you to bed. It was Christmas. We were putting presents under the tree when we heard a noise. It was you, peeking around the doorway."

She wanted to argue with him, to say she had been just a baby then and she was above that now, but of course she couldn't, not when he had caught her red-handed.

"How much did you hear?" Clay asked.

"All of it."

He studied her face, wondering if she would feel differently about him, now that she had heard it all. He had told her parts of it before, but not all of it. He had sugar-coated the killing, hoping to spare her the raw ugliness of it.

Hallie nodded, and Clay felt his stomach clench. And then she was kneeling in front of him, clasping his free hand to her breast.

"Oh, Clay, why didn't you tell me all this before? I never realized how awful it had been for you."

"I'm sorry you had to find out."

"I wish you had told me before."

"Why? It wouldn't have changed anything."

That was true, she thought, but she could better

understand his need to avenge his wife's death now. Surely the men he had killed were burning in hell.

"Hallie, go back to the hotel and pack Clay's gear."

"Why? What are you going to do?"

A slow smile spread over McIntyre's face. "I think there's going to be a jail break."

"A jail break?" Hallie exclaimed.

"Yeah. I'll work out the details later. Go along now, get Clay's stuff from the hotel."

Hope surged through her as she kissed Clay, kissed her father on the cheek, and ran out of the jail.

Clay shook his head. "You're gonna turn me loose, just like that?"

McIntyre nodded. "I've been on both sides of law. This is one time when I think maybe justice was a little too blind."

"So, what do you have in mind?"

"I'm not sure, but I'll think of a good story. In the meantime, I want your word that you'll take good care of Hallie, that you'll change your name and settle down somewhere, and that you'll let me know where you are."

"You've got it." Clay lifted his shackled hand as far as possible, a question in his eyes.

"Oh, yeah." With a grin, McIntyre pulled the hand-cuff key from his pocket.

Clay glanced over his shoulder as the door swung open, surprised that Hallie had returned so quickly. Only it wasn't Hallie.

"Get those hands up, Sheriff."

"Will!" McIntyre exclaimed. "What the hell are you doing?"

"That bastard killed my brother and shot Bob full of holes. He might . . ." Will swallowed hard. "Bob might die."

"And he'll pay for it," McIntyre said, his voice calm. "He's been tried and convicted for killing five men, and he's gonna hang. Now, put that gun away before you do something stupid."

Will Sayers shook his head. He was a tall, slender kid, with light brown hair and blue eyes.

"I don't want him hangin' for what he did to somebody else," the kid declared, his voice rising. "He killed Clyde. I wanna see him squirm, and then I wanna finish him off." A malicious smile twisted his lips. "Real slow."

"You'll have to go through me to do it," McIntyre said. "Are you ready to do that?"

Indecision flickered in Sayers's eyes.

"Come on, Will, I've known you for three years. I've never known you to break the law. You don't want to start by killing somebody."

"But he killed Clyde!"

"And he'll pay for it." McIntyre put the key in his pocket and held out his hand. "Give me the gun."

Clay watched Sayers. The kid didn't look to be much older than eighteen or nineteen. His older brothers might have been killers, but it was obvious that Will Sayers wasn't cut from the same cloth. His eyes were worried, downright scared. His finger was white where it curled around the trigger. It wouldn't take much to push him over the edge.

The thought had no sooner crossed Clay's mind than the jailhouse door swung open.

"Hey, Sheriff, there's trouble brewing over at the . . ."

It all happened so fast, Clay wasn't sure who moved first. Will's head had jerked around when the door opened. As soon as his attention was elsewhere, McIntyre lunged forward.

The man at the door went white. Turning on his heel, he ran off down the street.

Will Sayers turned back toward McIntyre. His eyes went wide as he saw the sheriff reaching toward him. There was a loud blast as the gun went off. McIntyre staggered backward. A bright crimson stain spread slowly across the front of his shirt. He looked down at it, his expression one of surprise, and then he collapsed.

"Shit!" Will Sayers looked at the gun in his hand as if he had never seen it before. "Shit!" He dropped the gun, sent a last stricken glance at McIntyre, then bolted out the door.

"McIntyre!" Clay stood up. Dragging the chair behind him, he crossed the floor and knelt beside Hallie's father. "Dammit, Frank, can you hear me?"

The sheriff's eyelids fluttered open. "Damn, but you're bad luck." He took a deep, struggling breath. "Hallie? Where's Hallie?"

"She'll be back soon." Clay reached into McIntyre's pocket and pulled out the key to the handcuffs.

"Remember your ... promise ... make ... her happy."

"Take it easy, Frank." Clay unlocked the cuffs and tossed them aside. Removing the kerchief from the sheriff's neck, he folded it into a square and pressed it over the wound in the lawman's chest to staunch the bleeding.

"Never should have ... left her ..."

"Save your breath, McIntyre." Applying more pressure to the wound, Clay glanced over his shoulder. Where the hell was Hallie?

He heard the sound of footsteps on the boardwalk and then Hallie swept into the room. "I think I ... Papa!" She dropped the bag she was carrying on the floor and knelt beside Clay, her eyes wide with horror. "What happened?"

"Will Sayers came looking for me and, hell, there's

no time to explain now." Clay took her hand and placed it over the makeshift bandage. "Press down on this, hard. I'm going for the doctor."

"Hurry!"

Clay gave her shoulder a quick squeeze, then hurried out the door.

McIntyre's eyelids fluttered open. "Hallie?"

"I'm here."

"Sorry . . . I left you . . ."

"Shh, it's all right. Don't try to talk. You're gonna be fine, just fine."

"Sure."

"Please don't die. Please don't leave me."

"Don't . . . want to."

"Shh, shh . . ." *Hurry, Clay, please hurry!*

She stared at the blood spreading across her father's shirtfront. He would be all right, he had to be all right. Clay had been shot, too, and he was fine, just fine. But there hadn't been so much blood. It soaked through the cloth beneath her hand. She could feel it, warm and sticky, against her palm.

Never had time passed so slowly. It seemed hours had passed since Clay went for the doctor. She wondered, fleetingly, if he had decided to make a run for it and then felt a rush of shame for even thinking such a thing.

"Hallie . . ."

"What?"

"Forgive me."

"There's nothing to forgive, Papa. Please don't talk. You need to save your strength. The doctor will be here soon."

Hurry, Clay, please hurry!

As if in answer to her prayer, he burst into the room, followed by Dr. Smitson. The doctor didn't waste time asking what had happened. He quickly knelt beside her father and got to work.

She was hardly aware of Clay taking her by the arm, lifting her to her feet, turning her away so she couldn't see what the doctor was doing.

"I'm sorry, Hallie," Clay said. "It should have been me."

She stared up at him, mute, as tears flowed down her cheeks.

The doctor removed McIntyre's shirt and gun belt and tossed them aside, then unfastened the top of his long underwear to expose the wound. He grunted softly as he pressed a fresh bandage over the wound. "I'll need some hot water."

"I'll get it." Hallie stirred the coals in the potbellied stove and placed the coffeepot on top to heat.

"He'll be all right." Clay moved up behind her and drew her into his arms. "I'm sure he'll be all right."

She turned, burying her face against his chest, trying to shut out the harsh rasp of her father's breathing. Once, he groaned low in his throat. The sound made her sick to her stomach.

When the water was hot, she poured it into a bowl and handed it to the doctor. Tears fell, unnoticed, down her cheeks as she watched the doctor probe the wound. And then she felt Clay's arms around her once more, drawing her away.

"There's nothing you can do," he said quietly.

She lost track of time. Standing there in Clay's arms, she sent urgent prayers to heaven, begging for her father's life, promising to be good, so good, if only her father would live.

"Well, I've done all I can," Smitson said. Rising to his feet, he wiped his hands on a towel pulled from his black bag. "I don't want to move him too far." He looked at Clay. "There's a bed in the back room where

McIntyre sometimes spends the night. Give me a hand, will you?"

Clay gave Hallie a squeeze, then helped the doctor lift McIntyre. Hallie ran ahead to open the door and turn down the blankets on the bed. Once McIntyre was settled, Clay went into the office to clean up the mess while the doctor spoke to Hallie.

He was scrubbing the blood from the floor when the doctor entered the room. "How is he?"

"I'm afraid it's too soon to tell. He's lost a great deal of blood, but he's a strong man. I'll know more by tomorrow."

Rising, Clay tossed the bloody rag into the wastebasket. "Thanks, Doc."

"I've been right busy since you came to town," Smitson remarked as he packed up his black bag.

Clay shrugged. "Bad luck just seems to dog some people."

"So it seems. Well, call me if you need me. I think Frank will probably sleep through the night. I'll be by in the morning to look in on him."

"Thanks, again."

Smitson grunted in reply, then left the office.

Clay threw McIntyre's ruined shirt into the trash can, then picked up the lawman's gun and holster and placed them on the desk. After locking the door, he turned down the lamp, then went into the back room to check on Hallie.

She was sitting on a ladder-back chair beside the bed, staring at her father, as if she could will him to breathe, to live.

"Hallie?"

She looked up at him, her eyes red-rimmed.

"Why don't you go home and get some rest? I'll sit by your father."

"No, I can't leave him."

"Hallie . . ."

"No."

"If I bring one of the cots down, will you try and get some sleep?"

"I don't think I can."

"He's gonna need you in the morning, when he wakes up."

"I know, but . . ."

"I'll stay right here. I'll wake you up if anything happens."

She thought about that a moment, then nodded. "All right."

A short time later, Clay had a cot set up next to her father's bed.

"Thank you, Clay. Will you pray with me before I go to sleep?"

His first reaction was to refuse, but she looked so earnest, so hopeful, he found himself saying, "Sure." He knelt beside her as she drew her rosary from her skirt pocket.

Hallie bowed her head, the beads clasped in her hands.

"Hail Mary, full of grace, the Lord is with thee. Blessed art thou amongst women, and blessed is the fruit of thy womb. . . ."

Clay repeated the words after her. To his surprise, he felt a long-forgotten sense of peace steal over him as he repeated the once-familiar words. He had not prayed in years, not since Summer Wind died in his arms.

"Thank you," Hallie smiled at him. "I think maybe I can sleep now."

He stood up and helped her to her feet. "Try not to worry, honey."

She kissed him lightly, then sat down on the edge of the cot and removed her shoes. She smoothed a lock of hair from her father's brow and then, taking his hand in hers, she lay down and closed her eyes.

With a sigh, Clay sat down in the chair on the opposite side of her father's bed. It was going to be a long night.

Chapter 20

McIntyre didn't seem to be much better in the morning. Clay went after the doctor; then, while Smitson looked after Hallie's father, Clay went into the office and put on a pot of coffee. Waiting for the water to heat, he strapped on the lawman's gun belt. He felt better when he was armed again, though the rig felt strange. He drew the gun, getting the feel of it, testing the weight of it in his hand.

He drank a cup of coffee, then took one in to Hallie. She shook her head when he offered it to her, and he left it on the table. Murmuring that he'd be back later, he left the jail and went to McIntyre's house, letting himself in with the key he had taken from the lawman's trousers. It was a modest four-room house. He had only seen the parlor the last time he was there; now he explored the other rooms. In addition to the parlor, there was a small kitchen with a stove, a hand pump, a rough-hewn round table, and a couple of chairs made of dark oak. A narrow hall led to two fair-sized bedrooms.

He found shaving gear in McIntyre's room. Using the lawman's strop and razor and a bar of yellow soap, he shaved and washed up, then helped himself to one of McIntyre's shirts. Taking his own gun belt from the hall-tree, he slung it over his shoulder, and then, knowing Hallie probably wouldn't want to leave her father's side long enough to come home and change, he got a clean dress from her room, found her hairbrush and a package of pins, and headed back to the jail.

He felt more than a little vulnerable as he walked down the street. Where the hell was Will Sayers? Will had said Bob was still alive, but Clay was pretty sure Bob wasn't holed up anywhere in town. Had Will left town to take care of his brother, or was he lurking behind one of those windows, waiting for another crack at the man who had killed Clyde and wounded Bob?

A few businesses were open, and Clay was conscious of being stared at as he angled across the street toward the jailhouse. The short hairs prickled along the back of his neck, and he felt a curious itching between his shoulder blades as he contemplated a bullet in the back.

Hallie was sitting beside her father's bed when he returned to the jail. Her eyes were red and swollen, mute testimony to the fact that the doctor had given her bad news.

Clay dropped her belongings and his gun belt on the cot she'd used the night before, then lifted her to her feet. The minute his arms went around her, she burst into tears.

Clay felt a rush of guilt as he held her. If he hadn't come here looking for Bob Sayers, none of this would have happened.

He held her close, murmuring what words of comfort he could, until her tears subsided.

"I'm sorry," she sniffed.

"I'm the one who's sorry," Clay muttered.

"You? Why?"

"I should never have brought you here."

"Maybe," Hallie replied after a moment. "But then I never would have had the chance to see my father again." She looked up at him, her eyes filling with tears. "Oh, Clay, what if he dies?"

"What did the doctor say?"

"He said . . . he said to prepare myself for the worst."

Clay swore under his breath. What kind of man was Smitson? Couldn't the doctor have given her a little hope to cling to?

"Wipe your eyes, Hallie," Clay said gently. "Crying won't help."

"I know." She went to the small dresser beside the door. There was a pitcher of water and bowl there. She poured some water in the bowl, soaked a cloth, and wiped her face.

"That's better," Clay remarked. "Come on, let's go over to the hotel and get some breakfast."

"I can't leave him," Hallie said. "What if he wakes up while I'm gone? What if he needs me?"

Clay blew out a sigh. He'd known she wouldn't leave her father, but she had to eat, and so did he. "How about if I go over to the restaurant and get us something and bring it back?"

"Thank you, Clay."

He kissed her on the forehead, then left the jail.

He paused on the boardwalk, his gaze moving up and down the street. All the stores were open now. Several proprietors were outside, sweeping the boardwalk in front of their respective establishments. A small group of men were gathered at the livery. Looked like a horse auction. It reminded Clay that he needed to check on Romeo and Juliet before the day was out.

Crossing the street, he went to the hotel restaurant and ordered breakfast for himself and Hallie, then stood with his back to the wall so he could keep an eye on anyone entering the dining room.

Where the devil was Will Sayers? The man might not be a natural-born killer like Bob, but he'd already made one attempt at vengeance. Would he chance another? Clay grunted softly. He knew all about revenge, about the relentless need to right a wrong. He knew all too well what Will Sayers was feeling.

A girl brought his order on a covered tray. Clay paid for the meal, then left the hotel, the tray balanced on his left hand, his right had hovering over the butt of his gun.

Hallie was sitting beside the bed, wiping her father's brow with a damp cloth. She had changed her clothes while he had been gone. Her hair, neatly brushed, was coiled in a thick knot at her nape.

"How's he doing?" he asked.

"Not very well." She took a deep breath. "The doctor stopped by. He changed the bandages and said he would be back later on this afternoon."

Clay set the tray on the dresser and removed the cloth. The aroma of bacon, eggs, and fried potatoes wafted through the air. He spread some butter and jam on a biscuit.

"Here," Clay said. He handed Hallie one of the plates. "Looks good."

Hallie nodded.

"Eat, Hallie."

Obediently, she picked up her fork and took a bite of the potatoes.

Taking the other plate, Clay sat down on the edge of the cot. He ate without tasting a thing, his thoughts jumping from Will and Bob Sayers to Anna to Frank McIntyre and then, as always, to Hallie. She was his wife now. As much as that pleased him, it also worried the hell out of him. What was he going to do with a wife? He couldn't very well drag her around with him while he tracked Bob Sayers. If her father died, he couldn't leave her here, in Green Willow Creek, alone. He didn't know if Reverend Mother Matilda would take her back, but he doubted Hallie would go, even if the nuns welcomed her with open arms.

He put his plate aside and reached for one of the coffee cups, draining it in a couple of quick swallows.

He glanced at Hallie. She was staring at her father, the plate in her lap forgotten.

Rising, he put their plates on the tray, then offered Hallie the other cup. "Here, drink this."

"I don't want it."

He'd forgotten she didn't like coffee. Damn. He should have brought her a cup of tea or a glass of milk. He drained the cup and added it to the tray and then, too restless to sit still, he began to pace the floor.

He was on his tenth lap when McIntyre let out a long, low groan and opened his eyes.

"Papa!" Hallie was at his side immediately, one hand stroking his brow. "Papa, how do you feel?"

"Like I've been kicked in the . . ." He struggled for breath. "Kicked in the chest by a . . . loco bronc." He looked over at Clay and frowned. "Thought you were . . . leaving town."

Clay grunted softly. "I'd have been long gone if it wasn't for you."

McIntyre managed a weak smile. "Sorry I . . . didn't die."

"Papa, don't say that."

McIntyre took a couple of shallow breaths. "I'll be all right, Hallie. Take more . . . than a wild-eyed kid like . . . Will Sayers to . . . to put me under."

"Another inch to the left and you'd be cold by now," Clay remarked. "Hallie, go get the doctor."

"But . . ."

"Go on."

With a humph of pique, she flounced out of the office.

McIntyre stared at Clay, his eyes narrowed. "I take it you've . . . got something to say. Something . . . you don't want . . . Hallie to hear."

"Right."

"Sayers . . . you're going . . . after Sayers." He closed his eyes a moment. "You want to leave Hallie here."

"You're pretty smart, for a lawman."

"She's welcome . . . to stay with me . . . but she won't . . . won't want to."

"I don't intend to give her a choice."

"Just gonna run out on her, huh?" McIntyre glanced pointedly at the Colt holstered at Clay's hip. "I'd think you'd . . ." He drew in a deep breath. "You'd have had enough killing by now."

"That's none of your business."

Anger flared in the lawman's eyes. "Hallie is my business . . . don't want to see her get hurt."

"I'll come back for her."

"If you're able."

"Don't worry. Nothing's gonna happen to me. I've got too much to live for."

"Uh-huh." McIntyre glanced pointedly at Clay's shoulder. "Sayers . . . might not miss . . . next time."

"Neither will I. I intend to . . ." Clay's voice trailed off as he saw McIntyre shake his head. Glancing over his shoulder, he saw Hallie and the doctor walking toward them.

"What do you intend to do?" Hallie asked.

"Nothing."

Hallie glanced at her father, then back at Clay. "What's going on?"

"Nothing, Hallie. Let's go out in the other room so the doctor can examine your father." Taking her by the arm, Clay steered her out of the room.

"What were you and my father talking about?"

Clay shrugged. "Nothing much." Releasing her arm, he went to stand at the window. He could feel Hallie's gaze burning into his back.

"You're getting ready to leave, aren't you?"

"What makes you think that?"

"Aren't you?"

Clay shoved his hands in the pockets of his trousers, wondering what would be kinder, the hard truth, or a lie.

"You married me only because my father made you, didn't you? And now you're going to leave me here while you go look for Bob Sayers and his brother. You might get killed, but you don't care about that, do you?"

"Hallie, you don't understand."

"I understand more than you think. You're so eaten up with the need for revenge you don't care about anything else. Not me, not your daughter . . ."

Clay swung around to face her, his expression cold and hard. "Dammit, Hallie, that's not true!"

"It is true! It was horrible what those men did to your family. I can't blame you for wanting to see them dead. But what has your killing accomplished? Your family is still dead and nothing you can do will bring them back. You've left your daughter for two years, and for what?" She pressed her hands over her abdomen. "I could be carrying your child, Clay. But you don't care about that either, do you?"

"Hallie . . ." Clay stared at her, surprised that he wasn't bleeding. Every word she'd said had hit him with the force of a bullet. He'd been so eaten up with guilt for not being there when Summer needed him, so filled with rage and hate for the men who had violated her, he'd abandoned his daughter and gone looking for revenge in the hope that it would somehow salve his conscience.

Hallie fisted the tears from her eyes. She never should have left the convent, never should have followed him. Never should have fallen in love with him.

"You're right," Clay said, his voice heavy. "I've been a damn fool."

Hallie blinked at him. "What?"

Clay shook his head. "I've wasted two years of my life for nothing."

He raked a hand through his hair as an old, half-forgotten scripture rose in his mind. *Vengeance is mine, saith the Lord. I will repay. . . .* What had he hoped to gain by killing the men who had murdered his family? Hallie was right. It hadn't changed anything. His parents and Summer Rain were still dead. Instead of staying with Anna and helping his daughter through a bad time, he had gone off on some stupid quest for revenge and in the process, he had become little better than the men he had gunned down.

"Clay . . ."

"I've been a fool." Crossing the floor, he took Hallie's hands in his. "Can you forgive me?"

"Oh, Clay, there's nothing to forgive. I love you."

"I don't know why."

"Someday I'll tell you." She smiled up at him, hope shining in her eyes. "Does this mean you're not going after Bob Sayers, that you're going to stay here, with me?"

"I reckon so," he murmured, and felt as if the weight of the world had just dropped off his shoulders.

"Oh, Clay!" She threw her arms around his neck and hugged him close.

"Uh, excuse me?"

Hallie glanced over her shoulder to see the doctor standing in the doorway. "Oh, Dr. Smitson, how's my father?"

Smitson nodded. "He's going to be fine, just fine. That man is as strong as an ox, but I don't want him getting out of bed for at least a month."

"You'll probably have to tie him down," Clay muttered.

"It wouldn't surprise me," Smitson replied, grinning. "While I'm here, I'd like to take a look at that arm."

"I'm fine," Clay said.

"I'd still like to have a look at it."

With a grimace, Clay sat on the edge of the desk and peeled off his shirt.

The doctor removed the bandage and studied the wound a moment, then nodded. "It seems to be healing nicely. I'll just apply a clean dressing."

"Have you treated any other gunshot wounds in the last day or so?" Clay asked.

Smitson shook his head. "No, why?"

"Just curious."

Smitson finished dressing Clay's arm. "I don't get many gunshot wounds," he remarked as he closed his satchel. "This is a pretty quiet town most of the time. I like it that way." He quirked an eyebrow at Clay. "Our town was a lot quieter before you got here. I'll be by this evening to look in on McIntyre."

"Thank you, Doctor," Hallie said.

"You're welcome." Taking up his satchel, Smitson left the building.

"I don't think he likes me much," Clay mused as he put on his shirt.

"That's okay," Hallie said, smiling. "I like you plenty."

"Do you? I can't imagine why."

"I could show you."

"I'd like that. We never had a proper honeymoon." Bending, he kissed her lightly. "I love you, Hallie."

Happiness bubbled up inside her, warm and sweet, as he held her tight. Everything was going to be all right. Closing her eyes, she sent a fervent prayer of thanks to heaven.

Clay rested his chin on the top of Hallie's head, a rare feeling of contentment washing over her.

"Maybe you could get a job as a deputy," Hallie mused. "I'm sure Papa could use the help."

Clay grinned in wry amusement. He doubted the people of Green Willow Creek would consider a half-breed outlaw a fit candidate for a deputy sheriff, but there was no point in mentioning it now. "Maybe. We can talk about it later."

"You won't mind if we stay here, will you? At least for a little while, until Papa can take care of himself."

"Listen, Hallie . . ."

She drew back and looked up at him. "What's wrong?"

"Nothing's wrong. I think you should stay here."

"Where are you going?"

"I'll be leaving in the morning."

"Leaving! So soon? But you said—"

"I want to go get Anna."

"Oh, of course."

"Is that going to be a problem?"

"What do you mean?"

"Is it going to bother you, raising another woman's child?"

"Clay, don't be silly. She's our daughter now. She belongs here, with us."

He blew out a breath he hadn't realized he'd been holding, then wondered why he had been worried in the first place. Hallie could no more refuse to love a child than she could fly.

"How long will you be gone?"

"I don't know. Depends on how long it takes me to find my people. They should be near the South Platte this time of year." So near, he mused, and yet so far.

His people . . . Hallie's gaze ran over Clay's face. The fact that he was half-Indian had never mattered to her; indeed, she had never really given it any thought. His skin was dark, and not just from being in the sun. His hair was long, black as a raven's wing. She studied his features—the hawklike nose, the high cheekbones, the shape of his eyes, and tried to imagine him in buckskin and feathers.

"Hallie?" Her father's voice, sounding slightly peevish, broke in on her thoughts. "Hallie, you out there?"

"Yes, Papa."

"Think I could get some breakfast?"

"Sure, Papa, right away."

"I'll get it," Clay muttered with a wry grin. "I'm getting pretty good at fetching and carrying. You go sit with your father."

"All right." She kissed him on the cheek. "Hurry back."

"Count on it."

Whistling softly, he left the office.

Chapter 21

"**I** want to go with you."

"No. I'll be back as soon as I can."

They were sitting on the sofa in McIntyre's house. Earlier, with the doc's help, they had settled McIntyre into his own bed. Hallie had fixed her father some broth, then sat with him until he fell asleep. Later, she had fixed dinner for Clay.

It was the first meal Hallie had ever cooked for him. He had stood in the doorway, one shoulder propped against the door jamb, watching her bustle about the tiny kitchen, her hair pinned atop her head, a frilly white apron tied around her waist.

Dinner—steak, potatoes, and corn—had been surprisingly good, considering her claim that she had never cooked before. If the steak had been a little too done for his taste, and the potatoes a little raw, he hadn't seen any reason to mention it.

Now they were in the parlor. It seemed strange to be living in a house again, with a woman at his side. Images of Summer Rain flitted through his mind—

Summer learning to cook the white man's way; Summer laughing as she helped him plant their first garden; Summer lying beside him under the stars, her belly softly rounded; Summer sitting in the sunlight, watching him work as she nursed their child; Summer humming softly as she tucked Anna into bed at night;

and Summer lying close beside him, her supple body pressed against his own. . . .

"Clay?"

He looked up, startled to realize he wasn't alone, and the images faded away. "What?"

"How long are you going to be gone?"

"I don't know." He looked past Hallie, his thoughts turned inward. It had been several years since he had lived with the Lakota. What would it be like to go back? Would he still belong? Would the People welcome him home, or look on him as a stranger? He thought of the warm summer days spent on the plains, the buffalo hunts, the awesome power and spiritual renewal of the Sun Dance ceremony.

"You don't intend to stay there indefinitely, do you?"

"Of course not. You're here. I'll come back for you."

She reached over and took his hand in hers. "Please let me go with you."

"What about your father?"

"The doctor said he's pretty sure my father's out of danger, but that he's going to have a long recovery. Please, Clay. I want to see your people." It was true, partly anyway, but mainly she was afraid of being left behind, afraid something might happen to Clay while he was gone and she would never see him again.

"All right, sweetheart, if you're sure."

She smiled up at him, her eyes radiant. "I'm sure." She hesitated a moment. "Would you mind, that is, do you think we could wait a few days, just to make sure Papa's going to be all right?"

He didn't want to wait. He'd waited long enough, but he couldn't refuse her. "Sure, honey."

"I love you so much."

"I love you, too." He trailed a finger down her cheek. "It's getting late. We should turn in."

He had intended to leave town early in the morning,

but his decision to take Hallie with him had changed things. It might be easier on her if they took a stage as far north as they could. Tomorrow, he would go over to the ticket office and make arrangements.

Hallie ran her hand over his arm, her eyes glowing as she gazed up at him, and he forgot everything else. He smiled down at her. "Are you ready for bed?"

Hallie's eyelids fluttered down and a faint flush tinged her cheeks. "Yes, if you are."

"We haven't had much of a honeymoon, have we?"

"I'm not complaining."

"I know." He put his finger under her chin and tilted her head up. "You never do." He kissed the tip of her nose, then stood up.

"Where are you going?"

"I'll be back in a little while."

"But . . ."

He winked at her, and then he was gone.

Hallie frowned, wondering at his abrupt departure. She tried not to worry, and even though she knew he wouldn't leave town without telling her good-bye, all she could think of was that he had left her.

She was half-asleep when she heard the front door open, and then Clay was there, sweeping her into his arms.

"What are you doing?" she asked, blushing hotly when she saw Dr. Smitson standing behind Clay.

"Don't ask questions. The doc's gonna keep an eye on your father until we get back."

"Back? Where are we going?"

"You'll see."

"But . . ."

"Your father will be fine, sweetheart." He jerked his chin toward the doctor. "He'll be in good hands."

With a sigh, she wrapped her arms around his neck, content to let him take her wherever he would.

A couple of drunk cowboys whistled and made rude remarks as Clay carried her across the street and up the stairs into the Palace Hotel.

Hallie couldn't help staring at her surroundings as Clay carried her across the lobby. She had thought the Southwick Hotel was the loveliest place she had ever seen, but the lobby of the Palace was dazzling. Huge crystal chandeliers hung from the ceilings. Rich maroon-colored velvet draperies covered the windows. Curved settees, comfortable-looking chairs, and burnished oak tables were placed at intervals. A flowered carpet covered the floor.

The desk clerk smiled warmly as Clay approached. "Ah, Mr. Clayton, your room is all ready."

"Thank you."

"Is there anything else we can do for you this evening?"

"Just don't disturb us."

"Of course not, sir."

Hallie's heart began to beat faster as Clay carried her up a winding staircase and down a long hall to the room at the end of the corridor.

"Close your eyes, Hallie."

"What?"

"Just do it."

Obediently, she closed her eyes, her curiosity mushrooming.

Clay opened the door and stepped inside, kicked the door shut with his foot. Gently, he lowered her to the floor. "Keep your eyes closed."

She heard Clay cross the room. There was a rasp, the smell of sulphur, a flare of light.

And then she felt Clay's arms slip around her waist, felt his lips nuzzle her neck. "You can open your eyes now."

"Oh, Clay," she murmured, "it's beautiful."

The room was decorated in white with splashes of blue in the carpet and the bedspread. The bed was strewn with flower petals, a dozen candles filled the room with a soft amber glow, a bottle of champagne and two crystal glasses sat on the bedside table alongside a basket of bread and cheese.

"You like it?" His breath fanned across her cheek. It had taken the last of the money he'd won at cards to pay for the room. He had felt guilty, starting their marriage flat broke, until he saw the look on her face.

"I don't know what to say."

"Say you love me."

She turned in his embrace and rested her hands on his shoulders. "I love you, Clay."

"Come here," he said, and taking her by the hand, he led her into an adjoining room where a tub of hot, scented water awaited.

Candles burned in this room, too, their flickering light casting shadows on the walls.

Slowly, reverently, he began to undress her. "You're so beautiful, Hallie." He dropped butterfly kisses along her shoulders. "So beautiful."

She tilted her head back, her eyelids fluttering down as he pressed kisses to her throat, her cheeks. She gasped as his tongue traced lazy circles over her breasts.

When she was naked, he lifted her into the tub. She sighed as the water closed around her, felt a sudden, sensual stirring deep within her as Clay began to undress, revealing a broad chest that tapered to a trim waist and long, long legs. She doubted she would ever tire of looking at him. His skin was dark all over, and not just where the sun had touched him. Muscles rippled beneath his taut flesh, the sight filling her with excitement.

And then he stepped into the tub behind her, his big

body cradling hers, his arms sliding around her waist to draw her back against him.

Hallie sighed with pleasure as Clay picked up a bar of soap and began to wash her, his hands moving slowly and deliberately as he soaped her arms, her legs, her belly. He lingered over her thighs, her breasts, paused to rain fervent kisses along the slender line of her shoulders, her nape. The feather-light touch of his hands and lips inflamed her, making her shiver with desire.

When he had washed her from head to toe, she wriggled around in the rub, took the soap from his hand, and washed him in return. The act of washing him, of touching him so intimately, aroused him even as it added to her own pleasure, her own frantic need.

With a low growl, Clay stood up, carrying her with him. Heedless of the water that splashed over the edge of the tub and soaked the floor, he grabbed a towel and carried her into the other room.

Setting her on her feet, he quickly toweled her dry and then he removed the pins from her hair.

"My beautiful, Hallie." He tunneled his fingers into her hair, loving the feel of it, the way it fell down her back and over her shoulders like a river of rich chestnut silk.

He kissed her, then fell back on the bed, carrying Hallie with him. He was desperate to hold her, to kiss her, to sink himself deep within her.

He gloried in the touch of her hands on his flesh. She was his, only his. It pleased him that she had never known another man, would never know another man.

The scent of crushed flower petals filled the room with perfume as he rolled her over and settled himself between her thighs.

"Hallie, Hallie . . ." he whispered her name over and over again. "How did I ever live without you?"

His words filled her with joy. Clasping his head

between her hands, she drew his face down and kissed him, and shuddered with sensual pleasure as his body meshed with hers.

"Swear it," he said, his voice ragged with desire. "Swear you'll never leave me."

"I won't," she replied fervently. "You know I won't."

It was the most beautiful night of her life, a night when nothing else mattered, when there was no one else in all the world but the two of them, Adam and Eve alone in the Garden, surrounded by golden candlelight and the heady fragrance of crushed flowers.

She touched him everywhere, kissed the scar on his throat, plumbed the depths of his belly button with her fingertip, discovered he was ticklish behind his knees.

She had never known making love could be so wonderful, that it could be fun. And just when she thought it was over, he lifted her atop of him and taught her there were other ways to find pleasure, that she could be in control.

She cried his name as pleasure exploded deep within her, radiating outward, like ripples on a lake, felt his body convulse as his life spilled into her, filling her with warmth and contentment.

Much later, snuggled close together and covered by a sheet, he fed her bread and cheese. They drank champagne from the same glass, and then they made love again, more slowly this time, savoring each moment.

It was near dawn when she fell asleep in his arms, happier, more content, than she had ever been in her life.

Chapter 22

She woke to find Clay standing beside the bed, gazing down at her.

"Morning, sleepyhead," he murmured.

She smiled up at him. "Good morning."

He sat down on the edge of the mattress and she closed her eyes as he feathered kisses over her eyes and nose, wrapped her arms around his neck as his mouth slanted over hers. She felt bereft when he took his lips from hers.

"What a wonderful way to wake up." She couldn't seem to stop smiling, or to keep from touching him.

"I couldn't agree more," Clay remarked. He ran a hand through her hair, remembering how she had looked the night before, with her hair falling in wild disarray over her shoulders, brushing over his chest like wisps of silk. . . . His reaction to the memory was instantaneous and blatantly obvious.

Eyes sparkling, a seductive smile hovering over her lips, she ran her hand along the inside of his thigh.

Clay grinned at her. "I think I've married a wanton."

"Oh, I'm definitely wanting," Hallie quipped, then blushed to the roots of her hair.

Chuckling softly, Clay shucked his trousers and slid under the covers, eager to see if he could make Hallie blush some more.

* * *

It was much later when they left the hotel. McIntyre was asleep when they returned to the house. Smitson assured them that Frank was out of danger and admitted his first prognosis had been overly grim. Bidding them a good day, he left the house.

Hallie said she was going to sit with her father a while, so Clay went down to the livery to check on the horses. Juliet welcomed him with a soft whinny; Romeo laid back his ears.

Leaving the stable, he went to check the stage schedule. The next one headed in the right direction wasn't due for almost a month.

He frowned, then shrugged. Maybe it was just as well. Frank would need someone to look after him at least that long. Thanking the agent for his help, he left the depot and headed home. *Home . . . home to Hallie.*

The next few days passed peacefully, though time weighed heavily on Clay's hands. McIntyre got stronger every day. A week after he'd been shot, he was complaining about being forced to stay in bed.

"Dammit, I'm not an invalid," he protested on more than one occasion.

Hallie ignored his grumbling, glad that he was alive, glad that he was recovering so quickly.

It was a bittersweet interlude. Living there with Hallie reminded Clay of the days he had spent in the valley with Summer Rain. It had been a long time since he'd had a woman to cook and care for him, a long time since he had thought of anything but the need for revenge. There was an unreal quality to his days now. He spent a considerable amount of time playing checkers with McIntyre, or sitting out on the front porch, basking in the sun. There was little for him to do, though Hallie was busy, learning to cook, cleaning, looking after her father. No matter where she was, what task occupied her hands, he was ever aware of her nearness, of the fact that, come nightfall, she would be in his bed, in his arms.

The passion between them blazed anew every time he held her close. There, in the dark of night, with Hallie lying close beside him, he forgot everything but the pleasure of her touch, the wonder of her love. What a rare and delightful creature she was! She had changed his life in so many ways, given him hope, restored his faith, cleansed the bitterness from his heart.

Sometimes, when he knelt beside her while she recited her evening prayers, he hardly recognized himself.

Three weeks after he had been shot, Frank McIntyre got out of bed, declaring he'd been coddled long enough and he wasn't, by damn, going to spend another day in bed.

His timing couldn't have been better, Clay mused. Their stage was due in three days. As much as Hallie hated to leave her father, she knew he'd be all right. Clay had been patience itself in the last few weeks.

"Where are you planning to settle after you get your daughter back?" McIntyre asked at dinner that night.

Clay shook his head. "I'm not sure. It'll have to be someplace where no one knows who I am."

McIntyre nodded. "You'll let me know?"

Hallie laid her hand over her father's. "Of course we will. We'll want you to come visit us, won't we, Clay?"

He nodded, meaning it.

Hallie looked at Clay. "But we'll come back here before we do anything else, won't we?"

"Sure, honey."

"I'll miss you," McIntyre said gruffly. "Both of you."

They boarded the stage three days later. Hallie had bid her father a tearful good-bye, promising to write if she got the chance. McIntyre had promised to look after Romeo and Juliet.

Now, Clay stared out the window, watching the countryside pass, miles and miles of flat, treeless land covered with buffalo grass. He'd spent several evenings playing poker and had managed to win enough to pay for their tickets on the stage, and have enough left over to buy the horses and supplies they'd need on the trail. McIntyre had offered to lend them money if they needed it, but Clay had refused. He wasn't about to start borrowing money from his father-in-law. But damn, stagecoach tickets were expensive. Fifty dollars for the two of them.

Clay took a deep breath and blew it out in a long sigh. It would take two days to reach the last town on the route. When they arrived, he would buy a couple of horses and supplies to last them a week or so. Hopefully, it wouldn't take more than two or three days to find the People.

The farther they went, the more he began to question the wisdom of taking the stage. The brilliant yellow Concord coaches with their unglazed windows, curtains, armrests and upholstered seats, and small candle lamps, were touted to be the most elegant of all the coaches that traveled the West. But, for all that, it was still a bumpy ride. Dust boiled up from the horses' hooves and the wheels of the coach, filtering through the cracks to cover them with a fine layer of dun-colored grit. The man across the way had a permanent scowl on his face; his wife was trying to quiet a fussy baby, who'd been crying for the last twenty minutes.

Hallie drew his head down so she could whisper in his ear. "Are you thinking what I'm thinking?"

"If you're thinking we should have ridden horseback, I am. Romeo's bad temper would be easier to put up with than this."

"I think you're right," Hallie agreed with a grin. The coach hit another rut in the road, almost unseating her. "Oh!" she exclaimed, and clung to him as they bounced over yet another bump that threw her the other way.

"Maybe we'll ride back," Clay muttered, quietly cursing the dust, the rough road, and the crying baby.

They were sacrificing comfort for time, he mused, and wondered if it was a fair trade. But they couldn't push saddle horses this hard this long. The Concord stopped every twelve miles or so to change horses and allow the passengers to stretch their legs and answer nature's call. Pushing so hard enabled them to make good time. The only good thing was that the coach, which could seat from nine to twelve people, carried only five passengers, giving them all plenty of room.

Sitting back, Clay slid his arm around Hallie's shoulders, taking pleasure in the way she snuggled against him. He wouldn't have thought it possible for anyone to sleep amid the creak of wheels and harness and the baby's incessant crying, but somehow, Hallie managed it.

Clay's thoughts turned inward as the miles slipped by. He summoned a mental image of Anna. She had been a pretty little five-year-old when he saw her last, slightly plump, with straight black hair and dark, dark eyes. Bright and curious, she had been the joy of his life. She had been a happy, smiling child until that fateful day.

He blew out a deep sigh. He never should have left her. He knew that now. Killing the men who killed Summer hadn't brought her back, or lessened the pain of her death. It hadn't eased his loneliness or his guilt. Thank goodness for Hallie. She had made him see the error of his ways, made him realize what a fool he'd been.

Hallie . . . He glanced down at her, his gaze moving

lovingly over her face and figure. She was wearing a burgundy-striped traveling dress and matching jacket, a white bonnet adorned with burgundy streamers, and white gloves. She looked like an angel, he mused as he brushed a bit of dust from her shoulder. He had never known anyone quite like her. She was the epitome of innocence one minute, a temptress the next. Sometimes she seemed like a child; sometimes she was all woman. And now she was his wife.

He gazed out the window again. What would Anna think about having Hallie for a mother? What would Cloud Woman and Iron Shield think when he showed up with a *washicu* wife?

At noon, they stopped at a way station to change the horses and grab something to eat.

Hallie shook the dust from her skirts, grateful to be on solid ground. The station was a big square building, with thick shutters and a heavy door.

Inside, the passengers sat down at a long trestle table. The midday meal, served by the station master's wife, consisted of jerked beef, jack rabbit stew, baking powder biscuits, and black coffee.

The baby had finally stopped crying and now sat on his mother's knee, gurgling happily.

Hallie smiled at the baby's mother. "How old is your little boy?"

"Almost ten months."

"He's a handsome fellow."

"Thank you." The woman shifted the baby on her knee. "We think so."

"I'm Hallie, and this is my husband, Clay."

"Pleased to meet you. I'm Lila McKary, and this is . . ."

"Don't be talking to the likes of them," the woman's husband said, his voice harsh. He looked at Hallie, his gaze filled with contempt. "She's no better than a damned squaw."

Clay started to rise. "Don't talk to my wife like that."

Hallie clutched at his arm. "Clay, don't."

McKary glared at Clay. "You ain't fit to sit at the same table as decent folks."

"Listen, you sonofa—"

"Clay! Don't, please."

He glanced over at Hallie, his anger dissolving in the face of the tears she was trying not to shed.

Hallie folded her napkin and placed it very carefully on the table. "I'm not hungry anymore." She stood up, her face white, her hands tightly clenched. "Would you take me outside, please?"

"Sure." Clay tossed his napkin on the table, took Hallie by the arm, and led her outside. "I'm sorry, Hallie."

She looked up at him, her expression mirroring her confusion. "I don't understand."

"I'm a half-breed, Hallie."

She frowned. "I still don't understand."

"Some people think half-breeds are worse than full-bloods. They hate me because of it, and I'm afraid some of them are gonna hate you, too, just because you're married to me."

"But that's so silly. They don't even know you."

"It's the way of the world, Hallie." Clay stared into the distance. "White men killed Summer and no one cared. As far as they were concerned, she was just another dirty Indian. My father was a white man, but it didn't matter. He was married to a Lakota woman, and that made him a squaw man."

"Oh, Clay, that's awful. I never realized how bad it must have been for you."

"Maybe you should go back to Green Willow Creek and stay with your old man."

"No!" She stood on tiptoe and kissed his cheek. "Whither thou goest, I will go," she whispered, "and where there thou lodgest, I will lodge: thy people shall be my people, and thy God . . ." Her voice trailed off. "You do believe in God, don't you, Clay?"

"Which one?"

"There's only one. It doesn't matter by what name you worship Him."

"I know, Hallie. I was just joshin' ya."

"You mustn't joke about such things, Clay," she replied solemnly. "It isn't fitting. Do the Indians believe in God?"

"Of course. They call him *Wakan Tanka.*"

"Wakan Tanka." She said it slowly. "I like the way it sounds. *Wakan Tanka.*"

"My people have a lot of beliefs you'll find strange and hard to understand. Some might even shock you, but they're very religious, Hallie. They believe that everything has a spirit; rocks, trees, the grass, that everything is alive, a part of the whole. In spite of what you may have heard, they aren't godless savages. They're decent men and women who love their kids and hate their enemies and just want to be left alone to live the best way they know how."

"How can a rock be alive and have a spirit?"

Clay glanced past Hallie to where the McKarys were boarding the stage. "We'll have to finish this up later," he remarked. "Looks like the stage is ready to roll."

The last thing Hallie wanted to do was sit in the coach's quarters with the McKarys, but there was no help for it. Lifting her chin and squaring her shoulders, she marched toward the coach.

Clay followed her, admiring the angry swish of her hips. She had grit, his Hallie, he had to give her that.

Settling her skirts around her, she sat straight and tall beside him. Uncomfortable didn't begin to describe the tension inside the coach. Lila McKary focused all her attention on her baby. Clay knew she had been embarrassed by her husband's earlier behavior. McKary had his hat pulled down over his eyes and was pretending to sleep.

Hallie stared out the window, her back straight. He wondered if she was having second thoughts about being married to a half-breed. He'd gotten used to having some whites treat him like dirt a long time ago, but it hadn't bothered him because he'd had the love and support of his parents and Summer. But Hallie had been gently reared by her mother and grandmother, and then she had been shut up inside a convent, protected from the ugliness in the world. He doubted she had ever heard a harsh word in her whole life until she met him.

They traveled without incident until dark, then pulled into another way station where they would take supper and spend the night.

Inside, Hallie removed her hat, jacket, and gloves. Hallie and Clay sat at one end of the dinner table, the McKarys at the other. The station master and his wife sat in the middle. They introduced themselves as Rita and Joseph Clancy. They kept up a constant chatter, relieving the silence and the tension between McKary and Clay.

As soon as the meal was over, Hallie asked Clay if they could go for a walk.

"Best stay close to the house," the station master admonished. "Been some Injun trouble hereabouts."

"What kind of trouble?" Clay asked.

"Oh, them damn Sioux been prowling around, stealing horses, burning barns, that kind of thing. They killed a friend of mine, Jack Mallory, last year."

Clay grunted softly.

"Anyways, just thought you ought to know."

"Thanks," Clay said, "we'll be careful."

They walked in silence for a few moments. Hallie jumped when she heard a coyote howl, then laughed self-consciously.

"You don't think the Indians will attack us, do you?"

"I don't know. It's a possibility, I guess."

"Why are they burning the stage stations?"

"Trying to keep people from crossing their hunting grounds, I reckon."

"But it's such a big country," Hallie said. "Surely there's room out here for everybody."

"I don't know about everybody, but as far as the Indians are concerned, it's getting smaller all the time. More and more people are coming West, killing the buffalo, hunting for gold." Clay stopped walking and turned Hallie to face him. "Do you want to go back to Green Willow Creek?"

"No. No, I want to stay here, with you."

"Are you sure?"

She nodded, her eyes wide, and he thought how lovely she was, with the moonlight shining down on her, limning her hair with silver.

"Hallie . . ." Helpless to resist, he bent his head and kissed her. It was like touching a spark to dry grass. Passion flamed between them. He wrapped one arm around her, drawing her close, while his hand slid down her back. Cupping her buttocks, he pulled her up hard against him.

"Clay, we shouldn't. Not here."

"I know." Lifting his head, he glanced around, searching for a place where they could be alone. "Come on," he said, taking her hand.

"Where are we going?"

"You'll see." He stopped at the coach and pulled two of the lap robes from beneath the seat, then led Hallie behind a wall of boulders located about fifty yards away from the station.

She felt a moment of apprehension as she glanced around. Even though the boulders formed a rough semicircle, shielding them from view on three sides, they were still out in the open, should anyone pass by.

Excitement and yearning replaced her apprehension as she watched Clay spread the blankets on the ground.

"Come here, darlin'," he said, and held out his hand.

Her heart began to beat faster as she moved toward him. She had been yearning to touch him, to be touched in return, all day. It was as if there was a spark inside her, a tiny ember that grew each time Clay looked at her, each time she heard his voice, until the spark became a flame, a fire that only he could quench.

And then his hand closed over hers and he drew her into his arms once more. His gaze moved over her face, and she thought she might melt from the warmth radiating from his eyes.

"Hallie," he murmured, his voice husky, "you're the best thing that ever happened to me."

"Am I?"

He nodded. "The very best."

She pressed herself against him, loving the way he looked at her, the feel of his hard-muscled body against her own. A joyful warmth flooded through her as he drew her down on the blankets and held her close. The need between them was vibrant and alive, yet he made love to her slowly, as though he wanted to savor every moment. Their clothing disappeared effortlessly, and she thought there was nothing more wonderful, more exciting, than the feel of his bare flesh against her own, the whisper of his breath fanning her cheek, the touch of his heated skin beneath her hand, the sound of his voice as he murmured to her, his voice thick with desire.

She lifted her hips to receive him, sighed with pleasure as his body melded with hers, until they were truly one flesh, one heart, one soul. She ran her hands over his arms, down his back, over his buttocks, reveling in the way his muscles rippled beneath her fingertips. He was hers, fully and completely hers, as she was his, would ever be his.

She gloried in the touch of his hands and lips, wishing she could be closer, closer, though how that could be possible was beyond her. She couldn't tell where she ended and he began. It was the most wonderful feeling in the world.

A wild tide churned within her and she bucked beneath him, wanting him closer, deeper, until the current swelled, swelled to near painful pleasure, and then slowly receded, leaving her feeling weak, and smiling.

"I didn't hurt you, did I?" he asked, his voice gruff.

"Never."

Resting on his elbows, Clay gazed down at her. There was no doubt that she had been well and truly pleasured. Her eyes glowed, her lips were swollen from his kisses, her breasts slightly reddened from the abrasion of his whiskers.

When he would have withdrawn, she wrapped her arms and legs around him. "Not yet."

"I must be heavy."

He was, but it was a wondrous weight. "Don't go."

With a sigh, Clay rested his forehead against hers, wishing they could stay as they were forever.

Minutes ticked by. Hallie began to shiver as the perspiration on her skin started to cool.

Clay kissed her nose, her cheeks, her lips, then rolled onto his side, carrying her with him. Reaching for one of the blankets, he drew it over the two of them.

"Shouldn't we go back to the station?" Hallie asked.

"Later. I want to hold you for a while."

She didn't argue. It was too wonderful to be in his arms. She gazed up at the sky. A million twinkling stars sparkled in the heavens, and the Man in the Moon seemed to be smiling down on them.

"God's in His heaven, and all's right with the world," she murmured, and fell asleep between one breath and the next.

Chapter 23

She woke to the sound of gunfire, and a woman's screams. Clay's hand on her arm kept her from rising.

"Stay down."

"What's happening?"

"The station's being attacked."

"Indians?" She looked up at him, her eyes wide with fear and horror.

Clay nodded. "Get dressed. Hurry."

He was pulling on his pants as he spoke, shrugging into his shirt, strapping on his gun belt.

Hallie stared at him, thinking of Mrs. McKary and the baby. "Shouldn't we try to help?"

"There's nothing we can do."

"But, Clay, the baby . . . they won't hurt the baby?"

"No." Clay peered around the boulder. He guessed there were about twenty-five warriors. Most of them were firing at the stage station while a handful of others drove the horses out of the corrals toward the plains. The barn was on fire. The station itself would be next.

Clay studied the warriors. He knew most of them. Zintkala Sapa seemed to be in charge of the raid. Clay glanced over his shoulder at Hallie. She was on her knees, her rosary clasped in her hands, her eyes closed, and he knew she was praying for the welfare of the people inside the station.

"Hallie. Hallie."

"What?"

"Stay here. I'll be back in a few minutes."

"What are you going to do?"

"Put a stop to this, if I can."

She scrambled to her feet. It was what she wanted, what she had prayed for, but she was suddenly afraid for Clay.

"How can you stop it? What are you going to do?"

"I know these men. It'll be all right." He kissed her forehead, then left the protection of the rocks.

A warrior near the corrals spotted him immediately.

Clay lifted one hand. *"Hou, kola."*

Thew warrior lowered his rifle. *"Cetan Mani,* is that you?"

"Han."

A grin spread over the warrior's paint-streaked face. "Come," the warrior said, "join us."

"No. I ask you to spare these people."

The warrior frowned. "Why? They are the enemy."

"No, they are friends," Clay said, though the lie tasted like ashes in his mouth. "I would not see them killed."

"Tell them to surrender their weapons, and we will spare their lives."

Clay nodded. "It shall be as you say."

The warrior shouted for the fighting to stop, and, after a few moments, a great silence settled over the station, a stillness broken only by the crackling flames and the crashing of the barn as it fell in on itself.

The warriors gathered together off to one side. Clay glanced at them over his shoulder, then walked toward the stage station.

"The fighting's over," he hollered. "Lay down your weapons."

"Go to hell, half-breed!"

Clay grimaced as he recognized McKary's voice. "Listen to me, you stupid bastard. The Lakota have agreed to spare your lives in exchange for your weapons and the horses."

"Why should we trust you? You're one of them."

"Where's Clancy?"

"He's dead. I'm in charge now."

"Then don't be a fool. If you don't surrender your weapons, the Lakota will burn you out."

"Let them try."

"Dammit, McKary, use your head. You can't win. If you don't want your child to be killed, or raised by the Sioux, you'll come out here with your hands up. There should be another stage along in a few hours."

"How do I know they won't shoot us when we step outside?"

"Because I'm telling you they won't."

There was a long pause. Clay heard the women pleading with McKary, and then the door to the station opened. The two wranglers came out first, their hands held high. One was bleeding from a wound in his shoulder.

Rita Clancy came out next, followed by McKary and his wife. Lila McKary's face was almost as white as her bonnet. She clutched her baby to her breast, and Clay could hear her sobbing quietly.

"Is that everybody?" Clay asked.

"Yeah," McKary replied curtly. "Now what?"

"Move away from the house."

The little band of survivors followed McKary. As soon as they were away from the building, three of the warriors went inside and ransacked the place. When the Indians had taken everything of value, two of the warriors tossed burning torches inside the front door.

Rita Clancy began to wail softly as her home, and her husband's body, went up in flames.

"We go now," Zintkala Sapa told Clay. "Come with us."

Clay nodded, and one of the warriors brought him a horse. Swinging onto its bare back, Clay rode behind the pile of boulders and offered Hallie his hand. "Come on, we're leaving."

"Where are we going?"

"To get my daughter."

Hallie's eyes widened. "These are your people?"

"Yep." He grabbed her forearm and lifted her up behind him.

Hallie wrapped her arms around Clay's waist and hugged him tight. "What about the McKarys and Mrs. Clancy?"

"They'll be all right. There should be another stage in a few hours."

"What if there isn't?"

"I've done all I can. The rest is up to them." Clay placed his hand over her forearm and squeezed it reassuringly, then rode out to join the Lakota.

Zintkala Sapa stared at Hallie in surprise, then, raising his rifle above his head, he shouted, "*Hoppo!* Let's go!"

The Indians raced away amid a cloud of dust.

Clay held his horse back. "Listen, McKary, if the line ahead hasn't been hit, they'll send someone to look for you when you don't show up on time. Just sit tight."

Rita Clancy looked up at him through eyes red and swollen with tears. "Thank you for your help."

"Yeah," McKary said gruffly. "Thanks."

"Good luck to you," Clay said, and wheeling his horse around, he set out after the Lakota.

They rode for hours. Hallie clung to Clay, her arms tight around his waist, her cheek pressed to his back. She had known they were going to find his people, to find his daughter, but somehow, *being* on their way to find the Indians was far different from actually *finding* them. They were wilder, more fearsome, than she had ever imagined. Their long black hair was adorned with eagle feathers and bits of fur, their faces were painted in frightful designs. Some wore buckskin leggings and vests, some wore almost nothing at all. She was certain that several of the horses had scalps tied to their manes.

She stared at the horse running alongside Clay's. There was a red handprint painted on the animal's shoulder, a long zigzag lightning streak ran from its rump down its hind leg. A white circle had been painted around one eye. There were several horizontal lines painted above the animal's nose.

She glanced over Clay's shoulder. There was a kind of beauty in watching the Indians race ahead of them across the prairie, and yet she couldn't help being afraid. Afraid of the Indians, of the unknown, of meeting Clay's daughter.

After what seemed like forever, the Indians drew rein near a shallow stream where they rested their horses.

Hallie stayed near Clay, aware of the curious glances sent her way. She smiled as he introduced her to the men he knew, tried to tell herself that, underneath all that war paint, the Indians were just ordinary men.

"It'll be all right, honey," Clay said.

She nodded, not wanting him to know how frightened she was.

"They won't hurt you. Zintkala Sapa is my cousin. The others are old friends. Don't be afraid."

The Indians watered their horses, then sat down to eat. Clay handed Hallie a piece of what looked like leather, explaining that it was dried venison. She stared at it, then took a bite. It tasted like leather, too, she thought, but she was too hungry to be finicky.

An hour later, they were riding again.

* * *

Clay felt an overwhelming sense of homecoming as they neared the village. This was where he had been born and raised, where he had grown to manhood, become a warrior, a husband, a father.

Excitement and dread pulsed through him as he thought of seeing Anna again. Would she even remember him? Would she be glad to see him, or angry that he had left her for so long?

The village first appeared as a dark silhouette rising up from the Plains, and then individual lodges became evident. He saw the horse herd grazing beyond the village. As they rode closer, he saw tendrils of gray smoke rising from several lodges, heard the sound of dogs barking, the laughter of children. A soft summer breeze carried the scent of roasting meat.

Men and women stopped what they were doing as the war party rode into the middle of the camp. Zintkala Sapa proclaimed their victory, then slid from the back of his horse. His wife came forward to take the reins.

Women and children clustered around the returning warriors, all talking at once.

Clay glanced around the village, looking for Cloud Woman's lodge. He felt his breath catch in his throat as he saw Iron Shield emerge from a lodge across the way. A moment later, Cloud Woman stepped outside. And then he saw Anna.

In that moment, he forgot everything else. She had grown in the last two years. She was tall for her age, slender as a reed. Her long black hair had a slight wave, her skin was the color of dark honey. She smiled at something Cloud Woman said, and the expression was so like Summer Rain's that Clay thought his heart would break.

"Anna." Her name whispered past his lips as he slid from the back of his horse.

"Where? Clay?" Hallie tapped him on the arm, trying to get his attention. "Clay?"

"What?" He looked over his shoulder.

He had forgotten she was even there. Hallie told herself it was only natural, that it didn't mean anything, but she couldn't help feeling hurt. "Nothing."

"I'm sorry, honey."

"Is that her, your daughter?"

Clay nodded.

"Aren't you going to go say hello?"

"You're not going to believe this," he said with a wry grin, "but I'm scared to death."

"I know just how you feel."

"Yeah, I guess you do at that. Well, come on, let's get it over with."

Taking Hallie by the hand, he headed for Cloud Woman's lodge.

Iron Shield was the first to notice Clay. He stared at him a moment, then frowned. "So, you have come back to us at last."

"Hello, Iron Shield." Because the Lakota practiced avoidance, Clay did not look at or speak to his mother-in-law, but he could feel her unfriendly gaze on his back before she ducked inside the lodge.

Clay blew out a deep breath, then focused his attention on his daughter. "Hello, Anna. Remember me?"

She stared up at him for several long moments, and then she nodded. "You are my father."

The lack of emotion in her voice tore at his heart. He glanced at Iron Shield, wondering what her grandparents had said about him in his absence.

"That's right, sugar. I've missed you." He clenched his hands to keep from reaching for her.

"Why have you come back to us?" Iron Shield asked.

"I've come for my daughter."

"She is our daughter now," Iron Shield said. He held out his arms, and Anna went to him.

"No," Clay said.

"Yes," Iron Shield replied firmly. "You turned your back on your people when you took our daughter and left us, and then you turned your back on your own daughter. We have taken her into our lodge to replace the daughter you took from us, and here she will stay."

Clay looked at Anna. "Is this what you want?"

Anna glanced up at Iron Shield, and then she nodded. Her dark eyes were solemn, her lower lip quivered ever so slightly.

"Who is the white woman?" Iron Shield asked.

Clay took Hallie's hand in his and held it tight. "She is my wife."

"Take your white woman and go back to the *wasichu*. You are not wanted here."

"This is my home," Clay said, keeping a tight rein on his anger. "The Lakota are my people. I will not leave until it pleases me to do so. I'll come to see you again, Anna."

She didn't reply, simply stared at him, her expression one of confusion.

"Come on, Hallie, let's go."

"Well," Hallie said when they were out of earshot of Iron Shield's lodge, "that didn't go very well, did it?"

Clay grunted softly. Not well was putting it mildly. He'd been a fool to think he could just ride in and take Anna from Cloud Woman and Iron Shield. They had been angry when he took Summer Rain away from the People, heartsick when they learned of her death. When he left Anna with them, they had both begged him not to go, but, caught up in his own grief, in an overwhelming need for revenge, he had turned a deaf ear to their pleas.

"What are you going to do now?" Hallie asked.

"Find us a place to stay."

Hallie glanced around, and then she grinned. "I don't see a hotel."

"Very funny. Come on, let's go see Zintkala Sapa. He'll put us up for the night."

Hallie stared into the darkness. Clay slept peacefully beside her, but she couldn't seem to relax. Earlier, they had eaten with Zintkala Sapa and his family. Hallie had accepted the food she was offered with a smile, though she couldn't help wondering exactly what it was she was eating. The meat had a wild, gamy taste. She was sure it wasn't beef and was afraid to guess what it might be. Someone had once told her that Indians ate their dogs and horses.

After dinner, Clay and his friend had sat beside the fire, smoking a pipe, while Zintkala Sapa's wife removed the dishes, then put her two children, a boy and a girl who looked to be about six and eight, to bed in the rear of the lodge.

She rolled onto her side and stared at Clay. She could see his face in the faint light cast by the dying embers of the fire. He hadn't said anything about his daughter, but she knew he was sorely disappointed in Anna's reception.

With a sigh, she wondered how long they would have to stay here, and how Clay was going to convince Anna's grandparents to give her up.

She jumped as she heard a growl outside the lodge, blew out a shaky sigh as she realized it was just one of the camp dogs, which were everywhere. She had never seen so many large, fierce-looking beasts in her whole life. Of course, there were smaller, cuter ones, too. She had watched the Indian children playing tug-of-war with some of them. It had reassured her, somehow, to see the Indian children laughing and playing. The boys had played with tiny bows and arrows; the little girls carried buckskin dolls with long black braids.

Rolling onto her back again, Hallie placed a hand over her stomach. She might be pregnant even now. The thought made her smile.

Moments later, she was asleep.

Clay woke early the following morning. He considered waking Hallie, then decided to let her sleep.

Rising, he left the lodge and walked into the woods, then went down to the river to wash up. On his way back to Zintkala Sapa's lodge, he paused in a secluded thicket. Years ago, he had started every morning with a prayer to *Wakan Tanka*. Standing there, he gazed heavenward. Slowly, haltingly, the words came back to him:

"Great Mystery, thank you for the beauty of this day, for the Sky People who give direction to our lives. Thank you for the earth, the mother of all that lives. Thank you for the rain that washes the earth, for the sun that gives us light, for the moon and stars who light our way in the darkness. Thank you for my brother, the buffalo, who nourishes our lives. Thank you for all my four-legged brothers, for all our relatives who swim and crawl and live within the earth. They teach us much, and give us much. Thank you for the mountains that endure forever, for the sacred ceremonies of our people that enlighten us and give us wisdom and understanding."

He paused a moment and then added fervently, "Thank you for Hallie, who has given my life new meaning, and for my daughter, Anna. Please help me to win her forgiveness." He blew out a deep sigh. "And forgive me, *Wakan Tanka,* for the lives I took in anger."

He stood there a moment more, his eyes closed, feeling a sense of peace wash over him, and with it, like a healing balm, a sense of forgiveness, the likes of which he had never known.

Murmuring a silent prayer of thanks, he hurried back to Zintkala Sapa's lodge, the urge to see and hold Hallie strong within him.

Hallie smiled as she accepted the bowl and spoon that Zintkala Sapa's wife offered her. For the tenth time in as many minutes, she glanced at the door of the lodge, wondering where Clay was. How could he go off and leave her here alone? She knew there was nothing to fear. Zintkala Sapa and his wife had treated her with kindness, but they were still strangers. Strangers who didn't speak her language.

Hallie glanced around the lodge. It was quite large, perhaps twenty feet in diameter. The floor was covered with robes. There were several backrests made of willow. Near the doorway, there was a small stack of firewood. Cooking utensils and pots were arranged beside the wood. Bedrolls were spread near the rear of the lodge, the children's on one side, the parents' on the other.

Zintkala Sapa's children ate quickly, then left the lodge. She could hear other children outside, calling to one another in play, the sound of two women laughing together.

Zintkala Sapa put his bowl aside, took up a long curved bow and a quiver of arrows, and left the lodge.

Hallie finished her breakfast. Smiling her thanks, she handed the bowl to Zintkala Sapa's wife, then stepped out of the lodge. Where was Clay?

She stood in the shade, watching the activity around her. Several men, all armed with bows and arrows, were gathered together a short distance away. She couldn't help wondering if they were going hunting, or to war. She saw women standing in small groups, talking and laughing, while others knelt on the ground, scraping hides. Other women could be seen hanging clothes over rawhide ropes stretched between two trees. A beautiful young woman with glossy black hair sat in the shade, a fat-cheeked baby at her breast.

There seemed to be dogs and children everywhere. In the distance, she could see a vast horse herd.

And then she saw Clay's daughter emerge from the trees, a load of firewood cradled in her arms. She really was a lovely child, Hallie mused, with her long dark hair and big brown eyes. She wore a buckskin tunic and moccasins. Bits of red ribbon fluttered from the ends of her braids.

Hallie gasped as two dogs ran in front of Anna, snarling over a bone. Anna tried to avoid them and in so doing, she tripped on a rock and the wood went flying from her arms.

Hallie ran forward. "Anna, are you all right?"

The girl muttered something Hallie didn't understand as she scrambled to her feet and began picking up the wood.

"Here, let me help you," Hallie offered.

Anna stopped what she was doing and turned to face the white woman. "I do not need the help of a *wasicun winyan*."

Hallie stared at her, momentarily taken aback by the girl's disdain.

"Anna, apologize to my wife."

Hallie glanced over her shoulder to see Clay striding toward them.

"Hiya!" No.

"Anna, apologize. In English."

Twin flags of color rose in the girl's cheeks. "I am . . ." She paused, obviously searching for the right word. "Sorry."

Clay grunted softly. He doubted she meant it, but at least she'd said the words. He quickly gathered up the wood she had dropped. "Are you all right?"

"*Han.*"

"Come on, I'll walk you home."

Anna didn't argue, but she didn't look pleased either. Without a word, she turned and headed for her grand-parent's lodge.

Cloud Woman was sitting outside the tipi when they arrived. She looked up and smiled when she saw Anna, but her smile quickly turned to a frown when she spied Clay walking toward her.

Clay piled the wood near the entrance of the lodge, then turned his back to Cloud Woman. "Anna, tell your grandmother that I want to take you for a walk."

Hallie frowned. "Why don't you tell her yourself? And why are you being so rude?"

"According to custom, a man and his mother-in-law never look at each other or speak to each other."

"Really?"

"Really. Anna, speak to your grandmother for me."

Anna relayed Clay's message to Cloud Woman.

"*Hiya,*" Cloud Woman replied.

"I'm your father. Tell your grandmother it is my right to speak to you alone."

"*Hiya!*" Cloud Woman repeated, more vehemently this time.

"Anna, tell her we won't be gone long."

Cloud Woman started to shake her head again, then shrugged. "Anna, do you wish to go for a walk with this man who calls himself your father?"

Anna glanced at Clay. He was sure she would say no, but after a moment, she nodded.

"Very well," Cloud Woman muttered. "Go."

They walked down toward the river. It was pretty there, all green and gold this time of year. When they reached a quiet place dotted with boulders and shaded by a handful of willows, Clay sat down on a flat-topped rock. Anna stood a short distance away, making an obvious effort not to look at him.

Hallie sat at the water's edge, trying not to intrude on what should have been a private moment. The tension between Clay and his daughter burned bright between them.

"Anna?"

Clay called his daughter's name softly, a wealth of yearning in a single word. Hallie knew the girl heard, but she refused to answer.

"Anna, look at me."

Reluctantly, the child did as she was told.

"Anna, I'm sorry I left you. I didn't mean to hurt you."

"*Unci* said you killed my mother."

"That's not true!" Clay stood up, his hands clenched at his sides. "I took her away from here because I knew that war was coming with the white man. I thought I could keep her safe. I loved your mother. I would never have done anything to hurt her. Or you."

"I don't believe you. *Unci* says the *washicu* can't be trusted. She says the *washicu* are nothing but liars."

"Your grandmother is wrong, Anna. Not all white men are liars. I would never lie to you."

"You did!" she cried. "You said you would come back soon! I waited and waited, and you never came back!"

"Anna, Anna." Dropping to his knees, Clay took his daughter in his arms.

"I hate you!" She pummeled his chest and face with her fists as she screamed the words. "I hate you!"

Clay didn't flinch as she struck him, didn't back away or try to avoid her violent outburst.

"I hate you!" she cried. "I hate you!"

"I know," Clay said softly. "I know."

"I hate you." She hit him again and again, releasing

years of loneliness and unhappiness and insecurity and then, with a long, shuddering sigh, she collapsed in his arms and began to cry, her slender shoulders shaking with the force of her tears.

Clay held her tight, his heart breaking for the pain he had caused her, for the years he had wasted seeking vengeance. "Anna, please don't cry."

"Why did you leave me?" she wailed. "Why?"

"I was hurt. Angry with the men who had burned our house and killed your mother. I wanted revenge." Clay gazed into her tear-swollen eyes. "You know what that is?"

Anna nodded.

"I know now that I was wrong, but at the time it was something I felt I had to do."

"Did you find them, those men who . . . who . . . ?"

Clay took a deep breath, wondering how much Anna remembered of what she had seen and heard that terrible day. Had she watched while those bastards raped Summer? "I found them, Anna."

She looked up at him, her dark eyes intense. "Are they dead?"

"All but one."

"I am glad they're dead," she said, and then she looked up at her father, her expression troubled. "Is it wrong for me to be glad they are dead?"

"No. They deserved to die for what they did."

"You should have taken me with you."

"I know. I love you, Anna. I never stopped loving you, or thinking of you. Can you forgive me for what I did?"

Hallie held her breath as she waited for Anna's reply.

"Anna?"

"*Unci said . . .*"

"Never mind what *unci* said. I want to know how you feel."

She stared at him, unblinking, for several moments. Clay held his breath, waiting for her answer, needing her forgiveness.

"I missed you, *ate*," she replied, and threw her arms around his neck.

Hallie wiped the tears from her eyes as she watched father and daughter embrace. They held each other close for several minutes. Tears ran down Clay's cheeks as he held his daughter, one hand gently stroking her back. Anna buried her face in his shoulder, her arms clasped around his neck as if she would never let go.

After a while, she drew back a little so she could see his face. "Are you going to stay here now?" she asked, sniffing back her tears.

Clay glanced at Hallie. "I don't know. I came here to get you and take you away with me."

"I don't want to leave *unci* and *tunkashila*."

"I know." Among the Lakota, if a child's parents divorced or were killed, a child Anna's age was allowed to chose who she wished to live with, but he didn't intend to give Anna a choice. She was his daughter, and her place was with him.

Clay wiped the tears from her cheeks, then kissed the tip of her nose. "We can talk about it later, okay?"

A smile spread over Anna's face. "Okay."

"I love you, Anna," Clay said, his voice thick with emotion. "I swear I'll never leave you again." He hugged her a long, long time and then he stood up. "Anna, this is Hallie."

"She is pretty," Anna said after staring at Hallie for several moments. "Not as pretty as Mama, though."

Clay grinned at Hallie, then shrugged.

"Of course not," Hallie said. "No one could ever be as pretty as your mother."

"Did you know my mother?" Anna asked.

"No, but you're very pretty, and I'll bet you look just like her."

Anna flushed at the compliment, and Clay breathed a sigh of relief. Maybe everything would work out, after all.

Chapter 24

Hallie ran her hands over the front of her dress, wishing she had a mirror so she could see how she looked. She had expected the doeskin tunic to feel rough against her skin, but it was soft and smooth, almost like velvet in its softness. She wondered what Clay would think when he saw her wearing an Indian dress and moccasins, her hair in braids.

"So," she mused, turning to face Anna. "What do you think?"

Anna lifted her shoulders and let them fall. "You really want to know what *ate* will think?"

"Yes, I guess I do."

"He will probably not even notice what you have on," Anna remarked with a grimace. "He looks at you like one who has had too much of the white man's firewater."

Hallie grinned. "Does he?"

"You know he does." There was a long pause. "He used to look at my mother like that."

"I'm not trying to take her place," Hallie said. "But I love your father very much."

"Does he love you, too?"

"Yes, but that doesn't mean he doesn't love you, too."

"He wants me to go away with him."

"I know."

"I don't want to go. I don't want to leave *unci* and *tunkashila*."

"There's a big world out there, Anna," Hallie said, echoing words Clay had once said to her. "Wouldn't you like to see it?"

Anna shook her head. "No," she said, "I like it here." But there was less conviction in her voice now. She slid a furtive glance at the dress and petticoats and black kidskin boots Hallie had just taken off. She had never seen such fancy clothes before, never seen such bright colors.

"Do you like it?" Hallie asked.

Anna shrugged. "Do all white women wear so much clothing?"

"Not always. Would you like to try my dress on?"

"Me?"

"Sure. Haven't you ever played dress-up? No, well, come on, it'll be fun."

Clay paused outside the lodge, listening to the sound of his daughter's laughter. She was so like Summer Rain, sometimes just looking at her broke his heart.

They had reached a truce, of sorts, in the last few days. He could feel Anna's resentment slipping away. Hopefully, in time, she would be able to forgive him.

Cloud Woman and Iron Shield watched him like hawks, certain he was going to grab Anna and run away like a thief in the night the minute their backs were turned, but he was willing to give Anna time to get to know him again, time to trust him, before he took her away from here. He grinned ruefully. If he couldn't persuade his daughter to leave with him, he just might have to steal her away, but he was determined it wouldn't come to that. He was in no hurry to leave. And whatever he decided, Anna was his daughter. The Lakota would not interfere in his decision.

He quirked an eyebrow as he heard Hallie say, "There, you look just like a princess."

Curious, he ducked inside the lodge.

Both females whirled around to face him.

"Hi, Clay."

"Hello, *ate*."

Clay grinned as he glanced at the two women in his life. Hallie wore a doeskin tunic and beaded moccasins; his daughter wore Hallie's traveling dress and boots.

"You're both looking very pretty this afternoon," he remarked.

"Thank you, sir," Hallie replied, grinning.

"Thank you, sir," Anna repeated.

"What do you think?" Hallie asked, pirouetting before him. "Zintkala Sapa's wife made it for me."

"Looks good on you."

"What about me, *ate*?" Anna asked. She twirled around in front of him, and almost tripped on her skirts.

"Like this," Hallie said. "You have to lift your skirts so you don't step on them."

Anna held up her skirt and whirled before Clay, careful not to step on the hem.

"You look like a fine lady, Miss Anna," Clay said. A quick image of his daughter as she would look in another ten years' time flashed before his eyes.

"I like this dress." Anna ran her fingers over the velvet sash at her waist. "If I go away with you, can I have a dress like this one?"

"If you want."

"Hallie said *washicu* dresses come in all the colors of the rainbow. Could I have a yellow one?"

"Sure, sweetheart."

"And cake? I remember Mama made a cake that was as sweet as honey." Anna looked up at Hallie. "Can you make cake?"

"I don't know how," Hallie said, and then she smiled. "But we could learn to make one together."

Anna toyed with a lock of her hair, her brow furrowed in thought. Clay held his breath, waiting, hoping.

"I think I would like to see the city." Anna glanced at Hallie. "Is she going to live with us?"

"Yes. Hallie's my wife. She goes where I go."

"Is she going to be my mother?"

"If you want her to."

Anna looked thoughtful. "If I don't like the city, will you bring me back here?"

"Yes."

"You promise?"

"Yes, I promise to bring you back here if you're unhappy living with me."

Anna frowned thoughtfully. "Would you bring me back here to visit sometime?"

Clay nodded. "Of course I will. Anytime you want."

A slow smile spread across Anna's face. "I think I would like to see the city, and wear pretty dresses. And petticoats. Can I have lots of petticoats with lace and yellow ribbons on them?"

Joy rose up inside Clay, bubbling and overflowing like one of the hot springs he had seen in the Yellowstone country. With a wordless cry, he stood up, lifted Anna in his arms, and twirled her round and round, until they were both laughing.

"I'll buy you as many dresses and petticoats as you want, sweetheart!" he promised.

"Can *unci* and *tunkashila* come with us?"

"I'd like that very much," Clay replied, "but I don't think *unci* will leave her sisters."

"Then I don't want to go."

Joy drained out of Clay like water through a sieve as he placed Anna on her feet. His first instinct was to tell her she would damn well go where he said she'd go and like it. Instead, he took a deep breath. Patience, he thought. You've got to be patient with her, convince her that you love her, that she can trust you. You've got to give Iron Shield and Cloud Woman time to get used to the idea that Anna is leaving. You owe them that much.

Anna slipped out of Hallie's dress and put on her own clothes. Without a word, she left the lodge.

The next day, Cloud Woman and Zintkala Sapa's wife erected a lodge for Clay and Hallie so they could have some privacy.

Hallie was amazed at how quickly the lodge went up. It took but a few minutes to set up the poles; the heavy cover was in place, pinned together, and staked down in another fifteen minutes or so.

In addition to erecting the lodge, the Indian women had provided two bedrolls, two backrests, and a few cooking utensils. They had dug a pit in the middle of the lodge, then Zintkala Sapa's wife had cleared a little space of bare earth behind the fire pit. With a last look around, the two women had left the lodge.

Hallie stood in the middle of the floor, a bemused expression on her face. She finally had a home of her own, and it was an Indian tipi out in the middle of nowhere. For some reason, the thought made her smile.

She turned at the sound of footsteps, felt her heart skip a beat and her blood grow warm as Clay entered the lodge. For a moment, she could only stare at him, wondering what had happened to the man she knew. Surely this tall, bronzed creature clad only in a deerskin clout and moccasins, his long hair falling over his shoulders, was not the man she had married.

Clay stopped in his tracks, surprised to feel himself blushing under Hallie's scrutiny.

"What's wrong?" he asked gruffly. "As long as you're wearing buckskins, I thought I would, too."

Slowly, Hallie shook her head. "Nothing's wrong. You just look so . . . so different."

"Is that good?"

"Oh, it's very good," Hallie murmured, her gaze moving appreciatively over his lean, well-muscled body. "Very good indeed."

Clay tossed his clothes and boots in the back of the lodge.

"You keep looking at me like that," he drawled as he dropped his gun belt near the doorway, "and I won't be responsible for what happens next."

"Really?" Hallie said, stifling a grin. "What might that be?"

"Come here, little girl," he growled, "and I'll show you."

She was grinning now; she couldn't help it. "Show me what?"

"It's a surprise."

"Really?" She batted her eyelashes at him. "Will I like it?"

"Oh, yes," Clay said. "I can promise you that."

"Is it something I've seen before?"

Laughing now, he walked toward her. "Come here, woman."

She went into his arms gladly, her hands eager for the touch of him, her lips hungry for his.

She was breathless when he drew away. Heart pounding with excitement and anticipation, she watched him strip off his clout and moccasins to stand gloriously naked in front of her.

Conscious of her heated gaze, he knelt at Hallie's feet and removed her moccasins. She giggled as his fingers stroked the bottom of her foot.

"Ticklish, hmm," he remarked. "I'll have to remember that."

He eased her tunic over her head, laughed softly when

he saw she was wearing her lace-trimmed chemise and ribbon-bedecked drawers underneath. Leather and lace, he mused, surprised she hadn't kept her corset on, too.

"Clay, what if someone comes in?"

"No one will come in," he said as he tossed her chemise aside. "If we wanted company, we would leave the door flap open. When it's closed, it means we want to be alone."

She hoped he was right, but then he was laying her back on the buffalo robes, kissing her as he eased her drawers over her hips, and everything else ceased to matter. There was no one else in the world, only the two of them. The furry robe was soft beneath her, a delicious contrast to Clay's hard-muscled body and urgent caresses. She ran her hands over him, delighting in the muscles that bulged and quivered beneath her fingertips, amazed that her touch could enflame him. It gave her an odd sense of power, to know that she could arouse him, that her touch could make him groan with pleasure.

He whispered her name, his breath hot against her cheek, as hot as the fire that burned between them.

"Clay, oh, Clay!" Just his name, again and again, as he fanned the flames of desire until they consumed her in a bright flash of ecstasy.

Later, lying in his arms, she thought how wonderful it was that she had found him. Who would have thought that a woman who was going to be a nun would find herself married to an outlaw? Surely Fate must have had a hand in their lives, to bring them together, to lead them to Green Willow Creek, and her father.

"What are you smiling about?" Clay asked.

"Us."

"What about us?"

She shrugged. "I think we were meant to be together."

"What makes you say that?"

"Think about it. We should never have met, but we did."

Clay grunted softly. "I guess that's true." If he hadn't been shot, he never would have ended up at the convent. He would never have met Hallie. He felt a catch in his heart at he contemplated what his life would have been like without her.

Hallie sighed. "I know it's true."

"You're not sorry, about not being a nun?"

"No."

"You don't mind staying here awhile, do you?"

She shook her head. She didn't care where they lived, as long as they were together.

The summer days blended together, one into the other. Surprisingly, Hallie felt more at home among the Lakota than she ever had at the convent. It didn't matter that she couldn't speak their language, or that their customs were strange. They were Clay's people, and she loved them. She learned that the little cleared space behind the fire pit was the family altar. It was called "a square of mellowed earth." Sweet grass, sage, or cedar were burned as incense to the spirits. The Lakota believed the smoke carried their prayers to the Great Spirit.

She quickly picked up a few Indian words and soon, using the words she knew and gestures that were universal, she was able to communicate in the most elemental way with Cloud Woman and Zintkala Sapa's wife when Anna wasn't there to interpret for her.

She thought it very strange that Clay was forbidden to speak to his mother-in-law, or that a man might not speak to his daughter-in-law. Try as she might, she could find no logic to explain such behavior.

She learned to cook over an open fire, though her

first attempts left much to be desired. Sometimes they laughed about the first venison steak she had roasted over the fire. It had been scorched on the outside, raw on the inside. Clay teased her, saying even the camp dogs wouldn't have been able to stomach that burnt hunk of meat.

But she learned quickly, and Clay was patience itself as he taught her Lakota ways. She found the customs and beliefs of the Lakota fascinating. She marveled that they believed that everything was alive, that everything had its own spirit and was therefore a part of the Great Mystery. They called the deer and the buffalo their brothers and whenever they killed an animal for food, they said a prayer, thanking the animal for giving up its life. Later, when they ate the meat, a small piece was put aside for the animal's spirit.

The Indians ate animals she would never thought of as food. Red squirrels, badgers, raccoons, muskrats, and skunks found their way into the Lakota cook pot, as well as prairie chickens, deer, and the buffalo. The buffalo was the main staple of the Sioux diet. Hallie had never seen one, but judging from the size of the robes she had seen, she decided they must be huge animals indeed.

Children were loved by the Lakota, and never spanked, nor were they permitted to cry. Hallie watched in fascination as a little girl cried, and when nothing her mother did seemed to help, the girl's grandmother began to cry, too, to keep her company. Young children were never told what to do; rather, they were asked. They were taught to love their parents, which, among the Lakota, meant more than just father and mother. Uncles were also called father, aunts were called mother, so that a Lakota child might have several fathers and mothers in the camp, all of whom gave love and instruction.

At the age of four or five, children were given their

own clothing and eating utensils, as well as a bed of their own, and were expected to care for these things, thus instilling in them a sense of responsibility. They were taught their place in the village by example, and were expected to imitate their elders.

Children were children, no matter what their color, Hallie mused as she watched the Lakota boys and girls at play. The little boys played with small bows and arrows; the girls played house with their dolls. She watched them mimic their elders as they played house and moved camp. The boys went hunting; the girls pretended to cook whatever the boys brought home.

Among the Lakota, the old people were revered for their wisdom. Many a night was spent in listening to the old ones tell stories of days gone by, passing the history of the People from one generation to the next, relating the stories of Coyote and *Iktomi*.

She learned that stealing from a member of the tribe was unheard of; stealing from an enemy was considered a coup.

The only thing that troubled Hallie was that the Indians believed in many gods. *Wakan Tanka* was the Supreme Being, but the Lakota believed there were other gods, as well. *Inyan,* the Rock; *Maka,* the Earth; *Skan,* the Sky, and *Wi,* the Sun. Each of these were considered to be gods. And there were more: *Hanwi,* the Moon; *Tate,* the Wind. Evil was personified by *Iya; Iktomi* was a deposed god. Hallie compared him to Lucifer, who had been cast out of heaven for rebellion.

She learned that the number four was a sacred number. There were four classes of gods; the Sun, the Moon, the Sky, and the Stars made up the four elements. There were four directions; time was composed of four parts: day, night, month, and year. There were four classes of animals: crawling, flying, two-legged, and four-legged. The life of man was divided into four stages: infancy, childhood, maturity, and old age. There were four great virtues: bravery, fortitude, generosity, and wisdom. Of these four, bravery was the most coveted, the most revered.

The Lakota considered the circle to be a sacred symbol. The Sun, the Moon, the Earth, and the Sky were round; the four winds circled the earth; life, itself, was a circle, thus Lakota lodges were round, and the camp circle was round, a constant reminder of the endless circle of life and death.

The strangest thing to understand were the men that clay called *winktes*. These were men who, for one reason or another, were unable to take on the responsibilities of men and chose to live as women. They dressed as women and followed feminine pursuits of tanning and quilling. Though these men were not abhorred, they were feared and treated with respect. They lived in their own lodges at the edge of the camp circle.

The most difficult thing to accept was the fact that there were men who had more than one wife, and that the women saw nothing wrong with this. Clay explained that if a man's brother died, he was expected to marry his brother's widow or widows. Some women urged their husbands to take a younger wife because it meant someone to share the housekeeping burdens as well as giving her status as the elder wife.

It was a concept Hallie found totally unacceptable, and one Clay assured her she would never have to embrace.

Iron Shield and Cloud Woman remained cool and aloof. It was obvious they loved Anna and were afraid of losing her. They tried to keep the girl away from Clay as much as possible, but Clay refused to be put off, and he spent every moment he could with his daughter.

Sometimes, seeing them together, Hallie felt a twinge of jealousy. Clay was her husband and she wanted to spend every minute with him, to be alone with him. She chided herself often, reminding herself that he hadn't seen Anna for two years, consoling herself with the knowledge that the nights belonged to her.

She reminded herself of that now as she sat at the river's edge, her bare feet dangling in the water, while she watched Clay teach Anna to swim.

They had left the village early that morning. Hallie had packed a lunch, and they had gone for a long walk, following the river. They had played a game, seeing who could find the most wildlife. Hallie hadn't done very well. The only creatures she had found had been a squirrel and a blue jay. Anna had spied a deer, a raccoon, and a beaver. Clay had pointed out a rabbit, a skunk, a red-tailed hawk soaring in effortless grace, and, off in the distance scratching its back against a tree, a grizzly bear.

She grinned as Anna and Clay began to splash each other. Watching the two of them together made her think about her own father. She was anxious to see him again, and she wondered how much longer Clay intended to stay in the village.

She shrieked as Clay splashed her.

"Come on in," he called.

"I can't."

"Why not?"

"Because I . . ." She felt a blush heat her cheeks. Clay was swimming in his clout; Anna was swimming in the nude. It seemed all right for them, natural, somehow.

Clay walked toward her, his dark eyes alight with mischief. "Come on."

Scrambling to her feet, she backed away from the shore. "No, Clay."

"There's no one to see you but us."

"Come on, Hallie," Anna called. "It's fun."

Clay emerged from the river. Water dripped from his body. His hair gleamed blue-black in the sunlight.

"Come on, Hallie," he coaxed.

"No." She shook her head. "I can't swim."

"You can't?" He cocked his head to one side, then grinned at her. "I'll teach you."

"I'm afraid."

"Of what?"

"Of the water."

"There's nothing to be afraid of." He held out his hand. "Come on."

She cast an anxious glance around to make certain they were still alone, then stepped out of her tunic and drawers and removed her moccasins. Clad only in her chemise, she put her hand in Clay's and let him lead her down the gentle slope into the river.

The water felt deliciously cool against her sun-warmed skin.

"Don't be afraid," Clay said. "Just relax, and trust me. I won't let you go."

She stared at the deepest part of the river and swallowed apprehensively. "Promise?"

"I promise."

"It's fun!" Anna called. "Watch me."

Anna had taken to the water like a fish. She swam upriver a short distance, then turned and swam back.

"You see?" Clay said with a grin. "Even a child can do it."

"All right," Hallie said, stifling the urge to stick her tongue out at him. "What do I do?"

An hour later, tired but able to swim, Hallie climbed out of the water and sat in the sun. Clay and Anna followed her a moment later.

"That was fun," Anna said. "Can we come here again tomorrow?"

"Sure," Clay said. "If Hallie wants to."

Anna plopped down on the blanket beside Hallie. "You want to, don't you?"

"I guess so."

"I'm hungry," Anna said. "Is there anything left in the basket?"

"No," Hallie said, "I'm afraid we ate it all."

Clay glanced up at the sky. "We should be heading back," he remarked. "We've got a long walk ahead of us, and it'll be getting dark soon."

"I'll race you back," Anna said.

"Well, let's get dressed first," Clay suggested.

"All right," Anna said, giggling behind her hand.

Using opposite corners of the blanket, Hallie and Anna dried off. Hallie took off her chemise and put it inside the basket, then put on her tunic, drawers, and moccasins.

Clay slipped a buckskin shirt over his head, pulled on his moccasins, then picked up a rifle he had borrowed from Zintkala Sapa.

"Are you ready, *ate*?" Anna asked, a challenge glowing in her dark eyes.

Clay shook his head. "I'm too old to run all the way back to camp," he said. "How about just a short race?"

Anna made a face at him. "How short?"

Clay pointed down the path. "See that log?" he asked, pointing to a large dead-fall about a quarter of a mile away. "First one there is the winner." He glanced over at Hallie. "You wanna get in on this?"

"No, you two go ahead."

Clay grinned at her. "Start us off, will you?"

"All right. Ready. Set. Go!"

Hallie shook her head as she watched father and daughter race down the path. They ran neck and neck for the first few yards, and then Clay began to fall back.

"I knew it. I knew he'd let her win." She turned away

to pick up the basket, chuckled softly when she heard Anna's scream.

"I guess she's really glad she won," Hallie muttered. When she heard the same scream again, she realized it wasn't a shout of victory. It was a cry of fear.

Staring down the path, she saw Anna standing near the log, and rising up behind her, seeming twenty feet tall, was the bear Clay had pointed out earlier.

Clay stood in the middle of the path, about three yards from his daughter. "Anna," he said quietly, "don't move."

"Ate . . ."

"It'll be all right, Anna. Just don't move."

Slowly, Clay raised his rifle to his shoulder.

The bear stood motionless, its pointy black snout sniffing the breeze.

"Anna, walk toward me. Slowly now. Don't be afraid."

Clay sighted down the barrel, every muscle in his body taut.

Anna took a step toward him, then another.

"That's right. Just keep walking toward me. Don't look back."

Hallie took a deep breath, her hand tightening on the handle of the basket. Quick images imprinted themselves on her mind: the taut line of Clay's shoulders. The way the sun made silver highlights on the bear's fur. The trust shining in Anna's dark eyes as she walked toward her father.

The grizzly make a soft snuffling sound as it dropped to all fours and climbed over the log. Lowering its massive head, it sniffed the ground where Anna had been standing.

"Ho, Matohota," Clay said. "I am *Cetan Mani* of the Lakota. We are brothers. Let there be no blood shed

between us this day. Go away now. We mean you no harm."

A low growl rumbled from the bear's throat as it rose up on its hind legs again.

Moving slowly, Clay grabbed Anna by the arm and thrust her behind him. "Don't move."

"Please," Hallie murmured. "Please."

It seemed like hours passed as she stood there, waiting, wondering why Clay didn't just shoot the bear and be done with it.

"Go home, *Matohota*," Clay said.

The grizzly stared at Clay for a long moment. Then, with a mighty roar, it dropped down on all fours and headed toward the woods.

Hallie's breath whooshed out in a sigh of relief.

With a sob, Anna wrapped her arms around Clay's waist.

Clay dropped to his knees and held her close. "It's all right, Anna. He's gone."

"I was . . . was . . . so scared."

"Yeah," Clay said. "Me, too." He glanced up as Hallie came running toward them.

"I've never been so frightened!" Hallie exclaimed. "Anna, are you all right?"

"Fine," she said, sniffing loudly.

"Why didn't you just shoot it?" Hallie asked.

"The bear is my brother," Clay replied. He smoothed Anna's hair from her brow, ran his hands over her shoulders, down her arms, assuring himself that she was all right. "When I sought my vision, I dreamed of a red-tailed hawk, and of a bear."

Hallie stared at Clay. She believed in visions and angels. Saints of old had seen them all the time, but she had never heard of anyone receiving a vision from a bird.

"Are you saying you had a spiritual manifestation? From a hawk?"

"Every Lakota male seeks a vision, Hallie. During a vision quest, a man learns which animal will be his spirit guide through life."

Hallie looked skeptical. "Sounds sort of . . ." She bit down on her lower lip.

"Heathenish?"

She nodded. "You don't really believe in that, do you?"

"I'm afraid so."

"But . . ."

Anna tugged on Clay's hand. "I want to go home."

"All right."

"I want to hear more about this vision," Hallie said.

Clay sighed. He had known Hallie would have a difficult time accepting some of the Lakota beliefs, but he was certain this was one part she would never believe. "We can talk about it later, if you want."

Hallie nodded. She stared into the woods, wondering if it was just coincidence that the bear had wandered off after Clay spoke to it, or if there really was some sort of mystical connection between Clay and the bear.

Chapter 25

The scene between Clay and the bear niggled at the back of Hallie's mind the rest of the day. Was it possible for a man and a beast to communicate? Had the bear really understood Clay's words? It seemed beyond impossible, almost ludicrous. But what if it was true?

Later that night, lying with her head pillowed on Clay's chest, she asked him to tell her about his vision.

Clay took a deep breath, his mind wandering back in time. "It was in the summer," he began. "I was sixteen and eager to be a warrior, to have a vision of my own. I rode up into the hills until I found a clearing in a grove of lodgepole pines. It was quiet there. Peaceful, with only the sound of the wind in the leaves.

"I traced a circle in the dirt, then stood in the middle of it. The medicine man had given me a small pouch of sacred pollen, and I offered a little to *Wakan Tanka*, to *Skan*, to *Maka* and *Inyan* and *Wi*, and then to the four directions. When that was done, I sang a song, and then I began to pray.

"I prayed all that day and into the night, but nothing happened. Dark clouds gathered over the top of the mountain. I wrapped up in a blanket and stared into the darkness and listened to my stomach growl."

"Didn't you take any food with you?"

"No. One goes fasting when he's seeking for a vision."

"Oh."

"I got up early in the morning and made my offering to the gods again, and then I prayed. And prayed. But nothing happened. I've got to admit, I was pretty discouraged when I went to sleep that night.

"It was raining in the morning. I stood there, cold and wet, and made my offerings to the earth and the sky and the four directions.

"I guess it was about noon when the rain stopped. I was thinking maybe I was wasting my time when the clouds parted and a rainbow spread across the sky. Biggest rainbow I'd ever seen. And then a red-tailed hawk just sort of dropped out of the rainbow and landed at my feet. At the same time, a big old silver-tip peered over the top of the hill."

"A silver-tip?"

"Grizzly bear."

"Weren't you scared?"

"Oh, yeah. I remember wishing I'd brought my bow, but I'd left all my weapons back in the village. My horse took one look at that grizzly and hightailed it down the trail."

"What happened?"

"Well, I stood there for what seemed like forever. And then the hawk began to speak."

"It talked to you?" Hallie asked in astonishment.

"Yeah. The hawk gave me one of its feathers and said I should take its name as my own. It told me that, because I have mixed blood, I would need the ability to fly fast from one world to the other. It also told me that if I remained true to my vision, I would have the strength of my brother, the grizzly bear, in times of trouble."

Hallie shook her head. "You don't believe that bear today was the same one you saw in your vision, do you?"

"No."

"Well, I don't know what to say. It's incredible, just incredible."

"I don't expect you to believe it."

"But I do. That's what's so incredible. Do you still have the feather? I'd like to see it."

Clay shook his head. "No." It had been destroyed the day Sayers and his gang killed Summer Rain. For a moment, he relived the anguish of that day, of coming home to find his home in flames, his daughter sobbing at Summer's side. And Summer ... he would never forget how she had looked, her body bruised and bloody, her eyes brimming with tears as she kissed Anna for the last time, the grief in her voice as she whispered that she loved him. He clenched his hands at his sides, fighting the same urge that had sent him after her killers two years ago, the urge to destroy the men who had murdered his wife and his parents.

"Clay, are you all right?"

"Yeah."

But he wasn't all right. She knew something was troubling him. She could hear it in his voice, feel it in the tension radiating from him like waves of heat off hot desert sand.

"Won't you tell me what's bothering you?" she asked.

"I don't want to talk about it, Hallie."

"I just want to help."

"You are helping, just by being here."

"You're thinking about her, aren't you? About your wife."

"Hallie . . ."

It was awful to be jealous of a dead woman, but she couldn't help it. He had loved his first wife, still loved her. How could she compete with a ghost?

Clay blew out a sigh as he drew Hallie into his arms. Holding her eased the anger in his heart. What was past was past. Nothing he did could change that. Summer Rain was gone, but Anna was still here, and she needed him. And Hallie . . . he needed her, needed her in ways he had never needed anyone else.

"Hallie, I . . ." His voice trailed off as he sought for words he could not find. He considered and rejected a dozen phrases, thinking they all sounded maudlin or contrite or just plain silly.

"What?" She closed her eyes, afraid he was going to tell her their marriage was a mistake, that he didn't love her, had never loved her.

Clay combed his fingers through her hair. "I'm glad you're in my life."

"Oh, Clay . . ." Tears stung her eyes as she wrapped her arms around him and drew him close. "I'm glad, too."

Living with the Lakota took some getting used to. There were no clocks. No bells called Hallie to prayers or to meals. The Indians ate when they were hungry and slept when they were tired. The men went hunting when they needed food. The women seemed endlessly busy— cooking, sewing, tanning hides, looking after their children. By comparison, the men seemed idle. It seemed to Hallie that Zintkala Sapa sometimes did little more than eat and sleep.

But there was little time to worry about it. Her days were filled with adventure. Zintkala Sapa's wife was teaching her to quill. Anna was teaching her to speak Lakota. And Clay was teaching her about love and life.

Hallie paused in the act of straightening their sleeping robes, a smile spreading over her face at the mere thought of him. He was the most wonderful man she had ever known. He made her feel beautiful, desirable. She basked in the love she saw in his eyes, reveled in the touch of his hands, his lips.

She couldn't seem to stop touching him, or wanting him to touch her in return. They had made love every night since they had been here, and it was always new and wonderful. Sometimes he coaxed her and aroused her until she thought she would expire with need, and sometimes he possessed her quickly, almost roughly. There were nights when he whispered sweet words, when he worshiped her with his kisses, and nights when he seemed driven by a need that was almost frightening in its intensity. She learned that love and desire had many faces, and that there was nothing to fear from any of them.

Tender or passionate, he was ever thoughtful of her needs, her desires. He learned what pleased her most, what made her smile with delight, what made her groan with pleasure. He had made love to her last night and again early this morning. She closed her eyes, remembering how ardently she had responded to him. He had assured her that it was perfectly natural for her to want him in return, but sometimes it embarrassed her, the way her body reacted to his touch, the wild yearning that rose up inside her, the need that bordered on desperation.

She glanced over her shoulder, felt her cheeks flush as the object of her thoughts entered the lodge.

"Hallie, Anna wants to know . . ."

Clay paused inside the doorway, his breath catching in his throat as he looked at Hallie. Startled, her eyes wide, her cheeks flushed, she looked young and vulnerable, like a doe poised to take flight. It took but one look at her expression to know what she had been thinking.

"What does Anna want?"

Clay shook his head. "I forgot." Crossing the lodge, he drew Hallie into his arms. "What were you thinking about when I came in?"

Her gaze slid away from his. "Oh, nothing."

"Hallie."

She traced the design on the yoke of buckskin shirt. "I was just thinking about a man I know."

"Do you like him, this man?" Clay asked.

"Oh, yes."

"Why?"

She lifted her gaze to his. "Why? Because he's tall and handsome and because he's a good man."

"Is he?"

She nodded solemnly. "He has a good heart, a good soul."

"A black heart," Clay muttered, thinking of the men he had killed, the rage that had engulfed him for the last two years. "A black soul."

"No. I couldn't love him so much if he was as bad as he thinks."

"Do you love him, Hallie?"

"You know I do. Does he love me?"

"Oh, yes. Never doubt it."

"Clay . . ."

"*Ate,* did you ask her? What did she say?" Anna burst into the lodge like a ray of sunshine.

Clay gave Hallie a squeeze. "I didn't ask her yet."

"Well, ask her."

"Anna wants to know if you'd like to go berry picking with Zintkala Sapa and her children."

"Of course I would," Hallie said, though what she really wanted was to spend the day in Clay's arms.

"Are you ready?" Anna asked. "They're ready to go now."

"Yes. Just let me get my moccasins."

"Well, I'll leave you two ladies to your berry picking," Clay said.

"What are you going to do today?" Hallie asked.

"I don't know. Maybe I'll see if I can't find a good piece of wood for a bow." He kissed Hallie, then ruffled Anna's hair. "Have fun you two."

"We will," Anna replied. "Come on, Hallie, they're waiting for us."

Clay grinned as he watched Anna practically drag Hallie out of the lodge. It pleased him beyond words to see the two of them together. He had been afraid Anna would resent Hallie, that she would never accept her, when, in fact, it was quite the opposite. And Hallie seemed to truly care for Anna.

"Life is good," he murmured. "Very good indeed."

Those words came back to haunt him three hours later. He was sitting outside his lodge, stripping the bark from a mulberry branch, when he looked up and saw Zintkala Sapa riding toward him.

"Come," his friend cried. "The Crow have taken our women and children."

"What?" Clay surged to his feet, the branch tumbling to the ground.

"*Han.* One of the herd boys saw it happen. When he tried to interfere, one of the warrior's struck him over the head."

"How long ago did this happen?"

"About two hours ago." Zintkala Sapa tossed a rifle to Clay. "*Hoppo!* Let us go!"

Clay vaulted onto the horse Zintkala Sapa had brought for him. It was a big-boned chestnut gelding, with a blaze face and one white stocking. Other warriors met them as they rode out of the village.

Anger boiled up inside Clay as he raced after Zintkala

Sapa. He had not found Anna only to lose her again! And Hallie . . . the thought of another man touching her filled him with rage. She was his, only his, and he would kill any man who dared defile her.

They rode to the place where the women had been abducted. Zintkala Sapa quickly located the tracks of the Crow ponies. Eight of them.

Moments later, they were riding north, toward the land of the Crow.

Hallie had never been so frightened in all her life. Not when Reverend Mother found Clay in the barn. Not when the grizzly had loomed over Anna. Fear was a cold hard lump in her belly, an iciness in her veins, a dull throbbing pain in the back of her head.

The rope that bound her wrists bit deep into her skin. The Indian mounted behind her held her close against him, his arm wrapped around her waist. He was the most frightening thing she had ever seen. Heavy black paint covered his face. His eyes were dark and cruel.

They had appeared out of nowhere. Almost before she knew what was happening, she had found herself bound and gagged and tossed on the back of a horse. Before she had time to fully comprehend what was happening, it was done.

She tried to see behind her, to make sure Anna was there, but she couldn't see anything but the Indian's broad chest and shoulders. She had hoped, for one crazy minute, that it was Clay playing some horrible joke, but one look into her captor's eyes had quickly stilled that hope.

She closed her eyes and tried to pray, but she couldn't remember the words, couldn't think of anything but the fact that Clay was certain to come after her and that he might be killed and she would never see him again.

Clay. Clay. Clay. The sound of the horse's hooves seem to echo his name.

Clay reined his horse to a halt, chafing at the necessity to let the horses rest. He paced restlessly back and forth, fighting the black rage that engulfed him as he imagined how frightened Hallie and Anna must be. The only thing that saved his sanity was the knowledge that the Crow had most likely taken them to be slaves. Had they been looking for scalps, the Crow would have killed the women where they found them.

He stared northward, his hands clenched at his sides. *I'm coming, Anna. I'm coming, Hallie. Be brave.*

"We will find them, *kola*."

Clay nodded at Zintkala Sapa. "I know."

"Let us ride."

They were never going to stop. Hallie sagged against the warrior riding behind her. Earlier, she had tried not to touch him but she no longer had the strength. Exhausted, thirstier than she could ever remember being in her life, her face burned by the relentless prairie sun, she slumped against him, no longer caring where they were going or what would happen when they got there. All she wanted to do was sleep.

It took her several minutes to realize the horse had stopped moving.

Opening her eyes, she saw that darkness had fallen and that the Indians had stopped near a shallow water hole. The warrior who had captured her slid over his horse's rump. Pulling her off the horse's back, he indicated she should sit down.

Hallie shook her head, her gaze searching for Anna.

The warrior didn't argue. Instead, he put his hands on her shoulders and forced her to the ground. He growled something at her and even though she had no idea what he said, there was no mistaking the warning in his tone. A few minutes later, he dropped a water skin in her lap, then handed her a thick piece of jerky.

But it wasn't food or water she needed. She needed to know Anna was all right. She needed to relieve herself.

Summoning her courage, she tucked the jerky in her sash, laid the water skin aside, and stood up.

The warrior was beside her instantly. As best she could with her bound hands, her cheeks flaming, she tried to make him understand what she needed.

He stared at her, uncomprehending, and then, with a grunt, he gestured toward a clump of underbrush. *"Kussdee."*

Hallie cowered behind the brush. With her hands bound, it was difficult to lift her skirt and lower her drawers, but she finally managed it. Never had she felt more vulnerable, or more exposed, than she did at that moment, squatting in the dirt while more than half a dozen men stood nearby.

"Hallie?"

"Anna! Over here." Hallie stood up, tugging at her drawers.

Anna ran to Hallie and threw her arms around her waist.

"Are you all right?" Hallie asked. "They didn't hurt you?"

"No. I'm all right. Are you?"

"Yes."

"I'm scared."

"I know." She was scared, too, but she tried not to show it. "I don't think they mean to hurt us."

"I want *ate*."

"He'll come for us, Anna. I know he will." She spoke the words, hoping to reassure the child, and herself. "Anna, let's pray."

"All right."

Hallie knelt, and Anna knelt beside her. Hallie thought a moment, but none of the prayers she had learned seemed right for their situation and so, for the first time in her life, she spoke from her heart, begging the God she had always believed in to spare their lives, to give them strength to endure, to protect Clay and the Lakota who were sure to come after them. She made the sign of the cross, then stood up.

"Do you think the *wasichu* god will hear us?" Anna asked.

"I'm sure of it, Anna. *Wakan Tanka* and my God are the same."

"Truly?"

"I believe so. I was taught there is only one God."

Before Anna could reply, the warrior who had captured Hallie strode into sight. Grabbing Hallie by the arm, he dragged her back to where the Indians had made camp for the night.

Anna followed. When the warrior pushed Hallie to the ground, Anna sat down beside her. *"Ina!"* she cried when the warrior tried to send her away. *"Ina!"*

The warrior frowned at her.

"Ina," Anna repeated. "My mother."

The warrior's eyes narrowed. *"Isahke?"*

"Yes," Anna said. "My mother."

With a grunt, the warrior turned away. There was a flurry of activity as the warriors made camp for the night. Two of them stood guard while the others ate, then rolled into their blankets and went to sleep.

Hallie glanced over at Zintkala Sapa's wife, who was sitting on the other side of the fire, her children close beside her. It was comforting, somehow, having them there, even though she couldn't communicate with them very well.

The warrior who had captured Hallie was one of the ones who kept watch. He had washed the war paint from his face, revealing a harsh countenance comprised of sharp planes and angles. There was no softness in that face, no pity. His hair was longer than Clay's and he wore it in braids wrapped with fur. A black-and-white feather painted with red stripes was tied in his hair near his left ear. He wore buckskin leggings, moccasins, and a buckskin shirt. A bear claw necklace circled his throat.

Feeling her gaze, he turned toward her. There had been a time when she wouldn't have recognized the look in his eyes. But no more. It was the look of a man who wanted a woman, a look that filled her with a deep and utter dread.

She turned her back to him.

"I'm hungry."

"What? Oh, of course you are." Hallie pulled the jerky from her sash and handed it to Anna.

"Don't you want some?"

"No, I'm not hungry."

Hallie could feel the warrior watching her as she took a drink from the water skin, then offered it to Anna. Knowing there was nothing she could do and no way, at the moment, to escape, she stretched out on the ground, determined to get some rest.

Anna curled up beside her. "I'm glad you're here," she whispered.

A moment later, the warrior who had captured Hallie covered them with his robe. Hallie glared up at him. She hated him for taking her away from Clay. She didn't want him to show her any kindness, didn't want to accept it, but she was too tired to argue. Tomorrow would be time enough.

Tomorrow, when she was rested, she would think of a way to escape.

Tomorrow. . . .

Chapter 26

Clay stared up at the clouds hovering low in the sky, every fiber of his being rebelling at the idea of stopping for the night. He'd never been any good at waiting. He wanted to be on the move, riding, doing something, anything, but there was no way to trail the Crow in the dark. He glared at the clouds. If it rained, it would wash out whatever tracks the Crow had left.

He swore, then swore again.

Zintkala Sapa looked at him from across the campfire. Although the warrior didn't understand English, there was no mistaking the angry tone of Clay's voice.

"We will pick up their trail at first light," Zintkala Sapa said.

"Unless it rains."

Zintkala Sapa studied the sky a moment then shook his head. "It will not rain. Be patient, my brother. We will find them."

Clad nodded, but it was hard to be patient when he thought of Anna and Hallie at the mercy of the Crow. There was a measure of comfort in knowing that they had each other.

Rising to his feet, Clay muttered something about checking on the horses and walked away from the others.

When he was out of their sight, he bowed his head. "I haven't prayed much in my life," he said quietly. "But

I've always known You were there. Maybe I don't deserve to be heard, but Hallie says You are always listening, so I'm begging You, please let them be all right."

He stood there in the darkness for a long time, listening to the wind as it whispered secrets to the pines, listening to the soft snuffle of the horses, the distant screech of an owl.

When he returned to the campfire, the men were all asleep save for the two standing guard. Clay nodded to them, then rolled up in his blankets. Arms folded beneath his head, he stared up at the sky. The clouds were moving south. Zintkala Sapa had been right again. It wouldn't rain.

They were on the move before first light. An hour later, they found the place where the Crow had bedded down for the night. Clay felt a rush of relief as he studied the ground. There, among the larger prints, he found one that could have only been made by a child. Anna. Thank God.

"We will catch them soon," Zintkala Sapa said.

Clay nodded. They were making good time. With any luck, they would catch up with the Crow before dusk and be on their way home in the morning.

Hallie stared back the way they had come. Was Clay out there somewhere in the shadows of the night? She had been so certain he would come after them, so certain that he would be there by now. But it was almost dusk and there had been no sign of anyone in pursuit. Maybe he wasn't coming . . . She shook the thought aside. He would come. It was too soon to give up hope. Clay would come.

She smiled reassuringly at Anna. Clay would come.

* * *

Clay watched Hallie and Anna bed down for the night. As far as he could tell, they hadn't been mistreated. It had taken longer than expected to get close to their quarry. The Crow, knowing they would be followed, had doubled back on their tracks several times, but Zintkala Sapa was the best tracker the Lakota had and he had not been fooled.

And now they were in position, waiting only for the Crow to settle down for the night.

Clay took a deep breath in an effort to calm his nerves. Waiting was always the hardest part. If all went as planned, the battle would be quickly over.

Crouched in the darkness, his hand fisted around a rifle, he closed his eyes and offered a quick prayer to *Wakan Tanka,* praying for strength in battle, for the courage to die well if he were killed. He prayed for the safety of his wife and daughter, for victory over their enemies.

A hand on his shoulder told him it was time. He nodded that he understood, and rose to his feet.

Hallie rolled onto her back and stared up at the sky. Try as she might, she couldn't sleep, couldn't shake the feeling that Clay was close by.

She glanced over at Anna and as she did so, she saw a shadow move through the darkness. Her heart slammed into her throat as that shadow was followed by another. She heard a muffled cry, followed by a dull thud, and then a sharp piercing cry of warning.

Instinctively, she pulled Anna into her arms and held her tight, trying to shield the child's body with her own, as the battle exploded all around them.

It looked like a scene out of Hell, she thought, watching the dark bodies struggling together in the flickering light of the dying fire. There was the sound of flesh striking flesh, the sharp retort of a gunshot, the acrid scent of gunsmoke.

She saw Clay fighting with the warrior who had captured her, and everything else seemed to fade away. She forgot about Anna, forgot everything else as she watched the two men who were locked together in a silent, deadly struggle.

Abruptly, they broke apart, and she saw that each man held a knife. They circled slowly for a moment, then came together, blades slicing through the air. When they parted again, there was a fine line of crimson across Clay's left shoulder.

Panting hard, the two men faced each other again. Only then did Hallie notice that, except for Clay and this one Crow warrior, the battle was over. A quick glance showed the bodies of the dead lying where they had fallen, grotesque in the moonlight. Zintkala Sapa and his warriors stood in a loose semicircle, watching the fight. Why didn't they stop it?

Time and again Clay and the Crow warrior came together, and each time they parted, there was fresh blood on one of them.

Anna squirmed in her arms. "Hallie, what's happening?" she asked, her face muffled against Hallie's breasts.

"Don't look."

"Why not?"

"Just don't."

But Anna wriggled out of Hallie's grasp, her eyes widening when she saw her father. "*Ate,*" she whispered, her voice filled with horror.

"Be still!" Hallie admonished, grabbing the child's arm when she would have rushed forward. "Don't distract him."

The two men came together one last time. Hallie leaned forward, her hands clasped tightly together.

Please, please, please . . . please don't let him die. . . .
Don't take him away from me . . . please. . . . Anna
needs him. . . . I need him. . . .

"No!" Hallie covered her mouth with her hand, stifling her own cry of horror when the Crow knocked Clay off balance. As Clay stumbled backward, the Crow shouted exultantly. Certain of victory, he lunged forward, his knife poised to strike.

Knowing he couldn't regain his balance, Clay went limp. He struck the ground, rolled quickly to the right, and brought his knife up in a quick powerful thrust. Helpless to stop himself, the Crow pitched forward, his own momentum driving Clay's blade deep into his chest.

It was over.

Hallie scrambled to her feet and ran to Clay, her gaze moving over him. There seemed to be blood everywhere, but she couldn't tell how much of it was his and how much belonged to the Crow.

Clay gripped Hallie by the shoulders, needing to touch her. "Are you all right?"

"I'm fine. Are you?"

"I'll be all right."

"Ate, ate!"

Clay knelt, wincing as Anna threw herself into his arms. "I knew you would come for us. I knew it!"

"Anna, we need to look after your father's wounds."

Anna hugged her father another moment, then let him go. "Did I hurt you?"

"No, sugar, I'm all right."

"Well, some of that blood is yours," Hallie said. "We need to clean it up."

Clay sat on one of the buffalo robes while Hallie tended his wounds. Though he had sustained several cuts, none of them were serious.

Zintkala Sapa and his men went through the Crow

camp, taking supplies and weapons. One Lakota had been killed in the fight, two others had been wounded. All the Crow were dead.

Hallie turned away, gagging, when she saw one of the warriors take a Crow scalp.

Clay put a finger under her chin. "Hey, are you all right? You look like you're gonna faint."

She pointed to the warrior. "How can he do that?" She shuddered. "*Why* is he doing that?"

Clay blew out a sigh. How to explain the Lakota custom of taking scalps? Among the Plains tribes, warfare was a way of life. A man gained honor and recognition on the battlefield. A scalp was proof that he had slain the enemy. A Lakota warrior took pride in his accomplishments on the battlefield. He painted his victories on the dew cloth of his tipi. When he rode to battle, he painted coup marks on his horse so that the enemy would know of his bravery. A rectangle meant the rider had led a war party, a handprint meant he had killed an enemy in hand-to-hand combat. A warrior gave the scalps he took to his women, who painted their faces black and sang of his bravery while dancing with the scalps suspended from a pole. The taking of scalps, counting coup, stealing the horses, these were worthy pursuits and deserving of praise among the Lakota.

"Clay?"

"Can't we discuss it later, honey?" he asked wearily.

"I guess so," she replied, but something in her tone told him she would never bring it up again, and maybe it was just as well. She had been raised in the Church. He wasn't sure there was anything he could say that would make it acceptable. Most whites thought the practice of scalping barbaric, which he had always thought odd, since there were white men who paid money for Indian scalps.

A short time later, they rode away from the Crow

camp. Hallie didn't look back, didn't like to think of the
bodies left behind, unburied, didn't like to think that
Clay had killed a man because of her.

Later than night, lying beside him, she knew she
wanted to go home, wanted to see her father again.
Surely Clay would understand.

It was midafternoon two days later when they returned
to the Lakota camp. It had been a long two days.

Clay glanced over at Hallie as they rode into the village. The events of the last few days had left her emo-
tionally drained. She hadn't said anything, but he had the
feeling she wanted to go back to Green Willow Creek,
that she needed to be with her own people, to see her
father again. And he couldn't blame her.

Cloud Woman and Iron Shield were among those who
clustered around them. Anna had been riding double
with Clay. He didn't object when Iron Shield lifted her
from the back of the horse and held her tight. Cloud
Woman met his gaze. She stared at him for a long
moment, then, just before she turned away, she smiled
at him. Clay smiled back, though he was not smiling on
the inside. He had come here with the sole intent of
taking Anna away from her grandparents. He hadn't
stopped to think about how that would affect Iron
Shield and Cloud Woman. Anna was his daughter, not
theirs. She belonged with him. But she belonged to
them, too. Family ties ran deep among the Lakota.

He watched Anna walk away with her grandparents,
relating the details of her ordeal, and knew he couldn't
take her against her will. She would have to be the one
to decide whether to stay with her grandparents or go
with him.

Dismounting, he helped Hallie from her horse.

"What's wrong, Clay?" she asked.

"I was just thinking about Anna, and how hard it's

going to be for her to leave here if she decides to go
with me." He tethered their horses to the picket pin outside the lodge, then followed Hallie inside. "And I was
thinking about you, and how anxious you must be to go
home, and wondering how I was going to make everybody happy."

"I am happy," Hallie said.

"Are you?"

"Of course. Why wouldn't I be?"

"What if Anna doesn't want to leave here?"

"What do you mean?"

"I can't take her if she doesn't want to go. I thought I
could, but . . ." He shrugged. "I can't. She loves her
grandparents. God knows they've always been there for
her. I can't take her away from here if she doesn't want
to go."

"I don't understand."

"I can't take her against her will, Hallie, and I can't
leave her."

"Oh."

"Where does that leave us?"

Wither thou goest, I will go . . . The words popped
into her mind, as loud and clear as if she had spoken
them aloud. She had said them to Clay not long ago.
Had she meant them? Would she truly be happy to stay
here, with his people, for the rest of her life?

"Hallie?"

"I don't know."

"Think about it, okay? I'll be back in a little while."

"Where are you going?"

"I need some time alone."

Hallie watched him swing effortlessly onto his
horse's back and ride out of the village. She felt a con-
striction in her chest, an ache in her heart, as if he had
taken part of it with him.

Once he cleared the village, Clay urged his mount

into a lope, then gave the horse its head, content to let the big chestnut go where it would. The horse ran tirelessly, long legs eating up the miles.

Pushing everything else from his mind, Clay lost himself in the joy of riding across the Plains, of the feel of the wind in his face, the power of the horse beneath him. A jackrabbit cut across the chestnut's path and the horse crow-hopped for a few yards, then lined out in a dead run.

Hair whipping across his face, Clay leaned over the gelding's neck and urged the horse to go faster. It was madness to race across the Plains this way, when one false step could mean disaster, but he rode on, heedless of the risk.

The chestnut was breathing hard when it began to slow. Clay pulled the horse to a stop beneath a scrawny cottonwood near a narrow stream. Dismounting, he stripped the blanket from the chestnut's back, then gathered a handful of scrub grass and began to rub the horse down. When he was finished, he walked the chestnut along the narrow creek until the horse had cooled out.

Kneeling, he drank his fill from the stream, then let the horse do the same.

He sat there for over an hour, staring at the slow-moving stream, while the horse grazed nearby.

Hallie wanted to go home.

Anna wanted to stay with her grandparents.

What did he want?

He didn't want to let Hallie go. He loved her desperately, needed her goodness, her sweetness, but he couldn't leave Anna again.

"Help me, *Wakan Tanka,* show me what to do. . . ."

Stretching out on the grass, he gazed up at the clear blue sky. Time lost all meaning as he lay there. The sound of the stream faded away, and he felt as though he were caught between heaven and earth. And then he heard the swish of wings and he saw a red-tailed hawk soaring effortlessly overhead.

Ho, brother, the hawk called, *I have blessed you with my name, with wisdom and courage. Only have faith in yourself, and in your woman, and all will be well.*

Suddenly, the hawk plunged to earth, straight and true as an arrow shot from a bow. Clay marveled at the bird's speed and grace, felt a sudden apprehension as the bird arrowed toward him. Clay swore as the eagle plummeted closer, only to pull up at the last moment. And then, as if it had never been there, the eagle was gone.

Sitting up, he took a deep breath. He would have thought he'd imagined the whole thing if not for the feather resting on the ground beside him.

It was near dark when he rode into the village. Hallie was standing outside the lodge, a blanket draped around her shoulders, waiting for him.

"Clay!" She threw herself into his arms as soon as he dismounted. "Where have you been? I've been so worried!"

Dropping the reins, he wrapped his arms around her and held her tight.

"Are you all right?" Her gaze moved over his face, searching, anxious.

"I'm fine, Hallie."

"Ate."

Clay glanced over Hallie's shoulder to see Anna standing near the door of his lodge. "Hi, sugar," he said quietly. "I didn't see you there."

"We've been waiting and waiting for you."

"Have you? I'm sorry."

"Where did you go?"

"I needed some time alone."

"Are you hungry?" Hallie asked. "I kept some soup warm for you."

"Yeah, thanks."

Inside the lodge, he sat beside the fire, watching Hallie as she filled a bowl with rabbit stew. He never tired of watching her. She moved with a kind of quiet grace and serenity. He had noticed the other nuns moved the same way, never seeming to hurry yet accomplishing much. Quiet hands, he thought, remembering how the good sisters kept their hands out of sight unless they were working. When they walked down a hallway, they kept close to the walls, their skirts hardly swaying, their heads bowed. He had never heard any of them say a cross word, or lift their voices in anger.

Hallie handed him a bowl, then sat at his right. Anna was seated on his left, a rag doll cradled in her lap. He realized with a shock that it was the same doll he had brought her from town that fateful day. It seemed a lifetime ago.

"Hallie wants to go home," Anna said.

Clay nodded. "I know."

"I don't want her to go."

"Me, either, but she misses her father. He was hurt when we left. I'm sure she wants to go and make sure he's all right."

"Her father left her, too."

Clay nodded, unable to speak past the lump rising in his throat.

"She said he explained why he had to go, and she forgave him."

Clay put the bowl aside, his appetite gone.

"She said sometimes grown-ups do things that are hard for children to understand."

Clay nodded again, wondering what Anna was leading up to.

"Are you going to take Hallie back to the city?"

"Yes. I know I promised I'd never leave you again, so I guess you'll just have to go with me to take her home. Is that all right with you?"

Anna nodded, her dark eyes wide. "Hallie said I'd like it in town. She said I could have lots of pretty dresses, and she said if it was all right with you, that maybe I could spend summers here, with *unci* and *tunkashila*."

Clay glanced over at Hallie. "I think that's a splendid idea," he said, and wondered why he hadn't thought of it himself.

"Hallie wants to leave right away."

"Does she?"

Anna nodded. "Can we leave day after tomorrow?"

"If you want."

"I want to spend tomorrow with *unci* and *tunkashila*."

"Sure. I guess I'd better go have a talk with Iron Shield."

"I already told him," Anna said.

"You did? What did he say?"

"He wasn't very happy at first, but I told him it would be all right, that I wanted to go to the city. Hallie said I should learn to read and write, and that if I didn't want to go to school, she would teach me."

"She did, huh?" Clay grinned at Hallie. "Sounds like you two worked everything out while I was gone."

"Pretty much," Hallie said. "I told Anna that she was part-white and she needed to know about that part of her heritage so she could decide where she wanted to live."

"I see."

"And I told her how I'd always wanted a little girl of my own, and how unhappy I would be if she stayed here, and how unhappy you would be if you had to choose between us."

"Who would you choose, *ate*?" Anna asked solemnly.

Clay took a deep breath, hoping that Hallie would

understand. "You, of course. You're my daughter, my blood. I was wrong to leave you before. I never will again."

"Papa!" With a cry, Anna threw her arms around Clay's neck. "I love you, Papa!"

"And I love you." Feeling like he could laugh and cry at the same time, he swung Anna round and round until they were both dizzy and breathless. Then, holding out his hand, he said, "Come here, Hallie."

"We're a family now, aren't we?" Anna asked.

"That we are, sugar, that we are." Clay nuzzled Hallie's neck. "I love you," he whispered. "More than you can imagine."

"And I love you."

"Thank you for this," he murmured. He spoke the words aloud for Hallie, but repeated them silently in his heart, hoping that his spirit guide, the hawk, would hear.

They spent the following day getting ready to leave. Zintkala Sapa insisted Clay keep the chestnut gelding, and gave him a fine-boned red roan Appaloosa mare for Hallie, and a pretty little dun mare for Anna. His women immediately named their horses—Hallie called the roan Candy because, she said, she was so sweet. Anna called her mare Hitonkala because she was the color of a mouse.

He had shook his head when Anna asked him what he had named the chestnut. Except for the warhorse he'd ridden when he was a young man, he had never named any of his horses.

"I'll think of something," Anna said, and skipped off to help Hallie finish packing.

On the day of their departure, Cloud Woman prepared several parfleches of food for their journey; Iron Shield insisted Clay take his rifle.

Clay had expected Anna to cry when it came time to

leave, but there were no tears in her eyes as she kissed her grandmother and hugged her grandfather. Dark eyes shining with excitement, she promised them she would be back next summer.

Clay helped Hallie mount her horse, lifted Anna onto the dun's back.

"Travel in safety, my brother," Zintkala Sapa said. "Come back and see us soon."

"Pilamaya," Clay replied. "Look after Cloud Woman and Iron Shield for me, will you?"

"Han. Do not worry about them."

Clay nodded, and it was time to go. All their good-byes had been said.

Chapter 27

Clay had expected traveling across country with Hallie and Anna would be a lot more difficult than it was. Surprisingly, they made good time. Anna had learned to ride before she was two; Hallie never complained, no matter how many hours they spent in the saddle.

Both of his girls seemed to regard the journey as a lark, neither one truly realizing the dangers facing a man, a woman, and a child riding across the Plains alone. Hallie was constantly thinking up games for them to play to pass the time. Who could find the first animal, the first bird, the first red flower, the first water hole; who would need to stop first to rest. She sang hymns and taught them to Anna. She tried to get Clay to sing, too, but he refused, declaring that he couldn't carry a tune if she gave him a bucket to put it in.

Hallie told Anna fairy tales and related funny things that had happened at the convent, like the time she had accidentally put salt in the sugar bowl, and the time she had tried to help Sister Dominica in the garden and pulled a whole row of tomato seedlings, thinking they were weeds.

Anna was ready for bed as soon as they ate dinner and was soon asleep, giving Hallie and Clay a chance to spend some time alone.

Hallie couldn't get over the way she yearned for

Clay's touch, the way she came alive in his arms. She thought about him every minute of the day, looking forward to the time when they could be alone, when she could crawl into his arms and hold him and kiss him. He had only to look at her, and she burned to feel his hands caressing her, yearned to hold and touch him in return. She wondered if there was something wrong with her, some terrible malady that made her so desperate to be near him. She felt the need to touch him all the time. Some nights it was all she could do to wait until Anna was asleep.

She had mentioned it once to Clay. It had taken all the courage she possessed to ask him if it was normal for her to want him all the time. He had given her a hug and assured her it was perfectly natural for her to want him that way, and that he felt the same way about her.

They traveled without incident, seeing no one, red or white. Hallie had assumed they would take a stage back to Green Willow Creek, but Clay decided to bypass the stage stations. Hallie didn't argue, the memory of the Indian attack still vivid in her mind.

Anna was fairly bubbling with excitement when they reached the outskirts of Green Willow Creek. Hallie had told her about the mercantile and the sweet shop and Anna couldn't wait to have a new dress—a yellow one, *Ate,* you promised—and buy a bag of candy. She remembered candy. Clay had always brought her back a small bag of peppermint sticks on the few occasions when he had gone into town.

Clay insisted they wait for nightfall before they rode into town. The fewer people who saw them, the better. He hadn't forgotten that he was a wanted man, or that Will Sayers might still be in town, looking for revenge.

Clay and Hallie both changed clothes before they rode into town. Hallie was surprised at how restricted she felt wearing her petticoats, dress, shoes, and stockings. The

Lakota women had the right idea, she thought as she folded her doeskin tunic and placed it in her saddlebags along with her moccasins.

They left their horses at the livery. Jax, the owner, seemed surprised to see them. Clay checked on Romeo and Juliet, pleased to see they had been well cared for in their absence.

"We should probably take the horses back to the convent," Hallie remarked as they left the livery.

"That might be difficult," Clay said as he took Anna's hand. "I'm in no itching hurry to go back to Bitter River, but I've been thinking maybe I should send Mother Matilda some money so she could replace them."

Hallie smiled at him, pleased with his decision.

The stores were all closed up for the night. Clay kept his head down when they passed by the saloons, hoping no one would see and recognize him.

Frank McIntyre was bent over his desk, frowning at the paperwork spread before him, when they entered the jail. "Be with you in a minute," he said, not looking up.

"Take your time, Papa," Hallie said.

McIntyre's head jerked up and a smile spread over his face. "Hallie!" Surging to his feet, he rounded the desk and swept her into his arms.

Hallie laughed, pleased and relieved to see that he was fully recovered.

McIntyre gave her one last hug, then released her. "So," he said, looking at Anna, "who's this pretty girl?"

"This is my daughter, Anna," Clay said. "Anna, this is Hallie's father."

Anna smiled shyly at McIntyre. *"Hau, tunkashila."*

McIntyre lifted one brow. "Doesn't she speak English?"

Anna blushed and pressed closer to Clay. "Hello, Grandfather," she said.

McIntyre grinned at her. "I'm glad to meet you, Miss Anna." He looked up at Clay. "So, what are you planning to do now? You can't stay in town. Much as I'd love to have you here, it's not safe. Too many people know who you are."

Clay nodded. McIntyre was right. "Any trouble since we left?"

"Nope. Been real quiet, except . . ." McIntyre took a deep breath. "Jake over at the Three Queens said he thought he saw Will Sayers skulking around down by the livery the other night."

Clay swore softly. He could only think of two reasons why Will would risk coming to town: either Bob had died and he was still looking for vengeance, or he was scouting for Bob. Neither possibility was particularly encouraging.

"Might be a good idea for you to lay low while you're here," McIntyre suggested. "Why don't you all go over to the house? I'll lock up here and see you at home in a half hour or so."

Clay nodded. McIntyre was right. The fewer people who knew he was in town, the better.

Hallie gave her father a quick hug, then followed Clay and Anna out of the office.

"What do you think it means, Will Sayers coming back here?"

Clay shook his head. "I'm not sure. Nothing good, I'll wager."

"I was hoping we could stay here for a while," Hallie remarked as they walked down the alley that led to her father's house.

"I know, honey, and I'm sorry."

Anna tugged on Clay's hand. "When can I get my new dress?"

"Tomorrow, sugar," Clay said. "Hallie can take you shopping."

Anna smiled up at him, her eyes shining with anticipation. "And buy candy?"

"Sure."

Anna skipped ahead, unaware of the tension between the adults.

"You're worried, aren't you?" Hallie said, taking Clay's hand.

He didn't deny it. Before, he'd had no one to worry about except himself. Eaten up with bitterness and the relentless desire for revenge, he hadn't cared about anything else, hadn't cared if he lived or died. Not too long ago, he would have gone looking for Bob Sayers with the same single-minded intent he had hunted the rest. But not now. Dying was no longer as appealing as it had once been, not now, when he had everything to live for.

He glanced at Hallie, grateful for the changes she had wrought in his life.

"Clay?"

He squeezed her hand. "It'll be all right, sweetheart. Don't worry."

Clay sat in the deep shadows on the porch of Frank McIntyre's house. He'd told Hallie not to worry, that everything would be all right. He wished he could believe it.

Staring out into the darkness, he was aware of the tension building within him. Sayers was out there, waiting. Once, he would have gone looking for the man, but not now. *Vengeance is mine, saith the Lord. I will repay. . . .*

He grinned into the darkness. Being around Hallie was starting to rub off on him, he mused. She'd changed him in so many ways, sometimes he didn't recognize himself anymore. She'd made him realize that what he'd been doing was wrong and, not only that, selfish. She had made him realize that caring for the living

was more important than avenging the dead, that it was
more important to be a Father to Anna than to avenge
Summer Rain's death. Hallie had made him realize
what a precious gift life was.

Hallie. He would never deserve her, but he intended
to hang on to her just as tight as he could.

He'd watched Hallie as they put Anna to bed that
night, felt his heart swell as Hallie tucked Anna in, sat
beside her and told her a story, kissed her good night.

Warmth enveloped him as he heard the sound of her
laughter coming from inside the house. It was good
to know that, if anything happened to him, his girls
wouldn't be alone. McIntyre would look after Hallie,
and Hallie would take care of Anna.

But for now they were his responsibility. It had been
two years since he'd felt the weight of responsibility on
his shoulders, but he felt it weighing heavily on him
now. He was a wanted man with a wife and child to care
for, and no way to support them.

Damn! He thought about the land he'd left behind. It
was still his; he had a deed in the bank to prove it. If he
could sell the property, he could use the money for a
stake, maybe buy a ranch somewhere where no one had
ever heard of him. Sitting there, alone in the dark, he
prayed that he hadn't lied to Hallie when he told her
that everything would be all right.

"I've got a share in a cattle ranch over in Montana,"
McIntyre said. "Been planning to settle there when I
retire. What would you think about going up there to
keep an eye on my interest for me?"

Clay sat back in his chair, his brow furrowed in
thought. They were sitting in the kitchen, just the two of
them. Hallie and Anna had gone into town.

"How'd you manage that?" Clay asked.

"Won it in a poker game. Man by the name of Husk

owns the other half. He's an old codger, in his seventies if he's a day. He'd probably welcome the help."

Clay grunted softly. "Think he'd sell me a share of the place?"

"I don't know. He might. He's got no kin. I always thought I'd buy him out when I got the money."

"How big a place is it?"

"Close to a thousand acres. Pretty place. I went up to take a look at it after I won it, just to see if there really was a ranch." McIntyre nodded. "I think you'd like it."

"I'll talk to Hallie, see what she says." Clay glanced out the window. "They've been gone quite a while."

McIntyre pulled his watch from his pocket and checked the time. "Almost two hours," he remarked, "but you know women and shopping."

"Yeah," Clay agreed. Pushing away from the table, he went to the window and looked outside. Anna had been excited about her first trip to town. She had probably tried on every dress in the mercantile, not to mention hats and shoes and whatever else caught her eye. He grinned as he imagined her dragging Hallie to the confectionery, stopping to look in every window along the way. There was probably nothing to worry about, so why did he have the feeling something was wrong?

He wasn't surprised when there was a sudden, urgent knock on the front door.

He stood out of sight, his hand on his gun butt, while the sheriff opened the door. A boy of about nine or ten stood on the porch.

"Hi, Tommy," McIntyre said. "What can I do for you?"

The boy held up a folded piece of paper. "A man asked me to give you this."

"A man?"

The boy nodded. "Paid me two bits to bring it to ya."

McIntyre nodded. "Wait a minute, son. He might want an answer."

McIntyre unfolded the sheet of paper. Clay couldn't see the sheriff's face, but, judging by the way his whole body tensed, it wasn't good news.

"Who gave you this, Tommy?"

"I don't know. Never saw him before."

"What did he look like?"

The boy shrugged. "I don't know. Just a man."

"What color was his hair?"

"Brown."

"What color were his eyes?"

"I don't remember. Blue, I think."

"One more question, Tommy. How big was he?"

"Not very. Shorter than you. Kind of skinny."

McIntyre nodded. "Thanks, Tommy. Here's a dollar for your trouble."

"A dollar! Wow! Thanks, Sheriff."

Clay waited until McIntyre closed the door. "What is it?" he asked. "What's wrong?"

"Here." McIntyre thrust the paper at him. "Read it for yourself."

Clay hesitated a moment before he took the letter.

We have the woman and the girl. If you want to see them alive again, you'll meet me at the crossroads at midnight. Bring Walking Hawk. Handcuff him to the cot inside the shack, then take his horse and ride away. No tricks, Sheriff, no games, or you'll never see your daughter or the 'breed kid alive again.

Clay crumbled the paper in his hands. "That dirty sonofa . . ." He took a deep breath, fighting back the rage that roiled within him.

"Exactly," McIntyre said.

"The crossroads," Clay said. "Where is it?"

"About a mile outside of town. There's an old miner's shack out there and not much else. The place doesn't have any windows and only one door. There's plenty of cover along both sides of the road."

Clay glanced at the mantel clock. It was almost four. Eight hours to wait. Eight hours to try and think of some way to find Hallie and Anna.

"I'm gonna go take a walk through town," McIntyre said.

"I'm going with you."

"No. You're still a wanted man, remember? I've got a flyer in my office with your name on it."

"Dammit, he's got my wife and my daughter!"

"He's got my daughter, too," McIntyre reminded him quietly.

"I know that," Clay exclaimed. "Don't you think I know that? But I can't just sit here. Dammit, if Sayers knows I'm in town, you can bet everybody else knows it, too."

McIntyre blew out a deep breath. "You're probably right, but you're the one Sayers wants. If some gun-happy cowhand decides to try to take you down to collect the reward, we've got nothing to bargain with."

"If some hothead kills me, then Sayers has no reason to hold Hallie and Anna."

"That's true, but if he did what you say he did to your first wife, what makes you think he'll just let them go?"

Clay sucked in a deep breath as the memory of finding Summer Rain flashed across his mind. "All right. I'll stay."

"See if you can't come up with some kind of plan while I'm gone." McIntyre plucked his hat off the hall-tree and settled it on his head. "And keep that gun handy."

Clay locked the door behind the sheriff, and then,

because he couldn't just sit there and wait, he began to pace the room.

A plan, he thought, they needed a plan.

"Hallie?"

"I'm here."

"I'm scared."

"I know, Anna." Hallie squirmed on the hardwood floor, wishing she could see where they were, but a rag covered her eyes; her hands were bound behind her back.

It had all happened so quickly. They had been walking home, laughing together, when someone had come up and grabbed Hallie from behind. She'd had no time to see who it was, no time to scream. A strong hand had pressed a cloth over her nose and mouth. She didn't remember anything after that.

There was a soft scuttling sound. A few moments later, she felt Anna pressing against her side.

"Anna, are your hands free? Can you untie me?"

"No." Anna sniffed back a tear. "The rope hurts my wrists, Hallie."

"Can you see where we are?"

"No, it's too dark."

"Do you think we're still in town?"

"No. They took us for a long ride. I couldn't see where, though, because they covered my eyes. Who are they, Hallie?"

"I don't know. Try not to worry. Clay will find us."

"What . . . what if he can't?" There was a decided quiver in Anna's voice, the sound of unshed tears.

"He will," Hallie said, forcing a note of certainty into her voice. "He will."

But what if he didn't?

"Well?" Clay asked. "Did you find out anything?"

"Not much." McIntyre tossed his hat on the rack.

"Just that Will was seen in town late last night. One of the dealers at the Crooked Ace was on his way home a little after midnight. He remembers seeing Will talking to Jax down at the livery. He said they had their heads together, then Will slipped something to Jax. Hobart said it was too dark to see what it was."

"A payoff," Clay mused. He followed McIntyre into the kitchen and sat down at the table.

"A payoff?" McIntyre frowned as he sat down across from Clay. "For information, you mean?"

Clay nodded. "I thought Jax seemed real surprised to see us last night, but now that I think about it, he seemed a little nervous."

McIntyre frowned. "So. Will paid Jax to keep an eye out for you. Jax sent word to Will that you were back in town. Will shows up for the payoff."

"So Will must be close by."

"That's my thinking."

"What do you say we go have a little talk with Jax?"

"Let's wait until nightfall. I'll fix us some dinner, and then we'll go find out what he knows."

"Howdy, Sheriff," Jax said. "What can I do fer ya?"

"I need you to answer a couple of questions for me."

"Sure, sure. Always glad to help the law when I can."

"I'm glad to hear that. When's the last time you saw Will Sayers?"

Jax swallowed hard, then cleared his throat. "Ah, not fer a couple weeks."

"You're sure?"

Jax slid a sideways glance at Clay. "I'm sure."

"Hobart says he saw you talking with Will late last night."

Jax shook his head vigorously. "No."

"You're sure?"

"Plumb sure."

Clay had been standing well behind McIntyre. Now, he moved up to stand beside the sheriff. "You're lying. I want to know where Sayers is staying, and I want to know now."

Jax looked offended. "You gonna let that 'breed talk to me like that?"

"Just answer the question, Jax, and there won't be any trouble."

"I told you I didn't . . ." The man's words trailed off as Clay pulled a knife.

"I don't have all night to play games," Clay said, his voice as hard as flint. "I need answers. Now."

Jax sent a pleading look at the sheriff. "You gonna let him cut me?"

"I'm gonna help him if you don't give me some straight answers damn quick."

Clay took a step forward. Lamplight glinted off the blade.

Jax took a step back. "All right, he was here."

McIntyre smiled. "What did he want?"

"He just wanted me to keep a eye out for him." Jax jerked his head in Clay's direction. "Said he'd make it worth my while if I let him know when the 'breed . . ." His eyes widened with the realization of what he'd said. "I don't mean nothing by that," he added quickly.

"Go on," Clay said.

"Said he'd make it worth my while to let him know when you come back to town. That's all."

"Where is he?"

"I don't know. He said I should leave word with Clementine if you was to come back to town. That's all I know."

Clay looked at McIntyre. "Clementine?"

"She's one of the doves over at the Crooked Ace. Bob Sayers is sweet on her."

"Is Will still in town?"

"I don't know." Jax looked at Clay. "Honest, I don't know."

McIntyre grunted softly. "Seems unlikely that Will and Bob could have been holed up at the saloon all this time."

"But it's possible," Clay replied.

"Well, sure, anything's possible."

"Let's go."

"If you see Will, keep your mouth shut about this."

Jax nodded vigorously. "I will, Sheriff."

Clay ran the edge of his thumb along the knife. "You'd better," he said, "or I'll cut out your tongue and feed it to you."

"Yessir," Jax said quickly.

"What were you trying to do?" McIntyre asked when they were outside again. "Scare that poor old old man to death?"

Clay shrugged. "He wasn't afraid of you. So, how do we play this?"

"I'll go over to the saloon and question Clementine. You go back to the house and wait for me."

"No."

"How did I know you'd say that?" McIntyre muttered.

"Is there a back entrance to the second floor of the saloon?"

"Yeah, in the alley."

"I'll wait at the top of the stairs. Holler if you need help."

"Right."

Keeping to the shadows, Clay entered the alley and climbed the rickety wooden staircase that led up to the second floor of the saloon. The door at the top of the stairs was unlocked and he opened it a crack and peered inside in time to see McIntyre knock on one of the doors not far from where he was standing.

It was opened by a tall woman wearing a long silk wrapper. She had the reddest hair Clay had ever seen.

"Hi, Clementine."

"Evening, Sheriff," she replied in a deep, sultry voice. "What can I do for you this evening?"

"Answer a few questions."

Clementine put one hand on her hip and puffed out her chest. The upper part of her wrapper opened a little more, revealing an expanse of milky white flesh. "Is that all?"

"That's all. You alone in there?"

"I sure am, honey."

"Quit it," McIntyre said curtly.

"Can't blame a girl for trying," Clementine said with a shrug.

"I'm looking for Will and Bob Sayers. You seen them lately?"

A shadow passed over the woman's face, and then she shook her head. "No, not for weeks."

"Mind if I come in and look around?"

Clementine took a step backward. "Help yourself, honey," she purred.

McIntyre went into the room, his gun drawn.

Clay eased open the alley door and padded quietly down the hallway. He paused at Clementine's door and peered through the crack.

The dove stood in the middle of the room while the sheriff looked around. There wasn't much to see. A brass bed, a four-drawer chest, a commode, a small wardrobe.

"You're sure you haven't seen Will in the last day or so?"

Clementine fiddled with the tie on her wrapper. "I'm sure."

"You're lying, Clementine. Why? How much is he paying you?"

"I don't know what you mean."

Clay slipped into the room and eased the door closed behind him. "You're wasting your time, Frank. She's not gonna talk to you."

Clementine whirled around, her eyes widening in surprise. "You!" There was no mistaking the fear in her voice. "You're that Injun. The one who killed all those men, and shot Bob!"

Clay smiled. It was the same smile Summer's attackers had seen before he pulled the trigger "I'm looking for Will," he said, a quiet edge of menace underlying his soft-spoken words. "Where is he?"

Clementine backed up until she was standing beside McIntyre. "He's staying at Morton's."

Clay looked at McIntyre. "Who's Morton?"

"He works at the bank. His mother took sick and he went back east to look after her. His house is located about a half mile out of town." Frank looked at Clementine. "Is Bob there, too?"

The dove nodded.

"So," Clay mused, "he didn't die, after all. Has he got my wife and daughter out there?"

"I don't know." She pressed closer to McIntyre. "Honest."

"Don't tell anyone we were here," McIntyre said.

"No. No, I won't."

"You think we can trust her?" Clay asked.

McIntyre grinned. "Oh, yeah, I think we can trust her."

Clementine nodded. "I won't say anything. I promise." She turned beseeching eyes on McIntyre. "Please, don't let him hurt me."

"Just keep your mouth shut, Clemmie."

"I will."

McIntyre jerked his head toward the door. "Let's go."

Clay nodded. He checked the hallway to make sure it

was empty, then went out the back door. The sheriff followed him down the stairs.

"You stay here," Frank said. "I'll get our horses."

Clay nodded. Stepping into the shadows, he watched the lawman walk down the street.

Chapter 28

The Morton house loomed ahead. It was a pretty little place, with a wide veranda and a red-brick chimney. Washed in a sea of moonlight, it looked like something out of a fairy tale. Lights burned in the downstairs windows; the upstairs was dark. Two horses were tethered to a hitch rail alongside the porch.

Clay reined his horse to a halt in the shelter of a grove of trees. Dismounting, he tied the reins to a low-hanging branch.

McIntyre reined his horse up beside Clay. He sat forward, his arms folded on the pommel, and surveyed the house.

"Two horses out front," McIntyre whispered. "Bob and Will are probably both inside." He glanced at his watch. It was a quarter-past ten.

"And the girls?"

"Probably upstairs."

"How do you think they'll play it?"

McIntyre shook his head. "I don't know. But one thing's for sure, they aren't planning to make a trade. They've both got to know that no matter how tonight turns out, I'll be coming after them."

"So, you figure they planned to ambush both of us?"

"That's the way I see it. What do you think?"

"I think you're right. I'll go in the front. You take the back."

"Maybe we should wait and take them out here."

"No. I don't think Bob will leave any witnesses behind. I'm going in."

With a nod, McIntyre slid from the back of his horse. "Give me five minutes to get around the back."

"Right. If anything happen to me . . ."

"Don't worry. I'll look after both of them."

Clay nodded. He checked his Colt, slid it back into the holster. Dropping down on his belly, he snaked toward the front of the house.

A figure passed in front of the window and Clay froze in a pool of shadow, becoming one with the earth and the night. He held his breath, waiting, and then he began to move again.

He rose to his feet at the foot of the porch, padded noiselessly up the stairs. McIntyre should be at the back door about now. He waited another minute, then put his hand on the latch.

The door opened on silent hinges. The entryway was dark. Clay slid inside and closed the door behind him, then stood against the wall, waiting for his eyes to adjust to the darkness.

He heard voices coming from the next room.

"It's almost time to leave. I'll check on the woman and the girl."

It was Bob Sayers's voice. Clay felt a surge of such relief it left him feeling almost light-headed. Hallie and Anna were here, alive.

"Bob . . ."

"We've discussed this, Will. Be ready to go when I get back."

Clay tensed as he heard footsteps coming his way. And then Bob Sayers was standing there, not three feet away. Clay's finger curled around the trigger. He had hunted this man for two long years and now Sayers was there, in front of him, like a gift from the gods. There was a moment when he almost pulled the trigger, when the memory of what this man had done to Summer Rain surged up within him, hot and bitter as bile, and then he thought of Hallie, and how disappointed in him she would be if he killed Sayers in cold blood, and the rage drained out of him.

"Hold it right there," he called softly.

Bob Sayers whipped around to his left, his hand streaking for his gun, his eyes searching for a target, and Clay shot him where he stood.

Sayers cursed as he dropped his gun and grabbed his shoulder.

"You all right?" It was McIntyre's voice.

"Fine," Clay called. He stepped out of the shadowy hallway and into the parlor.

Bob Sayers glared at him. Blood oozed from his right shoulder. McIntyre and Will Sayers emerged from the kitchen doorway. Will's hands were cuffed behind him.

"I'm going after the girls," Clay said, and McIntyre nodded.

Taking one of the lamps, Clay climbed the stairs to the second floor.

He found Hallie and Anna in the first bedroom at the top of the stairs. Hallie was sitting on the floor; Anna was pressed close beside her. They were both bound hand and foot and blindfolded.

He saw Hallie's body stiffen as he entered the room.

"It's all right, Hallie. Anna. It's me."

Holstering his gun, he placed the lamp on a table, then went to kneel in front of his girls.

"You two okay?" He removed the blindfolds, untied Anna's hands, then Hallie's, and drew them both into his arms.

"Fine, now," Hallie said. She slumped against him, weak with relief.

"Hallie said you'd come," Anna said. "I was afraid, but Hallie said you'd come."

"Did they hurt you?"

"No," Hallie replied. She stared into Clay's eyes. "I heard a gunshot."

"Sayers drew on me."

Hallie's eyes widened. "Are you hurt? Did you . . . is he . . . is he dead?"

Clay grinned at her. "I'm fine, and so is he."

"I'm glad you didn't kill him, Clay."

"It was tempting." He took Anna in his arms and stood up, then offered Hallie his hand and drew her to her feet. "You sure you're all right? They didn't . . ." He glanced at Anna, snuggled in his arms, her face buried against his neck. "You're sure they didn't hurt you?"

Hallie knew what he was asking and she smiled reassuringly. "I'm fine, really."

Clay slid his arm around her shoulders and kissed her lightly. "Let's go. Your old man's waiting downstairs."

Chapter 29

McIntyre was waiting for them in the parlor. Will Sayers was standing beside the sofa; Bob was sitting down, his kerchief pressed against his wounded shoulder. Will looked scared; Bob's expression was sullen, his eyes narrowed with pain and anger.

"Everything all right?" McIntyre asked.

"Fine," Clay replied.

McIntyre nodded. "Let's go then. Bob needs a doctor."

Clay nodded, but didn't reply. As far as he was concerned, Bob Sayers could bleed to death.

"Let's go."

Will Sayers glanced at his brother, then started walking toward the front door. Bob stood up. He groaned softly, took a step forward, then seemed to lose his balance. He reeled backward, his uninjured shoulder ramming into McIntyre, throwing the lawman off balance.

Pivoting sharply, Sayers drove his fist into McIntyre's face, then grabbed the lawman's gun.

Hallie screamed as her father fell. Time seemed to slow down and she saw everything in vivid detail . . . the stunned expression on her father's face, the blood trickling from his nose. She saw the startled look on Will's face.

And then Bob Sayers was turning to face Clay, pointing the gun in their direction. And Clay was pushing her and Anna out of the way, stepping in front of them, lifting his own weapon. Too late, she thought, too late.

The sound of gunfire echoed through the parlor like thunder.

Hallie screamed as Clay sank to the floor. Blood ran from a wound in his head.

Bob Sayers stood where he was for a moment and then, as if someone had cut a string, the gun fell from his hand, and he toppled backward onto the sofa.

Hallie ran forward and knelt beside Clay, oblivious to everything else.

Blood covered his face, her hands, the floor. So much blood.

"Clay! Oh, no, no. . . . Clay . . ."

She looked up as her father came to kneel beside her. "Papa, do something!"

McIntyre removed his kerchief and wiped the blood from Clay's forehead, revealing a long shallow gash along his left temple.

"Clay, don't die. Please don't die."

"Ate . . ." Anna came to stand beside Hallie, her dark eyes filled with tears. *"Ate . . ."*

McIntyre glanced over his shoulder at Will, then looked back at Hallie. "He's dead."

Hallie stared at her father. "No!"

"I'm sorry, honey." Taking her by the arm, he forced her to her feet. "Go outside. Take Anna with you."

"No." Hallie shook her head. "No!"

"Hallie," her father said sharply, "do as I said."

Feeling as though her heart were breaking, Hallie lifted Anna into her arms and carried the sobbing child outside.

"All right, Will, let's go."

"What about my brother? You can't just leave him here."

"I'll come back for him later. We'll need a wagon t
carry the bodies back to town. Let's go."

Hallie and Anna were waiting for him on the porch
They looked at him through grief-stricken eyes. John
Walking Hawk was dead. Soon, he'd be laid to rest
With a sigh, McIntyre took his daughter by the hand
and urged her down the stairs, knowing he would neve
forget the wounded look in her eyes.

He lifted Hallie and Anna onto the back of a horse
then handcuffed Will to the porch rail.

"I'll be right back," he said. "I forgot something."

Clay was sitting up, one hand pressed against hi
temple, when McIntyre entered the house. "Where'
Hallie?"

"She's outside."

Clay started to rise, but McIntyre put a hand on hi
shoulder, restraining him. "I want you to spend th
night here."

"What the hell for? Where's Hallie? Is Anna al
right?"

"They're fine." McIntyre lifted a hand. "Hear me out
Will Sayers thinks you're dead, and I want him to go o
thinking that."

"Go on."

"I'll come back later with a wagon and couple of cas
kets. We'll fill yours with rocks. We'll bury you to
morrow morning. After the funeral, you can take Halli
and Anna and leave town. John Walking Hawk will b
dead and buried. You follow me now?"

"What about Hallie?"

"She thinks you're dead. I know, I know, but it wa
necessary. I'll tell her and Anna the truth as soon as I ge
Sayers locked up. How's your head?"

"Hurts like a sonofagun, but I'll be all right."

McIntyre grunted softly. "Sit tight. I'll find something to bandage it up with. Hang on."

Clay watched McIntyre go into the kitchen. It was a good plan, he mused, one that just might work.

McIntyre returned a few minutes later with a bowl of water and a couple of dishcloths. He quickly washed away the blood, then tore the second cloth into strips. He made a thick pad and placed it over the wound, using the remaining strip of cloth to hold it in place.

He nodded as he stood up. "Hope you don't mind spending the night with Sayers," he remarked.

Clay grimaced. "Bob never looked better, as far as I'm concerned."

McIntyre laughed softly. "We'll be back tomorrow afternoon."

Hallie stared at her father, unable to believe her ears, unable to believe he would have let her and Anna believe Clay was dead for even one minute, let alone for the past two hours.

"How could you!" she exclaimed.

"Hallie, calm down and let me finish."

With a sigh of exasperation, she sat down on the sofa and took Anna's hand in hers. The child had wept silent tears all the way back to town. Now she stared up at McIntyre, her dark eyes filled with hope.

"Is my papa alive?" she asked. "Truly?"

McIntyre nodded. "He's fine. Bullet just creased him. I'm sorry I had to let the two of you think he was dead, but it was necessary. After the funeral tomorrow, you can leave here. As far as the law's concerned, John Walking Hawk is dead."

It was a simple plan. A brilliant plan, Hallie thought, and worth the temporary anguish she had suffered. Clay could start a new life with a new name.

Hallie jumped off the sofa and threw her arms arour
her father. "Thank you, Papa!"

"You're welcome, Hallie. Just take good care of eac
other."

"We will." She beamed at him. "You're the best fathe
a girl ever had."

They held the funeral early the following mornin;
Aside from the minister, Anna, Hallie, and her fathe
there were only a few others in attendance, townspeop
whose morbid curiosity had drawn them out to see
moderately notorious outlaw laid to rest.

It was a short service. The grieving widow wept be
hind her black veil, the child blinked back tears. Whe
it was over, the widow dropped a handful of earth on th
coffin, whispered, "Rest in peace, John Walking Hawk
then took the child by the hand and walked back t
town, followed by her father. No one thought it strang
that she packed up and left town that afternoon. Th
place had only bad memories for her now.

Clay was waiting for her at the Morton place. H
grinned when she alighted from the buckboard.

"You look right pretty in black," he drawled a
he pulled her into his arms and kissed her. "Right prett
indeed."

"Just make sure I don't have to wear it again anytim
soon," Hallie retorted.

"I promise. Hey, sugar, you look pretty, too."

"Grandpa McIntyre said I was a good actress."

"I'll bet you were." He scooped his daughter up wit
one arm, and drew Hallie close with the other, and kne
he was holding heaven in his arms.

Epilogue

Double Bar H Ranch, Montana
Five years later

Hallie sat on the front porch, nursing her youngest son while she listened to her father and her husband arguing about some matter of ranch business. They argued all the time, and she no longer paid any attention. It amazed her that two men who got along so well, and ran one of the biggest cattle ranches in the country, always squabbled like old ladies when there was a decision to be made, yet, in the end, they always agreed on whatever decision they reached. Men. There was no understanding them.

It had been a wonderful five years. They had left Green Willow Creek immediately after Clay's "death" and come here. Old man Husk had been glad to have help. Clay had learned the cattle business; Hallie had taken over the housekeeping chores and taught Anna to read and write. True to his word, Clay took Anna to visit her grandparents every summer.

Hosiah Husk had sold his share of the ranch to Clay the year before, with the stipulation that he could continue to live there. For all his years, he was still spry. He lived in his own house, but took his meals with the family.

Their first son, John, had been born the year after they moved to the ranch; their daughter, McKayla, had been born a year later. Hallie had been afraid Anna might be jealous of the babies, but it had been a foolish fear.

Hallie smiled at the infant in her arms. Young Clay was the spitting image of his father.

She looked up at the sound of her husband's footsteps. "Well, did you two get everything settled?"

"Oh, yeah," Clay replied. He smiled as the baby curled a tiny fist around his finger. "Your old man finally saw things my way."

Hallie grinned, knowing that, if asked, her father would insist that Clay had finally seen things *his* way.

Hallie sighed as Clay enfolded her and the baby in his arms. "Like holding my own piece of heaven," he often said, and she couldn't agree more, for she had surely found heaven in his arms.